All Sorrows Can Be Borne

All Sorrows Can Be Borne

by Loren Stephens

Rare Bird Books
Los Angeles, Calif.

THIS IS A GENUINE RARE BIRD BOOK

Rare Bird Books
453 South Spring Street, Suite 302
Los Angeles, CA 90013
rarebirdlit.com

Set in Minion Pro
Printed in the United States

10 9 8 7 6 5 4 3 2 1

Publisher's Cataloging-in-Publication Data available upon request.

To Dana

"All sorrows can be borne if you put them into a story..."

—Isak Dinesen

PART ONE

Chapter 1

ICHIRO TOLD ME OUR son would be better off living with his sister and her husband in America; I was too weak to argue with him. My mother said I had lost my mind to give up my child. Her judgment was cruel, but I knew she was right.

"You are like a monk for three days," she said.

"What do you mean?"

"You give up too easily. You carried your baby for nine months and took care of him for nearly three years, and after all that you give him away. Do you not love him, Noriko?"

"Of course, I love him, but what if Ichiro dies, then what? The doctors can't tell us anything, and we have no money. I could be a widow with a toddler. I don't have the courage to face such a fate." Hearing how defeated I sounded shocked me. A year of trying to buoy my husband's spirit was dragging me into a sandpit of sorrow and regret.

"The family will find a way to help you if it should come to that. In the meantime, you must stand up to Ichiro. You are not just an obedient Japanese wife who walks behind her husband staring at his ass. What has become of you? You used to be such a rebellious child. Now you are like a pillow with all the goose feathers pulled out."

"Ichiro says I am selfish to want to hold on to Hisashi. He sneers and says, 'What kind of life can we offer him?' I have no answer."

I cannot testify that this is exactly how the argument with my mother went, but I did not ask for help or turn to my brother or sister. I felt too ashamed of the situation Ichiro and I found we were in, even if it was no one's fault.

And now here we were in a sparse room at the old Dai-Ichi Hotel in Tokyo, the rain falling against the window blurring the edges of the Shinsaibashi train station across the street. Hisashi was still asleep next to me, his body warm, his black bangs covering his forehead as he gently breathed in and out, in and out. When I touched his rosy cheeks and brushed a few strands of hair from his forehead, he opened his innocent eyes and greeted me with his beautiful smile.

Pressing his hand against his pajama pants, he looked at me. "Shee-shee, Mama. I have to go to the bathroom."

"Can you wait a few minutes? Your daddy is just finishing his shower."

"I'll try."

"That's my good boy." I kissed his head and breathed in his sweet scent.

Ichiro opened the bathroom door, a cloud of steam behind him. Pulling his belt to the tightest notch, he looked as if he was wearing a larger man's business suit. The medication was stealing his appetite. He complained that nothing but liquor had any flavor.

"So, our little man is up. We don't have much time. The train to the airport will be leaving in less than an hour. I want to be at the terminal early so we get a seat. I don't have the energy to stand for the entire trip."

Taking the gold lighter he inherited from his father off the table, Ichiro spun the flint and took a deep drag on his cigarette.

"Should you be smoking, Ichiro?"

"What difference does it make? Please don't annoy me with your questions. Smoking is one of the few things I enjoy."

Hisashi pulled my hand, reminding me he needed to use the bathroom. I picked him up. "You are getting so heavy. All the weight your daddy is losing he must be giving to you."

Ichiro ignored my comment. Turning on the radio, he flipped the dial to the classical music station. "Do you recognize this? Beethoven's *Ninth*. His last and greatest symphony. No composer has written a Tenth—not Mahler, not Bruckner, not Schubert. They all died trying. Sad, isn't it?" How easily Ichiro distracted himself from what we dreaded: this day, this hour, this moment.

Hisashi sat down on the toilet seat as I instructed him so he wouldn't make droplets on the tile floor. I wiped the fog off the mirror, quickly brushed my teeth, and combed my hair. The fluorescent light exaggerated the faint scar on my forehead where a shard of glass hit me, marking me forever as a *hibakusha*—a survivor of the bomb that destroyed Hiroshima.

I opened Hisashi's suitcase and took out the new outfit I bought at Takashimaya Department Store. Ichiro said I was wasting our money, but I wanted him to look his best for the trip to America. I had washed the shirt to soften the fabric and cut the label so it wouldn't scratch his neck. These small gestures showed that I was a good mother. I helped him close the buttons of his shirt and then, holding up the short trousers, Hisashi stepped into them and pulled the suspenders over his shoulders. I thought, *Keep going. Tell him what to do next.*

"Here. Put your socks on."

"Left leg. Now right leg. Done, Mama."

I sang out: "Put your left leg in. Put your left leg out. Now do the hokey pokey and turn yourself around…"

Hisashi finished the song: "And that's what it's all about." We listened together to the records my sister-in-law Mitsuko sent from America, and he knew the lyrics by heart even if we didn't speak English.

Ichiro turned up the volume on the radio, signaling we were annoying him. "Do you hear it, Noriko? The final movement of the *Ninth*, the famous chorus? *Wer ein holdes Weib errungen / Mische seinen Jubel ein!*"

"What does that mean, Ichiro?"

"If I remember correctly, my professor said it means 'whoever has found an obedient wife let him join our songs of praise!' I couldn't agree more."

Laughing, he grabbed Hisashi and put him on his knee.

"Horsey, Dada."

"Hold on tight." Ichiro lifted our son up and down on his knee but stopped when he was struck by a coughing fit that lasted several seconds. Beads of sweat appeared on his forehead.

Unaware of his father's distress, Hisashi took out an imaginary coin and tried to put it in his father's pocket. "Here, Dada. Again, again."

"That's enough for now," his father said. "You'll ruin your expensive suit. Your mama wants you to look your very best for your new parents."

Wide-eyed, Hisashi hit his father. "No! No! No!"

Ichiro pinned his son's arms down by his sides as tears rolled down his chubby cheeks. "Calm down. It's time for us to go. Put on your jacket and your shoes. I don't want to hear another 'no' out of you." Hisashi's lower lip quivered. Inside I seethed with anger at Ichiro for speaking so harshly to Hisashi, but I held my tongue.

Ichiro opened his briefcase and held up the documents: "Passport, tickets, letter to stewardess..." The news interrupted the music. "Good morning, listeners. Today is February twenty-ninth, 1964. Leap Year. Don't forget, ladies. You may ask your boyfriend to marry you if you dare."

So next year there would be no February 29. I thought, *Will I light a candle on February 28 or March 1 and say a prayer for my little boy, wishing that someday I will see him again, if not in this lifetime, then in the next?*

I put a framed wedding photograph of Ichiro and me on top of Hisashi's clothes so he would remember what we looked like, and I tucked a heart-shaped box made of paulownia wood between the layers in his suitcase. Inside the box was Hisashi's umbilical cord that all good Japanese mothers save as a symbol of the connection between mother and child. After today, the flesh we had shared for the nine months of my pregnancy would no longer belong to me. It was to be passed on to Mitsuko, who awaited his arrival in America. Hisashi, her son at last. I closed his suitcase. The sound of the latches snapping shut echoed off the suffocating walls of the hotel room.

∽

THE LATE FEBRUARY AIR was damp and the cloudy sky promised more rain. Blackbirds swooped down on the branches of the trees that would be pregnant with cherry blossoms in a month, the city parks clogged with viewing parties organized by happy families and visiting tourists reveling in the beauty of the pink-petal snow. I tried pushing the thought out of my mind, but a voice kept repeating, *Hisashi will not be here to see the cherry blossoms. You and Ichiro will be alone.*

Ichiro and I clasped our son's hands and lifted him over the mud puddles in the street to make sure that his new shoes did not get wet. "Higher, higher," Hisashi shouted, as if we were playing a game. Ichiro stopped to catch his breath. He leaned over and rested his hands on his knees, taking shallow breaths to clear his lungs and bring the blood back into his head.

"Are you all right, Ichiro?"

"Just a little dizzy. Give me a moment, and I'll be fine."

Distracted, I didn't realize Hisashi had escaped my grip. He jumped into a puddle, splashing his shoes with mud. Ichiro grabbed him by the arm, spun him around, and slapped him on the behind. "You naughty boy. Your mama is going to have to wash off your shoes when we get to the airport."

"Ichiro, go easy on him. He's just trying to hold our attention. We can't expect him to always be an obedient child. Especially today..."

Ichiro wiped his mouth with his handkerchief and tucked it back into his breast pocket. "I shouldn't be so harsh, but this is as difficult for me as it is for you—even if I don't express it."

We found a seat in the front car. The doors closed and the train pulled out of the station, picking up speed as it headed toward Tokyo's Haneda International Airport. Hisashi sat on my lap next to the window and called out the names of the passing images: bicycle, dog, car, wagon. His vocabulary was expanding rapidly, and he was speaking in complete sentences, the result of all the books his father read to him. He was smart like Ichiro, but he was also a very emotional and sensitive child—which he had inherited from me. It occurred to me that our son was like a cup filled with tea poured at the same time from two cracked kettles. After what we were about to do, neither of us deserved him.

Ichiro scanned the Help Wanted section of yesterday's *Osaka Shimbun* he brought from home. He meticulously circled ads: "salesclerk needed in menswear department at Daimuru Osaka Shinsaibashi," "bookkeeper position at Nippon Steel." After hesitating a moment, he marked "chauffeur, HELLO Limousine Service." I knew he considered the job beneath him, but the pay would probably be good during the Olympics. He folded the paper and put it back in his briefcase. The rocking of the train made him sleepy, and he struggled to stay awake. I watched his eyes begin to flutter behind his glasses, which he had recently taken to wearing regularly as his eyesight worsened and his cheekbones became more prominent as he continued to lose weight. There were days I didn't recognize my husband.

Hisashi pulled his cap off and hid his face. "Where are you, Dada?"

"Right next to you," his father answered, lifting his head and seeming to struggle to keep his eyes open. "Where did you think I was?" He then tickled his son's stomach, and Hisashi squirmed in my lap.

"Let's keep him quiet so that he doesn't get overheated," I said, and I unbuttoned his maroon jacket and gave him a glass bottle filled with water. He sucked on the worn rubber nipple until there was nothing left in the bottle but air.

The voice over the loudspeaker announced, "Next stop, Haneda International Airport. All passengers must disembark. Please check around your seats to make sure you have all your belongings."

Ichiro picked Hisashi up off my lap, and I carried his suitcase and my husband's briefcase. A long flight of stairs leading to the main terminal loomed in front of us. Ichiro's steps slowed until, as we approached the stairs, he turned. "Take him. I can't carry him any longer." I clutched Hisashi's warm body against mine as I climbed the stairs. I could feel his heart beating just as it had when he was inside me, or did I imagine it? I kissed his neck and sang softly into his ear the words to "You Are My Sunshine."

When I reached the last line, I choked back tears. Hisashi kissed my cheek, which was wet with tears I could no longer stifle.

Ichiro ignored us and walked directly up to the agent at the Northwest Airlines counter, handing him Hisashi's one-way ticket from Tokyo to San Francisco. The clock overhead read nine. The black second hand juddered like a rusty music box, marking the minutes until Hisashi's departure. I wanted to turn back time to the day that Hisashi was born, to the day I held my perfect baby in my arms for the first time and promised to never let him go.

The agent looked through the documents. "I see everything is in order, Mr. Uchida. Since your son is traveling alone, we have assigned a stewardess— Miss Yume, I believe—to take care of him during the flight. There is one stop in Hawaii, but he can stay on the airplane with the other passengers who are also continuing on to San Francisco. Does he have any luggage?"

Ichiro answered, "Only this small suitcase. I measured it, and it will fit neatly under his seat."

The agent stamped Hisashi's passport and handed Ichiro a boarding pass. "Mr. and Mrs. Uchida, I'm afraid that you can't go onto the airplane with your son. When it is time to board, the stewardess will escort him to his seat."

I said, "No. It's not right. We want to be with him until the very last minute."

"I'm sorry. These are the rules. Only ticketed passengers can go onto the plane, Mrs. Uchida. "

"Are there no exceptions? Hisashi is only two and a half. What if he is afraid?"

The agent crossed out something he had written on a pad of paper in front of him as if he was trying to get rid of me. Pausing a moment, he said in a low voice, "You should have thought of that before, Mrs. Uchida." Turning to my husband, he asked, "Who will be meeting your son in San Francisco?"

"My sister Mitsuko Mishima and her husband, Harry. They paid for my son's ticket and made all his travel arrangements."

The agent filled out a form and handed it to Ichiro. "Give this to the stewardess. She will make sure your son is turned over only to his aunt and uncle. Northwest Airlines is responsible for his safety, and we want to be sure he is placed in the proper hands upon his arrival."

A line was forming behind us and the agent looked impatient. "If you have no other questions, you can wait in the lounge area. There will be an announcement when the airplane is ready to board." He leaned over the counter. "Have a good trip to San Francisco, Master Hisashi."

The three of us found a place to sit. I retrieved a hard candy from my purse and handed it to Hisashi. The syrup dribbled down his chin. I was afraid that he'd mess his new shirt. "Why don't we go to the bathroom one more time? I can wash your face and clean off your shoes, my angel."

Hisashi mumbled to himself as he followed me. "What are you saying, Hisashi?" I asked, waiting for him to catch up and take my hand.

"San Francisco, Mama. San Francisco."

"Yes, that is where you are going."

He hesitated for a moment and then asked, "You and Dada are going too, Mama?"

"I don't think so, but there are lots of surprises waiting for you." I forced myself to smile. "Now be a brave boy and do just what your papa and I tell you. Will you do that for me?"

"Yes, Mama."

I had tried to prepare my son for what lay ahead, but how could I really explain that Ichiro and I would no longer be part of our son's life?

In the ladies' room, I washed the sticky syrup off Hisashi's face. Then I leaned down and scraped the mud off his shoes. Hisashi wrapped his arms around my neck. "Carry me, Mama."

I lifted my son and held him close. I wanted to run away with him, to get back on the train and take him to Hokkaido, to Kyushu, anywhere, never to be seen or heard from again. But I had no money, and I had made a promise to Ichiro to give our son away. "For a better life." The words sounded hollow now that the moment had finally arrived. How was I going to live without him?

Ichiro stood at the gate holding Hisashi's suitcase. He was speaking with a stewardess. He waved me into the line. "This is Miss Yume. She will take good care of you, Hisashi."

Trying to remain calm, I said, "Miss Yume, please be sure that Hisashi eats all his meals. When he says 'shee-shee,' that's his way of saying he needs to go to the bathroom. In case he starts to cry, I put a photograph of my husband and me in his suitcase. Perhaps if you show it to him, it will calm him down."

"Don't worry, Mrs. Uchida. We will do everything to make your son feel cared for. It is not often we have a toddler traveling alone. I don't mean to hurry you, but perhaps we should get on board so I can settle him into his seat ahead of the other passengers."

Ichiro crouched to our son's eye level. "You go first. Mama and Papa will come later. We will be on the very next airplane." Handing him his red wooden truck, he said, "Don't forget your zoom-zoom." Then he hugged his son for the last time.

I kissed Hisashi hard, as if my lips were burning a permanent scar into his cheek. Miss Yume took Hisashi's hand. "Wave goodbye to your mama and papa." He did as he was told, then followed Miss Yume down the ramp. At the last moment he turned around. I could see his cheeks were glistening with tears, but he didn't call out. He pulled his cap down over his eyes and, like a brave soldier, kept walking.

Ichiro and I stood at the window until the airplane taxied down the runway, lifted off, and was devoured by rain clouds. Burying my face in Ichiro's neck, I asked, "Why did you say we will be on the next airplane when that is a terrible lie?"

"I thought telling him we would be coming soon would make it easier for him to leave us. I didn't want him fussing and whining in front of all the other passengers." Shrugging his shoulders in defeat, he said, "Even if we had enough money to buy tickets, the US Immigration people would send me right back to Japan like a piece of battered luggage stamped CAUTION, TUBERCULOSIS INSIDE."

I felt a sharp pain in my chest as if my heart were cracking open like a clay urn firing in a *noborigama* kiln. I turned away from Ichiro. I wanted to ask him, "How could you do this to me? To Hisashi?" But I knew I had only myself to blame for agreeing to his demand.

⌒

THE NIGHT MANAGER OF the Dai-Ichi Hotel looked up from his reservation ledger as Ichiro and I walked through the empty lobby. "Good evening, Mr. and Mrs. Uchida. Would you like some tea and rice balls sent up to your room?" Before Ichiro could answer, he continued, "And if I might inquire, where is your son? Such an enchanting child. So happy."

Ichiro answered, "He's on his way to visit relatives in America. We are expecting a call from San Francisco to let us know that he has arrived safely. Please connect the call to our room no matter what time it comes in. And have our bill ready for us. We are returning to Osaka tomorrow morning."

"With pleasure, sir. I wish both of you a good evening."

Halfway up the stairs, Ichiro turned around. "On second thought, send a bottle of hot *sake* to our room. This weather is giving me a chill."

I opened the door to our room and felt along the wall for the overhead light switch. The maid had stored our futons and comforters in the closet. I slid the wardrobe door open and unrolled the bedding, leaving Hisashi's comforter on the shelf. Ichiro turned on the radio to the news station: "Takamatsu Construction Group reported the addition of one thousand full- and part-time workers to meet the deadlines for the 1964 Summer Olympic Games in Japan."

I thought, *If there is so much demand, maybe there will be a job for Ichiro.*

As if reading my thoughts, he said, "With the economy so brisk, I might have better luck now."

There was a gentle knock on the door. A waitress entered with a bottle of sake on a lacquered tray and placed it on a low table in the center of the room. Bowing as she retreated, she closed the door behind her.

Turning my back to Ichiro, I unbuttoned my blouse and stepped out of my skirt while he quickly undressed. Sitting on a cushion, I watched Ichiro fill two porcelain cups with sake. His hand was shaking. Offering me a cup, he drained his cup in a single gulp. I took a few sips, then slid under the comforter. Ichiro turned off the light and lay down beside me. He kissed me gently, and then with more force. He caressed my breasts. I smelled the familiar scent of his cologne mixed with hints of sake and tobacco. Even in such pain, our sadness threatening to overwhelm us, the power of our physical attraction to one another was overwhelming. Like two survivors on a life raft, we clung to one another, riding each wave of desire as if it might be the fatal one that would wash us overboard and into a roiling sea. Our passion was all that we had left to keep us from drowning in our unspoken sorrow.

～

JUST BEFORE DAWN, THE telephone rang. The night manager said, "As you instructed, sir, I am putting your call through from America."

I could hear Mitsuko's voice through the receiver. "I'm holding Hisashi in my arms. He is such a precious child—so smart and lively. The minute I put him down, he escapes and Harry has to chase after him."

Ichiro asked, "Is he smiling?"

"Yes. The stewardess says that he was a good passenger, running through the airplane and saying hello to everyone during the flight."

Ichiro said, "Promise me, Mitsuko, that you will take good care of him. You must give him a good life—the kind of life Noriko and I cannot afford. From now on he is your son, not ours."

I tried to grab the telephone, but Ichiro pushed my hand away. "Let me say hello to Hisashi. I need to hear his voice, and I want to tell him I love him, that he is my sunshine."

"Hearing your voice will only confuse him. My sister will let us know how he is doing in a few days. Then maybe, when he is settled, I'll allow you to speak to him."

I left Ichiro still talking with his sister and went into the bathroom. Turning on the shower, I let the steam engulf me and the heat scorch my skin. Sliding to the tile floor, I wailed like a mother in mourning for her dead son.

Chapter 2

IT WAS SPRINGTIME 1943. I was an impatient five-year-old and asked my father repeatedly, "When will we be there?" as the train headed toward the Akiyoshido Caves in the Yamaguchi Prefecture, two hours from our home in Hiroshima. It was my father's idea to take us there for a brief family vacation before my sister, Setsuko, was sent to military headquarters up north. Lucky for us, my father didn't have to serve our great Emperor Hirohito. He was too old—at least forty—and he was allowed to keep the doors of his sushi shop open despite the government edict: soldiers first; citizens second.

My father answered my question, "Why don't you enjoy the scenery, Noriko? We'll be there soon enough." I looked out the window at the deep green fields that looked like an ocean of waving ferns. My sister sat next to me, flipping through the pages of a glossy movie star magazine, and my mother jostled my baby brother on her knee. When he started to cry, she stuck the rubber nipple of a milk bottle in his mouth to keep him from annoying the other passengers who rode on the train with us. I made a peevish expression at Tadashi. Truthfully, I was jealous that my mother paid so much attention to my little brother, which is one of the reasons I was sad that Setsuko was leaving. She was like a mother to me; she taught me how to read so that I would be ahead of my classmates when I went to school, how to count coins to make change for the bus driver, and how to fold my clothes—most of which had been hers when she was my age. Hand-me-downs because nothing in our house was to go to waste.

When the train arrived at the station, we walked the ten minutes to the caves, each of us carrying a light overnight bag. I was so excited that I nearly forgot mine on the train. Setsuko had to remind me to get mine from under my seat and cautioned me to stay close to the rest of the family or I would have bounded off even though I didn't know the direction of the caves.

There were few tourists at the entrance booth buying tickets. Hardly anyone was traveling these days, worried that there might be a surprise attack from enemy airplanes. Better to stay home or go deep into the countryside where there was enough food to feed a family of five. Most of the shelves in the Hiroshima markets were barren, which is why we were so lucky. My father always found a way to feed us, and he didn't share his neighbors' concerns about the war.

My father bought our tickets to the caves. Reading the pamphlet he announced, "These are the largest limestone caves in all of Japan." And then he cautioned me, "Noriko, stay on the platforms. You could fall into one of the pools, and I don't intend to fish you out." He didn't really mean it, but he used to speak to me that way, knowing I'd take chances. I was like a wild horse that didn't want to be tamed.

Setsuko held my hand tightly once we were inside the cave. It was cold, and I buttoned up my yellow sweater over my sleeveless pinafore. I was happy to put it on because there was a patch on the back of my dress where my mother had mended a tear, and I felt embarrassed by it although there really was no one looking. I was already developing a taste for fashion and the fine things that money could buy. Someday I'd have a fancy wardrobe and sparkling jewelry. I wondered if other five-year-olds were as ambitious as I was.

I could see my father and mother, my baby brother strapped to her body, crossing a wooden bridge in front of us over a deep pool, lit by a lantern, its color an azure blue. In the dim light the limestone formations in the cave looked like millions of jellyfish climbing a wall. Shadows bounced off the red and gray stones, some of which extended high up into the cave. Setsuko read me the sign: "That is the Golden Pillar. It is as high as a four-story building—higher than most of the buildings in Hiroshima except maybe the bank." She looked down at me and asked, "Can you guess how it was made?"

I was filled with fairy tales and ghost stories so it didn't take me long to come up with an answer. "A fairy princess and her samurai warrior stood on a ladder and built it."

"That's a good answer coming from an imaginative little girl like you. But the truth is it was made by dripping water that seeped through the cracks in the cave carrying tiny stones—one on top of the other like grains of sand—over millions and millions of years, way before you and I were born."

"I like my story better."

When we came out of the cave, my father and mother waited for us at the exit, and we boarded a bus to take us to a *ryokan* in Yamaguchi where we spent the night together in one large room. Before the maid brought us our dinner on lacquered trays, my mother and father took a soak in the communal hot baths. I wasn't interested. Instead I begged Setsuko to read me one of the stories from her movie magazine about a famous star who had just left the Takarazuka Theater to marry. I told her, "That's going to be me someday, Setsuko."

It had been a perfect day. I fell asleep with images of princesses and actresses visiting my dreams. In the morning, my father took us to the Brocade Sash Bridge, in Iwakuni, before we boarded the train back to Hiroshima. My father told me, "A long time ago only the samurai were allowed to cross this bridge over the river. Everyone else had to take a boat struggling against the strong current. But things are changing, and Japan is shedding some of its feudal habits and turning toward modernity. That's why we commoners can walk on this bridge now."

I didn't understand what my father was telling me. He was using words that were beyond that of a five-year-old's mind although I was told again and again how smart, imaginative, and clever I was. Also pretty, which was more important than the other three. I wanted to appear interested in what my father was telling me so I asked him, "Is the bridge strong enough to hold us, Papa?"

"Noriko, this bridge has been here for hundreds of years, and it will be here for hundreds more. Our ancestors were excellent bridge builders. They made this bridge without using a single nail. Every piece locked in place. Not even a samurai could break it."

I looked out at the valley past the river. The fog settled among the branches of the thick pine forest. Egrets soared above the trees on their journey to the inland marshes. Awkward on land, they were graceful and delicate in the air like a ballerina *en pointe*. I was already taking dance lessons (my father was generous with me), and one day I would take singing and acting lessons. If I was honest with myself, he spoiled me, and I thought of myself as his favorite child.

～

SITTING NEXT TO THE train window, I tried to catch sight of the egret, but it was nowhere to be seen among the thick groves of trees. Arriving at the station in Hiroshima, the evening sky was lit up from the burning cedar branches piled outside the nearby Buddhist temple. The air was filled with the smell of pine. We stopped at the temple to watch the monks walking barefoot across a path of burning coals, their faces showing no sign of pain. The monks invited the few onlookers to join them. No one was brave enough to respond to their invitation. A wooden carving of the god Izuna Daigongen, with a head of a raven, standing on top of the body of a fox, stood guard over the monks and the temple.

There was an alms box outside the temple. My father took my hand and we dropped a few coins into the box. I heard my father telling the god, "We have already had enough fighting. You need to put an end to this." I couldn't wait to leave the temple. The face of the god was frightening, but I comforted myself by thinking, "Maybe he is just as evil-looking to our enemies and that will scare them away."

That night I said a special prayer to Izuna Daigongen to keep my sister Setsuko from leaving, but it didn't reach his ears, and a few days later, she packed her bags and boarded a bus for the military base to the north. I didn't know how long she would be away, but even a day was unbearable to me, and I spent many nights crying myself to sleep. I missed her so much and was afraid that something might happen to her, or she would forget me.

Chapter 3

1945

THERE WERE NO AIR-RAID signals that morning. I begged my father to let me go to school so I could show off my new birthday shoes—the first time I didn't have to wear Setsuko's hand-me-downs. My father had read the leaflet the Americans dropped from the sky the previous day warning that a bomb, the likes of which we had never seen, could hit Hiroshima.

"I should probably keep you home today, Noriko, but the sky looks clear," my father said. My mother had a worried expression that turned to anger when my two-year-old brother banged his toy mallet to knock out the pieces stacked underneath the *daruma otoshi*.

She snapped at him, "Can't you be quiet for a few minutes, Tadashi?" I had never seen my mother so irritated at my brother. He hid in a corner. I wanted to comfort him but I would be late for school. Everyone in the house was tense. Some of our neighbors had moved to the countryside to escape danger, but my father was stubborn and didn't think it was worth the trouble. He also wanted to keep a careful eye on his sushi shop and continue to serve what customers remained to buy the scarce supply of fish, rice, and seaweed. My father was a resourceful man.

I grabbed my book bag and ran out the door. The sun was bright in the early morning, and a light breeze blew the leaves on the trees, making them look like silver fish. The bus stopped at the end of our street. Where the driver had found the gasoline was a mystery. Fuel was being rationed throughout the city, reserved for military jeeps and hospital ambulances.

Most seats on the school bus were empty. I thought, *Well, if there are fewer children at school, my new shoes will stand out. Lucky for me!* I could be very single-minded, closing off thoughts of danger others took seriously.

The Shinonome Elementary School was a solid brick building with large glass windows that opened out onto a courtyard. As I entered school, a butterfly hovered over a rose bush I had planted with my first-grade class the week before. Our teacher, Mrs. Okazaki, promised that we would make a vegetable garden next spring, and we could take the vegetables to the temple orphanage since most of my classmates had their own private family gardens. Of course, my family's garden was the nicest. My father made sure of that.

I took my seat and opened my song book. The clock on the wall above the blackboard read 8:14. Mrs. Okazaki addressed my first-grade class: "Students, let us all sing our national anthem. Please stand."

As I smoothed my skirt and pulled my knee socks up, there was a blinding flash of light. Glass and debris flew into the classroom, and I stood terrified, looking through the empty window frames as a building next to the school caught fire. Mrs. Okazaki screamed for us to follow her into the cellar. We held one another's hands as we stumbled down the stairs.

It was hot and humid in the dank cellar. Mrs. Okazaki handed me a handkerchief and told me to press it against my forehead. A shard of glass had cut me, but I hadn't noticed in the confusion.

Mrs. Okazaki cranked the radio, then turned the dial, trying to find a station that would explain what was happening, but all we heard was static, like paper being wadded into a ball, echoing against the cellar walls. My teeth chattered, and I couldn't catch my breath. My white blouse was splattered with blood. Some children moaned and cried out in pain, while others sat on the benches in stunned silence.

Handing out padded air-raid helmets, Mrs. Okazaki instructed us to put them on and hook the straps under our chins. Mine was so big that it slipped beneath my eyes, but I was afraid not to wear it in case the ceiling collapsed. We looked as if we were wearing turtle shells for hats. Mrs. Okazaki told us that any minute our parents would arrive to take each of us home. "For now, I'm going to tell you the story of the brave Little Peach Boy, Momotarō. Noriko, you have such a pretty voice. Why don't you sing the song about Momotarō, who slayed the evil foreign devil?"

I didn't want to disappoint Mrs. Okazaki, but I was too weak to stand up. Instead I sat on the bench and did my best to control my breath so I could sing:

Momotaro, Momotaro, You have dumplings in the pouch at your waist
Please give me one.

I'll give you one, I'll give you one,
For the future of the [enemy devil] expedition,
I'll give you one if you come.

Let's go, let's go,
I'll go with you wherever you go,
I'll go as your servant.

Let's attack the enemy-demon island at once,

Great! Great!
We've attacked and pinned down the demons,
Let's get the treasure back!

The other children joined in, and then Mrs. Okazaki used a flashlight to read the story to us, the beam making shadows on the craggy walls. I had a hard time concentrating on her words. Instead, I thought about my father—where was he? How long would I be trapped underground? I closed my eyes—fear giving way to exhaustion—and drifted off.

The sound of heavy footsteps on the stairs woke me. It was my father, Ryo. He was covered in dust and dirt, his pants torn and his shirt filled with big holes. He yelled out my name, and holding a flashlight, he made his way into the cellar. "Here, Papa. I'm right here." As he rushed toward me I knew I was saved. Nothing more to worry about.

He grabbed my hand, and we hurried toward the steps. As we passed Mrs. Okazaki, she whispered, "Please, Mr. Ito. Tell someone there are twenty-three students waiting to be rescued, and some of them are severely injured. I don't know how long we can stay down here. They should be seen at the hospital."

"Who am I supposed to tell, Mrs. Okazaki? It looks as if half of Hiroshima is no more. There is a firestorm out there and the streets are all torn up. Anyone who could has sought shelter, and the rest…It is unbelievable."

My father's hand felt strong and safe as we climbed up the stairs and came upon my classroom. Mrs. Okazaki's desk was in splinters and the blackboard had come off the wall and was tossed on its side. Jars of bright finger paint stained the floor. The glass windows were all blown out and the bricks that had promised to withstand a bomb blast lay in tumbled heaps. Books and papers had been sucked out the window. The rosebush I had planted was blackened; its leaves curled like burned paper on their scorched stems.

I felt something prick my foot and realized I had lost one of my birthday shoes. "Papa, can you help me look for it?"

"Noriko, be sensible. There is no chance we'll find your shoe in all this mess. I'll buy you another pair when I can. We need to get home. I've left your mother and your brother to fend for themselves."

My father's bicycle leaned against a charred tree stump in the schoolyard. After tying Mrs. Okazaki's handkerchief around my nose and mouth, he lifted me into the basket on the handlebars and instructed me to sit still as he pedaled his bicycle around the puddles and debris in what remained of the street. Huge boulders made of street pavement blocked our path, and my father had to avoid black holes that went down as far as the cellar I had just been freed from.

In the distance, I saw skeletons of bombed-out buildings; gray steam rose up from the ground, burning my nose and eyes. Charred bodies cluttered the streets, and the living looked to be walking around in a daze, many with blackened skin hanging from their faces and arms. A woman beside the road lifted her sleeping baby out of its carriage, and then holding the child in her arms, collapsed. I prayed that the mother would get up, but she lay motionless while her baby gripped at his mother's breast for milk with his tiny hands.

A light rain fell, misting my face and mingling with the tears that ran down my cheeks. Within minutes, black water drops fell from the sky. Survivors opened their parched lips trying to catch the drops. I had never seen black rain before. My father yelled in my ear, "Keep your mouth closed, Noriko. This is poison."

Electric poles listed off their moorings. Wires waved ominously in the wind, sending sparks into the air. People along the way asked politely, "Help me, I'm burning to death," but my father had nothing to offer and so we did not stop. I heard a man cry, "Give me water!" His face was like a cake of blackened tofu, his eyes, nose, and mouth boiled beyond recognition. Miraculously, my father found our way home despite the charred landscape. My father lifted me out of the basket and carried me up the five flights of stairs to our apartment, which, except for a gaping hole in the roof, had withstood the bomb. Many of the other houses in our neighborhood were not so fortunate. The clay roof tiles next door melted in the fire and heat.

My mother Kimie was sitting at our table holding my brother, four-year-old Tadashi, on her lap. Our apartment looked as if it had barely been touched by the explosion. The tatami mats lay flat on the floor, and the painted screen of an owl sitting on a pine branch covered with puffs of snow hung in the alcove undisturbed. An orange metal teapot sat on the stove and firewood was piled in the corner. On the porch, the laundry, normally white from my mother's scrubbing, was blackened as it flapped in the wind. Despite the intermittent sounds of neighbors screaming for help, my brother was fast asleep.

My mother asked me, "What's happened to your forehead, Noriko?"

"Something hit me."

"Come here so that I can clean your wound with some peroxide. We don't have any water right now."

While my mother tended to my wound, I confessed, "Please don't be angry, but I lost my shoe."

"Don't worry. There are plenty of extra pairs in Setsuko's wardrobe closet that are too small for her."

I stomped my foot. "Now that I'm in first grade, I want to wear a nice pair of shoes, not my sister's hand-me-downs." Looking back on this, I am ashamed for being so petulant.

My mother stuck a barrette in my hair so it wouldn't infect my wound. "We're going to have to make do with what we have for the time being. And I'll thank you to stop complaining. We are lucky to be alive."

"What's happened, Papa?"

"The Americans bombed Hiroshima to let us know who is going to win the war. But we are stronger than this bomb. The Emperor will find a way to fight back and the gods will protect us."

For the first time in my life I didn't believe my father. It was not my place to argue with him, and I wanted to believe him with all my heart.

〜

MY FATHER WAS A member of the Neighborhood Volunteer Crew. With the other men who had escaped injury, he went out into the streets in the days immediately following the blast with a wheelbarrow and moved the dying into temporary shelters. The corpses—many quickly covered with maggots and vermin—were buried in mounds under the smoking ash to avoid the spread of disease. The main hospital in Hiroshima had been destroyed by the bomb and all the doctors and nurses working there were killed so survivors were on their own taking care of wounded family and neighbors.

In the immediate aftermath of the blast, I saw many people jumping into the city canals when their bodies caught on fire, but the water was fuel and their bodies burned like parchment paper. I heard rumors that fish turned upside down as they swam into the tributary of the Ota River where I used to skip stones. I hated going outside. The stench of dead bodies was sickening. All I wanted to do was go back to school. I had to stay at home with my mother and brother and wait for the news of the day. Nothing made sense. Why did the Americans hate us so much that they would destroy our city and kill our people? Were they devils who wanted to steal the riches of the Empire and make us all their slaves?

When my father came home at night after working all day on the street crew, he dumped his work clothes in a basket outside and wore them again the next day. The water had been turned back on, but it was in scarce supply, and we didn't want to waste it by washing clothes. I couldn't go to sleep at night, and during the day a black cloud floated over the city. I wondered if the sun would ever come out again. People said that what had happened was because the gods were angry with us. No one went outside without wearing face masks to block the stench of death and dying. I didn't recognize anyone until they spoke, and even when they did, their voices sounded strange, as if someone was choking them. They were like croaking frogs and chirping cicadas.

Three days after the big bomb was dropped, there was news that a second bomb—even bigger—was dropped on Nagasaki and the Americans were threatening to launch an attack against Osaka and Tokyo, where the Emperor lived in the Imperial Palace. How could that be? The Emperor was a god and protected from the American devils.

I tried to make myself useful by amusing my brother while my mother mended the pleated skirt of the uniform I wore the day of the bombing. I held up a rabbit sock puppet and asked Tadashi, "Do you have a carrot, kind sir? I am sooooo hungry."

Tadashi ran to the ice box. When he opened the door, it was dripping water from the melted ice. He squealed, "No, I don't have a carrot. Be quiet. I will find you a carrot in the garden," he answered. Turning to my mother, he asked, "Can we go outside, Mama?"

"No, my angel. It's safer for you to stay indoors. Noriko, put down the puppet and tell your brother a happy story." I couldn't think of one—all the stories that popped into my head were about devils, demons, and ghosts.

I looked up, startled by the sound of the door to our apartment opening. My father, still in his dirty work clothes, said to my mother, "Kimie, turn on the radio. The Holy Emperor Hirohito is going to speak to us for the first time. He must have something important to announce."

In a squeaky, high-pitched voice so unlike what I imagined the Emperor's voice to be, and speaking in a language I barely understood, we were told, "To our good and loyal subjects. After pondering the general trends of the world and actual conditions of our Empire, today we have decided to accept a settlement of the present situation. The enemy has begun to employ a new and most cruel bomb, the power of which to do damage is, indeed, incalculable. Should we continue to fight, not only would it result in the ultimate collapse and obliteration of the Japanese nation, but it would also lead to the total extinction of human civilization."

I asked my father what all this meant. After taking a long gulp of water from the tap, he said, "The war is over." I couldn't tell from the tone of his voice if this was a good thing. Hadn't our soldiers said they would fight until the bitter end? My mother opened the window to our apartment. Neighbors were gathering in the street and singing our national anthem: "*May your reign continue for a thousand, eight thousand generations / Until pebbles grow into boulders lush with moss.*"

My father grumbled, "We should write a new anthem. The Emperor does not deserve our allegiance now that he has chosen to surrender."

My mother said, "Haven't we had enough death and destruction?" All I could think of was that I'd be able to go back to school and see my friends and my teacher, Mrs. Okazaki. And then I remembered that my school was in shambles, and my rosebush blackened liked burnt toast.

My father's anger was like a disturbed hornets' nest. When he heard that a US general, a man named MacArthur, called us a "Fourth Rate Nation," he stormed out of the apartment, but not before swearing, "This devil will learn to eat his words. We will prove the bastard wrong." I had never seen my father so enraged. My mother told me to ignore him. Tadashi, afraid of my father's booming voice, hid under a blanket and whimpered.

Each day something was fixed: water, electricity, and then the streets were swept of rubble and the corpses disappeared. But a month after the bomb was dropped, the skies opened up. A typhoon made landfall, and what the bomb had missed was swept up in the wind and rain of Makurazaki, as the typhoon was named. Our city—or what was left of it—was hard hit. We stayed indoors, listening to the wind and the rain pelting the windows and drumming on the roof. Puddles formed on the kitchen floor where the rain seeped through the holes.

My father stood on a chair trying to stay ahead of the rain that fell ceaselessly. "Noriko, hand me a nail so I can fix the hole in the roof."

I was grateful I could help my father, who looked weary from weeks of cleanup and repair. When the rain finally subsided, the hills surrounding Hiroshima burst into a wild profusion of flowers despite predictions that nothing would grow for the next seventy-five years. The hills looked as if they were draped in a golden cape, and sunbeams spotlighted its brilliance. I was relieved to see the sun come out again.

My father and I walked through the muddy yard behind our apartment. My rubber boots kept getting stuck in the ground, and I had to lean over and pull one foot and then the other out with my hands. I spotted the first blades of grass poking through the earth, which soaked up the rainwater like a parched victim of the bomb. My father planted a vegetable garden because the supply of food from the countryside was dwindling to less than a basket a week. We were forced to eat barley rice, *eba dango* (weed rice cake), and hard donuts.

My father told me, "It will be your job to make sure no weeds choke the plants once the seeds take root." Within days plants and flowers burst forth from the earth. Under the foundation of ruined houses along our street, Spanish bayonets, goose foot, morning glories, and canna lilies sprang up, their enormous shapes distorted by some poisonous and unseen magical force. I was afraid that, like the plants, the black rain had done something terrible to me—that my body would become misshapen, too, and I might die.

Chapter 4

PUSHING A WHEELBARROW LOADED with a shovel, pail, and broom, my father and I found our way to what remained of his sushi shop next to Hiroshima's central train station. The sign, ITO'S FRESHEST SUSHI, banged back and forth on its hinges, rocked by the wind coming off the Ota River. My father climbed over the wreckage that had once been a neat and tidy counter. Carving knives were melted into the steel counters. The black-and-white checkered linoleum had peeled away from the floorboards, and the broken glass from the display cases glistened like icicles piercing the leather stools. Delicate plates and bowls decorated with bright orange koi and lotus flowers lay cracked amidst the ashen rubble.

My father raked his fingers through his graying hair and then picked up the cash register, which no longer held its drawer. I held my breath, afraid of what Father might do or say. Instead of cursing the gods, he dropped the cash register and cried, his shoulders shaking with each heaving sob.

I turned away, not wanting to see my father so defeated. Looking into the middle distance, I stared at a girl in the street dressed in rags and wearing sandals that kept slipping off her feet. Around her neck was a rope and attached to it was a small white box. She looked so sad. I waved at her, but she ignored me and kept walking toward the railroad station, where people were gathering. A line of uniformed soldiers shuffled into the train station seeking shelter. There was no train service, but the trolleys were again running in parts of the city where electricity had been restored.

I took a broom out of the wheelbarrow and brought it to my father. "Papa, I saw a girl about the same age as me with a white box hanging from her neck. What's in it?"

"The bones and ashes of her parents. She is trying to find a place to bury them."

"Where does she live now that her parents are dead?"

"Probably in an orphanage run by the church or in one of the camps along the side of the road."

I hesitated and then asked him, "Can we take her home? Setsuko's room is empty."

"Not for long. She will be home soon. And what gives you the idea that we have enough food to feed another hungry mouth? You see what has become of my shop. It will be months until I can reopen for business. And where are my customers? Most of them are in a white box or near death in a makeshift hospital." I felt foolish asking whether we could take care of the girl, but she was about my age and I felt sorry for her. And more than that, I couldn't comprehend that our situation was so terrible. I had always counted on my father to take care of our family no matter what was happening outside our door.

My father picked up a shovel to clear a path through the shop. The back of his shirt was stained with sweat and his hair was covered in dust. The stench of decaying fish burned my eyes, and I had to keep swatting the flies. My father leaned against his shovel. "Put these gloves on and see if you can find some pieces of matching pottery."

"What will you do with them?"

"When something breaks, we shouldn't throw it away. We can repair it. We'll fill the cracks with liquid gold or silver and it will be more beautiful and unique than it was originally. Potters call this practice of repair *kintsugi*." He kissed me on my forehead and then traced my scar. "Just like your scar. Someday you will see it as a mark of your uniqueness, Noriko, and you'll be able to tell your children how you survived. You should be proud of it. "

"I'll try, Papa. I promise. And you will be part of my story."

～

IN FEBRUARY, MY SCHOOL reopened in an old heavy masonry bank building that had withstood "Little Boy," the name given to the bomb that destroyed Hiroshima. Mrs. Okazaki was no longer my teacher. The principal told my class, "Mrs. Okazaki's husband was a soldier and he gave up his life for our country. He is a real hero, but Mrs. Okazaki cannot smile, and she would rather stay at home so she does not make you sad, too." Some of my classmates did not return either. No one explained where they were, but I guessed they had either moved to the countryside or died. Many people in our neighborhood were sick with what some called Disease X because we had no idea what its true name might be, which caused their hair to fall out in chunks and their skin to shrivel up or turn bright red with weeping welts. The doctors who came into Hiroshima from other cities to help us didn't know what to do with those who had this mysterious illness other than feed them miso soup and pumpkin and keep them away from sugar and meat. If they knew what Disease X was, they were keeping it a secret.

My mother told me it was not catching, but every day, when I brushed my hair, I'd look to make sure that the bristles weren't filled; and when I got dressed in the morning, I'd examine myself for a rash. I decided that, if I found something terrible, I would not admit it to my parents but just wish it away. The children in my class were silent about what went on in their homes, but their drawings told stories of illness and death: a blackbird picking up a baby in its beak; someone's mother washing a gravestone at the cemetery in Onomichi; a boy shining shoes while a young girl looked on with a white box, that terrible white box, hanging from her neck.

And yet, even with all the sadness, we found time to play pop the ball or to chase one another across the school yard. Out of habit, we'd still stare at the sky looking for a war plane; but there were only puffy clouds and flocks of birds overhead.

My half-sister, Setsuko, returned from the military base where she was working, and after a few months of arguing with my parents, she moved to Osaka and married Hideo Fujiwara. They opened a tearoom in the Namba district, and some of the customers were Americans and English who were part of the rebuilding effort in Osaka. My sister and her husband lived on the third floor above the tearoom, as was customary among Japanese restaurant owners. In four years, they had a boy and a girl and a third baby on the way.

My father disapproved of her husband. "Hideo is part Chinese, and he's a good for nothing, spending all day at the pachinko parlor, wasting the money that your daughter makes." Setsuko was his stepdaughter but that didn't stop him from passing judgment on her choice of a husband.

My mother said, "Well, if she's unhappy with him, she can get rid of him. Divorce is not illegal."

"Where did you come up with such an idea? A single woman with children is like a bowl of day-old rice. No man will bother to look at her."

"You looked at me after my first husband died and I was left with Setsuko."

"That was different. You were a widow when I met you. In this case, Setsuko would be a divorced woman."

My mother argued, "Setsuko can take care of herself, and she has her rights. Women are no longer second-class citizens. We're going to have the vote soon, and we're going to make our own money."

My father sat down with a groan. "Is that what the war has done, given women such ideas? Maybe I should stay home and let you run the sushi shop."

"Don't tempt me, Ryo. If I knew how to cut fish as finely as you do, I would, but since I haven't your skill, we'll just have to live as we have. You cut fish and I'll watch the cash register and smile for the customers."

Ryo slapped his knees. "That's a pretty picture, but in a few years, you're going to be toothless and bald from old age. And then what?"

My mother was cutting a head of cabbage for soup. She picked up her knife, and in a threatening tone, she said, "Enough, Ryo. Noriko is listening to every word you're saying."

I was tired of hearing my parents fight. I loved them both equally and hated the ugly way they spoke to one another sometimes. I assumed there had to be some secret between them, an angry secret, that made them speak to one another in such a way.

I was relieved to be in middle school to get away from their arguments. As soon as I got home, I'd go to my room and, instead of doing my homework, I'd pore over the latest issue of *Women's Gazette,* devouring the articles and photographs of the glamorous actresses of the Takarazuka, an all-women's theater company in Osaka and Tokyo that had reopened after the war. I'd imagine performing in one of their lavish Broadway-style musicals when I was old enough to try out for the company. I wrote in my school notebook, "Noriko Ito Wins Adoring Fans in a sold-out performance of *The Rose of Versailles.*" I knew this was to be my destiny, and I vowed to do whatever it took to get there.

The photographs I found most intriguing were of actresses playing male roles—they were the real stars of the company and my classmates and I had crushes on them. These women were dressed in tight-fitting tuxedos, their hair cut short and greased back; and they penciled in sideburns and heavy eyebrows. I joined a fan club for the biggest star, Yachiyo Kasugano, pinning her picture up on my bedroom wall. The members of the troupe were expected to dedicate themselves entirely to their profession and forbidden by the producer from having boyfriends or from marrying until they left the company, which I thought was a small sacrifice to make to be famous. I didn't see the point of marriage anyway when my parents were constantly bickering, and my sister was married to a lout who lived off her hard labor. Some of the stars went into the film business after they left the Takarazuka and married politicians and rich businessmen. Maybe that would be my fate.

⌒

WHEN I TURNED FIFTEEN, eight years after the bombing of Hiroshima, I begged my father to send me to an expensive all-girls high school with a reputable drama club. I knew his sushi business was doing well again and he was able to pay for more than just the bare household necessities. It didn't take much convincing. I think he shared my ambition. He told me, "What is money for but to spoil my only daughter?"

"What about your only son? He's going to need to go to a good school. He'll be twelve on his next birthday. Or do you want him to be a sushi maker like you instead of a professional man?" asked my mother.

"Let me worry about Tadashi's future. And what's wrong with being a sushi maker, if I might ask? When did you get so high and mighty, Kimie?"

I thought the matter settled, but then she bargained with my father. "Well, if you have enough money to send Noriko to this fancy school, what about buying us some fresh tatami mats and a new carved lacquered table?"

"Fair enough, Kimie. But don't ask me for anything else. At least not right now."

Winking at me, she continued, "What about the vacation you promised us?"

He must have been feeling very guilty about something because he looked as if he had been backed into a corner. "You don't give up, do you? I can't leave the shop, but in a few months, we can discuss this again." All I could think of was that he had merely left the door open for another argument. And I knew my mother wouldn't leave him alone until she got what she wanted. I should have learned something about how to treat men from my mother, but I did just the opposite.

Chapter 5

I HELD A CANDLE up to my face, moving it from left to right and staring at the shadows playing across my cheeks and nose in front of the full-length mirror in my darkened room. Time had faded the angry, red scar on my forehead. It was hardly visible, and my black bangs made a curtain that hid what remained. I practiced my part in the drama club's production of *The Third Man*. I had been selected by the director for the male lead, American pulp fiction writer Holly Martins, the part played by Joseph Cotten in the film version. Ten other girls had tried out for the role, including my best friend Mizuki. Some girls were jealous I was chosen, but I didn't care. My father told me, "Ambition is nothing to apologize for."

My mother chimed in. "Even if Noriko is the most talented actress, that doesn't give her an excuse to put her nose in the air. You know what they say: 'The nail that sticks out gets hammered down.'"

"Mama, I'm nice to everyone. I can't help it if they are jealous of me. If they're not happy for me, they aren't truly my friends." That was the end of the discussion.

After turning on the phonograph player, I tipped the gray felt fedora at a jaunty angle, tightened the belt of a beige raincoat, turned up the collar, and sang out, enunciating each word to "The Third Man" theme as my teacher instructed.

I lowered my voice and repeated the lyrics so I sounded more masculine while trying to capture the yearning and sadness behind the words: love, supreme rapture. But what did I know of any of it? Trapped in Hiroshima, I had hardly lived. It seemed as if the world was spinning faster and faster and I, an impatient sixteen-year-old, was standing still, eager for my life to begin.

～

I WAITED FOR THE overture to *The Third Man* to end, and then, in the darkness, I took my place on stage with the rest of the cast. The lights went up slowly to reveal a turning Ferris wheel, its twinkling lights blinking in time to the music. The trees of Vienna's pleasure park were sketched on the canvas. A cast member pushed a cart selling make-believe frankfurters and sauerkraut, and a couple walked arm in arm across the shadowed stage. I couldn't see the audience over the footlights, but I sensed my parents and my brother sitting among them. As the spotlight followed me across the stage, my legs barely carried me, and I thought I might faint from the powerful potion of fear mixed with excitement. My teacher had said, "Use your fear. If you feel nothing you are not fully invested in your performance, Noriko, and the audience will be easily bored."

My body remembered from arduous practice exactly where I needed to go and so I didn't think about where I should be on the stage at any given moment, and I dug deep within myself to pull out all the emotions of each song and each scene. I could feel the knot in my stomach slowly loosening, and before I knew it the audience was clapping and the cast members were all standing next to one another taking our bows. I felt as if I was coming out of a trance when my proud father climbed onto the stage and handed me a bouquet of purple orchids. I bowed, took off my fedora so that my black hair fell dramatically around my face as I had practiced in my mirror, and then handed the delicate flowers to our director, Mrs. Nakamura, even though I felt I deserved them just as much as she did.

The school newspaper carried a review of *The Third Man*. I read it repeatedly in order to memorize it. "Here's what it says, Mama and Papa." I noticed my brother wasn't paying attention. "Are you listening to me, Tadashi?"

"Yes, Noriko. You're standing on a chair so how could I not be?" My thirteen-year-old brother had developed a wicked sense of humor and loved to tease me, but from the look on his face I guessed he was proud of me.

"Well then: 'Noriko Ito gave a natural and convincing performance of Holly Martins. She is a chameleon with an androgynous yet delicate face. She has a lovely voice and is light on her feet. At the risk of overstepping my role as a reviewer, may I say that Noriko will certainly find her way to the Takarazuka Theater Academy. We look forward to seeing her in the limelight and making our drama club most proud.'" I folded the newspaper, climbed down from my perch on the chair, then cut out the review and pasted it in my scrapbook.

Late in the day, my mother's older sister, Auntie Sanae, came to our apartment to take me to the evening service at the neighborhood Tenrikyo church where she worshipped twice a day. I insisted on reading the review of my performance to her. Gently placing her hands on my shoulders, she admonished me, "Remember, Noriko, the worst sin in our religion is arrogance. Don't think you are better than someone else because of your talent and beauty. They are nothing compared with the traits of generosity and selflessness. That is what God the Parent teaches us and what is essential to leading a joyous and fulfilling life. You will hear this message during prayers, and you must imprint this in your heart."

"What if I pray to God the Parent to forgive me for my arrogance for the time being and ask that She be patient and wait for me to become a virtuous person after I have earned a place in the Takarazuka Academy?"

My father snickered. "That's my girl. I like your pragmatism."

Auntie Sanae sighed. "Don't encourage her, Ryo. Just because you and Kimie have turned your backs on religion, that doesn't make it right. And what if she doesn't get into the Academy? You are just setting her up for disappointment."

I interrupted my aunt. "If I don't get in, I'll die. I swear it."

My father's face turned the color of a red radish. "Don't you dare say such a thing. You're lucky to be alive!"

My father's words were like a slap across my face. He was right, and I felt so ashamed. He continued, "Had you been at the Shima Hospital where everyone was incinerated when the bomb fell, or at my shop or a few steps closer to the window at your school…" He was out of breath and could not continue his rant.

Auntie Sanae came to my defense. "We don't want our youth to live in the shadow of the bomb. It's better that they try to forget what happened and think about their future. They shouldn't be punished for what happened."

I asked for my father's forgiveness. He reached into his pocket and gave me a few coins. "Put these in the charity box at the church. Ask your God the Parent to forgive you."

∼

THE CHIRPING OF THE crickets accompanied the sound of our footsteps along the freshly laid pavement as Auntie Sanae and I made our way to church. The moon was rising, casting a silver sheen over the newly constructed house rooftops. An occasional truck heading toward farmland passed us. I waited for my aunt to tell me something that would make me feel better and lessen the throbbing in my head. She did not disappoint me. "Noriko, try to understand your father. It is only because he loves you that he speaks harshly. His mood swings—that's what we call them—are not unusual among the hibakusha. The wounds of the explosion-affected people are not only physical. They are also mental. Many feel guilty to have survived, and others hold in their anger but sometimes they explode in unpredictable ways toward those they love the most. Do you understand what I'm saying?"

I nodded, but truthfully it was hard to follow my aunt's logic. If someone loved me, why would they be mean to me? I had a lot to learn about love.

Taking quicker strides so as not to be late for the evening service, she continued, "One reason many people have joined the Tenrikyo church is to overcome their anger. We preach the importance of leading a joyful life, no matter our circumstances, and that giving to others is where we find the greatest joy." This lesson would one day give me the strength to carry me through my darkest hours.

When we entered the church, a calmness came over me. Six male and female priests led the evening service, singing prayers accompanied by familiar hand gestures. I liked seeing women, unlike what was customary in the Buddhist and Shinto temples, leading the service. After all, why shouldn't women have the right to become religious leaders when the religion's foundress was a woman? Many worshippers had scars on their faces and were blind. When some raised their hands, I saw they were missing fingers or their hands were gnarled like the branches of a tree, and yet they all had smiles on their faces. The priests reminded us we could not control what happens to our body but that we have dominion over our minds. Our first duty, they said, is to sweep away the evils of our mind in order to attain salvation. Then, singing together accompanied by the beat of the drums, clappers, and gongs, they repeated, "Throughout the world, God is the broom for the sweeping of the innermost heart. Watch carefully and find ways to bring joy to others." I squeezed Auntie Sanae's hand to signal my gratitude for her bringing me here.

After the service, I dropped the coins my father had given me into the alms box. As they clanked to the bottom, I said my own silent prayer that the church foundress, Nakayama Miki, would help me get into the Takarazuka Theater Academy because my acceptance would bring joy to my mother and father. Wasn't that one of the messages in the service, to bring joy to others? That was the way my sixteen-year-old mind chose to interpret the prayers.

The next day, my drama teacher announced she planned a field trip for the club to see a performance of *Veronique* presented by the Takarazuka Theater Company at their grand theater on the outskirts of Osaka in the Hyogo Prefecture, a six-hour train ride from Hiroshima. I had never been anywhere without my parents, and I was afraid they might not give me permission, but my mother reasoned, "If you get into trouble, you can call your sister, Setsuko, in Namba, and she'll come to your rescue. You haven't seen her in such a long time or met her children. She would be delighted to see you."

My father said, "Of course, you can go. I wouldn't want your classmates to think I don't have the money to pay for a hotel or train tickets."

⌒

Mrs. Nakamura instructed us to stay close to one another as we walked from the train station to the Takarazuka Theater. "I don't want you getting lost in this crowd." She handed our tickets to us, and together we climbed the stairs into the grand theater like a long row of ducklings following their mother. I was so excited I could hardly breathe. Until the lights went down, I read the program describing the background of each actress and listing the songs in *Veronique*, which is based on a French opera in nineteenth century Paris, mainly in a flower shop. The two stars are Hélène, a lady of the court, and Flouristan, a ne'er-do-well his uncle hopes to introduce to Hélène so they might marry and she would then be able to pay off his debts.

The audience went wild when the haughty duchess said, "Men! I'm totally bored with them. Sticky as oil, to say the least. Inconsiderate and ever hungry for more power, conceited animals! Overconfident as if no sex is superior to theirs, shamelessly do they resort to violence against us. Oh, that filthy sex, holding themselves so superior, the pride unsubstantiated. Don't they kneel begging for love of women? Erotic beasts, that's what men are." I could not believe the playwright lauded the superiority of women over men, but it pleased me to no end because I agreed with him.

After intermission, the story veered away from the classic *Veronique*. From the back of the stage, twenty women—some dressed in pink taffeta ball gowns and others in tight-fitting sequined tuxedos—sang and strutted their way down the stairs, which were lit with twinkling lights. The audience broke out in thunderous applause as the *otokoyaku* top star, Chikage Ogi, bathed in a single spotlight, walked across the stage. She was dressed in a black tuxedo with glossy black feathers attached to her back and arms. Spreading them wide and commanding center stage as the chorus twirled around her, she sang out in a low voice, sounding more like a man than a woman. She floated off stage and then the entire company reappeared to sing the final number and take their bows. I sat glued to my seat. My best friend Mizuki pinched my arm. "We're leaving, or are you just going to sit there dreaming until the next performance?"

"I wish I could see it all over again." The performance made such a lasting impression upon me. Even when I got older and my life was far removed from the theater, I could close my eyes and recall every moment. It became one of my many escapes.

Mizuki took my hand and yanked me out of my seat. "Come on. We have to get back to the hotel."

Hundreds of women and young girls patiently waited for the stars to come out of the side door of the theater to present them with gifts and get their autographs. I tried to break away to join the line, but Mrs. Nakamura hurried us back to the train station for an overnight stay at a hotel.

I spoke up. "Can't we stay? It can't be so difficult to find my way back to the hotel. I can always ask someone for directions."

"No. A polite Japanese girl doesn't speak to strangers."

I whispered to Mizuki, "I don't like being treated like a child. And I do know how to read a map. At least I think I do…"

Mizuki laughed. "Really, Noriko. You have a lot of nerve. I wish I were as brazen as you, but everything scares me."

"That's why you need to try new things. We can't lead a sheltered life if we expect to get anywhere." I wasn't sure I could follow my own advice, but I thought, if I kept repeating these ideas, eventually I would become a more courageous person. However, I decided for now I'd follow Mrs. Nakamura's orders. I had a secret plan that I was about to execute and I needed Mizuki's help.

Mizuki and I shared a room at the hotel. I handed her a pair of sharp scissors I packed in my leather satchel. "Here, cut it all off."

"Are you serious, Noriko? You are going to look like a boy with nutshell breasts."

"Don't be ridiculous. I want to look like one of the Takarazuka stars. Here's a picture of Chikage Ogi in the program. Copy this!"

Skeins of black hair fell to the bathroom floor as Mizuki cut away. I ran my wet hands through my short hair, arranged it in a style, and asked Mizuki how I looked.

"Just like a Takarazuka star, Noriko."

Lowering my voice and pressing Mizuki's hand to my lips, I asked, "Mademoiselle Hélène, may I have this dance?" Feeling uninhibited, we waltzed across the tatami mats and then fell on top of one another laughing.

Mizuki shyly undressed in front of me. Turning around, she showed me the keloid scars on her back. "They aren't so bad, are they?"

I gulped, not knowing what to say. They looked as if a wild beast had torn into Mizuki's flesh. "The makeup artist will do a good job covering them up; the audience won't even notice them under the lights."

I brushed my bangs from my forehead, exposing my scar. "You already saw this. Does it look awful?"

Mizuki shook her head. "It's nothing. Nothing at all." Sitting on the floor, she asked me, "Where were you when the bomb exploded over the city?"

"I was at my school. My father saved me. He was the first person to reach us. And you?"

"I was near the epicenter. My mother was walking me to school that day. She pulled me out of the rubble, but a few weeks later, all her hair fell out, her gums started to bleed, and she had a terrible case of diarrhea. She died two months later. It was the saddest day of my life. My father has remarried, and my stepmother is pregnant. She is worried sick that something will be wrong with the baby even after all this time. There are people who believe that they have a time bomb inside them just waiting to go off—even after eight years."

"Because of radiation?" We had learned this word when some details were no longer kept a secret.

Mizuki swallowed hard and then asked, "Do you go to the doctor every year for a checkup, Noriko?"

"What for?"

"The Japanese and American doctors have been keeping track of the health of some of us to see who gets sick. They want to know how far we were from the epicenter so they can gauge the bomb's effects on us. Their examinations weren't so bad when I was younger, but now the doctors make me stand on a stage and slip a surgical gown down to my waist so they can examine my breasts. It's mortifying."

Just another indignity of being a hibakusha, I thought. I answered, "Mizuki, you and I are lucky to be alive. That's what my father likes to remind me and he's right. I'm sorry your mother can't see what a beautiful daughter she has. If you weren't my best friend, I'd be jealous of you."

"You have no reason to be jealous of my looks. You're just as pretty, and you've earned the top roles in our club performances. No one else stands a chance against you."

"Coming from you, that is a very high compliment. I always think of you as my stiffest competition. I wish we could always be on an equal footing so neither of us would win or lose." Mizuki nodded and promised that we would be friends for life.

Realizing I was tired after such a long and exciting day, I yawned. "Let's get into bed." I opened the window to let in some fresh air, and from the street below we heard a man singing a jazzy American tune. I looked out the window and there was an American GI dressed in a uniform with his arm draped around a Japanese woman, who looked to be a little older than Mizuki and I, wearing a low-cut green dress and balancing on a pair of high heels. They stopped underneath a streetlight, and putting his arms around her, the soldier kissed the girl. She leaned against him. He lightly grazed her breast with his hand, and then the couple disappeared into the darkness. Mizuki and I sat there for a time, embarrassed and, speaking for myself at least, aroused by this intimate gesture.

I asked Mizuki, "Do you believe in love?"

"I don't know anything about it except what I read in the *Women's Gazette* and see in the movies. I've never been out with a boy. I wouldn't know what to say to him."

"Me neither. Love will have to wait. All I care about is getting into the Takarazuka."

Mizuki smiled. "Let's see if we can find a shooting star to wish on." And just as she said this, a bright light streaked across the night sky.

I felt enveloped in happiness. "Good night, Hélène."

Mizuki answered, "*Bonne nuit*, Flouristan."

In unison, we sighed and exclaimed that this had been the most exciting day of our lives. At the risk of sounding arrogant, I said, "It's just the beginning!"

Chapter 6

I CELEBRATED MY SEVENTEENTH birthday in August and graduated high school. My parents—relieved I got through school despite the distractions of acting and singing—gave me permission to move to Osaka the following January. Lucky for me, my half-sister, Setsuko, offered to put me up in the apartment she shared with her husband, Hideo Fujiwara, and their three children. The apartment was above the Aki-Torii Grille Room, one of the two restaurants they owned and managed. The other restaurant was the European-style Tesagara Tearoom in the upscale Namba district, where I'd be put to work while I waited for my classes at the Academy to begin in May (that is, if I got in). Other than helping my father in his shop, I'd never had a job, but I felt confident I could play the role of tearoom waitress.

Before leaving for Osaka, Mizuki and I took French and English elocution lessons so we could sing the Takarazuka repertoire. We also studied tap and ballet and practiced interviewing skills so that we would convey the Takarazuka standards of "Beauty, Purity, and Honesty." My father spent a lot of money to prepare me for my audition but I think he saw it as a wise investment. One day I'd be a star able to support myself, and when the time came to leave the Takarazuka, I'd have my pick of wealthy men to marry. The competition to get into the Academy was ferocious—there were only forty spots with more than a thousand girls competing. Would I be one of the chosen few? And what about Mizuki? We wanted to go together to support each other.

~

SETSUKO SENT ME A map and marked the route from the Umeda train station to the Aki-Torii Grille Room in Osaka's Kitashinchi district. Carrying my suitcase and a book bag with sheet music, a leotard, tights, and my dance shoes, I hurried through the streets and then into the entertainment center of Osaka. It was freezing cold and had I not had all my bags with me I would have broken into a run to stay warm. The area was crowded with brightly lit restaurants offering sushi, shabu-shabu, and tempura; stores with Frank Sinatra and Billie Holiday records; and bars smelling of smoke and beer, the acrid scent drifting into the alley. Women dressed in cosmopolitan outfits were steered through the crowd by their male escorts, looking proud to have an attractive woman on their arm.

At the corner of the cobblestone lane marked on the map with an X was a Buddhist temple dedicated to the god Mizukake-fudo. A statue of the god was covered in moss from all the years of worshippers dousing it with water as they prayed for good luck and a good marriage. I could not spare any money, but feeling insecure and unsure, I said a quick prayer, asking the god to bring me luck.

I turned into the lane and found my way to the Aki-Torii Grille. Pushing the cotton banner aside that had the name of the restaurant emblazoned on it, the name meaning Autumn Gate, I stepped into the crowded dining room. The patrons sat at the bar or at wooden tables with dishes of grilled meat and bottles of sake and beer. A poster with a couple dressed in ski clothes hung on the wall: "Kirin Stout: The Beer to Drink in Winter." Although it was January, a string of Christmas lights still hung in the window, blinking on and off as if winking at the New Year 1955.

I waited, hoping to find Setsuko in the dining room, but after a few minutes I stopped one of the waitresses dressed in a traditional kimono and asked her where my sister was. "She's on the third floor in her apartment. You can go on up. I believe she's waiting for you." I passed the private rooms on the second floor. People toasting with shouts of *kampai* followed by raucous laughter drifted through the shoji screens, which, as my sister had told me in a letter describing the place, were kept closed except when the waitresses served diners their order. By the time I reached the third floor I was out of breath. I was relieved to see my sister waiting at the top of the stairs, her baby daughter, Kazuko, in her arms. She was a pretty little thing but kept drooling all over my sister's blouse. I kissed both of them and followed Setsuko down the hallway to my room at the back of the apartment next to the children's quarters. "The children couldn't wait for you to get here, Noriko."

"I've brought them gifts," I said, handing eight-year-old Mitsuo a rubber ball and six-year-old Akiko a hand-painted mirror. "Is that why they were anxious for me to arrive?"

Mitsuo started to bounce the ball on the wooden floor. Setsuko reprimanded him, "Not in the house, and as for you, Akiko, put that mirror away before you break it." I had never heard Setsuko speak so sharply, but I could see that she had her hands full. I sighed to myself and swore that I would never become trapped by "family" circumstances.

Opening a tidy wardrobe, Setsuko held up a uniform. "Try it on and make sure it fits. I have instructed my manager, Ichiro Uchida, that you're joining the staff at the Tesagara Tearoom. I warned him not to show any favoritism toward you. You will be treated like any other employee."

"Am I supposed to start tomorrow? I was hoping to take a tour of Osaka, go into some of the fancy department stores, and maybe even catch a movie with my friend Mizuki." I could barely control my excitement over being in Osaka and sampling all it had to offer.

"That's going to have to wait. One of our waitresses at the tearoom quit yesterday and we are shorthanded. You are here to do a job, Noriko, not to amuse yourself. Life isn't all fun and games anymore. I had a hard time convincing my husband to allow you to stay with us, so you need to make yourself useful. When he gets annoyed, he is impossible to live with, I can assure you."

While I put on my waitress costume, Setsuko gave me a further warning: "I expect you to follow Mr. Uchida's instructions or you'll have me to answer to. I need him to pay attention to his duties and not get caught up in a romance with a lovesick girl."

"I have no intention of getting involved with him, Setsuko."

"Hmm, you haven't seen him. He's good-looking. Most of the waitresses have a crush on him. They keep it to themselves, of course, but I can see it in their eyes. Fortunately, he hardly notices. He wants to make something of himself. Maybe own his own restaurant one day."

I tied the lace-fringed apron around my waist. Setsuko looked me up and down. "The uniform fits you perfectly."

Hugging my sister, I said, "Thank you so much, Setsuko. Mother and Father would never have let me come to Osaka on my own, and to be honest, I'm not sure I would have had the nerve to live here by myself. You're really helping me out by giving me a job. I intend to pay Father back for all the money he's spent on my acting and singing lessons."

"He doesn't need your money. From what Mother told me, he's doing just fine. Besides, he's proud of you for your talent. He expects great things from you."

"Nevertheless, I made myself a promise, and I intend to keep it."

Turning on the overhead light, Setsuko told me to unpack and then join the family for a light meal. I looked at myself in the mirror attached to the back of the door, which Setsuko closed behind her. I did look pretty in the uniform, although I knew I shouldn't have been thinking that way. What did the Tenrikyo church preach: "Our bodies are lent to us from God the Parent. Only our minds are in our control." I vowed to remember that. As I hung my clothes up in the wardrobe, everything I brought suddenly seemed so shabby compared with the stylish clothing the women I passed on the city streets wore.

I unwrapped the photographs I brought with me: Mother and Father with Tadashi standing between them in front of my father's shop; publicity shots of some of the Takarazuka stars; and a scene from *The Eddy Duchin Story*, with Kim Novak and my favorite actor, Tyrone Power. Mizuki and I had seen the movie so often I could recite the dialogue between Eddy Duchin, a society bandleader, and his pregnant wife, Marjorie. I ran the lines for both characters as I stood before the mirror:

Eddy: Do you dance?

Marjorie: I have in my time.

Eddy: Shall we, just the three of us?

Marjorie (Patting my stomach): I am afraid that I'm keeping you at a distance.

Eddy: Yes. You have let someone come between us.

Marjorie (Quivering my lower lip): Do you mind terribly?

Eddy: Not so long as I have you.

Setsuko knocked on my door, interrupting my "performance." She opened the door and stood with her hands on her hips looking bemused.

"Should I be worried? I heard you talking to yourself."

"I was just practicing some dialogue. Do you want to hear it?"

"Not really. Get out of that uniform so it is fresh for tomorrow and come to the table. Or is the ingénue too busy to eat with the family?"

"Are you making fun of me?"

"I shouldn't have said that, but I'm a bit jealous. My little sister is free to pursue her dreams while I..." Her voice trailed off, interrupted by the cry of "Mama" from the far end of the apartment and laughter drifting up from customers on the second floor. I was curious as to why my sister chose to marry and have children so soon, but I knew she was like many other young Japanese women who were afraid that they would not find a husband. The war had killed off so many eligible men that the government had organized marriage bazaars. If I were ever to get married, and I didn't think I would as I watched my sister hurry off, it would only be for love and not for money or mere companionship. I trusted I could survive on my own, and I had ambitions that I swore to myself I would never allow a man to step on. I wanted a man who believed in me as much as I believed in myself.

Over the months leading up to my audition, I had endured terrible headaches brought on by worry. I knew that if I didn't make it through my audition, I would not have a second chance. The cutoff age for entrance into the Takarazuka Academy was eighteen, and I would be eighteen on my next birthday. Too old to catch a rising star.

Chapter 7

ICHIRO UCHIDA, THE GENERAL manager of the Tesagara Tearoom, unlocked the front door well before the first customer arrived at seven in the morning. His commute consisted of walking down the hallway and taking the stairs to the first floor since he lived right above the restaurant. His six-tatami-mat room looked out on the alleyway where the trash was kept and the cats prowled nightly looking for a saucer of milk. His accommodations were meager, but at least they were his and his alone.

All the tables in the tearoom downstairs were laid out with freshly starched tablecloths and purple irises in bud vases. He arranged for them with the local florist so that there were fresh flowers on the tables daily, even in winter. The smell of baking pastries from the kitchen indicated that, in just a few minutes, the cases would be filled with croissants, scones, and other European delicacies the regular patrons expected. He pulled back the lace curtains to let in the early morning sunlight. The black-and-white tile floor sparkled from the mopping that was part of the regular upkeep Ichiro insisted upon. Newspapers hung from the racks: the *International Herald Tribune*, the *Osaka Shimbun*, *Le Monde*, and the *London Times*. No detail was too small for his attentive eye.

Ichiro walked through the tearoom adjusting a spoon here and a fork there, then went to the cash register. The door boy wiped off the fingerprints from the glass and shined the brass door handles with a chamois. Ichiro watched him to make sure he didn't miss a spot. Cleaning the door had been his job when Mrs. Setsuko Fujiwara first hired him ten years earlier; he was eventually promoted to waiter and now he was the general manager of both the tearoom and the Aki-Torii Grille. Not a bad living for a man of twenty-four, but what he was doing hardly met his aspirations. He had wanted to be an accountant like his father, the top man at the Izumi Steelworks Company, but instead, when his father died right after the war, Ichiro ended up living on the street with his older sister, Mitsuko. If it were not for her, he reminded himself often, he would not have survived. She worked in a shipyard and stood in line, suffering from exhaustion, for a meager bag of rice and a box of grasshoppers. The family fortune was gone, his stepmother having stolen all their money when their father died.

Ichiro and his sister separated after the war ended. He took a train into downtown Osaka and found his way to the Tesagara Tearoom, and his sister, Mitsuko, traveled to the outskirts of Osaka to live with an aunt and uncle. She dropped out of high school and got a job as an elevator operator at the American Army base commissary. They eventually reunited before his sister married a Japanese-American army man who did his time during the Korean War. Ichiro paid for their wedding and saw Mitsuko off at the rail station in Kobe with her new husband, who took her to America. Her face was covered with tears as she climbed aboard the train, holding onto a portrait of their mother as the sole reminder of their life before…and before…and before. Ichiro turned away so that Mitsuko would not see that he was crying, too. Now an ocean separated them, but he held his sister deep within his heart, praying that someday he might see her again, if not in this world then in the next.

Ichiro's present circumstances were conscribed by what went on at the tearoom and the Grille Room. He rarely took a vacation and hardly spent any money on himself. His only luxury was his phonograph machine and his collection of American jazz and classical music records. He listened to Billie Holiday, Frank Sinatra, Tony Bennett, and the American big bands, committing the music to memory. Late at night, after all the patrons left, he'd play the upright piano sitting in the corner of the tearoom for his own pleasure, and then climb the stairs to his second-floor bedroom. The room was barely large enough to stretch his arms out, but since he had no one to share it with, it hardly mattered; and the rent he paid Mrs. Fujiwara and her husband was manageable. He built a bookcase for the few volumes he rescued from his father's library that Madam Tamae, his stepmother, had threatened to throw away: English versions of *The Little Prince* by Saint-Exupéry, *Sayings and Anecdotes* by Diogenes, *Kwaidan* by Lafcadio Hearn, and *Lady Chatterley's Lover* by D. H. Lawrence. He also saved the second-hand textbooks he studied when he went to night school to earn his high school diploma. He was fascinated by every subject but especially mathematics and music theory and composition. He graduated at the top of his high school class and would have qualified for any course of study at a university, but he couldn't afford to quit his day job. He wondered, *When did my life become an unending series of disappointments?*

～

Before Christmas, Ichiro received a surprise invitation from a former classmate to join him for a ski trip to Hakodateyama. He had not seen Norimitsu Suzuki since they graduated night school together, but he heard his friend had gone on to the Osaka University Business School and worked in a high-level position for an international corporation. Ichiro thought it might be a good career move to spend some time with Norimitsu in case his friend had a lead on a corporate job he might be suited for. Connections were the way to get ahead in this world, and he had few to count on.

His boss, Mrs. Setsuko Fujiwara, gave Ichiro two days off, and before his departure she lent him a heavy sweater, a pair of woolen overalls, and gloves that belonged to her husband. They were too big for him, and when he put them on, he looked bedraggled; but the clothes would keep him warm. He was embarrassed by the way he looked when he stood in front of the mirror, but it wasn't worth spending money on a new outfit when he probably would never go skiing a second time. He admitted to Mrs. Fujiwara, "I've never been skiing. Perhaps I should rethink this invitation before I make a fool of myself."

"Ichiro, it will be good for you to get away before the holidays. We're going to be working hard through Christmas and New Year's so now is as good a time as any. And by the way, my sister, Noriko, will be coming to live with me for a while. I've offered her a job as a waitress at the tearoom. You'll have your hands full. She is a strong-willed seventeen-year-old, but I'm sure you'll keep her in line."

"I'll do my best, Mrs. Fujiwara, but thank you for giving me fair warning." He thought to himself, *I should have been given the courtesy of interviewing her. All the more reason to be looking for another job. I'm never going to get ahead here.*

Ichiro met Norimitsu and his girlfriend at the train station. The two classmates embraced. Ichiro said, "Well, my friend, you are looking very spiffy." Norimitsu was dressed in a dark cashmere coat, a plaid scarf tied around his neck. He sported an expensive-looking gold watch. His attire made Ichiro feel like a beggar, but he put on a brave face. Norimitsu introduced him to his girlfriend, Maemi, and Ichiro bowed politely. When he looked into her eyes, which were as dark as obsidian, he blushed.

Maemi said, "Norimitsu, you didn't tell me how handsome your friend is. We should have brought a date for him."

Ichiro responded, "No worries. I will have enough on my hands just trying to stay on my feet. I don't need another girl as beautiful as you distracting me."

The threesome settled into their seats on the train for the one-hour trip into the mountains. Maemi took out a textbook. She was preparing for her anatomy examination to qualify for her nursing license. Ichiro watched her as she wound and unwound a long strand of shiny black hair around her finger, all the while silently mouthing the technical words she needed to memorize.

Norimitsu whispered, "I'm going to ask Maemi to marry me this weekend. What do you think?"

Ichiro felt a pang of longing. "You are a lucky man. She's beautiful, and she must be smart as well. Ambitious too."

"Right, on all counts. And what about you, Ichiro?"

"Me. I'm too busy running two restaurants to have time for romance, but I hope someday I'll meet someone. My work prospects aren't particularly good, and so I don't know if I'm much of a catch…"

"Nonsense. You graduated top of our class. Have you looked for another job?"

"Not really. I was going to ask you if you might have some ideas for me."

"Let me think about it. My father and I have a few connections, and business in Osaka is booming. The Americans and the Brits are pumping money into Japan's economy to keep the Commies from taking over."

Ichiro pushed the matter. "It would mean everything to me—just an introduction, you understand. It will be up to me to promote myself. What's the expression, 'What has this man done in the past that proves he can do a job in the future?'"

Ichiro asked Norimitsu to describe his job and where he hoped to be in five years. That was the way Norimitsu thought—he enjoyed the luxury of a self-satisfied man who gave himself permission to plan ahead. Ichiro was just living from day to day, but he hoped to change this pattern.

Their conversation carried the two friends all the way to Hakodateyama. Snowflakes fell as the threesome walked over the shoveled streets carrying their belongings to the Auberge Kokian, where Norimitsu had reserved two rooms. The roof of the traditional guest house looked like praying hands or the wings of a bird. As they entered the inn, the fire in the central hearth sent a tail of wispy smoke up to the ceiling beams, which had turned the color of ebony over the years. The manager led them down the second-floor corridor to their neighboring rooms.

Ichiro's guest room was simply furnished, but spacious compared to what he was used to at the tearoom. Stepping out onto the balcony, he looked down to a partially frozen river. Rocks and tree roots protruded above the ice, forming a river tooth that caught the dead leaves tossed into the water by the wind. In the distance, looking like a silver platter, was Lake Biwa. Ichiro breathed in the mountain air and his chest suddenly constricted. He bent over coughing and staggered back into his room to gulp down a glass of water. After a few minutes he was able to catch his breath. Nothing like this had happened to him before, so he didn't give it much thought, but he felt unusually fatigued.

Changing into his baggy ski clothes, he laughed at his reflection. He put on the knitted hat he had borrowed and dark glasses and ventured out. Maemi and Norimitsu were waiting for him in the greeting room.

Norimitsu asked, "Ready, old man?"

"That's a bit how I feel, like an old man who should be in a rocking chair by the fire rather than tackling a ski slope. I'm having a hard time catching my breath."

"We'll take it slow. The air is thinner up here. And if you don't get used to it, there's always the bar at the chalet."

"Please. I have already spent more than enough time in bars. A change of scenery will do me good, clear my head and my lungs."

"That's the attitude, old man." Ichiro cringed when he heard Norimitsu refer to him that way a second time. Did he really look so old? Maybe it was just his ill-fitting clothes, he thought.

After renting their equipment, Norimitsu offered to give Ichiro and Maemi a lesson. He demonstrated how to board the rope tow. "Grab it like this, putting one hand in front of the other. Lean back, just relax, and let the rope take you up the hill. Keep your skis in the tracks. When you get to the top there will be a level platform. Let go of the rope and head to the nearest available spot. We'll meet there and then you can follow me down. This is the easiest slope on the mountain. Maybe tomorrow we'll try something more advanced."

Looking uphill, Ichiro shook his head. "No, I think this is just about my speed."

Maemi went first. The tow was slow enough that she made it easily to the top without falling off. Ichiro followed, his skis fitting neatly in the tracks and carrying him smoothly with a faint "whooshing" sound. The snow continued to fall, snowflakes dusting his sweater and melting against his skin. A cloud of his breath hung in front of him. When he reached the top of the tow, he released his grip on the rope and headed toward where Maemi was standing. He had no idea how to stop. His arms waving and his skis sliding out from under him, he fell headfirst into a snowbank. Norimitsu was right behind him. "Grab onto my ski pole. I'll pull you up."

When Ichiro stood up he felt dizzy and as if his legs were melting underneath him. Maemi said, "Ichiro, you look pale. Do you want to rest for a minute?"

"No, I'm fine. Let's just get going. I don't know the first thing about getting down this hill, and even if it's the easiest one on the mountain, it doesn't look so easy from up here."

Norimitsu showed them the basic snowplow technique, positioning his legs in a V and digging the edges of his skis into the fresh powder. Maemi and Ichiro followed him as he slowly traversed the hill. By the time they reached the bottom of the hill, Ichiro was drenched in sweat. "Why don't the two of you take the next run without me? I think I need a break."

Skiers crashed into one another at the bottom of the hill, laughing at their clumsiness. Young children, their cheeks pink from the cold, sat on wooden sleighs that their parents pulled across the snow or were dragged on miniature skis with harnesses wrapped around their waists.

A young mother stopped in front of Ichiro. Her little boy was crying. She knelt down in the snow and wiped away his tears. "You are not lost, my angel. I was right behind you. Don't be scared. Mama will never leave you." Ichiro caught the little boy's eyes and waved at him. Startled, the toddler smiled over his mother's comforting shoulder.

Ichiro asked, "What is your name?"

"Go ahead," his mother urged him. "You can tell the nice man."

"Fumio."

"And I'm Ichiro. Are you having fun?"

The toddler shrugged. His mother said, "I don't think he's quite sure. But a few more times up and down the hill and he'll be very happy. Now wave goodbye to Mr. Ichiro."

The toddler did as he was told, and then his mother bent over to remove his skis. They headed into the chalet. Looking up the hill, Ichiro spotted Maemi's black jacket as she followed Norimitsu. They looked very elegant as they moved aggressively back and forth across the hill in rhythm with one another as if they were listening to a musical score played just for them.

When Maemi reached the bottom of the hill, she kicked off her skis and ran over to Ichiro; her cheeks were flushed and her eyes sparkled from the cold. "Come on. We're going back to the inn for dinner. We're famished."

Ichiro lifted his wooden skis onto his shoulders. They felt as if they had turned into heavy iron rods. He had to lean on his bamboo poles for support and had trouble keeping up with Maemi and Norimitsu. The snow had accumulated on the path back to the inn, and he was afraid he might slip and fall.

The next morning Ichiro did not feel well enough to ski. He spent the day in bed nursing what he thought was a cold, and by evening he felt well enough to join Maemi and Norimitsu. Norimitsu ordered a bottle of hot sake and announced their engagement. "Don't tell anyone yet. We have not asked Maemi's parents for their permission and, of course, we have to go through the formality of finding a go-between to make our engagement official."

Ichiro toasted them. Maemi said, "Perhaps you will be the next one to get engaged, Ichiro. Norimitsu says you don't have a girlfriend, but I know a few unattached girls at the college who will certainly find you most attractive. May I have your permission to introduce you to someone?"

Ichiro didn't know what to say. "I'm not ready for the responsibility of a wife."

Maemi laughed, "No one is asking you to get married. Just to go out on a date."

"Well, we'll see." He took a sip of sake and was struck with another coughing fit.

The look on Maemi's face communicated her concern. "Ichiro, I don't mean to pry, but have you seen a doctor about your cough? It might be more serious that you imagine."

Ichiro shook his head. She continued, "I can arrange for you to see a pulmonary doctor on the faculty of my school. As a favor to me, he won't charge you. I'm doing some independent research for him."

Resenting being treated like a charity case, Ichiro said, "That's very generous of you. If I don't feel better in a few days, I have someone I can see just as well. In the meantime, I think it's best that I stay away from skiing. In fact, if you will excuse me, I think I'll retire for the night and leave you two to enjoy what's left of the sake."

Ichiro shivered underneath his comforter. He put on his ski sweater for extra warmth. Tossing and turning until sleep finally overtook him, he was aware of a vivid dream: he was standing on his skis atop a high mountain covered with blood-red snow. As he pushed off, wings sprouted through his jacket. Kicking his skis off, he soared above the valley on a powerful updraft. As he flew past the village of Hakodateyama and westward to the peak of Mt. Fuji, he caught sight of the red torii gate separating earth from the spirit world. The moon shone over his shoulder, and by its light he saw a pale and fragile woman warming her hands by a fire at the top of Mt. Fuji. When she looked up at him he recognized his young mother, Toshiko. She beckoned to him, but as he tried to reach her his wings fell off and he tumbled blindly into the darkness.

He awakened. Surprised by the vividness of the dream, he thought that seeing the lovely mother caring for her toddler at the bottom of the ski hill had prompted memories of his own mother. As a child, he was forbidden by his father from speaking her name or mentioning the terrible disease that took her life. He owned nothing that had belonged to her, except for a delicate fan given to her by his father on the day they became engaged. He never knew what it was like to bask in the warmth of motherly love, to be cherished as an only son, and to be surrounded by affection.

Ichiro wrapped himself in a blanket and went out on the balcony. The face of the moon was partially hidden by fast-moving clouds and the sky was starless. From the next room he heard Maemi's muffled laughter, and then she said something to Norimitsu he could not make out. He imagined her telling his friend what Ichiro longed to hear someone say to him: "You are my perfect love." Their passion awakened a desire within him to find someone to fill his empty heart.

Chapter 8

THE WARREN OF ALLEYWAYS and cobblestone streets between the Aki-Torii and the Tesagara Tearoom confused me, and I took several wrong turns before I found the tearoom where I was supposed to report for work at seven thirty in the morning. I was already ten minutes late. The door boy opened the glass door and bowed as I came in. Patrons were seated at a number of tables, and there was a line at the pastry counter for those customers who did not have the time to sit at a table leisurely sipping a cup of coffee and reading one of the morning papers. I asked the door boy, "Where is the manager, Mr. Uchida?"

Pointing to a table in the corner, he said, "Over there, speaking to Mr. Yasujirō Ozu. When he's in Osaka he comes into the tearoom every morning."

"Please tell him Noriko Ito is reporting for work—a little late but here nevertheless."

I took a mirror out of my dance bag and smoothed my hair, which was windblown from running. When I looked up, I saw Mr. Uchida hand an order pad to one of the other waitresses. Then he walked toward me across the dining room. I could feel my heart beating in my chest. I had been warned by my sister, but I didn't expect the manager to be so handsome. Wearing a navy-blue suit that fit him perfectly and a beautiful silk tie, he looked like a matinee idol. I didn't know if he would chide me for being late.

Tying my apron around my waist, I waited for him to address me. "Well, Miss Ito, I'll excuse you for being late this one time because it's your first day, and you may not have calculated how long it would take you to get here from the grill room. Am I correct?"

"Yes, sir, and I also got lost. I thought I knew where I was going but I was wrong. I should have brought a map but it completely slipped my mind." I was so nervous I nearly tripped over my words.

Mr. Uchida let a smile cross his lips. "Osaka can be confusing, but I'm sure you'll know your way around in no time. Now, follow me." He led me to the pastry counter, the display filled with freshly baked delicacies. Pitchers of persimmon, cranberry, and freshly squeezed orange juice were embedded in sparkling mounds of crushed ice. "For today, you'll work behind the counter. In a few days, when you have familiarized yourself with our menu, I'll assign you to five tables. Have you been a waitress?"

"I helped my father in his sushi shop in Hiroshima, but to tell you the truth, I've never had a real job before. This is my first." I saw no point in lying to Mr. Uchida. He would soon find me out, anyway.

"Our clientele expects courteous and efficient service. For example, Mr. Ozu sitting in the corner is a famous film director. Whenever he's in Osaka, he comes here for breakfast. He looks over the menu but always orders the same thing—two chocolate croissants and strong black coffee."

"I'll be sure and remember his habits, and if you'll allow me, I'll tell him how much I admire his films."

"You've heard of him?"

"Of course. I'm going to be an actress someday, but for now I'll be in training at the Takarazuka Theater Academy. I'm auditioning later today."

"We always respect the privacy of our patrons, especially someone as famous as Mr. Ozu. Although he keeps looking in your direction, I suggest you don't say anything to him. If, in a few days, he comes in again and shows an interest in you, then there would be nothing wrong with engaging him in polite conversation."

"I'll be sure and tell him how much I admire *Late Spring*. His main female character is named Noriko, like me, and like me she doesn't really believe in marriage. Or maybe it's Mr. Ozu who refers to marriage as 'life's graveyard' and declares weddings and funerals two sides of the same coin." I could see from the expression on Mr. Uchida's face that he was puzzled by what I said.

"I wouldn't know. I'm not a very keen observer of romance and marriage."

"What about films?" I asked. "I adore the movies."

"From time to time I go to the movies, but I'm more inclined to attend a concert." He cocked his head toward the piano sitting in the corner. "I play the piano for my own amusement after the tearoom closes. It's just a hobby, but it gives me a lot of pleasure."

I was being very forward but I couldn't help suggesting, "Perhaps you'll play a song for me sometime."

He nodded and then excused himself. I suspected I had embarrassed him. Mr. Ozu was about to leave, and he and the manager engaged in a brief conversation. Mr. Ozu slapped Mr. Uchida on the back as if he was congratulating him about something, and then he walked out into the winter sun carrying a sheaf of papers.

Mr. Uchida kept me a few minutes past my shift to explain how to fill out the bills for the patrons and keep a running tally of the sales at the counter. As soon as I could, I slipped into the bathroom and changed into my audition clothes: a black turtleneck sweater, a red pencil skirt, and comfortable black pumps I could dance in if asked to by the director. Running past the Hozenji Temple, I almost knocked over the caretaker who was carrying a mop and heavy wooden bucket filled with soapy water. She yelled out, "Watch where you're going." I wanted to put a coin in the alms box, but there was a line of worshippers and if I waited my turn I was afraid I might be locked out of the audition. I'd just have to rely on my talent and not the gods to earn me a place in the Academy. I prayed I had not made a mistake.

～

I waited a moment while the clerk looked down the audition list, and then despite it being impolite I pointed impatiently, "There. There's my name. Noriko Ito."

"Yes, now I see it." She handed me a clipboard. "Sign in here and then go upstairs. Take a seat and wait for your name to be called." I picked up my dance bag and took the stairs two at a time.

My best friend Mizuki was already sitting in the back row, an empty seat next to her. She whispered as I sat down, "How was your first day at work?"

"You won't believe who I saw. Mr. Yasujirō Ozu. He is a regular at the tearoom when he is in Osaka, and it seems the manager knows him."

"You mean the director of *Barley Harvest*?"

"Yes, and *The Late Spring* and an earlier black and white film, *The Only Son*."

"I was worried you might not show up."

"The manager kept me past my checkout time. I don't know if I made a good impression on him and so I didn't want to tell him I was going to be late for my audition. I think I talked too much. He's really good-looking, but he's so shy and reserved. I feared his eyes were going to burn holes in his shoes. He barely looked me in the eye."

"He's probably intimidated by you."

"Why?"

"Have you seen yourself in the mirror lately?"

Suddenly the doors to the audition room swung open and a girl with her hair in long braids and wearing a plaid skirt and white blouse ran out, tears streaming down her face.

I said, "She must have gotten bad news."

Mizuki said, "Dressed like that, what do you expect? Lucky you had time to change out of your uniform. You look very French." That was the look I was going for. "*Merci, Mademoiselle* Mizuki."

I rummaged around in my purse for my Ballet Pink lipstick, reapplied it, and ran my hands through my short-cropped hair. Then I licked my finger and smoothed my eyebrows. "Well?"

Mizuki said, "You look like a Takarazuka star."

"I don't know about that, but let's hope the director thinks so."

The proctor banged on the floor to silence us. The doors opened again and Mizuki's name was called. Under her breath she said, "Wish me luck." I watched her run down the aisle and then the heavy black doors shut behind her. Soon it would be my turn.

I looked over my sheet music: "*Les Feuilles Mortes.*" "Autumn Leaves" was a risky choice. One verse in English and then one in French, but my singing teacher said, "It will make you stand apart from the other girls. No one but the most confident of singers would choose this. Just remember to breathe from your diaphragm. And don't forget the meaning of the song. You are telling a story—this is a love song. You have been in love, haven't you?"

I said, "No, but I've seen plenty of romantic movies."

"Well, use that, then."

I chose "When You Wish Upon a Star" for an encore if the director requested one. I was so engrossed in my music I didn't realize Mizuki had taken her seat next to me again. She tugged at my sleeve. "I'm in. I can't believe it. I've been accepted for the next class starting in May." Perspiration ran down Mizuki's face. I had never seen her look so happy or relieved.

"How was it?"

"I forgot some of the words to the song. I thought I'd die. The director told me to start over again, and I did it perfectly the second time."

"I'm not sure I would have been able to recover."

"Don't say that, Noriko. Besides, you've never forgotten a lyric, ever."

Someone called out from the front of the room. "Noriko Ito. Where are you?"

I raised my hand. For a moment I had the urge to turn around and run out of the waiting room, to run as far from the audition hall as I could, but I willed my legs to carry me forward. I felt like I was going to throw up. I tasted a lump of sour bile at the back of my throat. I never had experienced stage fright before but nothing had ever mattered so much to me as this audition.

Sitting at a long table flanked by two assistants, the director, wearing a white silk scarf, gestured me into the audition room. A pianist sat on his bench smoking a cigarette. There were mirrors behind the director; I pulled my sweater down over my hips and brushed my hair out of my eyes with my fingers. A nervous habit. Large windows on one side of the hall above the street let in the afternoon sunlight that reflected off the pianist's bald head, making him look like a lucky Buddha. I heard music coming from a room on the floor below. I recognized Anna's song, "Whenever I Feel Afraid," from *The King and I.* Should I take it as a good omen? I knew the lyrics by heart and the message was what I needed in that moment: "Make believe I'm brave and I will be!"

Looking at my application, the director tapped his pencil. "You graduated high school in Hiroshima. Were you there in August of forty-five?"

"Yes, I was, sir." Anticipating his next question, I lied. "I've been tested by the doctors every year, and I'm in excellent physical condition."

The woman to his left said, "Some of our Hiroshima entrants haven't made it through the training."

"In my case, you have nothing to worry about, I assure you."

"What?"

I repeated myself.

The director said, "You'll have to project better than that if you expect to earn a place in our company. I see that you want to try out for the men's roles. Is that why you cut your hair so short?"

"Yes, sir." Trying to impress them, I said, "Ever since I saw a production of *Veronique,* I've worn my hair this way. Do you think it suits me?"

The director frowned. "I'm supposed to be asking the questions, not you. You're not very tall, Miss Ito, even with high heels on. Our stars who take the male parts are at least five foot four. What are you, five foot two?

"I don't know, sir. I've never been measured."

"Not even by those doctors you say examined you? That's something they keep track of." I could feel my face burning.

This was beginning to feel like an interrogation, not an audition. Had I done something to annoy them? Perhaps they were testing me. I forged ahead, "I have always played the male leads in the drama club productions. I won top prize for Holly Martins in *The Third Man*."

His assistant interjected, "Isn't that special. I'll make a note of it on your application." She seemed to mock me.

"The sun is right in my eyes. It's irritating the hell out of me." The director put on a pair of dark glasses hanging from his neck. "Let's get on with this. We've got twenty other girls waiting out there. Why don't you show us what you've got, Miss Ito." The director laced his hands behind his head and leaned back in his chair, staring at me with a bored expression on his face.

I handed my music to the pianist. Placing his cigarette in an ashtray without putting it out, he played the introduction and then nodded for me to begin. I signaled for him to slow the tempo so I could hold the notes. When I reached the high note on "winter song" my voice cracked. One of the women wrinkled her nose as if she smelled a pot of boiled brussels sprouts. I forged ahead, hoping to redeem myself with the second verse in French. When I got to *les amants deunis*, I extended my arms toward the window as if begging my lover not to leave me. I had practiced this gesture often with my drama teacher, but catching myself in the mirror, I looked naïve and melodramatic.

The director said, "I think we've heard enough, Miss Ito. You have a beautiful face and a lovely figure, but your voice isn't strong enough for the men's roles."

"Please, sir, is there a possibility that you'd take me in if I were to agree to play one of the women's parts?"

"Not this year. Maybe next."

"There won't be a next. I'll be eighteen in August. I'll be too old to compete."

"*Tant pis, mademoiselle.* Now *au revoir* and *bonne chance*. Goodbye and good luck." The pianist handed me my music. Under his breath, he whispered,

"Little Sparrow, I thought you sang beautifully. Don't give up!" His comment seemed as if he were dropping a coin into a beggar's tin cup.

I walked out of the audition room forcing myself to smile brightly. "Mizuki, get your things. I'll tell you what happened when we're outside."

"From the look on your face, it's all good news."

I stopped at a water fountain in the lobby and took several gulps. My throat felt parched, and I thought I might faint. Mizuki pushed the heavy door with her shoulder and waited impatiently.

"I didn't make it. They seemed to be making fun of me. I was mortified. The director said I was too short."

Mizuki stamped her foot. "Did you ask them if they'd take you for one of the women's roles like me?"

"I did, but it was too late. They'd already made up their minds. I shouldn't have listened to our teacher. I was getting way ahead of myself. I should have been content playing a woman's part, and then, over time I could have been promoted to a man's role. I'm a complete idiot. How could I have been so foolish?" I tried not to cry but couldn't help myself.

Mizuki put her arms around me. "Something just as good will come along."

"Like what? This is all I have ever wanted."

"You'll figure it out." Shifting her dance bag from one shoulder to the other, she asked, "What about Mr. Ozu? One day he'll discover you in the tearoom, and before you know it, you'll be smiling in front of a camera instead of on stage at the Takarazuka. You'll invite me to the premiere, won't you?"

Pretending to believe her, I added, "And afterward we'll ride in a limousine to the opening night party and my costar will fall in love with me. After all, there are no rules about romances and marriages for movie stars."

"There you are. And I'll be a lonely spinster at the Takarazuka."

I held my head high and tried to be brave, but all my dreams seemed to have exploded into a million pieces. Putting our arms around one another's waists, we synchronized our steps. Men, rushing toward the subway station, gave us admiring glances. I should have been flattered, but all I felt was the ache of stunning defeat.

I ran up the stairs of the Aki-Torii to my room relieved that my sister was busy with customers in the dining room. Pulling my sweater over my head and stepping out of the red skirt, I opened the window onto the alley.

Overcome with fatigue, I lay down on my futon, replaying the humiliation and embarrassment I had endured. I hated myself for being jealous of Mizuki, but I secretly thought I was more talented. Why had she gotten in and I had not?

Through the window I heard the cook barking orders to a busboy and the whining of an orphan cat looking for scraps of food from the kitchen. "Don't give that little scoundrel anything to eat. He'll just come back tomorrow night, and if Mrs. Fujiwara sees you feeding him, you'll be sacked. Now stack those empty beer bottles carefully." And then the door slammed shut.

I asked myself, *Is this going to be my world from now on?* I couldn't bear the thought it might be true. I turned over, buried my face in the pillow, and cried myself to sleep.

Chapter 9

DELIVERY TRUCKS RUMBLED DOWN the alleyway, and shafts of winter sunlight fell on the floor of my room. My first thoughts of the day were dark. *What have I got to look forward to? Everything I wanted has been stolen from me.* I couldn't help feeling sorry for myself, but I managed to put on my uniform, make myself look presentable, and arrive at the tearoom on time. At least, if I kept busy, I told myself, I wouldn't slip into a fog of self-pity. Setsuko and her husband Hideo were still asleep, so I left the apartment without being questioned about my abysmal failure yesterday at my audition.

Mr. Uchida gave me an appreciative nod for being on time as I stood behind the pastry counter. I made sure to fill out the customer tickets legibly and hand them to the cashier, who was concentrating so hard on what she was doing that she barely noticed me. I would have at least expected a "good morning." By eight thirty in the morning there was a line of customers out the door. My feet started to hurt, but I kept a smile on my face to create what Mr. Uchida called "an atmosphere of friendly respect." I kept looking around to see if Mr. Ozu, the director, had returned, but his table in the corner was vacant. Maybe he had an early morning call, and would come in later.

By mid-afternoon, my sister arrived. After speaking with Mr. Uchida, she stepped behind the counter and, without wasting a minute, asked, "How did your audition go, Noriko? I assume you got in."

I sighed dramatically. "You would be wrong. My schoolmate Mizuki made it but the director rejected me. I don't think I'll ever get over it."

"I'm so sorry. I know how much you wanted this." Her sympathy made me feel even worse. "But as the saying goes: 'When one door closes another one opens.'"

"That's what Mizuki said. Fine for her to think that! She got in."

"I hope you don't resent her and her success won't ruin your friendship."

"I'll try not to, but it won't be easy. I keep reminding myself of what the Tenrikyo priests teach, that one of the dusts of the mind is jealousy. Right now, I feel like my head is full of dust and not much else."

"You are in charge of your mind, Noriko. Don't forget that." All this philosophical chatter gave me a headache. I had no desire to be rational. I just wanted to collapse in a puddle of disappointment. This was the first time in my life that I did not get what I wanted, and I wasn't prepared for failure.

Setsuko tucked a strand of hair that had escaped her bun. There were already streaks of gray in her hair and shadows underneath her eyes. Was it all the hard work, the three children, or the nuisance of being saddled with a gambler for a husband that had prematurely aged her?

She continued, "Mr. Uchida thinks you're a natural. Even after just one shift he has decided that instead of keeping you behind the counter like a little wallflower, he's going to promote you to waitress right away. One of our girls was offered a hostess job at another tearoom in Namba. They are thrilled to have her because everyone knows how well trained our waitresses are under Mr. Uchida."

"I guess I should consider myself lucky to be given this opportunity so soon." I tried to sound enthusiastic and grateful, but my words came out without the slightest expression, in a flat monotone.

"Yes. I suggest you stop thinking about the Takarazuka and figure out how you can make yourself useful here. If you do a good job, who knows where you might end up?"

"Setsuko, will you do me a favor? More than what you have already done for me."

"What is it?"

"Will you call Mother and tell her I didn't get in—and ask her to tell Father. He is going to be crushed, and I just can't bear to hear the disappointment in his voice. To make things easier, please let her know that I plan to pay him back. I know you don't think he needs my money, but it will make me feel better. Will you do that for me?"

"Don't you think you should be the one to tell them?"

"Yes, but I just can't, and they will find out soon enough. Mizuki's father will be bragging all over town. He'll probably put an announcement in the Hiroshima newspaper."

"All right. If it makes it easier on you, but you really should be the one to tell them. We can't always get what we want in life, and the sooner you accept this fact, the easier it will be for you to grow up." Then she hugged me, to soften the blow of her harsh words.

I untied my apron and hung it on a hook in the locker that had been assigned to me and took out my pocketbook. I refreshed my lipstick and applied a little powder to my nose. No point in looking washed out and tired. I felt a hand lightly touch my shoulder. It was the cashier. "Sorry I didn't greet you today, Miss Ito. I'm glad you are here, and if there is anything you have a question about, you have only to ask me. I used to be a waitress, but a few years ago, Mr. Uchida promoted me to cashier. My name is Hana."

"How long have you worked here?"

"I'm very lucky. It's been about ten years now. I came right after the war. My husband was killed, so I'm responsible for supporting my son—he's now twelve years old. We're all alone, but he's a happy boy and doing very well in school. The Tesagara is like family. You'll see."

I didn't want to tell her Setsuko was my half-sister. It wasn't my place. Instead, I turned to leave. From across the dining room, I saw Mr. Uchida lead a fashionably dressed woman to a table after giving the door boy her fur coat. Taking off her cat-eye tortoise-shell sunglasses, she smiled seductively, and in response, Mr. Uchida's face brightened noticeably.

As I passed by her table, I heard Mr. Uchida say, "Mrs. Tanaka, how was your trip to Arashiyama? It must have been refreshing to leave the city for the mountains at this time of year?"

Mrs. Tanaka pouted, "It was, but there were no single men to amuse my sister and me at the inn. It would have been ever so much more charming to have someone your age and looks to accompany us on our snow walks. Maybe next time you'd care to join us."

Mr. Uchida blushed. "I've just taken a vacation in the mountains. I don't think I'll have any free time for quite a while."

Shrugging her shoulders, she said, "What a pity. If you suddenly find yourself with a day off, you must be sure to let me know. I'll send a car for you." And then she reached into her pocketbook and handed him her card. "My private number."

Mr. Uchida bowed and then raised his hand to signal for a waitress to take Mrs. Tanaka's order.

It was as if I was watching a two-hander, a drama with two characters of different social standings. This woman was at least ten years older than Mr. Uchida, but she seemed comfortable extending this invitation. My curiosity was piqued. I wondered what would happen next, and I wondered if Mr. Uchida was the object of other flirtations.

〜

THE WINDOW DISPLAY OF the fancy boutique a few blocks from the tearoom featured a mannequin in a bathing suit and sarong holding a pair of sunglasses. I stood there for a long moment and then impulsively walked in. Still wearing my waitress uniform, I'm sure I looked out of place, but the salesgirl asked me in a high-pitched voice if I was looking for something in particular. "The cat-eye sunglasses in the window. I'd like to see them."

Taking a key out of her pocket, she unlocked the case and put the glasses on the counter. Tipping a mirror in my direction, she said, "Try them on." Emboldened by their effect, I pouted at my reflection. The salesgirl laughed. I took them off to inspect the price. "Oh, I'm sorry. They are much too expensive..." Wiping my hands on my uniform, I waited, hoping the salesgirl might make me an offer that would put the sunglasses within my reach.

"I can set them aside for you, and you can pay me a little each week out of your salary at the Tesagara. That is where you work, isn't it?"

"Just for the present. I'm hoping to audition soon for a famous film director. I want to be an actress."

"Hmm. That explains why your expressions are so dramatic." Was it my imagination or did the salesgirl suddenly look at me differently? "Wait here a minute. Let me talk to the owner and see what we can do."

Through the store window I saw a black limousine come to a stop, the window down despite the frigid temperature. Mrs. Tanaka was in the back seat. I half-expected to see Mr. Uchida sitting next to her, but instead there was a large Afghan hound. She absentmindedly petted the dog and then blew cigarette smoke out the window. When the traffic lightened, the car pulled away. I wondered what a woman of her means did with her time when she wasn't walking in the snow in Arashiyama.

The salesgirl came back. "The owner thinks it will be good publicity for us to have you wear these sunglasses. Can you manage three hundred sixty yen a week?"

"Let me think about it. Will you hold them for me for a few days? My name is Noriko Ito."

I walked out of the store as if in a trance. What came over me? I had no idea what my salary would be, and I wouldn't have money to spend on those glasses when I intended to pay my father back. As I stood at the corner, I held two images in my mind at the same time. One was a dream of riding along the French Riviera in a convertible like Grace Kelly in *To Catch a Thief* with Mr. Ozu at the wheel, and in the other I was strolling in the Kema Sakuranomiya Park along the Okawa River toward the Osaka Castle with Ichiro Uchida by my side. I couldn't decide which fantasy appealed more. All I knew for sure was that I had to go back to the boutique and tell them I had changed my mind. Fortunately, the salesgirl was busy. I left her a note, sparing myself the embarrassment.

Chapter 10

1958

AFTER THE TABLES HAD been cleared and reset for the following day, Ichiro went over the receipts and entered the amounts in his daily ledger. Then he checked the pantry shelves to make sure there was an adequate supply of flour, sugar, honey, nuts, and chocolate for the next week. Exotic tea leaves and coffee beans from the Far East emitted an intoxicating blend of aromas. All this abundance was a startling contrast to the famine and poverty of Japan during the war. Leaning against the shelves, he let his mind wander to the evening when his sister, Mitsuko, snuck into the kitchen of their house to steal some cooked rice for them to eat. The police commissioner was renting most of the rooms for himself and his family, and when he came home drunk he discovered Ichiro's sister hiding under the kitchen table with a bowl in her hand. He kicked it with his boot. The kernels scattered on the floor as he yelled, "Thief! You and Ichiro are to be out of here by tomorrow or I'll throw you both in jail." They had no way of challenging the commissioner's authority and quickly packed their few belongings and were gone by the next morning trying to find shelter. They went days without eating, searching through the trash bins for a morsel of food that wasn't gnawed on by rats.

Ichiro heard the busboy throwing a bucket of water into the back alley and the meowing of a cat. When he stepped to the door, the cat rubbed her nose against the screen, waiting for Ichiro to put out a dish of milk. The cat rolled over, exposing her belly for her nightly scratch, which he provided after opening the door, along with the milk, and then she stuck her head into the saucer, lapping up the milk quickly as if afraid it might disappear.

Laughing, Ichiro said, "Don't worry. There's more where that came from, you shameless orphan." Before locking the door, he told the cat, "I

cannot let you into the kitchen, but I'll see you tomorrow night, my friend."
He put on a heavy winter coat to ward off the icy wind. He'd need to walk
quickly to the Aki-Torii to stay warm on such a cold night. By this time, all
the customers at the Grille Room would have finished their meal, and he
could go over the day's receipts and make sure everything was in order. He
sighed, feeling as if he was on a treadmill where one day rolled into the next
with no surprises to change the course of his life for the better. He had given
up hoping that his friend Norimitsu might call him with a job lead. It was
too much to expect.

Ichiro was about to turn off the lights when he heard a noise coming
from the bathroom. He grabbed a knife and tiptoed to the door. "Who's in
there? Whoever you are, come out right now before I call the police."

"Don't do that. It's me, Noriko."

"What are you doing?"

～

I OPENED THE DOOR. "I didn't want you to see me like this, Ichiro." My face was
covered in tears and blotchy from crying. I handed him today's newspaper.
On the front page was a photograph of Mizuki Abe with the headline, "Newest
Junior Star of Takarazuka is Sensational in *Cinderella*." I blew my nose and
then explained. "Mizuki was my schoolmate. We tried out for the Takarazuka
Academy together. She got in and obviously I didn't. And now look where
she is, and look where I am. Still playing the part of a tearoom waitress while
Mizuki's name is up in lights. I should go back to Hiroshima. There's a small
theater company there and, if I apply myself, I can make my way up the ranks.
I'll be a big fish in a little pond instead of a Miss Nobody."

"Your father is a sushi maker, am I correct?"

"And your point is…?"

"He would appreciate your choice of words, Noriko."

"Are you making fun of me?"

"Just a little."

His eyes were so expressive. Fascinating dark eyes that looked sad and
strong at the same time. No wonder he never looked directly at me. I might
uncover secrets he didn't want to reveal. Taking my hand for the first time,
he said, "Please don't leave. I look forward to coming to work every day just
to see your lovely face." And then he led me over to the upright piano in the

corner of the tearoom. Sitting down at the bench, he asked, "Would you like me to play something for you, Noriko? You have such a sweet speaking voice and such an engaging laugh; I'd love to hear you sing."

"Where did you learn to play the piano?"

"I taught myself by listening to records. I have a good ear but I can't read a note. I sometimes play late at night when there's no one here. I've never accompanied anyone before so you'll have to forgive me if I make a few mistakes." He started warming up, his hands lightly running up and down the keys. "So, what will it be?"

"Do you know 'You Are My Everything?'"

Ichiro lit a cigarette and rested it on the lip of the ashtray on top of the piano. "It's the theme song from the American movie *The Eddy Duchin Story*, isn't it? The one about the bandleader married to a socialite who dies in childbirth. Tuberculosis, I believe. He's so heartbroken he abandons his son, but they finally reunite. It's very sad."

I agreed, the story was sad. "But it's one of my favorite songs. I've acted out a few scenes from the movie by myself. It seems like a million years ago. I hope I remember the words."

"Well, let's give it a try. We'll use our imaginations." Taking in the empty tables with his eyes he said, "This is a Manhattan nightclub; maybe Delmonico's. I'm dressed in a tuxedo, and you're wearing a red silk gown and a diamond necklace I've just given you for our first anniversary. Are you ready? Our patrons are holding their breath, waiting for you to begin." Pointing out the window at a beggar who was pushing a cart loaded with brooms and pails, he said, "See that man. He's the famous film director George Sidney. This could be your lucky break." It felt so natural for the two of us to be creating a romantic scene. I had never seen these qualities in Ichiro before—imagination, a wry sense of humor, and a romantic streak that could rival any matinee idol's performance.

I touched my neck as if to adjust the necklace, then nodded for Ichiro to begin. He played with easy assurance and did not need to look at the keyboard. Instead he focused all his attention on me. I could feel my heart beating as I looked into his mysterious eyes. I kept taking deep breaths to make sure my tone was full and clear.

When the song ended, Ichiro stood up and, without breaking character he asked, "May I have this dance, Mrs. Duchin?"

"But there's no music."

"Then we'll just have to keep pretending. What will it be? A foxtrot, a rhumba, or the waltz?"

Getting up my nerve, I said, "I don't care so long as it is slow and you can hold me in your arms and never let me go."

"Are you acting or do you mean that I have permission to kiss you, Noriko?"

"I thought you would never ask. What's taken you so long?"

"I was afraid you'd reject me."

"Well, you were wrong." And then I leaned in and, closing my eyes, kissed Ichiro on his lips. They tasted of tobacco and mint, and I inhaled the faint smell of some exotic blend of tea leaves and coffee beans that clung to his suit jacket. We were breaking Setsuko's rules not to become involved with one another, but at that moment, I didn't care. I felt like the rebellious girl I once was instead of the obedient tearoom waitress who could get into trouble for seducing the manager. Or was he seducing me?

Breaking from our first embrace, I asked, "Ichiro, will you walk me back to the Aki-Torii? I shouldn't be out alone at this hour."

"I was planning to go there anyway. I have at least an hour more work to do. But what if your sister sees us together?"

"You can walk me back without getting either of us in trouble. My sister has suspected for some time that there must be something between us."

"Well, then, will you let me take you out on a proper date?"

"Yes, but I need you to answer one question."

Ichiro furrowed his brow and looked apprehensive about what I might want to know.

"I see all those women at the tearoom giving you their cards and flirting with you, like Mrs. Tanaka. You put her card in your pocket. What do you do with them?"

"With the cards or with the women?"

"You know what I mean, silly."

"I save the cards. It would be rude to throw them away. But I have never once gone out with any of these women. They are not to my liking. I would be nothing more than a toy to them. They are just looking for entertainment while their husbands are busy making money so they can continue to live in the high style they think they deserve. And the rest of us, myself included, are just here to cater to them. So, I smile and bow and keep myself for a true love. Does that answer your question?"

Putting my coat on, I said, "Thank you for pulling me out of the doldrums. I thought this would be the worst day of my life when I read about Mizuki's success, but I was wrong." And then, without the benefit of the piano music to underscore my words, I said, "I'll accept a date with you if you promise to be my everything—my summer, fall, winter, and spring."

I waited for him to answer me as he locked the door behind us, but then we were startled by the rare sight of snowflakes falling like granules of sugar lit by the streetlight. The beggar had disappeared, but other people were hurrying by, their heads bent against the snow. Ichiro said, "How beautiful. Three years ago, I went skiing with my former schoolmate, Norimitsu, and his fiancée, Maemi. I was so jealous of them and wondered if I would ever find someone to love."

"And have you?"

Wrapping his arms around my waist, he answered yes, and this time, he leaned in and kissed me first. "I'll try and be your everything even if I haven't very much to offer you, Noriko."

I reached out and brushed off a dusting of snow from Ichiro's hair. "Let me be the judge of that. You don't have to act so humble with me. I like a man who has self-confidence, who knows what he is capable of, and a man who is not afraid of a woman who will speak her mind—a woman like me."

"I don't have very much experience around women. Let's see if I'm up to the challenge."

"Just be yourself and be honest. To tell you the truth, I don't have very much experience around men."

Our naïveté and purity were like the crystalline snow that followed us back to the Aki-Torii. I left Ichiro in the dining room, floating up the stairs to my room and imagining what might happen next. I was like a schoolgirl devouring the pages of a romance novel.

Chapter 11

I KNEW LITTLE ABOUT Ichiro's background other than what my sister had told me, that he had appeared at the Tesagara one day after the war, she gave him a job as a door boy, and that he had been there ever since. He eventually saved up enough money to graduate from night school, she told me, but he stayed on at the tearoom, abandoning his plans of becoming an accountant like his father. I suspected his abilities far exceeded the life he was leading, but I understood that sometimes people are trapped in a situation and don't know how to free themselves. We seem to have that in common. I wondered if together we could find a way out, and create a more exciting life for both of us. I knew I was getting way ahead of myself, but patience was never my strong suit. In that way, Ichiro and I were of opposite minds. He seemed to have all the patience in the world. He was kind even to the dullest of waitresses, and with his encouragement, they turned out to be reliable. I would have stamped my foot and shown them out the door.

Whenever Ichiro had a few extra coins in his pocket, he'd take us to dinner at one of the all-night restaurants, a few subway stops from Namba, so we wouldn't run into anyone we knew. I'd ask him questions about his past, and over many meals and bottles of sake, he revealed episodes from his life. "Do you mind my being so inquisitive, Ichiro?" I asked more than once.

"No, if we are going to be together, you must know everything about me, but it's hard for me to relive a lot of what I went through, and I don't want to sound like a victim of my circumstances."

"We both have wounds we carry, and we both have sorrows. I'm fortunate that I didn't lose anyone when the bomb fell. All I have to show that I was there is the small scar on my forehead." I brushed my bangs away.

"I wondered where you got that but I didn't want to pry." He gently touched my forehead and traced the raised skin above my eyebrow.

"Sometimes, I blame the bomb for not getting into the Academy. When I tried out they asked me where I had been on August sixth, and the director looked at me with mistrust. But then I remind myself that there are other girls who did get in, like my high school friend Mizuki. Once in a while I wonder if there is something hidden inside my body that will kill me one day. I've read about such things happening to other survivors."

"Don't ever say that again, Noriko. Look at you. You are the picture of health and have enough energy for two people. When I see you rushing from table to table without taking a breath, I wish you wouldn't work so hard."

"I'm just trying to make things easier for you." Ichiro refilled my cup with more cold sake. It was summertime and the drink was so refreshing.

"Tell me about your stepmother, Ichiro." Setsuko had shared a few facts about Ichiro's family, and I felt I could bring them up to prompt him.

"It's a strange coincidence, really. She was a dancer in the Takarazuka, of all things, beautiful with sea green eyes and long black hair. My father met her at the Café Absinthe in Minami and fell insanely in love with her. He lost his grip on reality and turned his back on me and my sister. Her name was Madam Tamae. She was like a black widow spider, and she set a trap for my father using her body as bait. My birth mother was from a wealthy family. She had breeding and manners. My father genuinely loved her, but after she died of tuberculosis, he was at loose ends. He had a brief arranged marriage with a peasant woman who loved my sister and me deeply, but he grew tired of her, calling her a 'lumpen bore,' and started seeing Madam Tamae secretly. Not giving us any thought, he got rid of his second wife and married Madam Tamae. We moved into her house so she could continue giving dancing and singing lessons to the pupils who found her through advertisements in the newspaper: 'The famous Madam Tamae Seto will turn your child into a star.' It was ludicrous."

"And did she turn children into stars?"

"Hardly, but she fooled everyone with her phony French accent. She promised my father to love us like we were her own children, but that was a lie too. She made us into her personal slaves behind my father's back. While he was at the office, she was spending his money on baubles. She decided to hold a recital called *The Princess and the Herd Boy*.

"I was expected to turn over the phonograph record when she gave me the signal. It accidentally dropped out of my hand and broke. She screamed at me and told my father that I would ruin her recital. Somehow, he was able, even in the midst of the war, to buy a replacement. She set up her studio like a theater for the recital, buying expensive velvet to cover the chairs and a scrim painted with scenery of shooting stars. She even had a program printed, which I was to hand out to the audience. She rented an usher's uniform for me with a cap that kept falling down over my eyes—a cap not unlike the one the door boy at the Tesagara wears—and had me stand at the door greeting everyone. I felt so humiliated. My sister Mitsuko was put in charge of raising and lowering the scrim and turning the house lights on and off. At the end of the evening Madam Tamae announced to the entire audience she was pregnant. My sister and I were aghast. She couldn't be bothered to take care of the two of us. What was she going to do with her own child?

"My father snuffed out the torches that lit the way from her treasure box of a theater to the house after the audience left her recital. I could hear my stepmother berating my father and bragging about all the money that the parents had given her that evening and how many of her students planned on returning in the fall after her baby was born."

I asked, "So she planned on keeping the baby?"

He lit a cigarette and watched the flame ignite the tip. "She thought of the baby as her meal ticket. Once the child was born, there would be nothing my father wouldn't do to please her."

"Discovering that I had lost my usher's cap after the recital, I stayed behind crawling around the floor trying to find it, fearful of what she might do if I lost it. My father must have realized that I was not in my room. He came back outside and discovered me crying underneath one of the theater seats. He helped me find the cap, then put his arms around me and carried me back into the house. That is the last time I remember anything kindly he did toward me. From then on it was pure torture living in the house."

"What happened?"

"I can't speak about it now. Maybe some other time. You've heard enough of my sad story for tonight. Self-pity is not an extremely attractive quality in a man." He paused for a moment and then was unable to stop. "My father eventually sent me away to live with an aunt and uncle. Meanwhile, my sister had to clean the toilets, mop the floors, dust the chandeliers instead of doing schoolwork. My father was disappointed that her grades had slipped, but he didn't realize that she had no time for her studies because of Madam Tamae. It wasn't until my sister got up the courage to write a letter to my father—hiding it in his bathroom under his shaving pot—telling him how evil his wife was that he understood what was happening right under his nose. But he refused to leave her, and instead, he sent my sister away, too."

"I can't imagine a father being so cruel and heartless as to abandon his children."

"After the war ended, he died, and we lived for a while with our grandmother, but there was no money to pay the rent and we took in boarders who took terrible advantage of us. We ended up on the street—and you know the rest. Not a happy story."

I sipped the sake slowly so I could buy more time. "Is there anything else?"

"Well, before my sister went to live in America with her husband, she visited Madam Tamae. She wrote to me of her intention to see our stepmother, and I couldn't understand her reasoning, but she explained that she wanted Madam Tamae to see that she had made something of herself."

I commented, "Madam Tamae must have been impressed. It wasn't easy for Japanese girls to get jobs at the American PX."

"You're right, but here's the irony. Madam Tamae was practically blind. She laughed at my sister and told her it was too late to get any satisfaction because she could barely see her. She put her sunglasses on—cat-eye sunglasses I believe—and shut the door in my sister's face."

I felt a shiver go up my spine. I wouldn't admit that I had coveted sunglasses like those worn by Madam Tamae, a coincidence that was unbearable. "And now your sister is doing well living in America?"

"I guess so. I miss her terribly. Perhaps, someday, she and her husband will come back to Japan and we can see them. I will never be able to thank her enough for the way that she took care of me, protected me, and loved me when no one else cared about me."

Hearing Ichiro say "we" was reassuring. He thought of us as a couple, and we were, but we had no plans for what to do with our lives moving forward. Ichiro used to say, "You can't be disappointed if you have no plans," but I encouraged him to change his way of thinking.

We left the all-night restaurant just as the sky was turning pink and the sun was coming up. It was already five; we would soon have to go back to work. I buried my head in Ichiro's neck and whispered, "Promise me you won't speak of all this again. It is now behind you."

Tilting my chin so our lips met, Ichiro said, "I want that more than anything in the world."

I felt a pain in my stomach. I understood from these stories that Ichiro carried terrible childhood wounds. Because I loved him, I knew it would be up to me to help Ichiro bury his anger and resentment and, as Tenrikyo teaches us, sweep the dust from his mind so he could lead a joyous life. Isn't that what we are put on this earth for? I didn't realize then how difficult a task that would be, not only for him but for me.

Chapter 12

1959

Ichiro led Mr. Ozu to his table in the corner of the tearoom next to the lace-curtained window. He waved me over. I would finally have a chance to meet the great director. I felt very self-conscious and unsure of myself. Ichiro introduced us. "Mr. Ozu, this is Noriko Ito. I believe you were here on her first day of work. I have come to rely upon her to keep our patrons happy."

Mr. Ozu smiled. "You are handing me over to her, Ichiro? She's certainly a lot better looking than you."

"Indeed, sir. I know from your films how much you appreciate beauty."

"And you as well."

Ichiro blushed, then returned to the front of the house to seat a party of four American tourists with cameras around their necks and folded maps in their hands.

Mr. Ozu boldly inquired, "When did the two of you begin a romance, Miss Ito?"

I gasped. "Is it that obvious?"

Mr. Ozu took off his dark glasses. "I specialize in reading facial expressions, and there is love all over your beautiful face, Miss Ito."

I tried to avoid reacting to his personal comment and asked, "Will you have your usual—two chocolate croissants and a cup of strong black coffee? We are offering a wonderful blend of mocha-Java from Sumatra today."

"You know what it is that I like?"

"Yes, Ichiro...I mean, Mr. Uchida expects us to remember all our regular customers' preferences. It's a way to make you feel at home here at the Tesagara."

"But I haven't been here in a long time. I'm in Osaka for a few days taking a break from preproduction for my next film." He pointed to a page in the script he was marking up. "There's a scene here in *Late Autumn* between twenty-four-year-old Ayako and her widowed mother Akiko that I'm trying to block. My heroine is about your age."

"I'll be twenty-one in a few weeks. An August baby."

"Hmm, I recall Ichiro…I mean, I recall Mr. Uchida told me you wanted to be an actress. Whatever came of that? I'm surprised to find you here."

"I didn't make it into the Takarazuka Theater Academy. To tell you the truth, I was devastated, but I made a commitment to my father to pay him back for all the acting and singing lessons and so I stayed on here."

"At the expense of a career in the theater or film? That's a very convenient excuse for giving up on your aspirations. Or perhaps it was something, or someone, else?" He cocked his head in Ichiro's direction. "Love often gets in the way of aspirations. In my opinion, marriage is a rather outdated way of living for the modern woman. My films explore this theme."

I found myself babbling, failing to defend myself. "I really had no idea how to look for opportunities. Osaka is a big city, and other than the tearoom and my room at the Aki-Torii, I haven't been many places or met many people. But there is a whole world right here. Just look around. We now have Americans coming in. I sometimes overhear their conversations and so I'm learning a lot." He looked me up and down with a quizzical expression on his face as if he didn't believe me. "A clever girl like you. I would have thought you could have navigated your way around the city and made inroads into the world of entertainment to advance your career. There are other theater companies that might have made a place for you, Miss Ito."

"If you'll excuse me, I'll run and get your order. I see Mr. Uchida watching me out of the corner of his eye."

In a sarcastic tone he said, "We wouldn't want to make him jealous, would we?" Mr. Ozu took his card out of his jacket pocket. "Here's my business card. If the camera likes you, I could offer you a walk-on part in *Late Autumn*. You'd have to come to Tokyo to audition and then back again once I start shooting if you get the part. I'd need you for about a week or two. Think about it. Of course, there are no guarantees, but who knows? I may just have discovered a new talent."

I tried to keep my hand from shaking. Slipping his card into my apron pocket, I said, "I've never been to Tokyo."

"It's about time. The men there will find you enchanting, just as they do here in Osaka."

I could hardly believe what had just happened. I went behind the pastry counter and took a drink of water. Hana looked at me. "What's going on, Noriko? You look like you just got a marriage proposal from the Crown Prince."

"Mr. Ozu invited me to Tokyo."

"Was he propositioning you? You know, older men have an eye for pretty young women. And directors are notorious flirts. The rumors about the 'casting couch' are more than just rumors."

"I don't know what you're talking about. He asked me to audition for his next film—but just for a walk-on part. Who knows what it might lead to…"

"Aren't you getting ahead of yourself? What about Mr. Uchida?"

I felt my cheeks turning red. "You know about us?"

"The whole staff does, but don't worry. We're happy for you both, Noriko."

"I guess I'm not a very good actress after all."

I was flattered by Mr. Ozu's invitation, but I did not like the way he spoke to me in such a condescending and self-important manner. And I kept thinking about Ichiro and how he would feel if I pursued this opportunity. I could not risk losing him. Even if he encouraged me to go, I knew it would hurt him deeply. He could just as easily interpret my ambition as abandonment, and he had had more than his share of abandonment to last a lifetime.

I realized I was arguing against Mr. Ozu's invitation. Carrying his order to his table, I fingered Mr. Ozu's card. "I believe you misjudge me, Mr. Ozu. I'm happy here at the Tesagara."

Mr. Ozu shrugged his shoulders. "Suit yourself, Noriko, but keep my card in case you change your mind. I have a sixth sense and can spot talent even without an audition. I think you have what it takes to be a star—the Takarazuka is not the last stop on the subway line." And then he added, "The only difference between you and my leading actress in *Late Autumn* is that, at the beginning of her career, she believed in herself and was willing to risk rejection. Apparently, you're not. Being an actress takes fierce determination, self-confidence, and sacrifice—not just talent. If you don't have these, it's just as well that you know it now so neither of us will be wasting our time."

His words stung, but there was truth in what he said. I could not allow myself to get my hopes up only to be rejected a second time. Whatever dreams I once had of becoming an actress seemed unattainable compared with the real prospect of one day becoming Ichiro Uchida's wife. I didn't know if that would make me happy forever, but I was willing to take a chance. And maybe once we were married and I had convinced Ichiro of my love for him, he would feel less threatened by my desire to pursue an acting career. He might even enjoy sitting next to me in a big black limousine with an Afghan hound resting obediently at our feet.

Chapter 13

STREET BANNERS ANNOUNCED THE appearance of American pianist Van Cliburn at Osaka's central auditorium. Although the concert was sold out in a matter of hours, Ichiro was able to buy a pair of tickets for my twenty-first birthday. I knew nothing about classical music and would have preferred to see a movie, but he was so enthusiastic and wanted to share one of his passions with me. He gave me a recording of Tchaikovsky's *Piano Concerto No. 1* from his collection, the piece that won Cliburn the competition in Moscow and made him an international sensation. Ichiro said, "Listening to this music makes me feel as if I'm in harmony with the universe. I hope it will affect you the same way."

"I've never been to a classical music concert. What should I wear?"

"Is that what women think about?"

"I certainly do. I want to be sure you can't take your eyes off me."

"You have nothing to worry about. My problem is just the opposite. Sometimes, I lose my focus at work because all I want to do is drink in your beautiful face and touch your soft skin. I imagine the two of us lying in bed together naked, exploring one another's bodies, and discovering the ecstasy of physical love." He spoke to me in such a poetic manner that I wondered if he practiced what he said to me. What it lacked in spontaneity it made up for in artistry.

I was very surprised by his confession. I had so much to learn about Ichiro. "We'll have to wait for that. Maybe I'm being old-fashioned but the first man I give myself to will also be my last."

"Nowadays girls in Japan want to experiment before settling on one man, but I respect your wishes, as difficult as they are to honor."

～

MY PARENTS SENT ME money for my birthday, and I knew exactly what I would spend it on—a new outfit for the concert. When there was a lull in the customers coming into the tearoom, I asked Ichiro for permission to leave.

"Where are you off to?"

"I have a quick errand to run. It's a surprise." I'm sure Ichiro knew what I was up to because he could practically read my mind, but he didn't want to steal my fun and so said nothing. I had been reading fashion magazines and studying the outfits of the women who came into the tearoom for the past several weeks, educating myself in the latest fashions. This time when I went into the boutique down the street, I had enough money to buy what I wanted. My parents were very generous; even my Aunt Sanae sent me money for my birthday.

～

I COULDN'T RESIST THE lavender silk dress with a cropped jacket in the window. The collar and cuffs on the jacket were trimmed in tiny rhinestones that caught the sunlight. When I put the outfit on and stood in front of the mirror, I had to keep myself from smiling. It fit perfectly. The salesgirl handed me a pair of white silk pumps. "Try these on, too. They are not easy to walk in but very flattering to the leg."

I twirled around, showing off, made a curtsey like a silly schoolgirl, and told her to ring everything up. Handing me the bill, which was the most I had ever spent on anything for myself, she said, "Forgive me for being nosy, but from the uniform you have on, I see that you are still working at the Tesagara. Whatever happened to your audition?"

"You remember me? It's been almost four years since I came into your shop."

"Of course, I do. You inquired about a pair of sunglasses and then left us a note to say you had changed your mind. It's not every day that someone comes into the boutique who is as pretty as you are. We were hoping you would buy the sunglasses. We have a similar pair if you'd like to see them now."

"No, thank you. They're no longer to my liking."

"You're certainly going to turn heads in this outfit. If someone takes a picture of you, please bring in a copy, and we'll put it on our board."

"I didn't answer your question. I actually changed my mind about the audition. I would have had to move to Tokyo and I just couldn't see myself living in such a big city. Osaka is enough for me, and I am very happy waitressing at the Tesagara."

The salesgirl shrugged her shoulders. "Sometimes life turns out very differently than we expect, and it is up to us to make the most of whatever opportunities we are given. Leaving something secure for the unknown can be daunting, can't it?" The salesgirl handed me a shopping bag. "I hope that this has the desired effect on some lucky young man."

"I'm sure it will."

⁓

AUGUST 3, 1959. MY twenty-first birthday. I finished doing my makeup and styling my hair, which I kept short but curled softly around my face. It was much more feminine than the way I wore it a few years ago. I laughed to myself remembering the night Mizuki chopped my hair so I'd resemble a Takarazuka star. It seemed like a million years ago when I was still an impulsive girl who had never experienced heartbreak or disappointment.

I asked Setsuko to zip up my dress as I stepped into the pumps. "I hope I haven't made a mistake buying this ensemble."

"Are you looking for compliments, Noriko? You look stunning. I feel sorry for Ichiro. He's not going to be able to concentrate on the famous Mr. Cliburn."

"I doubt that. He's been looking forward to this concert for weeks. He made me listen to a recording at least ten times. Honestly, I don't really understand classical music at all. All I know is that Ichiro loves it, and so I'm sure I will come to love it, too."

"And will he learn to love your rock and roll?"

"That I'm not so sure about. I think it's too lowbrow for him. His taste in music is much more refined than mine."

I buttoned the jacket and took out a black purse. "You're not going to carry that old thing and ruin your outfit, are you?"

"It's all I have."

"Well, I think I can solve that problem." Setsuko handed me a beautiful silk purse with a crystal clasp that matched my outfit. "Happy Birthday, my sweet sister."

I opened it, and inside were a pair of white kid gloves and a compact. "Everything is perfect, Setsuko. Thank you."

Looking at her watch, she warned me. "You'd better go outside. I'm sure Ichiro will be here any minute. He's always on time."

I kissed Setsuko goodbye and carefully walked down the three flights of stairs and through the Aki-Torii dining room. Smelling the grilling chicken and beef, I realized I had forgotten to eat. I hoped my stomach wouldn't grumble from hunger during the concert.

I waited outside the restaurant, looking in both directions. Ichiro was nowhere in sight. My feet were beginning to pinch in my new pumps, but the shoes were so pretty I tried to ignore how uncomfortable they were. Men in business suits glanced in my direction. I felt as if I was on display for their pleasure. Where was Ichiro? He was already five minutes late. Suddenly, an American soldier dressed in uniform stood next to me. In fluent Japanese he asked, "Mind if I take your picture?"

Before I could answer him, the flash went off, and then a picture came out of a tray on the camera. "You're as pretty as Jacqueline Kennedy in that dress. Hear of her?"

I shook my head. "She's a United States senator's wife. Her husband is John Fitzgerald Kennedy, a hero in World War Two who was wounded in the Pacific theater. Everyone thinks he's going to run for president. If he does, I'm voting for him, even if he is an Irish Catholic."

This was a lot of information to absorb. I could tell that the officer was trying to impress me. I hardly kept up with American politics or what was happening in Japan, for that matter. All I cared about was that business at the Tesagara was thriving, and that I was in love.

Tucking my picture in the pocket of his uniform, he said, "Hey, why don't I take another picture of you and you can keep it?" I blinked as the flash went off again. Plucking the photograph out of the tray, he waved it back and forth to dry the ink and then handed it to me. Wishing he would go away, I put it in my purse without looking at it. I didn't want Ichiro to catch me speaking with him, even if I hadn't initiated the conversation. I had learned that Ichiro became jealous when other men paid attention to me, even when he had no reason to think I was the least bit interested.

The soldier tipped his cap. "Where can I find you? I'm stationed at the Iwakuni base, and I get to Osaka every now and then. I'd like to take you out on a date, show you off. Be sure and wear that outfit again." I couldn't believe how brazen he was, but I didn't want to make a scene.

"I have a boyfriend and we work together, so that won't be possible, sir."

"Too bad. Most Japanese girls like going out with American military. And they sure like spending our money."

"I wouldn't know about that." And then I added, "I'm from Hiroshima. You've heard of it, I'm sure?"

The color drained from his suntanned face. Reaching into his pocket, he gave me the photograph he intended as a souvenir. "I guess I won't be needing this to remember you by." I watched him leave, quickening his pace as he walked down the street.

I was relieved to be rid of him. The air was hot and humid. I wiped the back of my neck with a handkerchief and brushed my bangs from my forehead, praying that Ichiro would get here before my makeup melted and my hair lost all its curl. And then there he was, running down the street. "Noriko, I have a taxi waiting for us at the corner. Sorry I'm late."

"You look as if you've run all the way from the tearoom to get here."

"Not really. I left in plenty of time, but I suddenly felt dizzy. I had to sit down for a minute. I haven't felt like that since I was skiing in the mountains. At the time, I thought it was the altitude. Maybe now it's the heat and the car fumes, but either way I'm sure it's nothing." He ran his hands through his hair while I adjusted his tie, which was slightly askew.

Settling ourselves in the taxicab, Ichiro gave the driver instructions to take Naniwasuji Street. "It should be less congested at this hour."

"Right, sir. I should have thought of that myself, and I'm the driver. It's my job to give you a smooth ride and get you where you need to go right on time."

Ichiro laughed. "But I'm the one who is running late. We don't want to miss the curtain." Turning his attention to me he said, "You look stunning, Noriko. You seem to have found something spectacular to wear after all that worrying."

"Do you like it?"

"It's beautiful. I wish I had brought my camera to take a picture of you."

"I think I can make your wish come true. Look at these." I handed him both photographs. "Which one do you like better?"

"Who took them?"

"An American. While I was waiting for you, he took my picture with an instant camera. He said I reminded him of a famous lady. It was my outfit, I think. I hope you don't mind that I let him. I was so startled by his request that I couldn't think what to say to stop him. But you should have seen his face when I told him I was from Hiroshima. I don't think he'll be trying to pick up too many other Japanese girls—at least girls he doesn't have to pay for."

"I wish I could have seen his reaction, although I might have had the urge to punch him for being so forward with you, Noriko." Ichiro examined the two photographs. "I'll keep this one and you take the other as a reminder of your birthday, which I hope will be the best one you've ever had."

He leaned over and kissed me on the lips. Then he touched his breast pocket as if he were tapping his heart. "I have a birthday gift for you, but it will have to wait until after the concert."

I teasingly stuck my hand into his jacket. I was shocked at how warm his body was, and his shirt was damp from perspiration. I wondered if he might be running a fever. He never mentioned his health before, but I had a sinking feeling that something might be wrong with him. I should have pressed the matter, but I didn't want to ruin our evening together. I came to regret this decision. Had I spoken up, Ichiro might have consulted a doctor and life would have turned out so differently.

Ichiro pushed my hand away from his chest. "Don't do that. You'll ruin the surprise. I've put a lot of thought into this gift."

The taxicab stopped at the steps to the main entrance of the auditorium. A group of photographers followed a woman and her escort. Turning around to wave at the crowd trailing behind her, I recognized the film actress Machiko Kyo, who had most recently starred in *Sorrow Is Only for Women*. She wore an outfit identical to mine. As we passed her, she took her sunglasses off and looked me up and down as if trying to decide which of us looked better in our ensemble. I wanted to ask her for her autograph, but Ichiro hurried me along.

Ichiro handed our tickets to the usherette, and we were led down the aisle to the orchestra section, ten rows from the stage and directly behind the piano. "Ichiro, these are the best seats in the house. How could you afford them?"

"Let me worry about that. This is your first classical concert, and I want you to have a good experience. We'll have plenty of opportunities to sit in the balcony. Here's the program. You can read about Mr. Cliburn. I don't know if it's true, but I have read that, when he competed in Moscow two years ago, the judges wanted to give him the prize but were afraid of Khrushchev's reaction. They asked Khrushchev what to do. He demanded,

'Is he the best?' They said he was. 'Well, then give Cliburn the prize.' It caused quite a sensation as Cliburn is an American and was playing Russian music in a Soviet competition."

I tried to come up with an intelligent response to Ichiro's story, but I could think of nothing. All that mattered was that we were together, I told myself, but I still wanted to say something smart about his tale. When I had just about given up, a question suddenly popped into my head. "Did Cliburn's win do anything to improve US-Soviet relations?"

An approving smile crossed Ichiro's face. "As a matter of fact, it did. Khrushchev loved to point out that giving the prize to an American was an example of Soviet fairness, but he hastened to add that Cliburn's piano teacher was Russian." As usual, I was so impressed with Ichiro's vast knowledge. But it was his heart and his beautiful face that I truly loved. Sitting next to him, I couldn't believe my good fortune. Of all the women who admired him, he had chosen me.

Every seat in the auditorium was filled. A hush came over the audience as Machiko Kyo came down the aisle, her entrance timed to the dimming of the lights. She settled into her seat in the first row, and although the auditorium was air-conditioned, she opened a magnificent deep purple and gold fan. I thought it was a brilliant choice, giving a nod to traditional Japan while wearing the latest Western fashion.

Van Cliburn strode onstage to thunderous applause. He was followed by the Soviet conductor, who took his place at the podium. Tall and thin with a thatch of wavy brown hair, Cliburn sat down at the bench, flicking the tails of his tuxedo behind him. After adjusting the bench to his unusual height, he closed his eyes for a moment and then signaled to the conductor he was ready to begin. The excitement in the auditorium was palpable; it felt as if everyone was holding their breath. I turned to Ichiro, and he lifted my hand to his lips.

The orchestra played the opening bars, and then Cliburn touched the keyboard. One minute his fingers were like delicate birds in flight and the next like crouching tigers striking the keys with wild abandon. He swayed back and forth, using his whole body in service to the music, playing without a score. Every once in a while, the veins in his neck seemed to pulsate in time to the music. He had an expression of "pained ecstasy" on his face as if he were somehow in touch with the soul of the universe, which was exactly how Ichiro described his own reaction to music.

When the concerto ended, the audience worked hard to earn an encore. "What is he playing?" I asked.

Ichiro whispered, "Debussy's 'Clair de Lune,' which means 'Light of the Moon.' It is a short piece but very romantic."

We waited a few moments for the crowd to thin out after the final applause. Walking up the aisle and into the damp night air, Ichiro said, "Did you enjoy the concert? I hope that bringing you here wasn't simply self-indulgence on my part."

"I loved it. It was thrilling to sit so close to the stage. I felt the music reverberating in my body."

"It's a lot different than listening to a recording, isn't it?" Without waiting for me to answer, he admitted, "When I was studying music at night school, our professor offered me a free ticket to a live concert conducted by his friend, but I couldn't go because it was a matinee and I had to work. I was disappointed to miss out, especially when the other students had a chance to go backstage and meet the conductor."

"Was this your first concert too? I thought you had been many times because you know so much about classical music."

"Just what I learned in school and what I've taught myself from listening to recordings and reading the liner notes. That's where I learned the Khrushchev story. Hearing Cliburn play tonight made me jealous. He's only twenty-four and I'm already twenty-eight, and I've accomplished so little."

"To some you would be considered young. We both have our whole lives ahead of us."

"You're right, Noriko. You always know what to say to cheer me up. I shouldn't compare myself to a genius like Cliburn. After all, how many other musicians come close to his talent? I need to break myself of this habit and be content with what I have accomplished."

"No more gloomy thoughts. This is to be a happy occasion." I paused and then continued, "I have a confession to make. As much as I enjoyed the concert, I couldn't stop thinking about you—about us. And when you put your lips on my hand, I felt a jolt go through my body. I had never felt anything like it before. Is that what love feels like?"

"That or lust. We'll just have to see which it is."

I smiled, "Maybe it's both. Nothing wrong with being passionately in love, Ichiro."

Ichiro took my hand and led me to a park across the street from the auditorium. It was a beautiful sultry evening, the gardens bathed in the silver light of the August moon. We sat on a bench next to a fountain and enjoyed the sound of the splashing water for a few minutes. Then Ichiro reached into his breast pocket. "Happy Birthday, my dearest Noriko." He handed me an antique fan. I undid the hinge and spread the ribs–the diaphanous paper was painted with purple irises and yellow butterflies. The bamboo ribs were elaborately carved in a lacy pattern of winding leaves, and the tips were painted gold. On the end of the fan, a silk tassel dangled in the moonlight. It was an expensive work of art that a bride would carry at her wedding, and even more beautiful than the one that Machiko Kyo wore to the concert.

"Does this mean what I think it means, Ichiro?" My heart was pounding as I waited for his answer.

"This fan belonged to my mother, and it is one of the few reminders I have of her. I think I told you this already—it was a gift from my father when he asked her to marry him, and I'd like you to have it for the same reason. A family tradition, you might say. Will you do me the honor of becoming my wife?"

I positioned the open fan below my eyes, hiding my lips. "Guess what my answer to you is." Before Ichiro could imagine I might be hesitating, I lowered the fan and answered, "Of course, I'll marry you. It is all that I have wished for."

Ichiro held my face in his hands and kissed me. I could feel his body shaking, as was mine. "I wish to be a good husband to you. You are my everything," he said, naming the song he played for me not so long ago, bringing that intimate first encounter at the piano to mind.

"And you are mine."

We walked along the gravel path, deliberately synchronizing our steps. A pleasure boat cruising up the Dojima River sounded a warning foghorn, although the fog had lifted, and boats coming in opposite directions could easily have been seen by their captains.

Chapter 14

1960

NORIKO'S PARENTS RELUCTANTLY GAVE Ichiro permission to marry their daughter. Arguing with his wife, Ryo said, "What does Ichiro have to offer Noriko?"

"She's not getting any younger, and Setsuko assures me he's an honest and hard-working man and comes from a good family. His father was an accountant and a high-ranking executive at the Izumi Steelworks Company before and during World War Two."

"…who died without leaving his son an inheritance," Ryo said. "He got wiped out by a woman who took him for all he was worth. Not very clever for a numbers man, wouldn't you say?"

Wiping her hands on a dish towel, Kimie said, "According to Setsuko, Noriko's head over heels in love with Ichiro. It would break her heart if we didn't give our approval. She'd probably go and marry him anyway."

Heaving his heavy frame into the kitchen chair, which groaned under his weight, Ryo grunted. "Let her marry him, but he better make something of himself or I'm going to wash my hands of Noriko. She's already disappointed me by not getting into the Academy. I went around telling everyone my daughter was going to be a star when she went off to Osaka, and I turned into a laughingstock."

Kimie waved a wooden spoon at him. "You brought that on yourself, Ryo. A bottle of sake and you turn into a loudmouth braggart."

Ryo snarled, "You prove the adage: 'Women's chief weapon is the tongue and they will not let it rust.' Next time you want to insult me, try coming up with something I haven't heard from you before."

Kimie wouldn't let the matter rest. "'Boasting begins where wisdom stops.' You really are foolish, Ryo. Why don't you hold up a mirror to yourself? Yes, you have a successful sushi business, but why are you judging Ichiro so harshly? We haven't even met him. What's to say that someday he will not also own his own restaurant and be more successful than you? Noriko believes in him."

"I don't put much stock in a man's potential. I want to know what he's already done that proves his success. Why do you fault me for wanting the best for our daughter? And what will you do if someday she comes knocking on our door asking for money because Ichiro turns out to be a laggard like Setsuko's husband?"

"You would have to bring that up, wouldn't you? Setsuko can take care of herself."

"I'm not so sure the same can be said of Noriko. Noriko doesn't always have her feet on the ground. She's too much of a dreamer. I wish she had more common sense."

"Have a little faith, Ryo."

"Arguing with you is a waste of time. It's like giving a pearl to a pig."

"Don't you have an original thought? Enough with your old-fashioned sayings. Honestly, if Tadashi weren't still living at home, I'd leave you tomorrow."

"Don't threaten me unless you really mean it."

⌒

ICHIRO RESERVED THE NANIWA Chapel of the Christian United Church of Christ in Osaka for our wedding ceremony on November 10, 1960—the date picked out by the go-between. My sister looked puzzled when I told her the venue.

"You two aren't getting married in a Buddhist temple or at the Tenrikyo church in Nara?"

"Ichiro says that modern Japanese couples are getting married in Western-style Christian churches. He says, 'Shinto for births, Christianity for marriages, and Buddhism for funerals.' I visited the chapel. Fortunately, it has a simple silver cross over the altar and beautiful green and yellow stained-glass windows. I would hate to recite our wedding vows with a statue of Jesus Christ bleeding on the cross looking down at us. I really don't understand a lot of what Christianity teaches. Why would God sacrifice his only son for the sins of the world? Tenrikyo makes more sense to me. If we want to get rid of our sins, we sweep them away like dust and follow the teaching of a smart woman."

"Since when is Ichiro a Christian?"

"He doesn't believe in any religion, but he likes the idea of getting married in a church. He thinks of us as a modern couple, and I do too."

Setsuko had a frustrated look on her face. "So, on what is surely the most important day of your life, you're letting Ichiro decide where you will be married?"

"I thought it was only fair since he agreed to Father's go-between and his choice of a wedding date, which was much further into the future than we would have liked. In fact, I think that Father was testing us to see if we could stay together. If Ichiro had his way, we'd already be married. Waiting has been difficult for both of us. We can barely keep our hands off one another. The other night…"

Setsuko put her hand over my mouth. "Spare me the details. I've almost forgotten what it feels like to want a man touching me. I'm grateful when my husband Hideo leaves me alone. And the last thing I need is another child. You will be careful, won't you, Noriko? You and Ichiro should have some time together before you start having children. You can't send them back where they came from."

"Or give them away. I know. I haven't had much experience with babies and toddlers. I don't even know if I'd make a good mother."

"You and Ichiro have a lot to learn about one another. He's been your boss for much of your relationship. It's a whole different story when you're husband and wife. Do you even know how he feels about children and being a parent?"

"We haven't discussed it, but I'm sure we'll figure it out when the time comes." I could always count on my practical sister to pour a bucket of ice-cold water over my head.

～

SETSUKO AND I ARRIVED at the Moda Japan Bridal Salon near the Shinsaibashi Metro Station. The store had an extensive selection of Western-style bridal gowns and traditional Japanese kimonos for rent. Setsuko asked if Ichiro was paying for my dresses. "He is. He instructed me to choose whatever I want."

My sister admonished me. "Don't take advantage of his generosity, Noriko. He's not thinking clearly, I can assure you. I see the look in his eyes every time you pass by him in the restaurant. He looks starstruck. He just wants to please you, even if it means emptying his pockets."

"I would never do that to him. I can be practical when I need to be, although this is for the most important day of my life..." I couldn't believe I was actually saying this. As much as I loved Ichiro, I felt as if I was taking a leap of faith. But didn't every bride feel that way? In only a few weeks I would be reciting my marriage vows to Ichiro, promising myself body, mind, and soul. Perhaps I didn't know Ichiro as well as I should to be marrying him, but I had faith that the more I got to know him intimately, the more I would love him. I suspected that he still had secrets he was keeping from me. On the other hand, do we ever really know everything there is to know about our partner?

When we consulted with him, the minister at the chapel gave us our vows. I had already memorized them as if they were a script in a movie that I was starring in: *This man I marry, no matter what the health situation is, I will love this person, respect this person, console this person, help this person until death, protecting fidelity I swear.* I asked myself if I was truly prepared to do that. My honest answer was: "I will try my best."

The minister delivered a solemn blessing in English over us, and then in Japanese, he added, "Japanese people have many proverbs and sayings that I have heard over the years. This is one to keep in mind: 'Eggs and vows are easily broken.' My advice to you is to never take one another for granted and be realistic in your expectations. Know that you will be faced with good times and bad but you are stronger together than alone."

〜

THE RACKS ON ONE side of the bridal salon were filled with white dresses of every style and material: tulle, silk, velvet, organza. Some were embellished with lace, crystals, and beads; others were simple. On the opposite racks were traditional kimonos in dazzlingly bright colors with brocade, appliqué, and obis. I was overwhelmed by the choices and relieved when a salesgirl approached to offer her assistance. She selected several gowns and led Setsuko and me to a dressing room. Holding each one up, I picked the first one she showed me to try on.

The salesgirl clapped her hands. "An excellent choice, Miss Ito. This is an exact replica of the wedding dress worn by the American socialite Jacqueline Bouvier at her wedding to US Senator and presidential candidate John Fitzgerald Kennedy. It's been one of our most popular dresses this year, and if her husband wins the election, it will be even more so. Wait just a minute." She returned with a large album filled with photographs and newspaper clippings. "Look here. This is her picture. You look a little like Mrs. Kennedy, although she is now pregnant with their second child."

"I've been told that before, not that I am pregnant, but that I resemble her. It might just be my hairstyle."

"No, although I can't put my finger on it, it's more than that. When is your wedding?"

"November tenth."

"In the United States, that is November ninth, so it's right after the election. Let's hope Mr. Kennedy wins. That will be a sign of good luck for you in that dress."

The salesgirl adjusted the full-length, three-way mirror, and instructed me to stand up on the riser. "Step into the dress, and I'll zip it up. Let's see if it suits you."

Made of ivory silk taffeta, the bouffant skirt featured interwoven tucking bands and tiny wax flowers. Underneath was a tulle petticoat that made the skirt stand out. The classic portrait neckline sat beneath my collarbone. I looked as if I was floating on a cloud. With a flourish the salesgirl waved a tulle veil through the air and then attached it to my curls, securing it with a headband of silk orange blossoms and crystals. Clasping the waistband from the back, she said, "We'll just need to take the dress in slightly. Don't lose any weight between now and your wedding. Lots of brides are so nervous they forget to eat."

Always the practical businesswoman, Setsuko asked, "Is the adjustment included in the rental fee?"

"Yes, and so is the veil, but you'll need to buy a pair of pumps."

"I already have a pair. They're not comfortable, but I think I can endure the pain on my wedding day. I'll probably forget all about my feet." I looked at the tag on the dress, and from the expression on the salesgirl's face she could see I was shocked by the rental fee.

"My dear, think of it this way. Your wedding marks the end of your past and the beginning of your promising future. It's no time to be frugal, is it?"

Setsuko raised her eyebrows. "Don't you think you should try on another dress? There might be one that you like just as well that is less expensive."

"This is the one I want. I'll contribute some of my own money, and I won't tell Ichiro how much it costs." Setsuko tried arguing, but I said, "It's decided. Now let's find a kimono for the reception."

Setsuko said, "Impetuous as usual, Noriko. But it does look lovely on you. Which kimono do you prefer?"

I picked out a red kimono with white egrets on it—the color a symbol of good luck and the birds a symbol of love-sick maidens. I was hardly sick, but as for the "love" part, guilty as charged.

Standing behind the cash register, the salesgirl said, "We'll have both the wedding dress and kimono delivered to the church the morning of your wedding. We don't want you going to the trouble of picking them up. And we'll send someone there to help you change. We can also provide you with a photographer for an extra fee. Are you interested?"

"Of course."

"Good. With your permission, we'll put your photograph in our book for future brides to see."

"Thank you, but I'd rather you didn't. For your sake. I'm only a waitress at the Tesagara Tearoom. We have many fancy ladies who come in regularly. If one of them should see my photograph in that dress, it might dissuade them from picking it."

"As you wish, Miss Ito, but I think you're wrong. You look very glamorous, and you're a very good model." Taking out an adding machine, she punched in all the numbers and gave me the total. I folded the rental slip and put it in my pocketbook.

As we headed toward the subway, Setsuko said, "What you said about being a waitress…You don't need to ever apologize or make excuses."

"I hope I haven't insulted you. I'm grateful for my job, and if it hadn't been for you, I would never have met Ichiro. But you know how snobbish our patrons can be."

"Is that the only reason?"

"I don't want anyone to tell Ichiro how much my dress cost either. He's a proud man, and he'd be mortified if he thought I had paid some of the cost."

"Well, I can understand that. It will be our secret, but next time you want to hide something from him, you should think carefully. Secrets can poison a marriage."

"Certainly, you have your secrets from Hideo, don't you?"

"Yes. But I gave up on him a long time ago. We stay together for the sake of the children and the business. Hopefully, you won't need to pull the wool over Ichiro's eyes, and even if you believe you have a very good reason for doing so, you should think about it one hundred times."

I couldn't imagine why I would find it necessary to lie to Ichiro. And doing so would probably prove futile as he usually could guess what I held in my mind and in my heart. Wasn't that why we were so perfectly suited to one another?

Chapter 15

THE NANIWA CHAPEL ENFOLDED everyone I loved, most especially my husband to be, in its splendid arches and pews festooned with white flowers. My father held my hand as we waited for the music that would summon us through the heavy wooden doors and down the aisle to start. He looked like a stranger in his wedding attire, but I could still smell the faintest hint of fish, which never left him after so many years of sushi making in Hiroshima. He had a stern look on his face that forced me to warn him.

"Father, promise me you'll be cordial to Ichiro."

"I hardly know him, and what I do know about him isn't very impressive."

"You'd find fault with any man who wanted to marry me."

"That's not true. If he had a big bank account, I'd be perfectly happy."

"We have our whole lives ahead of us to make money and lead a comfortable life. Ichiro is intelligent and ambitious. I cannot imagine my life without him. I thought I'd end up a spinster but God the Parent had other plans for me."

"Love wears off. Didn't you ever hear of the expression, 'It's just as easy to marry a rich man as a poor man?'"

"And have him think he owns me? No, thank you. When did you become so cantankerous?" I knew my father was keeping a secret from me. Setsuko told me that he had a mistress, which explained my parents' constant bickering, and that he intended to divorce my mother. They had very little reason to stay together other than responsibility for my brother, who would soon be off to the university, and their shared entanglement in the sushi shop.

Suddenly the organ music started and the doors to the chapel opened. Standing behind me, my sister Setsuko fluffed up the skirt of my wedding gown and picked up the back of my veil. My niece Akiko and nephew Mitsuo dropped rose petals along the white carpet and then slipped into a pew toward the front of the chapel next to my mother and my brother Tadashi, who looked very handsome in his rented suit.

My father slowly walked me down the aisle. Sunlight filtered through the stained-glass windows throwing beams of green and yellow light onto Ichiro's dove-gray morning coat. I held my bouquet of lilies tightly to keep my hands from shaking. All the guests were smiling at me, but the only person I concentrated on was Ichiro. With each step I took toward him I felt my nervousness melt away. Handing my bouquet to Setsuko, I stood next to Ichiro, who grasped my hand in his. In that moment I knew with glad certainty that we were meant to be together and nothing could ever destroy our love. The minister asked us to repeat our vows, and then, after we exchanged rings, pronounced us husband and wife. Ichiro raised my veil and kissed me gently on the lips. Taking a handkerchief out of his breast pocket, he delicately wiped a tear that rolled down my cheek. As Mendelssohn's "Wedding March" filled the church, Ichiro led me down the aisle. I glanced at my mother smiling at me; at least one of my parents looked truly happy for me and Ichiro.

Twenty of our friends and relatives gathered in one of the private banquet rooms at the Grille Room waiting for Ichiro and me to make our official entrance. Passing through the downstairs public dining room, patrons looked up from their bowls, wishing us, *"Go-kekkon omedetou gozaimasu!"*

Excusing myself, I asked Ichiro to wait while I changed into my kimono. The photographer's assistant helped me put on the many layers and adjust the obi to just the right proportion to complement my figure. I pinned a white orchid in my hair and then picked up the fan Ichiro gave me on our engagement. Opening it, the melody of "Clair de Lune" replayed in my head, and I recited the words of the poem that inspired the music: "The sad and lovely moonlight that sets the birds dreaming in the trees and the fountains sobbing in ecstasy." Sobbing in ecstasy? Is that what awaited me lying in Ichiro's arms?

When I stepped into the hallway, Ichiro was impatiently pacing back and forth. "You took so long I thought maybe you had second thoughts and slipped out the back door."

"Hardly. It took me a long time to get into this kimono, even with the assistant's help. If it weren't for my aunties and uncles who are so old-fashioned, I wouldn't even have bothered."

"Your father didn't look very happy walking you down the aisle. I wondered if he might have planted a negative thought in your head about me."

"My father usually has a dour expression on his face. It means nothing." *My first lie as Ichiro's wife*, I thought. I prayed that he believed me.

The photographer ushered us into an empty banquet room where he had set up a stage for formal picture taking. I sat in a high-backed chair with my fan closed in my lap, and Ichiro stood behind me holding a pair of white gloves in his left hand, as is the tradition. We could hear laughter coming from the other side of the wall. The photographer peeked out from under the black-draped camera and slid a plate into the front. "I'll take a few pictures. Please do not smile as much as you might like to on this happiest of occasions. A smile on your lips will cause you to be embarrassed in the years to come. If you wish to show your happiness, express it in your eyes. You will look more sincere that way."

After taking several formal black and white pictures, the photographer folded his equipment. "We will make a very nice album for you, Mr. and Mrs. Uchida." He then backed out of the room, leaving us alone. Ichiro wrapped me in his arms and kissed me. When I opened my eyes, I was startled to see tears welling up in my husband's eyes.

"What's the matter, Ichiro? You aren't still concerned about my grumpy father, are you?"

"It's something else, Noriko. I wish my sister and her husband could be here with us. When she wrote saying she couldn't afford the airfare, it made me think that life is more difficult for her than she lets on. After everything we went through together, she deserves to be happy. And I wish the two of you had met one another before our wedding. I know you would love my sister, and she would certainly love you."

I pointed out, "Mizuki mentioned she and Harry are both afraid to fly. One day we'll visit them in Montana if they won't travel." I added, "Weddings should be such a joyous occasion, but they also remind us of who is missing in our lives. It would have meant the world to me to have my classmate, Mizuki, come to our wedding. She excused herself, saying she has a matinee performance. I don't mean anything to her now that she is famous."

"If you miss her that much, I'll buy us tickets for a performance. Would you like that?"

I didn't want to appear selfish. "Let's save our money for a trip to America. If our friendship meant that much to her she would have found a way to be here on our special day."

My nephew Mitsuo stood at the entrance to our banquet room holding a basket filled with decorative envelopes containing money in honor of our wedding. He slid the door open, and Ichiro and I took our cushioned seats at the long, low banquet table. I could hardly pay attention to the lively conversation and silly jokes; all I could think of was the song I had practiced for Ichiro and our guests. After everyone had eaten, three ceremonial cups of different sizes were filled with sake three times, and the men delivered congratulatory toasts, beginning with Ichiro's uncles. Then Ichiro's friend Norimitsu stood up. He recalled their ski trip to Hakodateyama. "I proposed to my wife Maemi there, and lucky for me, she said yes. And now we are having our first child." Smiling adoringly at his pregnant wife, he continued, "I hope Ichiro and Noriko will be blessed with as much happiness in their marriage as Maemi and I have found in ours." He added, "I recall at the time that Ichiro was pessimistic about his chances of meeting someone to love, but the gods proved him wrong. He has done very well for himself."

I drained my cup. I wasn't sure I could manage to swallow two more cups. My father signaled the waitress to fill the next cup, and even before the toast had been made, he gulped it down. I was afraid he might be getting drunk.

When it was Ichiro's turn to speak, I marveled at his poise and how elegant he looked in his morning coat. "First, I must acknowledge Noriko's parents for doing such a good job raising her. Thank you, Mr. and Mrs. Ito. I can only imagine what a special child Noriko must have been—headstrong too." My father rolled his eyes, and Mother nodded in agreement.

Ichiro continued, "I remember when Noriko danced into the tearoom, so full of life and joy. Those qualities are what drew me to her. Until I met you, Noriko, I only felt half alive. Your beauty and inner radiance light up my life. I promise to do my best to be worthy of your love, for now and for as long as we both shall live."

Auntie Sanae, my mother's sister, said a few words as a stand-in for my mother, who did not feel comfortable giving a toast. "I was not blessed with children, and so Noriko has been like a daughter to me. In my role as a second mother, I introduced her to Tenrikyo. She and I went regularly to their church. I hope that she will continue to observe their teachings and perhaps one day Ichiro will share in her devotion. We believe that marriage is the joyous acceptance between husband and wife. There should be no arguments. This may sound difficult at first, but with practice, I'm confident that you both will appreciate the value of harmony and the destructiveness of disagreements."

Ichiro politely nodded to indulge my aunt.

I took a letter out of the pocket of my kimono and stood up as my aunt took her seat. "Thank you all for your sincere wishes. To my parents, I am most grateful to you—first and foremost for allowing Ichiro to marry me." Looking up, I confessed, "Although, truthfully, I would have married him anyway."

I waited for the laughter to die down. "I owe everything to my father for rescuing me on that fateful day so many years ago." The guests nodded knowingly. "And to my mother, for showing me what it means to be a strong and independent woman, thank you. If Ichiro is unhappy with me, I'll tell him to complain to you."

My father reacted. "My advice to you, Ichiro, is that you always agree with whatever Noriko wants. That way you will be happy in your marriage." There was laughter at his joke.

Clearing her throat, my mother chimed in. "What Ryo says is absolutely true, but he doesn't follow his own advice when it concerns me." There was laughter once again, but it seemed an uneasy laughter, as if the audience sensed she meant it.

I hoped that my parents would remain cordial to one another, but they could not resist poking at one another even on my wedding day. After a moment of awkward silence, I signaled to Mitsuo to turn the phonograph record on. While the introductory bars played, I said, "I want to dedicate this song to my husband. I sang it for the first time with him at the piano in the tearoom, and it was at that moment we recognized the love between us that we had been denying. So, the song has special meaning to both of us. It's called 'You're My Everything,' and even if some of you don't understand the lyrics, it's my way of telling Ichiro that he is all I need to be happy."

Ichiro stood up and put his arm around my waist as I sang. We looked into one another's eyes, and my voice cracked with emotion. When the song ended, everyone clapped. My father raised his hand. Slurring his words, he said, "I can hear that you haven't lost your voice, Noriko. Too bad you're only using it to serenade your husband and all of us here who admire you instead of an audience of thousands as you planned." I cringed, hurt that my father chose this moment to remind me of my failure. Checking his pocket watch, he quickly changed the subject. "You two better leave now or you'll miss your train."

Hurrying out of the dining room so we could change into our street clothes, my father caught up with us. He was unsteady on his feet, and I smelled liquor on his breath from the scotch he drank between cups of sake. Handing Ichiro an envelope, he spoke loudly enough so I could hear him. "You've gotten yourself quite a prize, marrying my little songbird. I expect you to make something of yourself. You can't be a restaurant manager forever, Ichiro."

Before Ichiro could respond, I rushed to his defense. "The truth is, Ichiro plans on opening a restaurant of his own someday, and I'll be right by his side."

My father laughed derisively. "Well, you've certainly put my mind at ease."

Ichiro grabbed my father's shoulder. "Sir, I cannot accept your gift. I have already paid for the banquet and our honeymoon, and please be assured that you have nothing to worry about. I am perfectly capable of supporting both of us."

Without arguing, my father put the envelope in his pocket and went back to our guests. I tried apologizing for my father's rudeness. "He gets very surly when he's drunk."

Seemingly unruffled, Ichiro said, "Don't worry. I suspect he's jealous of me. That's the way fathers can be when they realize they're losing their precious daughter to another man. It's an old story."

I was proud of Ichiro for standing up to my father in so diplomatic a way. They were the two most important men in my life, and all I wanted was for them to get along. Perhaps I was being naïve, but I hoped that in time, my husband would earn my father's affection. And that my father would recognize I had made a wise decision to marry Ichiro.

Chapter 16

ICHIRO PICKED UP A newspaper and then we found our seats on the local train heading for Katsuura on the Kumano Sea, home to a port for whaling ships and religious shrines hidden in the mountains above the black water.

Ichiro sighed. "It will be so lovely to breathe in the salt air and feel the mountain breeze on our faces."

I touched his hand. "And to be alone with you at last."

"I won't have to hold myself back any longer," he said. "I can explore every inch of you."

"I hope you won't be disappointed in me."

"How could I be?" Pointing to the front page of the newspaper, he said, "There is Mrs. Kennedy with the newly elected president of the United States, John Fitzgerald Kennedy. You are even more beautiful than she is."

"Let me see." I studied her picture. "She looks very pregnant. Her baby must be due soon."

"What does the article say?" Ichiro reached into his pocket and pulled out a pair of wire-rimmed reading glasses.

"Since when did you start wearing those?"

"Oh, just recently. My eyes have been playing tricks on me, and the doctor recommended I wear them."

"You looked very distinguished."

Ichiro laughed. "Not like a silly old owl?"

"Definitely not. Now when is Mrs. Kennedy's baby due?"

"Before her husband's inauguration in January. They already have a daughter, so maybe this one will be a boy. They look very happy, don't they? Imagine. He's forty-three years old, the youngest man to ever serve as President of the United States."

"Certainly, the most handsome."

Ichiro took his glasses off, and with a twinkle in his eye asked, "Are you trying to make me jealous?"

"Not at all…Maybe just a little bit. It's healthy for a husband and wife to not take one another for granted."

"Is that what you read in your women's magazines?"

"Where else would I have picked up such an idea?"

Squeezing my hand, Ichiro whispered in my ear. "We'll have to teach one another how to hold one another's interest, although I can't imagine ever tiring of you, Noriko."

We carried on this banter until the conductor announced our arrival at Kii-Katsuura Station. Ichiro carried our valise from the railroad station for the ten-minute walk to the ryokan where he reserved a room. The leaves of the maple trees were bright red in the setting sun, and a cold breeze blew down from the mountains, hinting at the possibility of an early snow. He tied a scarf around his neck, then turned the collar of my coat up to protect me from the wind. I took a deep breath and smelled a hint of the sea. I imagined the whales playfully leaping out of the water and the priests high in the mountains saying their prayers to protect all living beings.

The ryokan glowed like a bright lantern in the fading autumn light. The manager of the inn welcomed us and led us to our room at the end of the corridor. After he had departed, I slipped into the private bathroom and changed into a cotton kimono. Sitting on a pillow on the floor, I waited for Ichiro; and when he entered, we separated at the men's and women's indoor baths to cleanse ourselves for a soak in the outdoor hot springs reserved only for us.

"Turn around, Ichiro. I'm taking my kimono off."

"Must I?"

"I feel embarrassed having your eyes on me. Please."

When his back was turned, I dropped my kimono and slipped into the hot water. I turned away to give Ichiro the same courtesy. We floated in the stone pool protected from the wind by an overhanging roof. Snowflakes fell, dusting the bamboo railing. The wind blowing down from the mountains grew in strength. I swam over to the edge of the pool and opened my mouth to catch the snow on my tongue. Ichiro swam up behind me, and then he dove underneath the water and nibbled gently on my toes. I felt a jolt of energy travel through my body. Slowly rising to the surface of the water, he enfolded me in his arms. Steam drifted off our entwined bodies into the frigid air. Ichiro kissed my closed eyelids as I floated on my back. He pulled me gently through the water toward the stone stairs. The branches of the evergreens cracked against one another, and from inside the inn guests toasted to shouts of *kampai*. I dove under the water and came up behind him, slipping my hands along his torso. He let out an involuntary groan.

Ichiro climbed out of the steaming water and quickly wrapped himself in his kimono. Handing me a towel, he asked, "May I watch you?"

I nodded and took my time drying myself off, feeling Ichiro's eyes drink in my entire body. He held out my kimono and tied the sash around my waist, and then he slid his hands, at first gently and then more aggressively, between my legs. My breath caught in my throat. I raked my fingers through his wet hair and then pushed him away from me. "Please wait, Ichiro."

"You're my wife. Whatever you say." And then he led me along the slippery snow-covered path back to our room.

The attendants had laid out our futons and pillows. A teapot and two celadon porcelain cups and a plate of honey cakes sat on a brazier heated by burning embers. The air smelled of incense and cedar branches. Hanging in the room's alcove was a parchment scroll with an ink drawing of a family of Japanese macaques soaking in the hot springs; a crackle vase filled with pine branches and red berries was the only other adornment. There was nothing to distract us from one another.

I poured Ichiro a cup of tea and then we greedily ate the honey cakes. Ichiro's fingers were covered in honey. I asked Ichiro if he would like me to lick the sticky honey off his fingers. "Yes, if you'll allow me to do the same." This simple act was deeply arousing.

I let the kimono fall off my shoulders and untied the sash; a thin trickle of perspiration ran between my breasts and pooled in the fold of my stomach. Ichiro leaned over and tasted my saltiness with his tongue. Turning off the lights, we lay on top of the comforter. The embers in the brazier threw soft shadows across the room and onto Ichiro's back.

I lifted my arms over my head so he could examine all of me. Ichiro clasped my hands in his and then gently guided himself between my legs. I gasped as we synchronized our rhythm to one another's urges. Outside the wind howled, muffling our cries of long-awaited pleasure. Closing my eyes, I could see stars shooting across an ink-black sky, and then I heard the strains of an unrecognizable theme—part earthly and part spiritual. I don't remember when we fell asleep wrapped around one another underneath the warm covers. In the morning, Ichiro woke me with his passion reignited, and I eagerly received him. When we had finished, suddenly thirsty, I didn't bother putting on my robe, and walking across the room took a few sips of cold tea. *How easily I lost my modesty and allowed Ichiro to stare at me.*

I slid the shoji screen open and sunlight streamed into our room. Melting snow dripped from the roof of the ryokan in a steady rhythm like the ticking of a clock marking off the minutes. I remarked to Ichiro how the mountainside was still awash in evergreens, dusted with snow, alongside brilliant red maples. "It's as if fall and winter are sharing the earth together."

"What a poetic image. You have such a vivid imagination. I would probably have said, '"Look how strange…Has Mother Nature become confused?"'

"I like that just as well, Ichiro, but my observation comes from the heart and yours is from the head. I'm more emotional and you're more intellectual, but that doesn't make either of us right or wrong. We complement one another perfectly." Ichiro slowly got out of bed. His ribs stood out from under his skin. "You look as if you don't eat enough, Ichiro."

"I don't have much of an appetite these days. Probably because I've just been anxious about our wedding, but now that we're married, I expect you to take care of me, to remind me when I haven't eaten enough, and fatten me up like a contented goose."

"In sickness and in health, that's what I promised. And you will do the same."

"You don't need to worry. You are perfect the way you are, Noriko." Squinting because of a sunbeam that stole through the window screen, Ichiro said, "We should get ready if we want to make something of the day. Although, to tell you the truth, I would just as soon stay right here and make love."

Picking up a tourist pamphlet the manager had left us, I said, "The waterfalls are a short walk from here. We'll have just enough time to take an excursion before our train leaves for Osaka."

Ichiro opened the shower door. "It's a bit tight in here, but why don't we take a shower together?" I squeezed in beside Ichiro, letting the hot water spray me and drench my hair. I traced the raised burn scars on Ichiro's back with my fingers, the places where Madam Tamae had repeatedly tortured him with lit sticks of moxa—punishment for just being alive. Ichiro winced and then relaxed as I continued to massage his back. Picking up a bar of pine-scented soap, Ichiro washed me between my legs and then pinned me against the tile wall, entering me again. I urged him on until we both were sated.

As we dried one another off, I asked my husband, "Do you think we'll always be as passionate as we are today? Or is this just what newlyweds do on their honeymoon and then their passion slowly fades, especially when children come along?"

"I can't say. And as for children, we have plenty of time for them. We should give ourselves a chance to enjoy one another as man and wife before being tied down by family responsibilities."

I took no precautions despite Setsuko's warning and my limited under-standing of a woman's body, but I was sure that I couldn't become pregnant at this point in my cycle. I did not mention this to Ichiro. Perhaps I was being foolish, but we had waited so long that I wanted nothing artificial to sep-arate us.

Dressing warmly and then packing our few things, we left our valise with the manager and followed the map to the waterfalls. A crowd of tourists gathered at the precipice opposite the jagged rocks to watch the water of the Nachi River tumble five hundred feet through the Mystic Mountain into a deep, black pool at the bottom of the ravine. According to the pamphlet, behind us was a three-story pagoda where the priests displayed their treasures. I read to Ichiro, "Each morning the Shinto priest makes offerings to the waterfall and many star-crossed lovers have leapt to their death from the top of the waterfall as a way of entering paradise." I asked him, "If they were truly in love, would they not see life on earth as a paradise?"

"This is why I don't believe in religion. Followers of any religion are convinced of the most foolish ideas. I'd rather rely on the ancient Greeks and sages of the Middle Ages to teach me how to live my life."

An owl screeched as it took off from the branch of a tree and disappeared into the mist above the waterfall. Its cry was unnerving, and I involuntarily grabbed Ichiro's hand. In a comforting voice he said, "Owls are good luck. Nothing for you to worry about, Noriko." But I was unconvinced and took the screeching as a bad omen. Ichiro led me back down the path, slippery with pine needles and patches of snow pressed into the earth by the tourists wishing to see the highest waterfall in all of Japan.

When we stopped at the ryokan to pick up our valise, the manager said, "I hope that we shall see you again, Mr. and Mrs. Uchida."

I loved the sound of my new name: Mrs. Noriko Uchida. As the train headed back to Osaka, I kept repeating it in time to the rumbling of wheels over the tracks. Every once in a while, I'd steal a glance at Ichiro, who had dozed off, a book open in his lap. Curious, I picked it up and read a page or two of *Magic Mountain*:

> *But Hans Castorp said as they walked on: "You see, I didn't mind it at all, I got on with her quite well; I always do with such people; I understand instinctively how to go at them—don't you think so? I even think, on the whole, I get on better with sad people than with jolly ones—goodness knows why. Perhaps it's because I'm an orphan, and lost my parents early."*

I wondered if Ichiro, who saw himself as an orphan, had the same opinion of himself. I doubted it, for if he had, he would not have married me. I was a woman who believed in happiness and shunned sorrow like a disease that must be avoided at all cost.

Chapter 17

FOR THE FIRST TWO months of marriage, we lived in my sister's apartment above the Aki-Torii because my room was bigger than the one Ichiro had rented over the tearoom. My sister's children were instructed never to enter our room without knocking, but they often couldn't resist and barged in. Ichiro had to devise ways to gently dismiss them. "Mitsuo, why don't you find a pail and carry my cigarette smoke outside?"

"I don't know how to do that, Uncle. You can't catch smoke in a pail."

"Well, try to figure it out, and when you do, you can come back into our room and not before then."

I pulled the sheet over my head so Mitsuo wouldn't hear me laughing. "Oh, Ichiro, that poor boy. He's going to be puzzling that out all day."

"That's the point. He'll stay away from us." Tracing my body with his finger, he said, "I'm going to install a lock on the door. I don't know why I didn't think of it before I moved in here with you."

"We should ask Setsuko's permission." Ichiro then rolled on top of me. I complained, "It's almost six a.m. Time to get up. Our customers will be lining up at the tearoom and we'll still be in bed."

"You're right. I'll be quick. Making love to you first thing in the morning always makes my day brighter. And then I don't have to be thinking about it all day long."

I whispered, "Sometimes, during the day, I close my eyes and imagine you are inside me, and I want to scream out in pleasure."

"I'm glad you control yourself. You'd frighten our customers with your moaning or make them jealous. Now, shhh." He gently put his hand behind my back and pressed his body against mine.

From the corridor we could hear the house stirring. Ichiro stepped into his slippers and wrapped himself in a kimono. Unable to resist philosophizing, he said, "We've only been married two months. It feels like a minute and an eternity. Does time slow down or speed up when one is happy?"

"I don't know." Still naked, I put my finger on the calendar hanging on the wall. "To be exact, it's sixty-four days. I've been keeping track." I wasn't sure this was the appropriate time to tell Ichiro, but I couldn't keep it a secret any longer. Putting my hands on my waist, I said, "Don't I look fatter, and aren't my breasts fuller?"

Speaking slowly, Ichiro said, "I did notice your uniform is a little tight but I thought it was because we've been spoiling ourselves by going out to eat after work more often."

I confessed, "I missed my period, and so I went to the doctor and he confirmed my suspicion. I'm pregnant." I tried to deliver this news in a neutral voice so that Ichiro would be free to express his feelings to me. I wanted him to be honest. I was prepared to terminate my pregnancy if he was against having a child so soon after we were married.

"I'm not sure what to think about this," he replied after a few moments of uncomfortable silence, the look on his face somewhere between studious and confused. "I was thinking it would be just the two of us for a while longer. I don't know if I'm ready to be a father yet."

I could feel my heart beating against my chest. I had hoped that one of us would feel sure that this was a happy accident. I assured Ichiro that we would have plenty of time to get used to the idea of becoming parents. "The doctor says our baby will be born around my birthday in August. He guesses that I conceived on our honeymoon." I confessed further, "I wasn't being very careful." Defending myself I said, "I thought it wasn't my time of the month. I relied on the rhythm method."

Ichiro lit a cigarette despite the lateness of the hour. "Obviously. It was foolish and irresponsible, but I won't hold it against you, Noriko. It was up to me, too, to keep us from getting pregnant." Trying to make light of the situation, Ichiro said, "So the baby is our 'love child'? Are you happy?"

"It feels like an enormous responsibility. I hesitate to admit it, but I can be selfish and self-absorbed and so I am not sure how good a mother I will be, but I feel a sense of relief that fate has taken the decision out of our hands. I know how you hate to plan ahead.

"I have started to imagine whether our baby is a boy or a girl and what it will be like." I placed my hands on my stomach and looked up at Ichiro for some measure of assurance that our baby would be born healthy.

Ichiro heard water running in the hallway bathroom. "Now I've missed my chance to take a shower. I'm going to have to get dressed covered with your scent still on my skin. Or maybe we can sneak into the shower together."

"You know where that will lead."

"About the baby. You have nothing to worry about. He will be gorgeous just like you. Unless he looks like me, of course. I remember reading what George Bernard Shaw said to the dancer Isadora Duncan when she proposed they have a child together. She said, 'Can you imagine what an amazing baby we will have with my looks and your brains?' Shaw responded, 'Ah, but what if the baby has my looks and your brains?'"

I threw the pillow at Ichiro. "What a nasty man. What did she say?"

"I don't know. The story might be apocryphal and, of course, they never actually married."

"Just as well. He must not have deserved a woman with her talent and beauty."

By way of apology, Ichiro kissed me. I tasted tobacco on his breath. Changing the subject, he said, "I think it's time for us to look for our own apartment. We'll need more room and privacy when the baby comes. What do you say?"

I interpreted his question as proof that this baby was to be part of our future. With a touch of humor, Ichiro added, "Tell Mitsuo he can forget about looking for a smoke pail. We'll be out of here in no time."

～

ICHIRO AND I RENTED an unfurnished second-floor studio apartment six subway stops from the tearoom. We moved in April, four months before my delivery date. The room was spotless and had a private toilet and shower. The kitchen sink was large enough to bathe a baby, and there was a balcony overlooking the street where I installed a profusion of pots filled with flowers and green plants. Ichiro hung a rope across the balcony so I could dry our laundry on sunny days. With the money we received as wedding gifts, I bought new tatami mats and silk pillows, a square, low, lacquered table for dining, a desk and chair, and a beautiful carved wood screen that divided the sleeping area from the rest of the room. In remembrance of our honeymoon, I found a copy of the scroll of macaques that hung in our room at the ryokan, and we placed a few photographs, including one from our wedding; one of Ichiro's father dressed in his cavalry uniform astride his favorite Arabian mount, Tariq; and one of his mother, Toshiko, her hair in a simple bun and wearing a black and white kimono. In this picture she is holding his sister Mitsuko in her arms, an expression of maternal love on her lovely face. Ichiro told me that, when this photograph of his mother was taken, she was already ill with tuberculosis but it had not yet stolen her beauty.

Mornings, I watered the plants and deadheaded the blossoms past their prime, and then I walked or took the subway to the tearoom with Ichiro. I intended to work right up until the time of our baby's birth so that we could save some money. Evenings, after Ichiro got off work, we'd sit on the balcony enjoying the spring weather, talking over the noise of the traffic below. Our conversation meandered lazily from the events of the day to what lay ahead of us.

On this night, Ichiro asked, "Shall I pour us a cup of sake and put on some music?"

"The doctor instructed me not to drink alcohol. It could be bad for the baby, but you go ahead. I'd love to hear some music—just keep it down so we don't wake the neighbors. We don't want them complaining to our landlady. Mrs. Masamoto might threaten to raise our rent or ask us to move. Renting the room to us knowing that we were having a baby was an exception to her usual practice."

Ichiro said, "I gave her more than she asked for as a security deposit when I negotiated the lease. It will keep us on her good side. And I think she's almost as excited about the baby as we are, so I don't think we have anything to worry about." He stood up and stretched his legs, returning with a cup of cold sake. Leaving the sliding door open, he asked, "Do you like the music? I bought the record the other day. I heard the music on the radio and just had to have it for my collection. It's one of my few indulgences, as you know. I couldn't live without music."

"What is it?"

"*Rhapsody in Blue.* The composer, Gershwin, said the entire melody popped into his head while he was riding on a train. He wanted to express America's 'unduplicated national pep and metropolitan madness.' He was quite a wordsmith and a great composer. I can hear the honking of the taxicabs and the roar of Manhattan's traffic as I listen to it. Some critics hated it at first—too much of a departure from the concerto structure—but it's now considered one of the greatest pieces of modern music. What do you think, Noriko?"

I stood up and swayed back and forth to the music, trying to find a beat to follow. Ichiro took my hand, and we twirled around the room faster and faster and then glided across the floor to the sound of the sliding oboes and clarinets. I felt clumsy from the extra weight of the baby and sat down.

Exuberant, Ichiro said, "Someday, we should go to New York City, take in all the Broadway shows, go to concerts and museums."

"Of course, we'd take our baby with us. I feel so attached, and I haven't even seen his face."

"Well, we don't have much longer to wait…"

I placed Ichiro's hands on my stomach. "Do you feel that? It's our baby kicking. I think he likes jazz."

"I doubt that, but who knows. I read in a science magazine that the unborn can recognize our voices and hear music at around twenty-four weeks."

"If that's the case, tell him you love him, Ichiro."

"I'll do better than that." He got down on his knees and covered my stomach with kisses.

Laughing, I said, "His mother likes what you are doing. Please don't stop."

⁓

AT THE END OF a long day at the tearoom, I insisted to Ichiro that we visit a local Shinto shrine for pregnant women so I could make an offering. I hadn't shared with Ichiro how worried I was that something might be wrong with our baby, but he reluctantly agreed to accompany me. I sometimes had terrible dreams that our baby was missing hands or feet or was blind and deaf, and I wanted to do everything I could to ward off any diseases or deformities.

At the temple, under the wooden portico, was a bronze statue of a dog and her pups. The priest gave me a sash with a picture of a dog painted on it and instructed me to wrap it around my stomach for the remainder of my pregnancy to guarantee a safe and easy birth. Wearing the sash underneath my uniform became part of my daily routine. I also scrubbed the toilet bowl every morning until it sparkled because my mother told me a clean toilet bowl ensures a good-looking and healthy baby.

To prove her point, Kimie said, "I scrubbed the toilet bowl every day when I carried you and look how you turned out. You are the beauty of the family."

Auntie Sanae reminded me to swallow the sacred rice powder from the Tenrikyo church for a safe birth. I had a bagful to protect me through my pregnancy. But I was still worried, and could hardly wait until I set eyes upon our baby, hold him in my arms, and make sure he was healthy.

Chapter 18

1961

April was the start of baseball season. Mr. Fukutake, one of the regular diners at the Aki-Torii Grille, gave Ichiro two tickets to a game at the Koshien Stadium in Osaka to see the underdog Hanshin Tigers play the Yomiuri Giants. Ichiro invited his nephew, fourteen-year-old Mitsuo Fujiwara, to join him. The boy craved his uncle's attention and was thrilled when Ichiro promised to teach him about the game. The boy's father showed no interest in him, and spent his time gambling at the pachinko parlor or hanging out at one of the neighborhood bars. Everyone kept their mouths closed when Hideo Fujiwara stumbled in late at night.

The green-turf outdoor stadium was packed with spectators stirred up to a fever pitch by the oendan cheering squad to watch the rivalry between the two Central League teams. As the game got underway, Minoru Murayama was in the Tigers' pitching lineup. Fans hoped he would turn the team's luck around since he had won the prestigious Eiji Sawamura Rookie of the Year award. Ichiro knew the batting averages of all the players, and as the game got underway, he kept up a running commentary so Mitsuo would understand what was happening.

"Are the Tigers your favorite team, Uncle?"

"Yes, now keep your eye on the catcher. He's going to signal to Murayama what kind of pitch to throw the batter."

"This is so exciting." With a sad look on his face he admitted that his father never took him anywhere.

"I'll tell you a secret, Mitsuo. My father never paid much attention to me either. He was too busy making money, and then he got sick. But I intend to take our child to lots of games—even if she's a girl. And don't worry.

I won't leave you behind. We'll all go together!" Seeing the look of pleasure on Mitsuo's face, Ichiro asked himself if this was what it could be like to be a loving and attentive father. He had no example to follow.

Ichiro and Mitsuo jumped out of their seats and waved their caps in the air every time it looked as if one of the Tigers was poised to score a run. Fans yelled, "Knock 'em dead, Tigers," to the beat of drumsticks and bells. Suddenly, Ichiro slumped back into his seat. He pulled out a handkerchief and covered his mouth; the white linen was stained with blood, and he felt a painful stab inside his chest.

"What's the matter, Uncle?"

Trying to catch his breath, Ichiro mumbled, "I don't know, but I feel like I'm going to pass out. Find an usher and have them call an ambulance right away, Mitsuo." Mitsuo ran up the stadium stairs to the nearest exit. Within minutes Ichiro was carried out on a stretcher. He clenched his teeth, stifling another painful cough. As the ambulance sped toward the hospital, every bump in the street caused a jarring pain up and down Ichiro's spine. He drifted in and out of consciousness.

When he opened his eyes, he saw that he was in a hospital room. A nurse wearing a face mask hovered over him, and Ichiro detected she was gravely concerned from the look in her eyes. Pouring a glass of water filled with ice cubes, she held it up to his lips and urged him to take a few sips.

Resting against the pillows, he asked, "Where is my nephew?"

"He's in the waiting room. I can't let him see you just yet."

"Please ask Mitsuo to call my landlady, Mrs. Masamoto. She will relay a message to my wife. Have him tell her that we stopped for a beer and a soda. I don't want my wife worrying about why I'm not home already. She's pregnant with our first child."

"Of course, but I need to draw your blood. Doctor's orders."

Ichiro winced as the needle pricked his flesh. As she collected the first of several vials of blood, the nurse asked, "Do you have brothers or sisters?" Ichiro suspected that she was attempting to distract him.

Not wanting to appear rude, he answered her honestly. "I have a sister who is three years older. She lives with her husband in the United States. I miss her terribly, especially because I will soon be a father. She should share in the joy of our baby."

The nurse, continuing with her tasks, said, "My brothers and sisters died in Hiroshima. I'm the only member of my family who survived. I was in school when the bomb dropped. The few doctors and nurses who escaped incineration performed miracles with what little they had. When I saw what they accomplished and how many people they saved, I decided to become a nurse."

"My wife also survived the bomb, along with her parents and her brother. Maybe that's why she generally looks on the bright side of things. You two are among the lucky ones."

"Women are usually optimistic. We have to be or we'd never choose to be mothers. So much can go wrong." Taking off her rubber gloves, she plumped up Ichiro's pillow. "I'm all finished—for the moment. Why don't you try to get some rest and I'll speak with your nephew?"

"Do you know what happened to me?"

"I don't, Mr. Uchida, but Dr. Shizumi will be in shortly to take a look at you. You have nothing to worry about. He's a good doctor." The nurse left Ichiro alone, but he wished she had stayed. She was so comforting and could distract him from the torrent of terrifying thoughts. He finally dozed off for a few minutes until the sound of the door swinging open jolted him out of his sleep. The doctor glanced at the chart hanging at the foot of his bed, then pulled up a chair next to Ichiro.

After introducing himself from behind his face mask, he asked, "Your age Mr. Uchida?"

"Twenty-nine. I'll be thirty in December."

"Are you married?"

"My wife, Noriko, is twenty-two; we're having our first child in August."

"Congratulations." Dr. Shizumi instructed Ichiro to lean forward and take a deep breath. He pressed the cold stethoscope against Ichiro's bare back. "What are these burn marks along your spine, Mr. Uchida?"

Embarrassed, he confessed, "Methodical punishments from a wicked stepmother—sounds like a Japanese folk tale but unfortunately it's true."

"No one stopped her?"

"My father was oblivious."

"Are they still alive, Mr. Uchida?"

"I haven't seen my stepmother in years, and my father died right after the war."

"Of what, might I ask?

"Heart failure. I think my stepmother drove him to his grave."

"And your birth mother?"

"She was diagnosed with tuberculosis when she was pregnant with me and died three years later. I have almost no memory of her."

"Children start to form memories at about three, so your experience is normal. Can you tell me how long you have had this cough?"

"It comes and goes. My first bout was while I was skiing several years ago. I should probably have seen a doctor then, but I chose to ignore it. I've never felt a severe pain in my chest before like I did at the baseball game. I thought I was going to pass out. I couldn't catch my breath. Maybe I overdid the cheering and jumping up and down. I'm a Tigers fan, and they need all the help they can get."

"Do you have bouts of fatigue?"

"I'm the general manager of two restaurants in Namba. I get to work at seven a.m. to open the tearoom and usually leave the Aki-Torii Grille Room around ten p.m., and so I'm putting in long days. But I can't complain. The money is good. My wife works as a waitress at the tearoom. At work I'm her boss; at home it's a different story. A typical middle-class couple. Nothing out of the ordinary."

"Perhaps you are both overdoing it. You might consider cutting back on your hours, Mr. Uchida."

"Dr. Shizumi, as I told you, we're getting ready for our first baby. If anything, I'll have to work more hours."

"And what about your appetite? You look very thin."

"It's all the running back and forth between the restaurants that keeps me in great shape. I don't eat regularly, but I eat enough."

Ichiro coughed into a tissue; answering the doctor's questions was irritating his throat and making him tired. He sank down into the pillows and pulled the bed covers up to his neck to hide his trembling.

"Given your symptoms and family history, I suspect you may have tuberculosis. TB could have been passed from your mother to you—even in utero. The strain can be dormant for many years if the body's immune system isn't compromised. We won't know the results of the blood tests for at least ten weeks. They will give us a definitive diagnosis."

The doctor's face kept fading in and out of focus as if a heavy mist from the ocean had blown through the hospital window. Ichiro tried to concentrate on Dr. Shizumi's voice, but his ears were ringing, and he had trouble understanding what the doctor was telling him.

"The best course of treatment is streptomycin. With luck you won't need to be quarantined and we can control your symptoms. If the blood test and X-rays confirm the diagnosis, I'll start you on daily injections at my clinic. Eventually you'll be able to take the medication orally, but I'll need to monitor your condition carefully."

"When can I leave the hospital?"

"You should go home now," Dr. Shizumi said, standing up to leave. "For the time being, you are to take cough medicine to relieve the congestion in your lungs. I'll have a prescription waiting for you at the front door. Expect a letter from me once all the tests are back, and we'll take it from there." He pulled off his mask. "Any questions, Mr. Uchida?"

Desperate for some assurance, he asked, "Am I going to die?"

"Eventually we're all going to die. But my job is to make sure that, in your case, it's later rather than sooner. Streptomycin is a miracle drug. Now, if you'll excuse me, I need to check on my other patients."

Ichiro's street clothes were hanging on a hook behind the door. His shirt was still damp with perspiration, and he regretted having to put it back on. Splashing water on his face, he ran his wet fingers through his hair, then put on his tie, making sure that he tied it straight. When fully dressed, he sat down on the bed until he stopped shaking.

Mitsuo flipped through a magazine when Ichiro found him in the hospital waiting room. Seeing his uncle, he rushed to his side, "Are you okay, Uncle Ichiro?"

"I'm fine now. I shouldn't have been jumping up and down like that. Too much excitement. Sorry I made you miss the rest of the game."

"The radio was on. Tigers seven, Giants ten. It was pretty close." He had a worried look on his face. "Are you going to tell the man who gave you the tickets we missed most of the game?"

"Can you keep a secret?"

Mitsuo put his Tigers cap on his head. "If you promise to take me to another game."

"You're a clever boy. It never hurts to bargain with your uncle. Here's what I need you to do: Don't tell anyone what happened—not even your parents. You know the final score so you can pretend we saw the entire game."

Mitsuo nodded like a good little soldier following orders.

As they were leaving, the nurse stopped Ichiro. "Here's your medicine, Mr. Uchida. Doctor's orders."

Slipping it into his jacket pocket, he adopted a confident tone for his nephew's benefit. "Thank you. I'm sure it will get rid of my cough in no time at all."

The train was packed with baseball fans sporting Tigers and Giants caps and carrying pennants; the riders entertained one another with play-by-play descriptions of each inning. Ichiro told Mitsuo to pay attention because he could learn much about the game. In truth he wanted the boy to back up his lie with facts. They squeezed into a seat when some of the passengers got off. Ichiro looked at his haggard reflection in the train window. He asked himself how he was going to tell Noriko what happened without alarming her unnecessarily.

Mitsuo tugged at his uncle's sleeve. "Here's your stop." Hesitating before he stepped onto the platform, Ichiro said, "Six more stops and that's where you get off. And don't forget to keep our secret safe." Mitsuo waved to communicate that he was a trustworthy coconspirator.

Ichiro had to catch his breath several times, walking like an old man, from the station. It was twenty steps from the front door of their building, past the landlady's apartment, and up to their room on the second floor. Each step felt like he was climbing over an enormous boulder. He held onto the banister for support and tried to breathe slowly to calm his beating heart. In his head he repeated the words in *The Little Prince*: "What saves a man is to take a step. Then another step. It is always the same step, but you have to take it." He finally made it upstairs. He clutched the key in his hand, the metal teeth biting into his flesh. He could hear Noriko singing "Blue Moon" to the music on the radio.

～

WHEN HE STEPPED INSIDE, Ichiro asked, "How's my lovely songbird?"

Drying my feet with a soft towel, I said, "Better now that you are home. I have been soaking my feet in a bowl of cold water. Standing all day at the tearoom makes my feet swell. Mitsuo said you stopped for a beer. I hope you didn't offer him a sip. That boy worships the ground you walk on. He wants to imitate everything you do."

"He should pick someone else to make his hero. Like Minoru Murayama. He pitched quite a game today."

Hanging the towel over the chair, I said, "You don't look well, Ichiro. I haven't wanted to mention it, but as I get fatter, you're getting thinner. You're working too hard."

"That's what the doctor told me, too."

"What doctor? What are you talking about?"

"The doctor at the Osaka Red Cross Hospital. I felt faint in the middle of the baseball game this afternoon. Mitsuo called an ambulance. I was so embarrassed. I had to be carried out of the stadium on a stretcher in front of all the fans. I only hope no one who knows me was in the stands. The doctor at the hospital, Dr. Shizumi, gave me some cough medicine. He's waiting for the results of some tests."

"For what?"

"He doesn't know for sure but from my symptoms he thinks I could have tuberculosis."

An involuntary gasp escaped my lips. Ichiro grabbed my hand and placed it on his chest. I could feel his ribs protruding through his damp shirt. "Noriko, I'm so sorry. Please forgive me. Had I known this might happen, I would never have married you or allowed you to carry our child. The doctor explained that I might have been infected by my mother when she was pregnant with me. I've been harboring the disease all these years but the bacteria was dormant until now, which is why I am having all these symptoms—fever, cough, temperature, loss of appetite, dizziness. What a terrible irony."

For the first time since I met Ichiro, I raised my voice against him. "Do you think I was selfish to marry you? How many Hiroshima women are rumored to have fallen ill and died years after the bombing from radiation poisoning? And what about the women who gave birth to deformed babies, which could happen to us too? Every day I worry that something might be wrong with our baby. I haven't wanted to mention it to you, and you never said anything because you love me. Another man might have considered me unclean and avoided me altogether." I threw my arms around Ichiro's neck and kissed his forehead. "We are meant to be together and we'll draw strength from one another, no matter what happens." Opening the cupboard, I shook out several kernels of rice. "Swallow these. They have been blessed by the priestess at the Tenrikyo church. If we both take a few each day, they'll help fortify us."

I handed Ichiro a glass of water and gestured for him to drink. Too weak to argue, he placed several rice kernels on his tongue and gulped them down.

Ichiro confessed, "I have sworn Mitsuo to secrecy with a bribe—tickets to another baseball game since we had to leave before today's game was over. What kind of bribe do I need to offer you to keep quiet until I figure this out?"

I murmured, "Be brave, my darling. That's all I ask of you."

～

As MY DUE DATE closed in on me, I gathered my courage to speak to the doctor about my mounting concerns. "What are the chances that something may be wrong with my baby? I was seven years old when Little Boy was dropped on Hiroshima, and I lived there until I was seventeen."

The doctor tapped his pen on his desk. "There is always a chance that a baby is born with something wrong, mentally or physically, as a quirk of nature, and the chances are amplified if the mother is a hibakusha. If we had a way of looking into your uterus, I could give you an accurate assessment of your unborn baby's condition. We would see if he is missing an arm or a leg or if his head is abnormally large. As it is, we must wait for the child to be born and assess his condition. But you're looking healthy, and you're gaining the normal weight for a woman at your stage of pregnancy. All indications are that your baby will be fine, Mrs. Uchida." His comments were of some relief, but I had more on my mind that worried me equally.

I felt a tear involuntarily escape from my eye. "Forgive me for crying. There is something else that I must ask you. My husband is not well. His doctor, Dr. Shizumi, suspects he may have an active strain of tuberculosis, although the results of the tests have not come back yet. The doctor believes that, because his mother had tuberculosis when he was born, he might have contracted the disease from her. Could this happen to our baby?"

The doctor stood up and paced back and forth as if he was trying to diffuse an overabundance of energy. I realized he might have been trying to buy himself some time before answering me. "Everything will depend upon the baby's immune system. Looking at the chart and how healthy you are, I am relatively certain that you're giving him all the necessary antibodies that he needs to protect him. But there are no guarantees. We will do the necessary tests when the baby is born just to assure ourselves he is healthy. After all, you are both my patients. That is one of the gifts of being an obstetrician. I'm in charge of both the mother and her child."

I was impressed with the doctor and thanked him for his concern, but I still felt uneasy.

"Mrs. Uchida, I recommend you stop worrying and hope for the best. It's not good for the baby to have an anxious mother. Some of my colleagues believe that a mother's emotional state can be transmitted to the unborn, and I hold the same opinion. It is in the best interest of your baby to maintain a happy disposition."

"Happy mother, happy baby, Doctor?"

"Happy baby, healthy baby. It's fascinating what we are learning about the mind-body connection. Not everything is due to physical causes."

"And what about the father's mental state?"

"Ah, that is something we haven't explored. But I suspect the same applies. A father's mood is important to a child. And, of course, a father should be engaged in raising a child. Both parents share in this responsibility these days."

Pushing on the arms of the chair, I stood up. "I've taken up enough of your time, Doctor. And I need to get back to work."

Walking to the tearoom through the early afternoon crowd, I put my hands on my stomach as if to protect my baby from being jostled by pedestrians.

"I hope you can hear me, little one. You have nothing to worry about. Mama will always take care of you," I said aloud.

My attempt to reassure my unborn baby sounded feeble to my ears; I would only truly believe my words when I held him in my arms and the doctor gave him a clean bill of health.

Chapter 19

NIGHT SWEATS MADE IT impossible for Ichiro to sleep. Too tired to go to work, he instructed me to tell Setsuko he had the flu. "I'll come in this afternoon if I'm feeling better. I don't want her to suspect there might be something seriously wrong with me. I can't afford to lose my job."

"Can I make you some tea before I leave for the tearoom?"

"No, I'm already feeling shaky. I don't need the caffeine. I'll just take some cough syrup and try to get some sleep." Without bothering to get a spoon, he drank directly from the bottle.

I said, "Let me see the label." Shaking my head, I expressed my concern. "This has got codeine in it. That's why you're feeling so nervous."

"What am I supposed to do? If I don't take it, I start coughing and I can't stop," he snapped.

"Don't speak to me in that tone of voice, Ichiro. I don't deserve it. I'm doing my best. I wish I could say the same for you." I put a light sweater on to ward off the early morning chill. "I'd better go now. It's almost seven. The tearoom early birds will be arriving, and they'll be looking for me..."

Ichiro smiled weakly. "You do have your fans, don't you?"

"Yes, but they aren't the kind I had imagined when we first met." Looking at the sadness come over Ichiro's face, I was ashamed I let this thought slip. As the tension between Ichiro and me mounted, I escaped into fantasies of being on stage, or standing in front of Mr. Ozu's camera.

∼

SEVERAL HOURS LATER THE doorbell rang, waking Ichiro out of a sound sleep. Putting on a bathrobe, he went downstairs and opened the front door. The post-man handed Ichiro a letter with the Osaka Red Cross Hospital's return address.

"Ah, I've been waiting for this. It must be our confirmation for a birthing room at the hospital," he lied.

"When is Mrs. Uchida's baby due? It must be very soon, I suspect."

"In about eight weeks. She is hoping for the fourth or the seventh of August."

"Good luck days? Not everyone believes these things, but why not? It doesn't hurt to have the gods on your side." Hopping back on his bicycle, the postman pedaled off with his heavy mailbag nested in his basket.

Although it was just noon, Ichiro wanted a stiff drink to fortify himself before opening the letter. He pried two ice cubes from the metal tray in the small refrigerator next to the stove and poured himself a gin and tonic.

Ichiro slid a sharp kitchen knife underneath the envelope flap and slowly unfolded Dr. Shizumi's letter:

June 10, 1961. To Mr. Ichiro Uchida. Diagnosis: Tuberculosis. Status: Active Strain. Treatment: Daily subcutaneous injections of streptomycin for one month at the hospital clinic followed by oral medication. Confinement to a sanatorium to be determined later if patient shows no signs of improvement. Quarantine unnecessary at present. Please make an appointment at my clinic immediately so we can start you on a reliable course of treatment...

Ichiro dropped the knife. He felt as if he was reading his death sentence. The only fact missing was the date of his execution. Tearing the letter into small bits, he dropped them in the sink and put a match to them, watching the pieces curl up and burn. As the smoke filled his lungs, he started coughing and went outside on the balcony. The glare of the sun hurt his eyes. Sitting down heavily on a bench, he stared at the traffic below. A woman with a baby strapped to her body carried groceries in a netted basket. She reminded him of Noriko. He remembered the look of joy on her face when she brought home the new basket where their baby would sleep and gently placed a toy lamb on top of the blanket, telling him, "We can keep the basket on the tatami mat right next to us so that I can nurse him during the night without getting up."

Remembering the hope in Noriko's voice and the sweet smile on her beautiful face, he covered his face with his hands and sobbed. She did not deserve this horrific diagnosis. Neither did he. Willing himself to stand, he straightened up the apartment, washed the glass, emptied out the ashtray, and folded up the futon so that everything would be neat and tidy when Noriko came home from the tearoom. Picking up the stuffed toy lamb, he clutched it against his heart for comfort and then replaced it in the basket. Talking to himself, he said, "This is another moment of soul-crushing sadness in the life of Ichiro Uchida."

~

THAT AFTERNOON ICHIRO WENT to Dr. Shizumi's clinic. He sat in the waiting room glancing at a pile of magazines to occupy his mind. An elderly woman squeezed into an empty chair beside him and fell into a deep sleep. She leaned against his shoulder snoring loudly, her sour breath filling his nostrils. He propped her up each time she listed in his direction. He was grateful when his name was called and he freed himself. He should have felt sympathy for her but he only felt disgust. Was she a reflection of what he would become if he survived to old age? A useless bag of bones.

Dr. Shizumi administered an injection to give the medication an immediate boost, and then handed Ichiro a large bottle of pills. "Two every day, and don't skip a single dose. We'll know in a few weeks how well you are responding. If you are feeling better and your temperature is normal, you can return to work."

As Dr. Shizumi predicted, Ichiro felt dramatically better and was assured that he was no longer contagious. Now that his diagnosis had been confirmed, Ichiro could not in good conscience keep his illness a secret from Setsuko. Noriko didn't say anything, but he suspected that she might already have told her sister. They were remarkably close, and Setsuko was the person Noriko turned to for advice and comfort.

Riding the subway to the Aki-Torii, he considered what Setsuko's reaction would be. All possibilities that occurred to him seemed disastrous. To his amazement, however, Setsuko assured him he was not in danger of losing his job. "Ichiro, you're part of the family. I wouldn't think of letting you go now. But I expect you to keep up with your duties. You know how I count on you. You're an excellent bookkeeper and the best manager we've had. But I must ask you, did Dr. Shizumi say you might be contagious? If that is the case, we'll have to make some adjustment to your duties. I can't let you be in contact with the customers."

Adopting a cheerful tone, he assured her, "I've been taking an antibiotic for two weeks, a miracle drug. So long as I keep up with the required dosage and see my doctor for periodic checkups, there is no danger of infecting anyone." Ichiro added, "I'm very lucky because I haven't had any side effects from the streptomycin. Some patients can't tolerate it, but Dr. Shizumi says I'm very strong—the advantages of youth. You have no reason to be concerned about my performance at work."

Putting her arms around him, she said, "If I close my eyes, I can still see you at fourteen, coming into the tearoom looking for a job. When I said I needed a door boy and offered you the job, you bowed so low I thought you would fall over. Many other boys had presented themselves, but there was something so special about you. You had such a sweetness and sincerity about you, I couldn't turn you away. I have never once regretted taking a chance on you."

"And here I am asking you for a job once again."

"The job is yours. You have earned it, and I can't imagine finding someone else—related to me or not—to replace you."

"Thank you, Setsuko." From the look on her face, it seemed that Setsuko had something else on her mind. "If anyone asks you where you've been these last two weeks, just tell them it was a bad case of the flu. I don't want to alarm any of our employees."

"Certainly. Always good to get our stories straight."

That evening, Ichiro stayed late at the office at the Aki-Torii to catch up on the paperwork piling up on his desk. Entering the receipts and bills in the ledger, he thought, *Numbers are concrete and unambiguous—add and subtract and you come up with an answer that you can count on. Nothing to wonder about; nothing to try and predict.* He wished that life were like that. There was value in certainty.

It was almost two in the morning but there were still a few customers sitting at the bar. The bartender, his face lit by the glowing neon clock, waved at Ichiro. "I haven't seen you in a couple of weeks, Mr. Uchida. Mr. Fujiwara had to pitch in. He's been as angry as a wild boar. Where have you been, sir?"

"Bad case of the flu. It's good to be back."

"How about a nightcap to celebrate? On me, of course." He made a show of taking money from his apron pocket and putting it in the cash register. Ichiro's rule was that no one working could take anything without paying for it.

"Thanks, but I still have some work to do at the tearoom. I'll see you tomorrow. Goodnight."

It was a few short blocks between the Grille Room and the Tesagara, but Ichiro was tempted to take a taxicab. His legs felt like they were filled with sand. The nighttime air was heavy with humidity. Fumbling his key into the lock, he turned the knob and pushed the door open. He turned on the dining room lights. The blackboard behind the patisserie counter listed the free "tea of the day" sample—Goddess of Mercy oolong—and the regular selection of black, herbal, green, white, and other oolong teas, French press coffee, hot chocolate, and lemonade.

The pastry chef was in the kitchen earlier than usual. Ichiro asked, "What are you doing here?"

"I'm testing a recipe for French macarons. They come in all flavors and look very pretty on a tea caddy. I thought we might add them to our menu, but I didn't want to suggest it to Mrs. Fujiwara until I was sure I could master them. If you wait a minute, sir, you can try one. They are just cooling."

"You don't need to check with her. As the general manager, I'm authorized to approve any and all additions and deletions to our menu."

Sliding a spatula underneath a row of baked macarons, the chef offered one to Ichiro. "Very good," Ichiro declared after his first bite.

"They're not quite finished. Imagine some chocolate ganache between two disks of meringue. That's the way they are meant to be served. Or we can put in almond paste, or vanilla."

"Let's offer some free samples this afternoon to go along with the Goddess of Mercy tea and see how the customers respond."

"Yes, sir. And if I may say so, you are looking very well. Your wife has been worried about you."

"Is that so?"

"She didn't say anything to me, but Hana, the cashier, and some of the waitresses were mentioning it, and I overheard them talking."

"My wife exaggerates. It goes along with her pregnancy. I just had a bad case of the flu, but I'm right as rain and eager to get back to work. But I see that everything is in order here. I'm lucky to have a conscientious staff."

"We all try and do our best for you and Mrs. Fujiwara, sir."

"Tell me. Who picked the Goddess of Mercy as the sample tea for today?"

"I did, sir."

"Well, change it. It's not the way to greet a customer. If they ask for it, that's one thing, but we don't need to promote it. Estate Darjeeling is a better choice." Knowing the value of complimenting his staff, Ichiro said, "It will be a nicer pairing with your macarons. They'll be the star of the show." It made little difference which of the two teas was offered, but Ichiro wanted to assert his authority and let the chef know who the boss was.

The pastry chef responded enthusiastically. "I'll change it right away." He took an eraser to the blackboard, and with a piece of chalk he wrote the new offering.

Turning off the overhead lights, Ichiro heard a loud tapping on the window. An old man dressed in rags and leaning against a pushcart filled with buckets and brooms, one of the many homeless in Osaka, stood outside. The man's face was covered in rheumy scabs, and when he smiled, Ichiro saw that he was toothless. His toes protruded out of his worn leather shoes.

Pressing his face against the windowpane, he mouthed, "Do you have anything to eat?" Ichiro signaled for him to wait, then went behind the counter, and put two chocolate croissants in a paper bag, opened the door, and handed it to the beggar. The man stuffed one of the pastries in his mouth, gumming the sweet, and shoved the other into the pocket of his jacket. He tipped his hat, and then, pushing his shoulder against the cart, disappeared into the gray morning fog. Putting a few coins into the cash register, Ichiro locked the door behind him and headed home. When he compared his life to the homeless beggar, he could only be grateful for what he had. Assuaging his anxiety he spoke out loud to himself, "Number one, a beautiful wife. Number two, a baby on the way. Number three, a steady job I can count on."

Chapter 20

IT WAS MY TWENTY-THIRD birthday, but I treated it as just another day and insisted on going to work. The doctor warned me I was just days from giving birth, but I wanted to keep myself occupied. I also didn't want to forfeit a day's salary. I managed to put a few coins in a glass jar, which I kept hidden behind a pipe underneath the kitchen sink.

When I came home from the tearoom, I poured out the coins in the jar onto the tatami mat and added up the amount. I was surprised that I had more than a month's rent put away, which gave me a feeling of security. I wasn't sure when I'd have enough to qualify for a checking account. I needed to ask Setsuko, who was much smarter than me about money and business. I scooped the coins back into the jar and stashed them in my hiding place.

The tatami mat smelled damp from the water that dripped over the edge of the sink every time Ichiro or I did the dishes or washed the laundry. It crossed my mind that the smell couldn't be healthy for Ichiro's lungs. Picking up the mat, I hung it over the balcony railing to dry out. In the apartment building across the street, a couple was dancing near an open window. I felt guilty spying, but I couldn't take my eyes off them. The man slowly unbuttoned the woman's blouse as they swayed back and forth to an unheard, but no doubt sultry, tune. The woman unzipped her skirt, and pulling it down, revealed black garters and lace-topped stockings. I was curious to see what would happen next, and then my baby kicked me hard in the stomach. "Ouch! Mommy is being very naughty, but you'll forgive me, won't you? After all, it is my birthday, little one."

The couple turned out the overhead light. I went back inside and waited for Ichiro to come home. It was well after two in the morning when I heard his hesitant steps on the stairs and then the sound of the key in the door.

Handing me a box, he said, "You told me not to get you anything, but you should have something for your birthday. It's not much, but it will come in handy." As I unwrapped the gift, he asked, "Am I right?" It was a book of baby names. We hadn't discussed it, but I thought Ichiro might want to name the baby Hide-Ichi after his father if it was a boy.

"And why would you think that, my darling?" he said when I mentioned this. "My father treated me and my sister as useless baggage. His only concern was for Madam Tamae, and then for their infant son. The baby's death was a stroke of good luck in a way because no child should have been cursed with her as a mother. My sister Mitsuko and I knew this only too well. It was my father who was blind to her faults."

Daring to challenge Ichiro, I pointed out that he obsessively compared himself to his father. "You always speak of your father's successes and compare yourself unfavorably to him."

"There's the paradox. My father exceeded his wildest expectations when it came to his career. But once my mother died, he ignored his motherless children who desperately needed him. As a father he was an abysmal failure. I would rather he had been more loving and less rich. Why would I pass on his name to our son? If the baby is a boy, I was thinking that Hisashi is a good name." He referred to the book. "The name means 'always with you' or 'an intention sustained over a long time.'"

"That's perfect," I told him. "If the baby is true to his name, he will be persistent toward his goals in life; and better yet, he will never leave us."

"I hope you're not going to smother him. A child needs his independence."

"In time, but certainly not for the first ten years. Anyway, what if the baby is a girl?" Tousling Ichiro's hair, I said, "That could happen, you know."

"You decide, Noriko. What name do you like?"

I turned the pages and "Aimi" jumped out at me. Pointing to the name, I read, "It means beautiful love and affection."

"Just like her mother. Beautiful and affectionate and also thoughtful and caring. I keep adding to the list of your attributes, Noriko. I don't know how I got so lucky." Seeing that Ichiro was in a romantic mood, I asked him for a favor. "That sounds serious," he replied.

"Not really. Would you dance with me even though my stomach is in the way of you holding me tight in your arms?"

"Of course. It would be my pleasure. And what would you like to dance to?"

"Surprise me."

Ichiro put an album on the phonograph and positioned the needle in the middle of the record. "You'll probably know the words. So, will you sing to me?" Taking off his jacket, he said, "Madam, if your card is not already full, may I have the honor of this dance?"

Playing along, I answered, "This dance has been spoken for, but the gentleman is nowhere to be found so you're in luck. To be truthful, you're much sexier than he is and perhaps a better dancer as well. He has two left feet and is constantly stepping on my toes."

Tucking myself into his open arms, I immediately recognized the song Ichiro had picked. As Ichiro confidently led me across the room, I sang, "*Give your heart and soul to me / and life will always be* La Vie en Rose."

"Do you feel up to one more dance? The next number is '*Je ne Regrette Rien*,' 'I Regret Nothing.'"

"I love that song, but I think I'm having contractions."

Ichiro looked panicked. "What should I do? Do you want me to call an ambulance? Should I pack your suitcase?"

"My suitcase is already packed and has been for a week. But let's wait. Maybe it's a false alarm. The doctor says I should check the timing of my contractions and only when they are five minutes apart should we go to the hospital. I don't want to get there only to be sent home. It would be so embarrassing and a waste of taxi money."

"You're sure?"

My contractions came and went in waves. Sometimes they were so painful I couldn't even do the deep breathing prescribed by the nurse; other times I barely felt them and was able to straighten the cupboards and sweep the floor like a bird preparing its nest.

Three nights later, I had a contraction that felt as if my insides were being ripped out of me. I told Ichiro it was time to go to the hospital. He hurried outside, and from the nearest phone booth, called for a taxi, which came in a few minutes. As we sped toward the hospital, the contractions were quickening. Ichiro held my hand tightly in his. I thought he might pass out from fright or excitement.

At the hospital, the baby took his time arriving, and there were long periods when I thought the doctor should just knock me out and pull the baby from my body. "No, Mrs. Uchida. You've come this far," he told me. "We can always give you a spinal, but the way things are progressing, I think that you can deliver the baby naturally, and it will be better for both of you if you do. So, hold on."

The nurse wheeled me into the delivery room. I remember the doctor telling me to push and pause, push and pause, and each time he told me to push I let out a bloodcurdling scream despite my best efforts not to do so.

Ichiro sat in the waiting room, and when our baby boy was finally placed on my stomach, all cleaned up and wrapped in a blanket, Ichiro was allowed to see us. Ichiro kissed me on my forehead, which was covered in perspiration. I was drunk with happiness and said, "Let's have another one right away."

Ichiro declared me crazy and said I was suffering from "birth amnesia." "Have you forgotten all the pain you've just been through? I certainly haven't. I don't think I could stand seeing you like that again so soon, if ever. Let's wait a while, at least four or five years."

The nurse wheeled our son into my hospital room in a bassinette. I inspected every inch of him, terrified that I might see some loathsome imperfection: a missing foot or hand, a bloodstain on his face, an ill-shapen head. All the terrifying mishaps I'd had nine months to conjure up, but he was perfect in every way. He had a tiny heart-shaped face, big brown eyes, and a thatch of black hair underneath his little knitted cap. I couldn't stop crying from joy and relief.

The doctor corroborated my assessment of our son: "Mr. and Mrs. Uchida, your baby merits an Apgar score of nine. Pulse, respiration, muscle tone, skin color, and weight are all at the high end of the scale. Well done!"

Hisashi's tiny rosebud lips emitted meowing sounds as he anticipated my milk. I pressed him against my breast and clumsily inserted my nipple into his mouth. At first he was frustrated, but he soon settled down, and I could feel him sucking my milk. I felt euphoric. Ichiro looked at me adoringly as if we had just created the most amazing miracle. And we had. I asked Ichiro to lift the shade from the window; outside the sky was filled with black clouds that spilled forth heavy rain. "What day is it?"

"August tenth, 1961."

"A lucky day; the number means plentiful or ample. That should stand Hisashi in good stead. He will always have enough of what he needs to be a satisfied man."

Ichiro smiled. "Believe what you will, Noriko. He will have enough if we are able to provide for him, and I intend to do just that. Provide for both of you." I know that he meant every word he said, but in the end he could not fulfill his pledge to me. Had I known what awaited us, I might have sought a way to escape with Hisashi, even then. And who would have blamed me?

◡

WHEN HISASHI STOPPED NURSING, I held him out to Ichiro. "Take him. He won't break. I promise."

Ichiro shook his head and whispered so that the woman in the next bed would not hear. "I should wait a few days until your milk passes the antibodies to protect him. You never know what I might have picked up on the subway or at the restaurant."

I read Ichiro's mind. *He's afraid he could be contagious.*

Quickly changing the subject, I said, "It looks as if Hisashi is smiling. Do you think he sees us, Ichiro?"

"A newborn's eyes are capable of responding to light and motion. In a couple of months, he'll be able to recognize our faces. Right now, it's as if Hisashi is extremely near-sighted and we are moving shadows."

I wrinkled my nose. "You're being so logical. I believe he sees us and that's why he's smiling. And he certainly recognizes our voices."

"I'm just reporting what I've read about newborns. He's probably passing gas or needs to be burped."

I felt exasperated. "You'll soon accept the fact that Hisashi is an exceptional child on all counts. And why wouldn't he be? He has us for parents."

"That's what every mother and father think until they're proven wrong and realize that their child is nobody special or becomes a thorn in their parents' side. Look at my father. He couldn't wait to get rid of me. Would he have done such a horrible thing if he thought I was exceptional? No matter how hard I tried to please him, it was never enough."

I covered Ichiro's mouth. His complaints were becoming tedious. "There's no need to keep bringing up these bad memories. You have a chance to right all the wrongs your father committed, Ichiro. Trauma like yours doesn't need to be passed from one generation to the next." I hoped in the years ahead he would remember our conversation and find the self-confidence to be an exemplary father. I suddenly felt so tired I could not keep my eyes open.

I asked Ichiro to sit by my bed, and before I knew it, I was fast asleep with Hisashi in my arms.

I woke up as the nurse tried to pry Hisashi from me. "Please leave my baby with me. I want to feel his heart beating next to mine."

"There will be plenty of time for you to attend to your baby, Mrs. Uchida, when you are home. Take advantage of this time to rest. I guarantee you'll wish there was someone to take him off your hands. Every mother's biggest complaint is not getting enough sleep. You'll see. And when he starts to crawl, he'll be following you everywhere. You won't get a moment's peace, even to go to the bathroom or take a shower. I should know. I have three children."

"I can't imagine ever feeling that way," I said. "He's my everything. Promise me you'll bring him back from the nursery the minute he wakes up."

Ichiro, who was still sitting by the bed, frowned. "So now I'm in competition with my son? I thought *I* was your everything."

"Do I have to choose one of you over the other? It's all so new to me. You both are my everything." Truthfully, I felt an immediate and fierce attachment to Hisashi that eclipsed anything I had ever experienced before. When the doctor gave me the umbilical cord for safekeeping, I burst into tears. Ichiro was helpless to calm me, and I could not explain to him this sudden bout of grief.

The nurse explained, "Women often have emotional swings after giving birth. Nothing to worry about. You'll feel better in a few days. It's all the hormones racing through your body."

"Can you give me something?"

"It's better not to take a sedative because you'll pass it on to the little one through your milk. I suggest you just try to relax."

⟿

SETSUKO AND HER THREE children crowded into my hospital room when visitors were allowed. Setsuko brought me carp fish soup and mochi made at the Aki-Torii to encourage my milk production. Mitsuo brought Hisashi a Hanshin Tigers baseball cap; Akiko knitted him a sunny yellow blanket; and Kazuko drew a picture in crayon of an angel baby sitting on the back of a white swan in flight. Beneath them stick figures of a man and woman waved goodbye.

Kazuko narrated her picture. "Auntie, the baby is Hisashi, and he's flying through the clouds to a place far away."

I was deeply disturbed by this innocent drawing and wished that I didn't have to accept it, but I didn't want to hurt Kazuko's feelings and so I told Ichiro to pin it up on the wall next to my bed. Looking at the children, I told them I loved all their gifts and added, "And so will Hisashi."

Akiko asked, "Can we see him now?"

"Ichiro, I shouldn't get out of bed. Can you take everyone to the nursery, and if Hisashi's awake, make sure to tell the nurse to bring him back to me as soon as they leave." I knew I would have to learn how to deal with separation from my baby, but for right now, I couldn't tolerate being apart from him for even a few minutes. I had carried him inside me for nine months, my blood nurturing him until he was ready to come into the world and embrace his destiny. Ten—the day of his birth. An auspicious number. Would it be enough to ensure his happiness?

Chapter 21

Aᴏᴛᴇʀ Iᴄʜɪʀᴏ ᴀɴᴅ I brought our baby home from the hospital, my mother arrived from Hiroshima to help me out and to attend our baby-naming ceremony. My mother busied herself making platters of red rice and beans and fresh sea bream for the invited family guests. I was so happy to see her. We had been apart since the day of our wedding. The distance to Hiroshima and my mother's obligation to help out at the sushi shop kept her from visiting us, and I was tethered to my job at the Tesagara until Hisashi was born.

Ichiro bought a blank cardboard plaque to write our son's name on. He dipped the brush into the ink, but his hand shook so violently he could not form the characters. Seeing his predicament, I took the brush and completed the task.

So my mother wouldn't hear, I whispered, "What's the matter, Ichiro?"

"I'm still adjusting to a different medication. The doctor warned me I might have side effects, but he said they should subside in a few weeks."

On the day of the *oshichiya*, my mother proudly dressed Hisashi in the gold silk kimono I had worn on my naming day and tied a white linen ruff around his neck. It looked as if it was irritating him, but he was such a good baby he didn't cry. At the ceremony, which was officiated by a Buddhist priest, I placed Hisashi's dried umbilical cord in a teardrop-shaped box made of paulownia wood for safekeeping. As I had been instructed, "It is what all devoted mothers do."

My mother and I reveled in the shared pleasure of taking care of Hisashi. Every morning after Ichiro left for work, she gave her grandson his bath in a round wooden tub and then, while I nursed Hisashi, she washed out his dirty diapers and hung them out to dry in the sun on the balcony.

Knowing I knew nothing about taking care of an infant, she gave me various tips. "The best way to wash diapers is to wring out the excess water and then shake them, and the sun will do its magic getting rid of germs. Never let dirty diapers sit for more than two days in a closed bucket or you won't be able to get the smell out. And rotate the diapers so they don't wear out from too much washing. When you put Hisashi down to sleep, wrap him tightly in a blanket and put him in a basket just large enough to hold him. That way he won't turn over when he gets a little older and risk suffocating himself."

"There is so much I have to learn about taking care of a baby."

"That's why I'm here. By the time I leave, you'll be a confident mother." When I tucked Hisashi into his basket, we used the time to speak seriously of what was on our minds. My mother spoke first.

"Noriko, your father and I are no longer living together. After your brother moved out of the apartment, Ryo had no reason to stay with me. It is no secret that we didn't have a happy marriage." She told me that my father moved north to Matsue, where he opened another sushi shop. He had left her in charge of the shop in Hiroshima.

"Is that why he didn't come to Hisashi's baby naming ceremony? I thought it rather strange. After all, Hisashi is his first grandchild. Setsuko's children, because she is his stepdaughter, don't belong to him. And he has never shown much interest in them anyway."

"Your father is living in Matsue with a Chinese woman who works as his bookkeeper. She has a five-year-old son from her first husband. She's not much older than you are. So long as the cash register is full and Ryo's bed is warm, he does what she tells him. He has put all of us out of his mind, very conveniently, including you. Once you married Ichiro, he didn't have much use for you, and he never really got over your being rejected by the Takarazuka."

"Please, Mother, don't bring that up. It still pains me." An idea popped into my head. "Why don't you divorce him?"

"I intend to once we arrive at a proper financial settlement. I have no interest in marrying again. Two husbands are more than enough. But I want to be sure I have enough money to pay for my old age. I don't want to be a burden on you, Setsuko, or Tadashi. Setsuko has her hands full, and I couldn't possibly expect you to help me out. I can see that Ichiro isn't the breadwinner I would have wished for you."

I cringed at my mother's thoughtlessness. "Ichiro has many dreams. Hopefully, he will be able to realize them someday. Working for Setsuko is a stepping stone to something bigger and better." Then, trying to change the subject, I said, "I'm sorry your relationship with my father has come to this unhappy ending."

"I'm not. I'm tired of pretending to be the obedient Japanese wife who always walks several steps behind her husband; I don't like the view." Groaning, she continued, "Ryo's ego is a lot bigger than what is hanging between his legs."

We burst out laughing, but my mood quickly changed as I looked at Hisashi sleeping contentedly in his basket. It was now my turn to unburden myself. "I don't quite know how to tell you this, Mother. Ichiro and I have had shocking news. He has been diagnosed with tuberculosis. His mother died from the disease when he was three years old, and the doctor speculates that he has carried the disease all these years, but now the bacteria has come to life and attacked his lungs."

My mother put her hand over her mouth. She could not hold back her tears. Sobbing, she asked, "How long have you known about this, Noriko? I hope you knew nothing of this when you agreed to marry Ichiro. It would have been foolhardy of you."

"We found out when I was five or six months pregnant. Had we known sooner, we might have chosen not to have our baby, but by the time we found out it was too late to stop the pregnancy. I'm grateful that I didn't have to face that choice. I cannot imagine my life without Hisashi. He is my proudest accomplishment!"

"What is going to happen to Ichiro?"

"He is doing well on his medication. He is being cared for by an excellent doctor whom I have the utmost confidence in. Ichiro doesn't share his fears with me, but he has become increasingly agitated and preoccupied. And who can blame him? He is ashamed of what's happened to him. There are moments when he drifts away from me, and when he looks into Hisashi's eyes, I think he feels bereft. I am doing my best to buoy his spirits, but some days even I have a hard time remaining positive."

I poured a glass of water and swallowed a handful of rice kernels. I offered some to my mother, but she turned them down. She didn't share my faith in Tenrikyo. Instead she put her arms around me and held me tightly, stroking my hair. I rested my head against my mother's shoulder, feeling the strength of her love.

Hisashi stirred in his basket and gave out a healthy wail.

"I'm getting used to the meaning of my baby's cries. He wants to be fed again." I picked him up and put him to my breast. He sucked eagerly as I rocked back and forth. Holding his warm body in my arms and breathing in his sweetness, I tried to empty my mind of all negative thoughts so my milk would flow freely as my son eagerly drank his fill.

⌢

Two weeks later my mother took the train back to Hiroshima, but not before promising she would tell my father about his grandson and ask him to visit us. Once upon a time he had been my hero, my savior, and I couldn't reconcile his indifference. It pained me to my core. Was he so disappointed in me that he kicked me to the side of the road in favor of his new family? Apparently so. I still remembered his harsh words to Ichiro on the day of our wedding.

One month after our child was born, I reluctantly left Hisashi with Ichiro so I could visit the neighborhood onsen for the first communal hot bath I was permitted to take after giving birth. Leaning my head against the edge of the pool, I felt the steaming water penetrate my muscles. An old woman swam up to me, her face barely visible behind the mist. She spoke directly to me, "The act of cutting is essential at the time of birth and again at the time of passing away toward rebirth. And between one cutting and the other, your choice, Noriko, is to be joyful. That is the way of Tenrikyo." I stared at her, and before I could respond, she drifted away, leaving me to wonder who she was and how she could have known my name. Maybe I was hallucinating.

I climbed out of the bath, dried off, and dressed quickly. Before leaving the onsen, I asked the attendant if she had seen an old woman leave a few minutes earlier. "Madam, you were the only person in the bath."

"Strange. I could have sworn there was someone there with me. My imagination must be playing tricks on me. Whatever the case, I received an important message, which I intend to follow."

The September breeze cooled my face, which was still warm from the steam bath. As I passed a neighborhood pasty shop, a line of women held sprays of pampas grass and the window display of round rice dumplings stacked in a pyramid reminded me that today was the Harvest Moon Festival.

Since Hisashi's birth, one day seemed to melt into the next, and I often lost track of time.

I entered the shop, and when I reached the counter, the proprietress said, "How many do you want? We are about sold out."

"I'll take two for my husband and me. My baby is much too young to eat one."

"When did you have your baby, Mrs. Uchida?"

"Exactly a month ago—August tenth. A boy."

"Hold onto him tightly. My son had his twenty-first birthday, and he's joining a monastery. I will never see him again once he takes his vows. When you have children, you never know how they are going to turn out, even when they are growing up under your nose."

"You must be proud that he's chosen to follow a spiritual path."

"Not really. I was hoping he'd do something more lucrative and help me out in my old age. But instead, I'll be working here until I collapse. But what's the use of complaining, Mrs. Uchida?"

"Every day I count my blessings and try to lead a joyous life." Did my words sound hollow? It was becoming more difficult to live by Tenrikyo's precepts.

Handing me my package, she said, "Enjoy the dumplings and take good care of yourself. You now have a little one relying on you. Becoming a mother is a monumental responsibility, I can assure you. And you aren't always repaid for your sacrifices."

⁓

Ichiro didn't hear me come into our apartment. He was standing on the balcony holding Hisashi in his arms. "What are you doing out there, my love?"

"I wanted to show Hisashi the moon. Not that he can really see it, but at least the light is shining on us. Look how bright the moon is."

I went out on the balcony. Ichiro put on a different voice and finished the story I had interrupted. "And so, the Old Man in the moon is up there with the rabbit protecting all of us. The End. That's always what my sister used to say when she finished telling me a story—the end. And then, of course, I'd beg her to repeat the entire thing word-for-word. I'm sure she used to tire of it, but she never refused. No one ever loved me as much as she did, not until you danced into my life."

I kissed the back of Ichiro's neck and then gave Hisashi a gentle kiss on his nose. "Come inside. I bought us some moon dumplings. Let's enjoy them, and then, if Hisashi will allow it, why don't we make love? It's been a while, and I feel so refreshed from my bath."

"Who but an idiot could refuse such a tempting proposal?"

After putting Hisashi in his basket, Ichiro slowly undressed me and then took his clothes off. He explored every inch of me with his lips, and I kept him from entering me until I could no longer stand it. Wrapping my legs around his body, I arched my back, inviting him in as deeply as possible, and then allowed myself to be carried away.

We lay next to one another, bathed in the moonlight streaming through the balcony door and listening to the even breathing of our love child and the beating of our hearts. The strength of Ichiro's passion for me gave me hope his health was improving.

Chapter 22

ICHIRO RECEIVED A LETTER from his sister Mitsuko with heart-breaking news. She wrote that she had suffered a miscarriage. He read aloud, "I had to have an operation and the doctor told me I cannot have children. Harry won't consider adopting a baby, which is sad, because there are so many children on the tribal reservations here in Montana whose parents are unable to care for them and love them. Harry and I don't have much, but we could give an unwanted baby a good home. I have always wanted to be a mother. I had plenty of practice taking care of you, Ichiro."

Ichiro put the letter down. "This was Mitsuko's second pregnancy."

"What are you talking about, Ichiro?"

"Before she married Harry she was in love with a white guy from New York—a soldier stationed in Otsu. His mother disapproved of my sister. He got her pregnant but she lost that baby. He abandoned her, went back to the states, and married his hometown sweetheart. He was a dog for treating my sister that way. Her husband Harry doesn't know anything about this. She's kept it a secret and hoped she could have another baby someday with Harry, but it wasn't to be."

Ichiro's eyes filled with tears. He picked up his sister's letter and continued: "But it's not all bad news. My husband and his brothers have gotten together and bought their mother, Kana, a ticket to Japan to see her family on Kyushu where she was born. She wants to visit you and Noriko in Osaka while she is in Japan. I hope you will agree to this, my dear brother. I wish I could accompany her, see you with my own eyes and meet Noriko and your baby. Unfortunately, Harry wouldn't think of allowing me to leave him on his own. He barely knows how to turn on the stove except to boil water. I miss you, Ichiro, and love you with all my heart. Your sister, Mitsuko."

I asked, "What are you going to tell your sister? We should agree to let Harry's mother stay with us for as long as she wishes. And I'd welcome an extra pair of hands to help me with Hisashi." I didn't believe her at the time, but the nurse at the hospital was right when she said that every mother needs a little help.

～

SEVENTY-YEAR-OLD KANA MISHIMA ARRIVED at our apartment carrying a small satchel and a large trove of maternal wisdom she had accumulated raising Harry and eight other children on a bean farm in Hillrose, Colorado. She was a picture bride brought to Hawaii and then Colorado by her husband. She never learned to speak English, relying upon her husband, and later her children, to navigate life in the United States. When her husband died and her children were adults, they made sure that she was well taken care of. She was a tiny woman with gray hair pulled back in a practical bun, and a calm and soothing manner.

She told us, "Harry is my youngest. When he came back from the Korean War and brought Mitsuko from Japan with him, I was so happy. The newlyweds lived with me on the farm for almost a year, and then Harry bought a farm of his own. But he had no luck and was forced to give up and move to Montana. He's got a good job and is paid very well. And Mitsuko works as an assistant general manager of the local hotel in Glendive." She caught her breath and then continued with her story. "Oh, Mitsuko would make such a wonderful mother. She has told me stories of how she took care of you, Ichiro, after your mama died. I know how disappointed Harry is that he won't be a father. Coming from a big farming family, it's as natural as the sun coming up in the morning to have lots of children."

Scooping Hisashi up in my arms to prove my point, I said, "Ichiro and I are so lucky to have such a healthy, happy baby. Not all hibakusha have been so fortunate."

Kana nodded. "Yes. I hope you and Ichiro will have more children—sooner rather than later. When they are close in age, if you teach them they have a duty to one another, the older ones raise the younger ones."

Lowering my voice so as not to agitate Ichiro, I admitted, "I've heard this advice, but Ichiro and I aren't in any position to think about having another child just now. I'm going back to work at my sister's tearoom soon, and I'm not sure how I'm going to handle one child, much less two, and work at the same time."

Kana smiled. "That's the advantage of raising children in the country. You work where you live and everyone pitches in. It's a good life. I couldn't imagine living in a big city like Osaka. I'm afraid to go out on the street. Too many people. Too many cars, and too much dirt and smoke. My son Harry takes after me. When they put up the first traffic light in his town a few years ago, he thought the place was going to the dogs."

I said, "I'm a city girl. I love the excitement of Osaka. When Hisashi is older, I plan to take him to the theater, the movies, and museums. And his father will fill his head with fascinating facts. You see that bookcase? He has read every one of those books and more. Ichiro has an insatiable curiosity about the world. He inherited some of that from his father, and I'm sure he will pass his knowledge on to Hisashi. I'm always learning something new from him. That is one of the traits I love so much about my husband." Kana smiled, but I sensed she had little appreciation for the intellectual stimulation I craved or the rhythm of city life.

As the days went by, I missed the excitement of the tearoom and our cosmopolitan customers. I didn't want to admit it, but in some ways I looked forward to going back to work. I justified this by telling myself that the time away from Hisashi would make me a better mother when I was with him.

"Kana, would you be brave enough to accompany me to the store? I promised myself I'd buy some new tatami mats for the apartment. Until now I haven't found the time, and I haven't wanted to take Hisashi out on the street. You can never tell what kind of germs people are carrying."

Hesitating, she suggested, "Why don't you go by yourself, Noriko? I'm more than happy to watch him. He's such an active baby. Sooner than you think, he's going to getting into all sorts of trouble. You'll need to keep your eyes on him all the time and I won't be here to help you."

"I'll just be gone for a few minutes." I grabbed my pocketbook and ran down the stairs, thankful to have a few minutes to myself. The apartment felt overcrowded with her there. I shocked myself with the thought that motherhood could be a drudgery and, no matter how hard I tried, I would never measure up to the kind of mother Kana was. I appreciated her helping hand, but I'd be relieved when the old woman left. I had gained enough confidence in my ability to take care of Hisashi at this point, and was proud of what I learned in such a short time.

Ichiro was impressed with her and concluded that Harry must be a wonderful man to have been raised by such an exceptional mother. He had only met Harry briefly before his sister's wedding, and he knew little about his brother-in-law other than what Mitsuko shared with him before she left for the United States. He tried not to be resentful that Harry had taken his sister away, but it was her choice to do with her life what she wanted. She saw Harry as her ticket to a better life.

And now Ichiro was saying another goodbye. As he settled Kana in the passenger seat of the taxicab that would take her to Haneda Airport for the return trip to America, he begged her to tell Mitsuko and Harry what an adorable baby Hisashi was, how clever he was even at two months old, and how much they would love him. I thought it odd how he made her promise to brag about our son, and I was hurt that he didn't instruct her to tell them something about me and how much I meant to him, and what a good mother I was.

Seeing the sad expression on my face she added, "And I'll be sure and tell them how lovely your wife is. Little Hisashi looks like her." She was psychologically more astute than I suspected.

Once Kana Mishima left, I could stop acting as if there was nothing wrong with Ichiro, and I was everything a mother should be to deserve such a perfect baby. I loved Hisashi with all my heart, but I missed my freedom. Was that the plight of every mother or just one as selfish as I judged myself to be?

Chapter 23

IN EARLY MAY, AS the evening sky held its dusky light longer, Ichiro was on his way home from the Aki-Torii Grille Room. Working at his desk earlier in the day, he imagined a hideous brown water beetle bit him on the calf with its sharp pincers and that blood trickled down his leg. When he rolled up his pant leg, his leg looked perfectly normal. He suspected his medication was causing him to hallucinate. Dr. Shizumi warned him this might be a side effect of the drugs along with sleeplessness and irritability.

Ichiro wanted to calm his nerves before going home to Noriko and Hisashi. He stopped at a bar and ordered a scotch and soda. The bar's loud music drowned out the hate-filled chatter in his head. He ordered a second drink and tossed it down. When the bartender cautioned him to go easy, Ichiro barked, "Mind your own business." Slapping a bill down on the bar, Ichiro left, sensing the bartender's eyes burning a hole into his back. He immediately felt ashamed of the way he had spoken, but he was in no mood to apologize.

Outside the bar, a vendor pushed a cart filled with flowers. Ichiro caught up with him and picked out a bouquet of red chrysanthemums for Noriko. Although she had not said anything to him about her mood, she seemed in need of cheering up as much as he did.

The vendor asked, "Are you going to a funeral, sir?"

Ichiro shook his head. "Why would you think that?"

"The chrysanthemums you picked are the appropriate gift to bring to relatives of the deceased."

"Obviously, I don't know that much about the symbolism of flowers. They're for my wife. My son was born nine months ago, and I want to bring her something special to celebrate. What would you suggest?"

"Perhaps she'd like these pale pink roses." When Ichiro leaned over to smell their fragrance, he started to cough. Turning his head, he wiped his mouth with a handkerchief, afraid to look if there was blood on it.

"Are you all right, sir?"

"Yes, probably just an allergy. What are these flowers called?"

"Star of Mine roses. A romantic name. Some of my customers bring them to the Takarazuka to give them to their favorite performers in the Star troupe."

"I'll take ten." The vendor counted out the flowers and carefully wrapped them in brown butcher paper, then tied them with a pink bow.

Ichiro could not find a seat on the subway and hung onto a strap as the train rocked back and forth. He struggled to keep his balance and hold onto the flowers. He opened the front door of the apartment building with great effort, then clutched the banister and slowly climbed the stairs to the second floor. His lungs were burning and his legs could barely hold him. He breathed in and out until he could feel the blood returning to his legs.

～

ICHIRO WAS SURPRISED TO see I was still awake. He handed me a bouquet of roses, and I looked at him suspiciously. "What are these for? If you want something from me you're going to have to do better than this." Seeing the disappointment on his face, I kissed him and said, "I'm just teasing you, my love."

"I bought these for you because Hisashi is nine months old today. Can you believe the months have gone by so fast?"

"Hisashi is desperate to stand up by himself, and so he keeps falling down and crying out of frustration, and I have to pick him up and comfort him. And then he tries again. I tell him that very soon he will stand on his own, and then he will take his first step, and before we know it he'll be running so fast I won't be able to catch him. And he'll turn around and with a mischievous smile he'll laugh at me. Today he pulled the cat's tail and she gave him a swat with her paw. I hope we don't have to give her away. Chaya is such a sweet thing. I love having her around. She's good company even if she is a bit of a vixen. Hisashi was so exhausted at the end of the day that, when I tucked him into his basket, he fell right to sleep."

"He'll eventually learn not to torment her, Star of Mine."

"What did you call me?"

"The flower vendor told me that is the name of these roses. I think the name suits you perfectly. You are my shining star, dearest Noriko." He leaned over and gently kissed me.

I smelled liquor on his breath, but I didn't want to mention it. "Were there many tourists at the Aki-Torii? It must be busy now that Sakura is almost over. The cherry blossoms are particularly beautiful this year, after all the winter rains. When I took Hisashi to the park today in his stroller, he kept stretching out his arms to catch the petals. He had the sweetest smile on his face. I shouldn't brag, but looking at the other babies in their carriages, he really is the most beautiful."

"That's because he looks like you, Noriko. You heard what Kana said, and I'm not going to argue."

"And if he takes after you, he will be the smartest child as well, if I recall what George Bernard Shaw and that dancer said about themselves. You always have interesting stories to tell me, Ichiro. That is one of the reasons I love you so much."

Whispering so as not to wake Hisashi, Ichiro said, "I have another story—a poem actually. Mr. Rexroth, an American writer, was at the restaurant today. We sometimes chat. He honored me by giving me a poem he's working on. I translated it into Japanese, using a dictionary, of course, but I think I got it mostly right. He told me it's supposed to be written by a woman to her lover. I thought you might like to hear it:

Making love with you is like drinking sea water.
The more I drink the thirstier I become
Until nothing can slake my thirst but to drink the entire sea.

I asked Ichiro to read it again. "Do you think you got all the words right? No one can drink sea water. Does it mean the woman is dying from her love for the man she is writing to?"

"I hadn't interpreted the poem that way. I was thinking what it meant was she could never get enough of her lover, that her desire for him is insatiable. Maybe we are both right. That is the magic of poetry. There can be many interpretations. Like music, meaning in poetry is what the listener brings to the poem as much as what the poet intends the words to mean. Sometimes even the poet is unconscious of all the layers of meaning." And then Ichiro slowly untied my robe. Smelling the scent of roses mixed with the odor of our passion, we made slow, languorous love and then drifted off to sleep.

～

Ichiro lay awake next to Noriko; the calming effect of the liquor and the balm of making love to her had worn off. He wished he could bury himself inside her skin and feel her hot blood reviving his decaying body. Too anxious to sleep, Ichiro slipped out of bed and silently dressed in the dark, trying not to disturb her.

He rode the subway as far as the Umeda station. The lights of a movie theater beckoned him. The marquee announced the science fiction thriller, *The Human Vapor*, a wildly popular special effects movie with science fiction superheroes, one of the many such films cranked out by Japanese filmmakers. A poster of a man in a business suit strapped to an operating room table with a gas mask over his face hung in the display case. Ichiro read the poster's advertisement: "Half Man, Half Beast! Born of Woman! Recreated by Outer Space Yet Loved Like a Man!"

Ichiro sat down in the last row of the theater. There were just a few patrons scattered among the rows; they had settled themselves far enough from one another to avoid any human contact. Ichiro noticed a woman sitting a few rows behind the screen; her cloche hat with its single feather was silhouetted by the film's light and shadow. He moved over a few seats so that the feather on her cloche would not obstruct his view.

Ichiro felt a chill from the blasting air-conditioning, but the cold temperature kept him alert. He was quickly engrossed in the movie's plot: a librarian working in a cancer sanatorium agrees to participate in a scientific experiment. He is turned into a vaporous mist and with his superhuman powers is able to slip through locked windows and doors, allowing him to rob a bank. Temporarily returning to human form, he falls in love with an out-of-work dancer who is indifferent to the shy librarian. The beautiful dancer only becomes interested in him when he showers her with extravagant gifts and helps her make a sensational comeback to the stage. Watching the librarian grovel at the dancer's feet, Ichiro was reminded of the way his father, Hide-Ichi, treated his stepmother, Madam Tamae. Ichiro silently cheered when the dancer is trapped in a fiery blaze set by the police and Vapor Man is condemned to live for all eternity without the woman he foolishly loves.

As the movie credits rolled, Ichiro stayed glued to his seat, stunned by the strange coincidences in the movie to his life.

The usher turned on the overhead lights and walked through the aisles pushing the seats up. He switched on a vacuum cleaner and dragged it along the carpet, picking up stray ticket stubs. The woman wearing the feathered cloche had fallen asleep. He turned off the vacuum cleaner, gently nudged her awake, and helped her to her feet. She looked around confused. Offering her his arm, the usher picked up a white cane and handed it to her. Tapping it from side to side, the two walked slowly up the aisle and into the lobby. Her hat partially obscured her face, but Ichiro noticed she was wearing dark glasses.

As she passed him, Ichiro heard her ask the usher, "Do you remember my telling you I was a famous dancer at the Takarazuka?"

"Yes. You must have been wonderful." Then in a solicitous tone he said, "Please watch your step, Madam Tamae."

Ichiro gripped the arms of his chair. He heard her cane scraping across the marble floor in the lobby of the theater.

Ichiro's heart was beating furiously. He wondered if he was having another hallucination from the medication and exhaustion. Or was that really his stepmother? Forcing himself to stand, he walked slowly into the theater lobby, fearing that she might be standing there, but the lobby was empty except for the usher, sweeping up with a broom and dustpan. Ichiro approached him.

"Is there anything I can do for you, sir? I am about to lock up."

"The blind woman you were helping up the aisle. Does she come here often?"

"I can't really say, sir. We don't give out information about our patrons unless, of course, you are a police detective."

"I'm not. But I heard you call her by her name—Madam Tamae—as if you know her. Do you?"

With a scowl on his face, the usher answered, "Do you want me to lose my job? I cannot answer your question. May I wish you a good evening, or should I say good morning. It's after three and the sun will be coming up soon enough." He held the door open.

Ichiro shivered from the damp air and his legs were stiff. He decided to walk home. A brisk walk might clear his head, he told himself, and sufficiently exhaust him so he could sleep for three hours before he had to get ready for work.

The skyline was punctuated by the red blinking lights of motionless construction cranes. Puffs of steam escaped from the subway grating, and the screeching of train brakes from underground interrupted the quiet of the sleeping city. Ichiro stopped at the corner of his street and lit a cigarette; blowing the smoke into the shaft of light from a streetlamp, he looked up at the balcony of his apartment. A soft breeze made the diapers hanging from the laundry line flutter and sway like headless ghosts. He crossed the street and climbed the stairs. Opening the door to the apartment, he was relieved that Noriko was asleep. He didn't want to tell her where he had been, and he didn't want to upset her with a story about Madam Tamae. No more horror movies for him. He'd stick to comedies, westerns, and romances to obliterate his waking nightmares, for surely that was what he had just experienced. Nothing more.

Chapter 24

A FTER WE MADE LOVE, Ichiro slipped out of bed, got dressed, and left.
I pretended to be asleep and didn't say anything to him when he returned
at three in the morning. I was too tired to think about why he was prowling
about the city. He didn't even say goodbye to Hisashi when he left for work in
the morning. Instead he shut the door as our darling boy repeatedly blurted,
"Dada," amidst a string of babbling noises. Hisashi hadn't yet mastered
"Mama," but I expected he would do so any day now. Was "Mama" harder for
a baby to say? It irked me when I was the parent who was giving Hisashi all
my love and attention. I could not have suspected that my devotion to him
would in the end make no difference.

I settled Hisashi into his highchair, and he banged on the tray with his
spoon. Trying to put on a stern expression, I said, "I know you're hungry but
you must learn to be patient and polite." I mashed up some freshly baked
squash and cut an apple into bite-size pieces. Taking the spoon from Hisashi,
he opened his mouth as we played our game. "Here is a bite for Dada. And
here's one for Grandma Kimie. And one for Kazuko." We continued in this
manner until Hisashi had eaten everything. I was thrilled that he had such a
healthy appetite. It gave me confidence in my mothering skills, which seemed
to come more naturally now despite having no experience with little ones.
I could feel myself relaxing into the role of Hisashi's mother, and I even
thought I might want another child when Ichiro's health improved. *But you
are getting ahead of yourself,* I thought. As my mother always reminded me,
"Noriko, you want to run before you can walk."

I filled the wooden tub with warm water for Hisashi's bath. As I washed
his back, he played with a little yellow rubber duck, pushing it under the
water and then squealing with delight when it popped back up. "Lean back

so I can shampoo your hair." Smiling, he did as he was told. I looked at his face and saw Ichiro and myself reflected in his features. I wondered what he would look like when he got older. Would he favor me or his father? I lifted him out of the tub, then dried him off with a soft towel and rubbed his thick black hair. Chaya whined for attention. Hisashi pointed at the cat and said, "*Neko.*" I almost dropped him. "When did you learn that?" Hisashi smiled and repeated the word.

"Well, if you can say 'cat,' how about 'Mama'?"

Hisashi put his hand over his mouth, shook his head, and laughed. I realized he was teasing me because, in the next instant, he said, "Mama," and then he kissed me. Tears welled up in my eyes. His kiss was just what I needed to lift my spirits.

After dressing him in a white shirt and short navy-blue pants, I settled Hisashi in my lap and picked out a storybook from his toy basket. He tried to grab the book. Gently prying his hand from the pages so as not to rip them, I asked, "Shall I read this story to you? It's called 'The Peach Boy.'" Hisashi nodded and then rested his head against my shoulder, a tuft of my hair between his fingers, which he brushed back and forth against his face. This was the most magical time of day for me—when it was just the two of us exchanging the warmth of our bodies.

"Once upon a time there was an old man and woman who had no children. One day the woman went down to the river and saw a big peach floating downstream." I stopped reading to point out a peach in the drawing and pronounced the word peach. "She brought it home and said to her husband, 'Let's divide it in half.' They split the peach open and a little boy— just like you—jumped out. His name was Momotarō. He told the man and woman he had come down from the sky. The old man and woman were so happy to have a child."

Hisashi rubbed his eyes and yawned, but he continued to show interest in the book, pointing at Momotarō and babbling a few unintelligible words that were part of his own private vocabulary. "He grew up and had many adventures. One day he sailed off to the island of Onigashima to kill a terrible demon. His parents were very worried, but they understood that this was what he wanted to do and so they let him go. And guess what? He slayed the demon and came home to them never to leave again. The End."

Closing the book, I told Hisashi I would never let him go away until I was very, very old. Hisashi patted my cheek as if to reassure me he never wanted to leave me, or at least that is how I interpreted his sweet gesture. Hisashi struggled to keep his eyes open. I tucked him into his comforter and told him that, after his morning nap, we would go to the park for an adventure. Rubbing his back, I sang him the childhood song about Momotarō until he fell asleep.

I filled a watering can and slid open the balcony door; my potted plants were neatly lined up on a cedar bench and thriving because I assiduously followed my father's instructions on how to take care of them. I could still hear my father telling me, "Noriko, when you take off a dead leaf, don't disturb the healthy flesh of the plant as you will kill it." Tending to the aralias, the lady fern, and the jade bamboo, I was struck by how much I missed my father. I thought about writing him a letter, but my pride stood in the way of reaching out to him. It pained me to think of myself as an estranged daughter. Maybe some miracle would bring us back together. I needed a strong man to lean on.

Looking at my watch I realized it was almost time to wake Hisashi and take him to the park as I promised. I tried to keep him on a strict schedule. When I turned around, Hisashi was already awake. I came inside and turned on the radio, which was set to my favorite music station, but instead of a lively tune, one of the saddest popular tunes of the year was playing: "Kanashii Sake." The singer tells of a broken love affair and begs the sake "to extinguish the agony of my heart." I turned the dial to the American station broadcasting programs for the US Army and Navy. Plucking a Star of Mine rose from the vase, I danced around the room to the catchy tune "Calendar Girl" and sang along while Hisashi, holding on to a chair, bounced up and down to the music on his chubby legs.

When the song ended, I asked Hisashi, "Shall we go to the park, my little lamb?" He nodded and smiled brightly. I ran a comb through his hair and put his shoes on. When I put him in his stroller, he swung his legs back and forth as if to telegraph, "It's time to go, Mama."

I found my pocketbook and looked inside my coin purse to make sure I had enough money to buy us a scoop of ice cream and a drink at the concession stand. Seeing that I had no money, I reached underneath the sink for my coin jar and was shocked that it was almost empty. I hadn't realized how often I'd invaded the jar to pay for something when there wasn't enough money left from the allowance Ichiro gave me each week for all our household expenses. I wondered why Ichiro didn't ask my sister for a raise, but knowing him as I did, I suspected he considered himself in a precarious position because of his health and so wouldn't dare speak up. And what if we were hit by an emergency? Then what?

I asked my doctor if it was safe to bring Hisashi to the tearoom and to go back to work. Setsuko had assured me she always needed my help, and I didn't question her loyalty to me. The other waitresses and Akiko and Mitsuo were willing to take turns watching him when they came home from school. Ichiro and I needed my salary if we intended to plan for our future. I hoped I wouldn't end up arguing with my husband and he would accept the reasonableness of my intention to go back to work.

⌒

ON ICHIRO'S DAY OFF we made a family outing to Osaka's Tennoji Zoo. At the wrought-iron gates, a vendor held a huge bouquet of animal balloons. A white and black penguin balloon slipped out of his grasp and floated up into the sky. Watching it sail high above the park and disappear into the clouds, Hisashi raised his arms, and when he realized he couldn't reach it, he started to cry. He was a sensitive little boy and was easily upset, but he was just as easily comforted and made to laugh.

Taking a handkerchief out of his pocket, Ichiro wiped away Hisashi's tears and assured him, "There are lots more balloons to choose from. Which one do you want?" He pointed to a green turtle. Hisashi clapped and reached for it. Ichiro tied the balloon to the stroller, assuring him that this one wouldn't drift away. Hisashi pulled the string and then let it go, watching the turtle snap back and forth in the breeze.

The vendor praised Hisashi. "That is a good choice, little one. The turtle represents a long life; and it is also a combination of heaven and earth. The shell is heaven and its flat underside is earth. You will be an explorer someday." Hisashi didn't understand what the vendor said, but he responded to the kindness in his voice by repeating, "Thank you."

Turning to me, Ichiro said, "And what would you like, Star of Mine? You deserve something special too." A shiny pinwheel caught my eye. "I'll take that. It will be my magic wand." When the vendor handed it to me, I blew on it and it threw shards of light across Ichiro and Hisashi's faces, making them look like characters in an old-fashioned movie.

Ichiro took his camera out of the case hanging around his neck. "Let me take a picture of you two to commemorate this day. We can send a picture to my sister and Harry. They'll be amazed at how big their nephew is."

"What's more amazing, the other day he said 'Mama' for the first time. I thought my heart would break from joy. I was beginning to feel I didn't matter to him, but I think he was just waiting to cheer me up!"

I detected Ichiro was barely listening to what I was saying. Fiddling with his camera, he directed me to stand next to Hisashi and hold my pinwheel up. I brushed Hisashi's hair out of his eyes so he could look directly into the camera. Ichiro stepped back, and as he pressed the button, he grimaced. I looked over my shoulder and there was a woman dressed entirely in black, a menacing expression on her face. She stared at Ichiro and then turned her face to reveal a dark red scar. Waiting for her to pass by, he took another picture. "I didn't want that woman ruining our picture."

"I don't blame you. I don't think she wishes us well. She's probably resentful of our good fortune."

Ichiro added, "She looks like someone out of a horror movie. I should have more sympathy for unfortunates like her, but I don't. And what does she know of what I am dealing with? My scars may not be visible but inside they are growing like a parasite."

"Please don't say such things, darling. Don't ruin this lovely day."

"I have no business speaking in such bleak terms. I have you and I have Hisashi. What more could I want? Will you forgive me?"

I took a deep breath and answered him with a lie. "Of course," but I was afraid he was about to ruin our one day together.

Ichiro pushed Hisashi's stroller through the park gates, past the circular flower garden, and toward the animal cages. The green turtle balloon did a crazy dance over Hisashi's head. Two elephants stamped the dusty ground in their display cage and waved their trunks in repetitive motions. Their back legs were chained to a stump to keep them from charging the iron bars. One of the elephants shook his head back and forth, his ears fanning out like giant butterfly wings. In the cage was a mud hole where a single white crane stood on one leg, eyeing the crowd that gathered in front of the cage to watch the miserable beasts straining for freedom. Ichiro echoed my thoughts. "They look sadly neglected. It's inhumane to keep these elephants tied up for the crowd's amusement."

A black-maned lion in a neighboring cage sat placidly on a high rock, waving his tail to ward off flies and yawning, from boredom I assumed, exposing his enormous sharp teeth and tongue. Hisashi swung his legs back and forth, and pointing, yelled, "Neko! Neko!"

Laughing, Ichiro corrected him. "No, Hisashi. That's not exactly a cat. That's a big lion, the king of the jungle. That's why he's sitting on the high rock. So that he can watch everything that is going on." As if on cue, the lion let out a roar, triggering screams from the children who were standing close to the railing. Hisashi covered his ears, and then grabbed my hand.

"Don't worry, Hisashi. He can't get out. He's just saying hello to us."

The lion's roar set the monkeys in a nearby cage howling. Agitated, a female monkey grabbed her baby and pressed him into her hairy breast while a large male monkey swung from vine to vine, apparently protecting his domain. In the next cage, a lone baboon rocked back and forth on her haunches. The stench from the cage was overpowering. Ichiro put on his sunglasses to protect his eyes from the vaporous stench.

We stopped at the aviary. Huge toucans flapped their wings, and tiny hummingbirds flitted from one trumpet flower to another, sucking on the sweet nectar. A hummingbird landed on Hisashi's shoulder and stuck his beak into his ear, tickling him. Hisashi tried to catch it, but the bird flew away the moment he felt Hisashi's fingers on its miniature feathers. Victorian crowned pigeons with their white tipped blue feathers rested in the highest branches next to the bleeding-heart doves. A scarlet ibis dipped its curved, black bill into the shallow water, and monarch butterflies waltzed among the thick vegetation. Children ran along the aviary path, deliriously happy with the profusion of color, movement, and light. Hisashi tried to get out of his stroller. I had to remind him he couldn't walk just yet.

"But who knows? In a few weeks, maybe on your birthday, you'll take your first steps, Hisashi." I obviously had no way to know if he understood me, but he had a proud look on his face.

Without warning, lightning bolts shot through the sky followed by several claps of thunder, and the rain came down in sheets. Ichiro and I gripped the handles on Hisashi's stroller and ran for cover in the nearby reptile cave. Other visitors pushed their way into the dark and dank cave to escape the rain. Behind a display window, a female python—its black and yellow diamond patterned skin shimmering in the dim light—was coiled around a single large egg. Suddenly her body began to undulate around her egg. Hisashi sat transfixed, and the crowd registered their astonishment with oohs and aahs.

Ichiro said, "Mother pythons wrap themselves around their eggs to keep them warm. They shiver like that to generate heat when the temperature of the egg drops. It's their way of protecting the egg until the baby hatches. The thunderstorm must be upsetting her."

"How do you know all this, Ichiro?" He shrugged his shoulders. "Someday you will tell everything you know to Hisashi. He's such a curious little boy. Look at the way he is staring at the snake. I'm surprised he's not frightened. He looks as if he'd like to go right into the cage and touch the snake."

"That wouldn't be a good idea. That snake could swallow him in a minute. She must be twenty feet long and weigh close to three hundred pounds. And when she's protecting her egg, she's dangerous."

"You're like an encyclopedia. I learn something from you every day, and so will Hisashi."

"A lot of good it will do him."

"Opening his eyes to the world is just as important as teaching him practical information." Ichiro jammed his hands into his pockets as if he were trying to control a silent rage building up inside him.

When the rain stopped, we escaped the cave; the air smelled fresh and clean, and shafts of sunlight broke through swiftly moving clouds. Hisashi pulled on the string of his balloon, flipping the turtle on its back, and the wind buffeted it about, turning it right side up again.

Riding on the subway, Ichiro said, "I hope you are satisfied with our little outing and it will keep you from bothering me with another request for a while."

I touched Ichiro's shoulder. "It wasn't just for me, Ichiro. It was for Hisashi and you see how happy it made him." I felt as if our family was beginning to crack apart, and that nothing would put it back together again.

Chapter 25

A FEW DAYS AFTER our visit to the zoo, Ichiro collapsed in the hallway. His key was in the lock but he didn't have the strength to open the door. I rushed down the stairs to the telephone booth on the street and called for an ambulance to take him to the hospital. Unable to go with him because I had to stay with Hisashi, I spent a sleepless night waiting for news of his condition.

The following morning, I asked our landlady, Mrs. Masamoto, to take care of Hisashi for an hour so I could go to the hospital. She was more than eager to accommodate me as she adored Hisashi and derived pleasure from his every little antic. I had no one else to leave him with on such short notice, and I didn't want to raise my sister's suspicions that something terrible had happened to Ichiro. I had never felt more desperate or alone.

I rushed down the hospital corridor. Dr. Shizumi was standing over Ichiro when I found him in a hospital room. I cradled Ichiro's face in my hands and let out an anguished sigh.

Dr. Shizumi said, "I'm glad you're here, Mrs. Uchida. I've advised your husband he will need to be here for the entire month. If he's better by the end of July we can send him home, but not before then. I'm going to start him on another course of treatment and it will take that long to determine if he's responding well to the medication. It's a lot stronger than what he's on."

"What is it?" asked Ichiro.

"A new drug we are using in combination with the streptomycin. You'll be given doses of both. And I want you to be on complete bed rest. Here you won't have any other choice. The nurses will watch over you to make sure you are getting enough sleep and eating well. Since the last time I saw you, you've dropped some weight. We need to bolster your immune system, and not eating properly is doing you no favors."

Dr. Shizumi expressed his concern for me. "This is hard on your wife, Ichiro. Oftentimes, an illness is worse for the family members than it is for the patient." Tapping Ichiro's chest, he said, "I suspect that somewhere inside you is a reservoir of bravery. After all, you managed to survive the war, which is not the case for many men your age, who died of various terrible diseases or did themselves in from despair. You pulled through, and I expect you to show the same resilience now. What do you say?"

Ichiro promised to do his best. "Not just for you, Noriko, but for Hisashi as well."

In a patronizing tone, Dr. Shizumi said, "There's the spirit, my boy. I want to count you as one of my success stories. I don't like losing a patient. It's bad for my reputation."

I didn't know how to react to his callous remark. I wondered if he was using harsh discipline rather than sympathy to spark Ichiro's fighting spirit. Maybe I needed to do the same, I thought. Instead of indulging Ichiro, perhaps the better path was to challenge him. I was in a foreign country without a map or compass to guide me—the country of tuberculosis.

As I was leaving the hospital, Dr. Shizumi stopped me. "Mrs. Uchida, just to be on the safe side, I think that you and your baby should be vaccinated. There is a vaccine called BCG, or bacillus Calmette-Guerin. Please make an appointment for both of you."

"Are there side effects, Doctor?"

"None, and it will put your mind at ease if you are worried that your husband may transmit the disease to either of you."

"I didn't want to mention my concern. It would only fuel Ichiro's shame and guilt, and he's carrying around plenty of that already as you can see."

"As I said, it's only natural for you to be worried. Especially with a little one. His immune system is not fully formed, but I must say, despite everything you are going through, you seem strong and healthy."

"It's an act, Dr. Shizumi. I was a drama student in high school, bound for the Takarazuka. You can thank my teacher. In truth I feel as if I'm dying."

"Well, make believe you're brave, and the trick will get you far..."

"Funny you should use those words. They are from one of my favorite musicals, *The King and I*. I once dreamed of playing Anna."

"Go see the show. It will cheer you up. My wife recently saw it in Namba, and she said it is utterly charming."

"When I find the time. For now, I have more important matters to attend to. *The King and I* will have to wait." I felt a pang of jealousy imagining Mrs. Shizumi attending tea parties, playing golf at the local country club, taking in a movie or a show at the Takarazuka. I imagined her as a lady of leisure while her husband labored at the hospital to create a comfortable lifestyle for his family. And then I talked myself out of this fantasy, because attached to it was the supercilious, self-important Dr. Shizumi, who held my husband's fate in his capable hands. He was our lifeline, and I prayed he would not let go of it until Ichiro recovered and was restored to the man I had cleaved my fate to.

⌢

DR. SHIZUMI, EXPECTING HIS patient to be resting in bed, knocked on Ichiro's door; but he found Ichiro packing his suitcase. "I haven't said you could leave yet. I want you under observation for another two weeks."

"I can't stay away from my job any longer. I don't get paid if I'm not there. It's not like I'm a company man with a guaranteed salary and a pension at the end of the line. That's why Mrs. Uchida is going back to work. And today is my son's first birthday. I want to be home to celebrate it. I already missed my wife's birthday last week. Who knows if I'll be around in a year's time to see Hisashi turn two?"

"Ichiro, you need to adopt a more positive attitude. We doctors have discovered that a positive mental attitude can have an impact on the body's ability to fight off diseases. Worry and stress are the enemies of recovery."

Ichiro said, "So I should paint a smile on my face and act like I haven't a care in the world?"

"The trick is not to over-exaggerate your optimism, because that is false and therefore delusional, but rather to trust that you are getting better bit by bit every day. Drugs alone are not going to heal you." Dr Shizumi wrote an additional note on Ichiro's chart. "I can't force you to stay in the hospital, but I need your assurance that you will continue to take both drugs. If you have a relapse, I'm going to have to take more drastic measures."

"And what is that?"

"I'll have to send you away to a sanatorium for an extended period. That is what I do for my sicker patients—or those that refuse to cooperate with me and follow a strict regime of rest and good food."

"And in the meantime, I should put on a happy face. That's my wife's philosophy. That and her unflagging belief in Tenrikyo, which dictates that our job in life is to be joyous. I don't disabuse her of that notion, but sometimes she takes it to an extreme, and as far as I'm concerned, Tenrikyo is a cult."

"I suggest you read Seneca. He had a lot to say about the mind-body connection." Dr. Shizumi wrote the name of the philosopher on his prescription pad and handed it to Ichiro. "The next time I see you I expect you to have gained a few pounds. Is that clear?"

Ichiro nodded and tucked Dr. Shizumi's "prescription" in his jacket pocket.

Leaving the hospital, Ichiro discovered the claim check in his jacket pocket for the photographs he had taken at the Tennōji Zoo. He stopped at the camera shop on his way home and picked up the photos. Flipping through them, he looked for the first two he took at the gate to the zoo. He wanted to destroy the one that caught the woman with the scar on her face standing behind Noriko and Hisashi. He was assured by the clerk that all the photographs had been developed, but the one that he was looking for was not in the envelope. "Were all the pictures developed? There is definitely one missing."

The clerk looked annoyed to be questioned. "Sir, I developed the entire roll."

"That's strange. Could one of the photographs have been cut off?"

"No. That is impossible. What you took is what you see."

"My mistake. I thought one of the pictures accidentally caught one of the hibakusha." He shivered just saying the word. Then he added, "Maybe she was like the 'Human Vapor Man.' Are you familiar with that movie? I recently saw it."

The clerk shrugged his shoulders. "I don't like those horror movies. As far as I'm concerned, we need to forget about the bomb and the war—that's what those movies are really about. I prefer comedies. Japan is better off burying that part of its past and focusing on our present and future."

Ichiro sized up the clerk as a university student. "Is that what they teach you in school?"

"Yes, our professors prefer to discuss the rebuilding of Japan with American money than dwell on the mistakes we made during the war. When I graduate, I'm going to take a job with Sumitomo Bank. Every enterprise needs money, right?"

"The optimism of youth." Looking at his watch, Ichiro said, "I'd better get going. My son is waiting for me, I'm sure."

"Good day, Mr. Uchida. Don't forget your photographs."

Chapter 26

No sooner was Ichiro admitted to the hospital than I went back to work at the Tesagara Tearoom. I regretted doing this behind his back, but we needed the money. I was apprehensive about leaving Hisashi with the waitresses or his two older cousins, but he was such an enchanting child and able to amuse himself with the slightest diversion that everyone argued over who would be lucky enough to watch him. When he was brought into the tearoom, he was the center of attention among the customers; and with so much stimulation, he flourished.

Before he went to sleep at night, he repeated "Dada," but I was unable to comfort him. I'd make up stories that he'd gone on a trip like Momotarō to slay the demon, or he was on the moon chasing after the rabbit, and he'd be back soon. Hisashi would cry and pull my hair or hit me with his hands curled up into fists out of frustration. I tried to keep my sadness buried deep inside, but there were evenings when my tears mingled with his. I'd hold him in my arms and rock him back and forth until he wore himself out.

~

I didn't know when Ichiro would be discharged from the hospital. He'd tell me he felt fine one day, and the next he'd be running a high fever and unable to drag himself out of bed, plagued with a wracking cough and blinding headaches. He finally admitted to me that he had frightening hallucinations—some of which were so vivid that he couldn't tell if they were real or imagined. I was afraid that he might not be able to go back to work if his health didn't improve. Or worse still, that he might become an invalid.

As I prepared dinner for Hisashi and me the evening of his first birthday, I heard a knock on the door. I thought it was Mrs. Masamoto looking for the rent, but when I opened the door, Ichiro stood there wearing the same clothes as when he was picked up by the ambulance weeks ago. I burst out into tears. I hadn't realized how much I missed him. His skin was pale, and his hair, although well groomed, had flecks of gray around his temples and needed a trim. He touched my face and then forcefully embraced me. Separating, he brushed my bangs off my forehead and traced my scar with his middle finger like a blind man wanting to reassure himself that here was his beloved.

Hisashi ran to him, abandoning the red wooden truck he was playing with. He grabbed his father's leg, yelling, "Dada, up, up." Ichiro picked him up and held him tightly against his chest.

"I can't believe you're home, Ichiro. I thought you'd be in the hospital for at least another two weeks."

"And not be here for my son's first birthday? Dr. Shizumi gave me special dispensation and a prescription for a book he's instructed me to read. He thinks it will improve my attitude."

"I've missed you so much, and so has Hisashi."

"You didn't bargain for this, did you, when you agreed to marry me?"

"Ichiro, we promised to love one another in sickness and in health. Are you questioning my feelings for you?"

"No. But I wouldn't blame you if you wanted to be rid of me."

"Do these tears look like the tears of a wife who doesn't love her husband?"

"No."

"Look at what I've done with the apartment to celebrate Hisashi's birthday." I had hung brightly colored paper cranes from one end of the apartment to the other and put up a cardboard poster with pictures of Hisashi from his first month to his first year. Ichiro took out a packet of photographs and added one to the display. Looking at it, I asked, "Is it my imagination or has Hisashi grown since you took this picture at the zoo?"

"It does look as if his shirt doesn't fit him properly now. It's a little tight."

"I've been putting off buying him something new. I've thought about asking Setsuko for one of Mitsuo's old shirts. She keeps all her children's clothes. I think she'll still have them by the time she's a grandmother. It's amazing how frugal my sister is."

Ichiro bristled. "That won't be necessary. I don't want my son wearing hand-me-downs. And I don't want you worrying about money. You sound like we're one step away from the alms house. I plan on going back to work tomorrow." I was startled he would consider returning to work so soon after being discharged from the hospital. It seemed foolhardy, but perhaps Dr. Shizumi had cleared him. Hisashi sat down at our table, unconsciously tapping his fingers.

"Would you like something to eat?"

"I'm dying for a home-cooked meal. I never want to look at another hospital meal again. I literally had to force myself to eat, and if I look thinner, that's the reason."

Putting Hisashi in his highchair, I portioned out ramen noodles, baked salmon, and steamed carrots. Ichiro watched Hisashi as he ate everything in his bowl. "He's got quite an appetite, hasn't he?" I didn't want to tell Ichiro that Hisashi had developed a sweet tooth from all the pastries and cookies offered to him by all his caregivers at the tearoom for being "such a good boy."

I cleared away the bowls and brought out Hisashi's birthday cake. Lighting two candles, I instructed him to blow them out, but he didn't understand and so Ichiro leaned over to help him. He coughed, his face turning red, and covered his mouth. I pretended not to notice and blew out the candles for him. When he recovered, Ichiro got out his camera and took a picture. The flash frightened Hisashi and he blinked, his lower lip quivering, but he quickly recovered when I gave him a piece of cake. He dug into the cake with his hands and smeared the icing all over his face. I burst out laughing.

Ichiro said, "Don't encourage bad manners. Where is his spoon, or has he forgotten how to use one?"

I lifted Hisashi out of his highchair, wiped the icing off his face, and gave him his wooden truck. He turned the wheels around and around and then announced, "Zoom, zoom," looking at his father with a proud smile on his face.

Ichiro seemed impressed. "Another new word. What else has he learned while I've been away?"

"Why don't you see for yourself? He can count to three and he knows where his eyes, ears, and mouth are."

Ichiro played a game with him. Pointing to his ears he asked, "And what do you call these?"

Hisashi answered correctly, and Ichiro continued to quiz him while I unwrapped a present from Mitsuko and Harry. With just a hint of pride in his voice, Ichiro said, "He's certainly a smart boy. But hearing him say all these new words makes me realize just how much I have already missed. I wonder when he's going to start to walk."

"Do you know when you started to walk?"

"No. The only person who would remember is my sister. I have no memory of it. Most children don't start forming memories until they are about three, which in my case is just as well. From the day I was born my mother was sick, and I'm told she was in bed and so weak she couldn't nurse me." I thought, *Apparently, Ichiro's stay in the hospital didn't disabuse him of his constant need to repeat stories about his tragic childhood.*

I snuck behind the wooden screen that divided our apartment and brought out a big package. "This came yesterday. It is from your sister and Harry." Ichiro lifted the lid off the J.C. Penney's box and held up a red and white checkered cowboy shirt and overalls. There was also a pair of leather cowboy boots and a canvas hat to go with the outfit.

Ichiro put the hat on Hisashi's head and pulled the string underneath his chin. It was too big for him and the brim slid down over his forehead, pushing his black bangs into his large brown eyes. Ichiro tipped the brim and took another picture. This time Hisashi smiled. "With the rest of the outfit on, you'll look like an American cowboy."

"What a happy coincidence. Look what my nephew Mitsuo and I bought for him at Takashimaya. It's perfect!" I pushed a plush white rocking horse into the middle of the apartment. It had a shaggy brown mane, a saddle with stirrups, and reins with silver bells and sturdy handles. Ichiro positioned Hisashi in the saddle and showed him how to hold the handles. As the horse tipped forward it gave out a loud neigh. At first Hisashi rocked back and forth cautiously, but as he gained confidence, he picked up the rhythm, and each time the horse let out a sound, he tried to imitate it.

Ichiro observed, "That's an expensive toy. Where did you get the money?"

"Mitsuko and Harry sent us fifty dollars this month, and they said they are going to try and send us the same amount every month to help us out."

"Why did they do that? Have you told them I haven't been working and we need the money? It's not your place to say anything to my sister. I plan to tell her about my diagnosis and our financial situation when things improve and I have good news to share. What's the point of making her worry about me?"

Stumbling over my words, I explained, "I didn't use all the money they sent us. I saved some for household expenses. Mitsuo contributed to the gift, too. He loves Hisashi so much he wanted to give him something special."

Ichiro lit a cigarette and blew the smoke into the air. Hisashi, trying to keep the smoke from getting into his eyes, waved his hands. Ichiro ignored him. "Where did Mitsuo get his own money?"

"Setsuko hired him to work in the kitchen. She wants him to learn how to be a chef so that someday he'll be prepared to take over when she retires. She certainly can't count on her husband to run the place."

"What about me? I'm certainly capable. Or has she already buried me?"

"Why would you say such a thing? She knows that someday you are going to want to start your own restaurant. At least that's what you've told me. Who knows? She may even want to be one of your investors. Life is always full of surprises!"

"Thank goodness I'm going back to work tomorrow. Had I stayed away much longer she might have made more changes to the staff." Now would have been the moment to tell Ichiro I had gone back to work while he was in the hospital, but I was panic-stricken he would react badly and I wasn't prepared for his reaction, which I assumed would be hostile.

Unable to help myself I said, "Perhaps you should rest for a few more days."

Ichiro stubbed his cigarette into the ashtray and poured himself a drink. Avoiding my eyes, he said, "I've been away long enough. I shouldn't test Setsuko's patience."

Trying to assuage his anger and hurt, I said, "You have been sorely missed by all the staff, and the customers too. Mr. Ozu came into the tearoom the other day and asked after you. He just completed his movie, *The End of Summer*. It's opening at a theater in Namba in a few weeks, and he offered us tickets."

"Did he ask where I was? You didn't embarrass me by telling him I was in the hospital, did you?"

"Why would I do that? No, I said you were taking an advanced accounting class. That's what Setsuko has told everyone. No point in raising their concern."

"Did he believe you? "

"Yes. I remember his exact words: 'You must be so proud of your husband for his ambitious nature.'"

Ichiro scoffed. "How would he know anything about me? I bow and scrape and compliment him on his films. He likes having an audience, that's all. And what's more, he was probably inquiring about me so he'd have an excuse to talk to you. I saw the way he looked at you when you came waltzing into the tearoom on your first day of work. I never told you this, but he encouraged me to go out with you. Do you remember that morning?"

I softly touched his cheek. "Of course, I remember. When I saw you, I thought I would faint. You were so handsome and so kind despite my being late for work. I had a crush on you from the first moment I saw you. I wasn't sure I could work for you feeling the way I did."

"And I could barely keep myself from putting my arms around you and kissing your lovely face. Honestly, I don't know how I managed to control myself for as long as I did. I hope we can rekindle those feelings."

"And why not? You are all that I want and need. Promise me you'll never leave me and Hisashi again, Ichiro."

"That's up to Dr. Shizumi's miracle drugs. I can't promise you anything. I might have to go back to the hospital. We need to be realistic about my condition."

I wrapped my arms around Ichiro and buried my face in his neck. "What we need is to stay optimistic and to be grateful for what we have—our love and a happy and healthy little boy."

We turned around and realized that the rocking of the horse had stopped and Hisashi's head was resting on his chest. He was fast asleep. "Why don't you put him to bed?" I said. "And then we should try to get some sleep."

"You do it. I need to press my shirt." He plugged the iron into the electrical outlet and filled the well with water. After a few minutes, the steam made gurgling sounds as he ran the iron across the wrinkled collar and cuffs. As if speaking to himself, he said, "Putting on a freshly pressed shirt makes me feel presentable."

"I can finish it for you."

"No offense, and you do an adequate job, of course, but you know I have a precise way I like my shirts ironed. Collar, cuffs, back, and then front." When he moved the fabric, he put the iron in the cradle at the end of the board. I saw his hand was shaking, but he persisted. Putting the shirt on a hanger, he inspected every inch. "The iron is heavier than I bargained for. I've lost strength in my arms lying around in bed all day with only a radio and a pack of cards for company."

I gently lay Hisashi on his futon and tucked the comforter around him. Suppressing my anger at Ichiro for not wanting to do this simple fatherly task, to feel the weight and warmth of his little boy, I washed the dishes and put on a nightgown, too tired and confused to quarrel.

Ichiro folded the ironing board. Lying down next to me after stripping off his clothes, he confessed, "I have missed you so much. Life would be unbearable without you."

"And what about Hisashi? Is he not just as important to you as I am?"

Ichiro hesitated. I waited, listening to the dripping of the water in the sink and the ticking of the clock. After what seemed like an eternity, he confessed, "I don't feel worthy of being Hisashi's father. I've thought about whether he might be better off being raised by a father and mother who are equally capable of caring for him. I could end up an invalid and then you'd be saddled with the two of us. You are too young to carry such a burden."

"I can't believe you are saying this to me. You aren't really serious, are you, Ichiro?"

"I don't know what to think right now. It's foolish of me to even bring this up. I think the weeks in the hospital, weeks of seeing so many patients wasting away—even some as young as I am—put me in a negative frame of mind. I'm sure that, once I'm back to work and have my feet underneath me, I'll be my old self again. You do believe me, don't you?"

"What choice do I have?"

Ichiro turned away from me and in a few minutes was in a deep sleep, snoring lightly and mumbling to himself. At some point he distinctly shouted, "Don't bite me," and then he fell silent. His outburst frightened me. What could he have been dreaming?

I heard Ichiro's breathing grow rhythmic, and unable to sleep, I wrapped myself in a robe and slipped out to the balcony in my bare feet. I touched my stomach where I carried Hisashi for nine months and examined my hands that had held him, bathed him, dressed him, wiped his tears away, fed him. I caressed my breasts that had nursed him, and I ran my fingertips over my lips that read stories to him, sung to him, and told him that he was the most lovable little boy on earth because he was of my flesh and blood, assuring him I would never let him go. Beneath the balcony, the traffic continued unabated and drowned out the beating of my broken heart.

PART TWO

Chapter 27

1962

MITSUKO MISHIMA, ICHIRO'S OLDER sister, was the Jordan Hotel's assistant manager in Glendive, Montana. At two in the morning, Mitsuko turned off the jukebox, shooed the last of the customers off the barstools, and counted the money in the cash register. Only the hotel night manager was in the lobby when she put the money in the safe, and he was fast asleep with his legs propped up on his desk behind the counter. It was a lonely place at that hour of the morning. Mitsuko never imagined her life would turn out this way when she said yes to Harry's marriage proposal. She thought she'd be a farmer's wife with lots of children. Instead, she had ended up in the badlands of Montana where Harry had taken a job as a dispatcher for the Halliburton Gas Company punching the clock at eight in the morning and returning at five in the evening as she headed off to the Jordan for a long evening and swollen feet. She and Harry were like two ships passing in the night, and their trailer home—instead of filled with children—was silent as a tomb with only the ticking of a clock for company.

Mitsuko buttoned up her woolen coat and put her shoulder to the wind. It was only October, but an early storm had blown down from the Arctic and the temperature was well below freezing even during the daylight hours. Mitsuko turned on the ignition of her secondhand green Chevrolet. For a nine-year-old car, it was still in good shape; the harsh winters had not rusted it out. She waited for the engine to warm up and the defroster to break up the ice crystals on the windshield. Even after living in the United States for nine years, she missed Japan: springtime when the delicate pink and white blossoms covered the tree branches; the smell of incense at the Buddhist temples; and most of all, her younger brother Ichiro. The adversity they had lived through during the war had brought them so close that Mitsuko could almost read Ichiro's mind across the thousands of miles that separated them.

Mitsuko turned on the radio to keep herself company. The announcer on KXGN-AM Radio said, "And now for you Roy Orbison fans out there, at a quarter after two on a cold October morning in 1962, let's listen to "Sweet Dream Baby." It's one darn sexy song, and it'll keep you awake if you're the only driver on the road!" Mitsuko still struggled with English, but she understood most of the lyrics.

Mitsuko pulled out onto Merrill Street, passing Couk's Furniture Store, Irene's Beauty Parlor, the Safeway Supermarket, and the First National Bank of Glendive. Crossing the Bell Street Bridge over the Yellowstone River, she drove past the used car lot where she and her husband Harry had bought her Chevrolet. They had just paid off the loan. Without the monthly payment they had a little extra cash, and so it was not such a stretch to send her brother Ichiro and his wife fifty dollars every month for whatever they needed for themselves and their little boy. She was grateful that Harry was so generous.

Except for an occasional gray light spilling out of a window from a television set, the houses on either side of the road were dark. She turned left into Knauff's Trailer Court. The "No Vacancy" sign flashed on and off. The tires made a crunching sound over the gravel as she drove slowly so as not to disturb her neighbors. Opening the unlocked front door of their trailer, she took off her high heels and tiptoed into the kitchen on her swollen feet.

Pulling the string to turn on the fluorescent light in the kitchen, she picked up an envelope Harry left on the counter. She immediately recognized Ichiro's handwriting, but the return address was the Aki-Torii Grille Room, Noriko's sister's restaurant, rather than their home address. Something about this change made her want to open the letter immediately. She quickly took off her brown woolen coat, and sat down at the Formica table to read her brother's letter:

October 13, 1962

My dear sister: Thank you for sending the cowboy outfit for Hisashi's birthday. He just started walking and the cowboy boots fit him perfectly. He's proud of himself, as you can imagine. He knows quite a few words beyond the usual Dada and Mama. When he falls down he just laughs and gets right up and walks again. He is a determined boy, and very happy despite everything Noriko and I are dealing with.

I haven't wanted to worry you, but I have been diagnosed with tuberculosis— the doctor thinks I have been carrying the disease since the day I was born— that Mother passed it on to me.

Mitsuko's hands trembled as she read Ichiro's words. How could this have happened? How had his luck taken such a tragic turn? Hadn't he already suffered enough? The last time she had seen him he was strong and healthy with a job he could be proud of.

She continued reading through her tears:

Whatever the cause, I must accept this. I am having a hard time staying on the job and have been in the hospital for a few weeks. I hope I won't have to go back. The doctor has warned me if my condition gets much worse I'll be sent to a sanatorium for an indeterminate period of time. If I can't work, we will be destitute since Noriko's income in the tearoom will not go far to support the three of us, and I have no savings to rely upon. (Madam Tamae made sure of that, didn't she?) I argued with Noriko about her going back to work because she has to take Hisashi with her, but honestly, we need her salary to make ends meet. It's humbling to think I alone cannot take care of my family.

I am embarrassed that you are sending us money, although I know you would do anything to help me out, even if it meant going without something for yourself. You have always been that way. I trust that, between you and Harry, you are doing fine and this is not too much of a burden.

The doctor tells me I should think positively and that I am doing myself a disservice by worrying, but I am unable to change my thinking. I want my son to have a good life and to be a successful man.

For this reason, I have hatched a plan I want to present to you. Would you and Harry consider adopting Hisashi and raising him as your own son? I know you are heartbroken that you are unable to have children. I don't know how difficult it is to give a Japanese child to a couple in America, but if Harry agrees, perhaps he can look into the mechanics of it. If you are wondering how I came up with this plan, it came to me when Harry's mother, Kana, visited us in Osaka. She is such a kind person that I am sure Harry is the same. Am I right? I hardly knew him when you got married, although he seemed like a decent fellow.

Mitsuko was stunned. How could Ichiro bring himself to do such a thing when she and her brother were both turned over to relatives by their father, suffering the consequences? It was inconceivable. Had he fallen into such a pit of despair that he saw no future for himself?

I do not want to ask this of you unless Harry is in complete agreement. Only then will I broach the subject with Noriko. I don't know how she will react any more than you know how Harry will take this news, but perhaps, between the two of us, we can convince them this is the proper course of action and what is best for Hisashi.

Will you let me know your decision soon? I don't want to wait any longer. If Hisashi gets much older, the separation from us will be that much more difficult. As it is, it's going to be a major adjustment for both Noriko and me as we love Hisashi very much. It is out of love that I believe this is the only solution. Please send your reply to me in care of the Aki-Torii. I would hate for Noriko to read your letter before I have had time to discuss this with her. Your loving brother, Ichiro.

Mitsuko buried her face in her hands and sobbed uncontrollably. For several months she suspected that Noriko was not revealing the seriousness of Ichiro's illness—she never actually mentioned tuberculosis. She reread the letter three times, letting her tears fall onto the thin paper. There was a black and white photograph in the letter of Hisashi in his stroller at the Tennōji Park Zoo with Noriko standing next to his stroller. A green turtle floated above their heads, and behind them was an old woman dressed in black with an angry scar on her face. Mitsuko wondered why Ichiro had picked this picture to send to her.

Mitsuko wanted to wake Harry but he needed his rest. He would be getting up in a few hours to go to work anyway so she resisted the urge to disturb him. She lay down on the sofa, wrapping herself in a warm knitted blanket. She listened to the ticking of the clock and waited for dawn. Sleep overtook her.

Mitsuko awoke to the smell of coffee brewing on the stove. She rubbed her eyes and threw the blanket aside.

"Why don't you get into bed, Mitzi?" Harry said. "I got tired of waiting for you. I must have dozed off before you came home. Did you see Ichiro's letter?"

"I didn't plan to go to sleep. I wanted to read you his letter the minute you woke up, but I guess I was so tired I fell asleep anyway."

Harry asked, "Is something wrong? It's always frustrating to see a letter from Ichiro. I can't read it so I have to wait for you to translate."

"I can hardly make sense of what he's written. He wants us to adopt Hisashi."

"What are you talking about?"

"Ichiro. He has tuberculosis, which is why he was sent to the hospital during the summer. He hasn't told Noriko of this idea. I don't know what's gotten into him. It's madness, but he says this is what he wants. As far as I'm concerned, giving away a child is an act of desperation."

Harry showed no emotion. Instead he got to the point. "Is that what you want, to raise this boy? How do you feel about accepting the responsibility of becoming Hisashi's mother?"

"Having a child of our own is more than I could ever have dreamed of once you shut the door on adoption after I lost our baby." Mitsuko put her hand on her stomach and sighed. It stilled pained her.

Harry argued, "Hisashi is the closest thing to having our own child. Remember how my mother bragged about him when she came back from Japan? She couldn't stop telling us how adorable he is, how smart, how clever, how sweet."

Mitsuko realized Harry was beginning to consider the idea. He wasn't totally against it, as she was afraid he would be. "What do you think? What should I write to Ichiro?"

"We aren't spring chickens. You're thirty-three, not exactly young to be a first-time mother. And if we agree to adopt him there's no turning back. Once we say yes, if Ichiro and Noriko realize they made a big mistake, it would just break your heart, and mine too, to give the child back. I know you would make a good mother, and I might not be such a bad father."

Harry zipped up his winter parka. Mitsuko handed him his lunch box and then stood at the front door as he maneuvered his pickup truck out of the driveway and into the flow of early morning traffic. Overhead a flock of Canada geese crossed the face of the autumn sun hanging low in the sky. The whistle of the Northern Pacific freight train heading toward the Glendive depot sounded shrill in the cold morning air.

Mitsuko was too distraught to go back to sleep. She turned up the thermostat and the electric baseboard heaters crackled and hummed. She took a shower and threw her clothes into the washing machine with Harry's flannel shirts and polyester trousers. Setting her wet hair in pink sponge rollers, she sat under her portable hair dryer. Mitsuko imagined telling Hisashi about being adopted when he was old enough to understand. She would never keep it a secret from him. She'd say, "Your parents loved you so much they gave you to us to give you a better life." She wondered how that might sound to the boy. She wasn't sure she believed it herself.

The telephone rang. She turned off the hair dryer and pressed the receiver to her ear. It was Harry. "Is something the matter, Harry? You never call me during the day unless there's been an accident on one of the rigs."

"This time I have good news. At least I think it's good news. I've given this thing about Hisashi a lot of thought all morning. As crazy as it sounds, if this is what you want, it's what I want too."

Mitsuko needed further affirmation before she could allow her heart to open up. "Are you sure, Harry?"

"You know I wouldn't say it if I didn't mean it." He stopped for a moment and then said, "The boss is signaling me. There is an emergency and so I need to get right off the phone, but you should write Ichiro to tell him we are ready to move ahead and see what's involved with adopting Hisashi from this side of the fence."

"Shouldn't I wait for you to get home and we can write him together?"

"No, you know what to say. You don't need my help."

Mitsuko was speechless. How could this have been so easy when all this time, Harry had resisted the idea of adopting a child? Perhaps Harry would change his mind, but he told her to write to Ichiro, so that couldn't be the case. Was this his way of paying her back for all the hardships they had encountered—not just losing the baby, but living in a place she was having trouble getting used to—so hot in the summer and freezing cold in the winter—with men who carried guns in the back of their pickup trucks and women who made her feel as if she didn't fit in?

"I have to go, Mitzi. See you tonight."

Mitsuko hung up the phone. Pouring herself a cup of warmed-over coffee, she checked the calendar above the gas stove to make sure of the date, and then sat down at the kitchen table and tried to think of what to write to Ichiro that would strike the right balance between joy and sorrow. After making several attempts, she stopped thinking and let her heart dictate her response:

Friday, October 20, 1962

My dearest Ichiro:

It will be Thanksgiving in a month; it's a big holiday here when we say thank you for everything we have been given. I don't know if I told you, but I have been promoted to assistant manager at the Jordan Hotel, so that's something I'm going to say thank you for. And Harry has been made head dispatcher at Halliburton. He's putting in long hours, but that's nothing unusual for us. Hard work never killed anyone.

Winter is here early this year. When I look out the window of our trailer, I can see the sparrows pecking at the ice in the fountain. You must still be enjoying the red maple trees and the last warm days of fall in Osaka. Hopefully, the weather is doing you good. I read your letter many times. To put your mind at ease, Harry and I are eager to adopt Hisashi. I must ask you to think about this one hundred times. You are not giving away a dog or a cat. You are giving away your firstborn son. Right now, you may think this is in Hisashi's best interest because you are not feeling well, but when you are better (which I am sure you will be) you may change your mind and come to regret your decision. This is life-changing for five people: you and Noriko, Harry and me, and, of course, little Hisashi most of all. Have you thought about the impact it will have on him in the years to come? Will he think of himself as a throwaway baby, or will he be grateful that you made this decision for him? He is too young to express how he feels, but he may be confused and wish he had never left Japan later on.

I often feel like a fish out of water in America. Hisashi may feel the same way, too, even if he comes here as a toddler.

Once Hisashi is ours, we will never give him back no matter how much you may regret your decision. I will be his mother and Harry his father. Do you remember what Father used to tell us: "Never step onto a bridge unless you know that it can hold you up." Our father made some mistakes in life but he was right about that. I sometimes wonder if I made the right decision marrying Harry. I wonder how my life would have turned out if I had stayed in Japan and married a widower with three children. It sounds like a gloomy existence, but at least I would have been warm during the winter and I would have been close to you.

Please take care of yourself and let us know what Noriko decides. She is his mother and has every right to hold onto her son forever, under any circumstances—good or bad.

With all my love, Mitsuko

P.S. The next time you send us a picture of Hisashi, please be sure that there are no scary women in the background. Perhaps you didn't notice her. Anyway, I'd like a nicer picture of Hisashi to keep on my mirror.

Mitsuko read the letter to herself and added a few more sentences that were intended to give Ichiro further encouragement. Then she carefully folded her letter, put it in an envelope, and addressed it to the Aki-Torii Grille as her brother instructed. Taking off her bathrobe, she put on a clean cocktail uniform, pinned her name badge—Mitzi Mishima—on the lapel, and sprayed her hair into a big bouffant. She looked at herself. Her face was still unlined and her dark hair shone. Maybe she wasn't too old to be a mother after all.

On her way to work she stopped at the Glendive Post Office. The sooner Ichiro received her letter the sooner she'd know whether this Thanksgiving she'd have something beyond her wildest dreams to be grateful for.

Chapter 28

SEVEN HUNDRED BRONZE LANTERNS were lit at the Sumiyoshi Taisha Shinto Shrine to commemorate the festival of Shichi-Go-San on November 15, the day children of three, five, and seven years old are celebrated and blessed by the local priests. It was Kazuko's big day, and the Fujiwaras, Ichiro, Hisashi, and I joined them to celebrate Kazuko's fifth birthday. Setsuko dressed her in a silk vermillion kimono and quilted vest. She wore wooden clogs and her long hair was pulled back with opalescent barrettes into tiny bunches.

I handed out the traditional red and white candy sticks in bags decorated with turtles and cranes. Hisashi sucked on his "thousand-year-old candy," which turned syrupy in his mouth and dribbled down his chin. I wet a handkerchief in a nearby fountain and wiped his face so it wouldn't dribble on to his navy-blue and white sailor suit.

Ichiro put two coins into the shrine's offering box telling me, "I hope the gods won't mind I'm making an offering for my niece *and* our son. I want to be sure that he has a long and prosperous life, too, even if it isn't his special day yet." Hisashi was just a little more than a year old. He ran after his cousin Kazuko, begging for her attention.

Mitsuo tossed a baseball to Ichiro. "Let's play catch, Uncle." Ichiro took off his jacket and handed it to me. I gave him a worried look. It wasn't good for him to be exerting himself, especially in the cool November weather, but Ichiro resented it whenever I mentioned he should take it easy. I called out to Hisashi and told him to sit next to me. I gave him a toy fire engine, and he pushed it back and forth in the pebbles and prattled to himself, "Stop. Go. Wait." I was amazed at how many words he knew and expected very soon he would be speaking in complete phrases.

At fifteen, my nephew Mitsuo was tall and gangly and very athletic. He threw the ball high in the air over Ichiro's head and it rolled toward the fountain. Ichiro ran after it and threw it back to Mitsuo, who caught it then yelled, "Uncle, you're out."

A few minutes later, Mitsuo held Ichiro's arm to steady him. Ichiro confessed, "I think I overdid it. We'll have to suspend the game." He sat down on the bench next to me, and I saw he was drenched in sweat and looked pale. He put his jacket back on and tucked his hands into his pockets to warm them. "I'll be thirty this Christmas, but I already feel like an old man. Noriko, you should turn me in for a younger guy."

I played along with Ichiro. "I would, but I can't find anyone who is as smart and handsome as you. Any other man would bore me in no time at all. You always have something fascinating to share with me."

Mitsuo interrupted our conversation. "Uncle, do you remember when you promised to take me to another baseball game? Mr. Fukutake gave me a pair of tickets for next season. Will you be up for it?"

"So now the tables are turned—you're treating your old uncle, huh? Of course, I'll go with you. Maybe this year the Tigers will finally win the pennant. Have you been studying the rules?"

"Yes, I'll be able to call a few of the plays, and we can see which one of us is up on the player stats."

"You're trying to compete with me, Mitsuo?" With a pained expression on his face, he added, "Before I know it, you'll be teaching me instead of the other way around."

The grounds of the shrine were emptying of worshippers. Hisashi was exhausted from chasing after Kazuko. I thought it best to take him home, but Ichiro insisted on going back to work. I hated being separated from him, and I felt that his duties at the restaurant were taking precedence over our time together as a family. Hisashi was becoming more needy, and I was feeling neglected as well.

I begged Ichiro to come home with us, but he argued with me, "If I don't show up at work now, it will just be harder for me to catch up on everything and I'll have to stay even later tomorrow night. This way I can spread things out. Don't expect me home until midnight at the earliest."

Riding home on the subway, I watched with jealousy as husbands and wives looked lovingly at the children they had just honored. Was I like a wife whose husband was away at war? Or one whose husband worked on a steamer sailing for months between Japan and China? Or a wife whose sick husband was confined to a hospital? I wondered which of these three scenarios might be the most difficult to endure. I hated feeling sorry for myself, but I was too weak to resist the urge. Looking at Hisashi's beautiful eyes and his rosebud mouth smiling at me as the train rocked back and forth, I resolved to stay strong for him.

⌒

THE PRIVATE DINING ROOMS on the second floor of the Aki-Torii were filled with partygoers feting children on their special day. Waitresses rushed up and down the narrow wooden stairs trying to keep up with patrons who poured into the restaurant for dinner. Mitsuo went into the kitchen to help the chef, and Setsuko stood at the front of the restaurant next to the cash register. Akiko went upstairs to her bedroom to do her homework. She would soon graduate middle school and was already making plans for her future—she thought about becoming a teacher. Unlike her brother, the restaurant business held no appeal for her.

Ichiro passed through the main dining room to his office at the back of the restaurant. The bartender greeted him, and some customers waved, pleased to see him. The smell of grilled chicken and pork ribs turned his stomach, and he tasted bile in his mouth. Taking a bottle out of his jacket, he swallowed a handful of pills without bothering to pour himself a glass of water. Sitting in his chair, he waited for the nausea to pass. His desk was piled high with a week's worth of bills, delivery notices, and receipts. He felt so tired, as he stared at the ledger, the lines receded and returned like seaweed floating on the surface of Osaka Bay.

Ichiro turned on the radio to drown out the clattering of dishes and shouts of *arigato* and *kampai* coming from the dining room. Mahler's *Fifth Symphony* was playing on the radio. Tonight, the exquisite beauty of the symphony was almost unbearable. He thought, *If I were asked what piece of music should be played at my funeral, this would be it.* Closing his eyes, he imagined himself sitting next to the composer at his villa on the shores of Wörthersee Lake in Austria, breathing in the fragrant country air while gray doves cooed to one another under the eaves of the villa and sailboats glided across the tranquil water. The music begins with a death march, but by the time Mahler reaches the *Adagietto,* written for strings and solo harp, the piece turns into a love letter for his bride, Alma. The brass instruments are cast aside to express his heartfelt desire for Alma.

Setsuko knocked on the office door. Picking up his pencil, Ichiro tried to look busy and ran his hands through his hair to make himself presentable. "There's a letter here for you, Ichiro. It must be from your sister because the return address is Glendive, Montana. Excuse me for being inquisitive, but why would she write here instead of to your home address?"

Ichiro thought quickly and came up with a plausible explanation. He had not anticipated that Setsuko would discover the letter since he usually went through the daily mail first. "I'm planning a surprise for Noriko. I didn't want her to see Mitsuko's letter before I've had a chance to read it. It involves her and her husband Harry."

"I hope whatever you're planning will do her some good. I only want what's best for my sister. I'm concerned about her. I don't know if it's such a good idea she's gone back to work. She's looking haggard, and she worries about you. Right now, you're like two trains going in opposite directions. That's no way for a marriage to survive, Ichiro."

Ichiro removed his glasses. He was in the habit of wearing them all the time when he worked because his vision was worsening. "What do you suggest I do? I wouldn't consider asking you for a raise, Setsuko. You have been more than generous to me, and very patient. The medicine that I am taking is expensive. The government pays for a good deal of it, but not everything and so I have to build up my reserves. And Hisashi is also costing us more than I had anticipated. Eventually I'm going to have to cover Hisashi's private school tuition. He is such a smart boy. I would hate to see him not being sufficiently stimulated and denied an excellent education. Without a proper education, he'll never get ahead in life."

"Children are happy with whatever you give them. It's not material things that count. What they really want is your love and attention. I'm sure you notice how Hisashi's eyes light up whenever he sees you. He is such an enchanting child, and he makes every effort to please you."

Ichiro felt as if Setsuko had stuck a knife in his back, but he forced a smile. "I suppose you're right. You know a lot more about raising children than I do. I'm still learning how to be a father. I didn't have a good example. My father devoted himself to his work and to my stepmother."

Setsuko looked as if she wanted to know what was in the letter, but she left it on his desk. Breaking the silence between them, she said, "Why don't you and Noriko go to Arashiyama? A day of forest bathing does wonders for the body and soul. I'll take care of Hisashi for the day. You'll have nothing to worry about."

Gesturing to the paperwork, he said, "I'm drowning. I don't think I can spare even a few hours."

"Your thirty-first birthday is this December, I believe. I'd like to give you and my sister an early present. You'll both come back relaxed and rested, and it will give you time to be together. You know how busy we get in December."

Feeling guilty and ashamed, Ichiro acquiesced.

"I'll leave you now. Kazuko is going to be sick from eating all that candy if I don't stop her." She quietly closed the door.

Ichiro picked up a letter opener and carefully cut the envelope flap. As he read Mitsuko's letter, he could hear her voice pleading with him: *You must think about this one hundred times.* She then said that she and Harry were ecstatic at the prospect of adopting Hisashi. *We will raise him as if he were our own son and give him everything we can to lessen your heartache. Knowing that he is well cared for by us and loved may be some consolation to you both and will give you the energy you need to get well.*

There it was—the answer he had been waiting for. He felt a mixture of relief and ineffable sadness like a man who was given a positive diagnosis after months of living with a mysterious illness. Now that he knew he could count on his sister and her husband to take Hisashi, he could plan whatever flimsy future he could carve out for himself and Noriko. And to make himself feel less grief-stricken, he thought, *If I am well eventually, Noriko and I can have another child. My sister is not so fortunate, and this will give her what she has so longed for. Hisashi will be her reward for taking care of me when we were growing up and restitution for all the pain and suffering we endured together during the war.* Ichiro immediately wrote back to Mitsuko, begging her once again to give his son a good life. The final movement of Mahler's symphony ended as Ichiro put his letter into the envelope. Mahler had infused the *Rondo* with a sadness and despair that spoke loudly to Ichiro's soul. Was this music a premonition of the tragedies that befell Mahler: the tragic death of his firstborn daughter and his premature death at fifty-one? Was this music a harbinger of the sorrow that lay ahead for him and Noriko?

Ichiro turned the dial on the radio, searching for music that would prepare him for the arguments he would present to Noriko in the river town of Arashiyama. A military march might be fitting, he thought, but he could find nothing to give him the courage to face Noriko and tell her of his intentions. If he could have written a piece of music to communicate his thoughts and feelings he would have. Instead he would have to come up with the words that expressed his plan as forcefully and compassionately as possible.

Chapter 29

THE DAY AFTER WE celebrated Kazuko's special day, Ichiro surprised me with an invitation to Arashiyama outside Kyoto for a day of forest bathing. He assured me, "Your sister offered to watch Hisashi, and Kazuko will help her. She loves playing the little mother to our son. And you needn't worry about the expense of the trip. Setsuko is paying for everything as an early birthday present for me."

I was elated at the prospect of spending an entire day with my husband. I yearned for his attention and the closeness that once came so easily to us. Such a trip would make all our sacrifices less burdensome and lift some of the gloom that hung over my head day after day. And I could store the pleasures within my heart to carry me through whatever we might be forced to face in the coming weeks if we received bad news from the doctor. I deplored the sound of Dr. Shizumi's name. Although he was Ichiro's lifeline, it seemed he was always bringing us bad news.

When we left Hisashi with Setsuko and Kazuko, he grabbed my coat sleeve and pulled hard, tears running down his cheeks. I told him to be a good boy and assured him that Mama and Papa would be back for him that evening. I'm sure he didn't know what "evening" meant but he understood the words "be back" and calmed down.

Kazuko, in a very grown up voice, said, "Hisashi, I have a kite for you. We can go to the park and fly it."

When she showed it to him, he shouted, "Airplane!"

She ran down the dark-paneled hallway toward her bedroom and Hisashi chased after her. Ichiro and I rushed down the stairs to catch the train before he realized we were gone. I felt guilty not kissing him goodbye, but he would have cried all over again; and by the time we settled him, we would have missed our train or I would have decided it wasn't worth upsetting him despite desperately yearning for time alone with Ichiro.

The train ride from Osaka north to the resort town of Arashiyama took an hour. I rested my head against Ichiro's shoulder and drifted in and out of a light sleep. Disembarking the train at the station, Ichiro told the driver to take us to the Togetsutei ryokan where he had reserved a room for the day.

From the window of the inn, we watched the Oi River flowing east underneath the pylons of the trestle bridge. In another month, the hillside would be wrapped in a gray shroud and the cedar branches laden with pillows of white snow. Traditional river boats with green peaked roofs powered by two rowers, one at the front and one at the back, strained against the river current. Tourists enjoying the changing fall colors on the mountainside dangled their fingers in the icy cold water trying to touch the fish swimming just beneath the surface.

An attendant dressed in a kimono slid the shoji screen open and brought a lacquered tray with a brazier, which she placed on the tatami mats in our room. The dishes of a traditional *kaiseki* appeared one after the other. Each course was no more than little bites, but the food was exquisite and the accumulation soon filled me up. Ichiro watched with pleasure as I relished each dish. I manipulated the chop sticks and fed Ichiro, who seemed disinterested in the feast placed in front of us.

He observed, "It's good to see you have such a hardy appetite today. It must be the crisp mountain air. In ancient times monks wrapped a heated stone to their stomachs beneath their robes to ward off hunger until they reached their temples at the top of the mountains. That's where the name of this banquet comes from—kaiseki. We are much more fortunate than the abstaining priests because we can indulge ourselves. We don't have to stave off hunger with a stone."

"In one way it's true. But in another we are not so fortunate because they were taught that abstinence brings enlightenment, which is the highest state of the human spirit." I took a sip of tea and continued, "Enlightenment is always a struggle and most of us never reach it. That is why our spirit returns time and again, each time learning a new lesson on how to be a good person who is able to bring joy to others." Feeling nervous, I brushed my bangs away from my scar. Something about Ichiro's mood and demeanor upset me. He struck me as more formal and professorial than usual. I continued, "Perhaps we would have greater clarity about our purpose in life, with more sacrifice from time to time."

"Is that what your Reverend Mother has taught you, Noriko? I was near starvation during the war, and all I could think of was finding something to eat. Most days I subsisted on grasshoppers and rats. All the rice available went to the soldiers. We were left with nothing. The Emperor told us we were sacrificing for the war and we should feel good about it. I cried my eyes out when my father took my bicycle away; and I worried every day that my sister would die from working in the factory. Children were put to work, and then in the end we lost the war and many lives. So, what was it all for?"

"I suppose you are right, but the Reverend Mother says that, when we sacrifice for others, it is not really a sacrifice. It is a way of bringing joy to another person, and that is the greatest virtue that any human can possess." I then added, "Of course, it's always better to simply give without taking something from yourself." I felt our conversation was leading nowhere, that we were trying to fill the cavernous space growing between us. *What I need from Ichiro is for him to pledge his desire to live,* I thought. *And to put his arms around me and hold me tight.*

Ichiro walked out on the veranda; I followed him. The sun was warm on our faces, but the breeze from the Oi River was cold and made me shiver. I dipped my hand in the steamy water of our private hot tub. Ichiro took his clothes off and stepped in. I could see his ribs protruding from beneath his ashen skin. He looked like a victim of the war. I was shocked to see how much weight he had lost since returning from the hospital. He had gotten into the habit of weighing himself every day, so I knew he must realize how much weight he had lost in so short a time. Knowing his habits, I was sure he kept a daily record, but he hid it from me.

I unbuttoned my blouse and skirt and slid into the water beside him. Ichiro pressed his body against mine. I cupped my hands to hold the water and slowly dripped it over his head and onto his face.

"What are you doing?"

"This is to wash away your worries, Ichiro."

"I wish it was so easy." I slid my fingers down his back, my signal to him that I wished to make love, and he let out a sigh. He touched me between my legs and kissed my neck. The twisted branches of the pine trees hid us from view, and we took advantage of the privacy. I could feel Ichiro gathering his strength to enter me. He murmured "Star of Mine" repeatedly. I closed my eyes, transporting myself to sexual arousal and release. I felt whole and complete for the first time in many months.

Stepping out of the hot tub, we wrapped ourselves in kimonos and poured ourselves steaming cups of tea set over the brazier. After taking a few sips of the bittersweet brew, Ichiro spoke. "There is something I must ask of you, Noriko. Do you remember when I told you I thought of myself as an incompetent father and feared I might have to go to a sanatorium if I didn't show improvement? Unfortunately, my health is continuing to slip. I have horrible nightmares, and sometimes I see things that aren't there and other times I don't see things that are. Just recently I sent Harry and Mitsuko a photograph of you and Hisashi at the zoo, and the image of that hideous woman was in the photograph. I thought she had disappeared but she hadn't.

"And I'm continuing to lose weight—that is obvious. When you add it all up, I'm a poor specimen of a man. Dr. Shizumi has told me I'm to be admitted to a sanatorium for a minimum of six months. This is the only way I can hope to rid myself of this disease, which is slowly eating me up. You must see that."

"I see the man I love, and I pray every day that you will get better. That is what I see, Ichiro. I cannot accept the possibility that you will die."

"Well, you had better because there is a good chance that is where I'm headed, and even if I do survive, what will I do for a living? I think the only recourse for us is to give Hisashi to my sister and Harry to raise. I am convinced he'll be better off with them than with us."

I felt as if a bomb was exploding inside my brain. I could not take in all this information at once, and I felt anger rising up inside me. I tried to remain calm as I listened to this nonsense. I argued, "My sister has promised that, so long as you are able to work, you are guaranteed a job. We're one family, and we have a duty to one another; *giri*, duty to family, is not just a feudalistic idea to be kicked to the side of the road when something unfortunate happens to one of us. We have an obligation to take care of each other."

"That's all well and good, but I don't have the stamina to do a proper job. My father told me that I must always do my best, and I'm defiling my father's memory by failing so utterly. I'm failing you as your husband and I'm failing our son Hisashi as his father."

"Have you concluded that, if you give him away, you will have one less obligation? Is that what you are arguing, Ichiro? And what happens when you get better? Then what? I swear you will come to regret this."

"We can always have another child. Fortunately, you are healthy."

"No other baby can replace our firstborn. I can't imagine another child would be as precious to me as Hisashi, and whether you want to admit it or not, you have become attached to him too. I see how proud of him you are. And he adores you. He could hardly wait for you to come home from the hospital. He was so frustrated when you were away that he beat me with his fists. I can still feel him pounding at me, and I had no way to tell him you were coming home." I gasped for air, then said, "Shall I now tell him that he will be leaving the only home he has known and the parents who love him? And for what?"

"Attachment is the curse of the human race. We must be willing to detach ourselves from people, possessions, and outcomes. That is what the Buddha teaches."

"Since when have you become a follower of the Buddha? As far as I can tell you live without a spiritual belief of any sort. I have wanted to take you to the Tenrikyo temple in Nara, but you always resist, and I have learned to pick my battles." I picked up a towel and started drying my hair, then used my brush to detangle my curls. For an instant I had the urge to throw my brush at Ichiro to startle him into rethinking what he was saying.

I put my clothes back on while formulating a potential solution. "I'll plead with my father to help us while you are in the sanatorium. That will carry us through until you are discharged. Mother tells me that his business is thriving in Matsue. My father saved me once. Why wouldn't he save me again, especially when it involves his grandson?"

Ichiro lit a cigarette and blew the smoke out the open window. "You can't be serious, Noriko. You haven't heard a word from him since we married. He disapproves of me. And what makes you think he cares about you or Hisashi? He has made a life separate from us." His words stung but I had asked myself the same question many times. He continued. "I won't allow you to ask your father for anything. I'd rather be a beggar on the street than accept a handout from him."

"Ichiro, don't let pride get in the way of doing what we need to do to save ourselves and our son." Tears rolled down my cheeks from sadness and disappointment. I said, "Look at me, Ichiro. No mother could love her son more than I do. You and Hisashi are my life now. If someone were to tell me I could be a star of the Takarazuka in exchange for giving my son away, even for one day, I would say no. I used to think that the stage was my destiny, but experiencing the love I have for you and Hisashi makes that alternative pale by comparison."

I needed all the ammunition I could gather, and so I revealed what had happened between Mr. Ozu and me. "I never told you, but Mr. Ozu offered to audition me for a walk-on part in one of his movies. I would have had to go to Tokyo, and, of course, there was no guarantee that I would have made the grade. He even compared me to one of his young actresses! But I turned down his offer. By then I was so in love with you that I didn't want to risk losing you. Mr. Ozu spoke to me in a sarcastic tone when I rejected his offer. I will never forget what he said: 'The only difference between you and the star of my movie is that you lack confidence and you don't believe in yourself. You have all the other qualities necessary to succeed.' So, you see, even then, before we married, I saw that you were my destiny. You were my everything and you still are...except I have made room for Hisashi." I couldn't go on. I sobbed uncontrollably and pushed Ichiro away when he tried to put his arms around me.

Ichiro said, "It is no life for Hisashi to have two parents who are struggling to get through each day. No one would judge us harshly. Other Japanese families have given away children when faced with adversity."

"I don't care about other families. I only care about us. If we give him away, what will fill up my starving heart? Will I need to tie a hot stone over my heart so that I don't feel its emptiness? Perhaps one of the monks will lend me a *kaiseki* to carry around for the rest of my life."

I was exhausted and had run out of arguments. Ichiro saw my weakness, and he used the last of his arguments to pin me like a dead butterfly against a piece of paper. "You must say yes. I am your husband and it is your duty to obey me."

Nothing could have riled me more. I found a second wind. "Since when did I promise to be an obedient wife? When you married me I was an independent woman. The only reason I have gone along with everything you asked of me is because of your illness. That argument is wearing thin like a piece of parchment paper. I can't give you an answer to this. I need to think it through. No husband could ask more of a wife than what you have just asked of me."

Ichiro showed his temper for the first time that day. "The longer we wait the more difficult it will be for Hisashi. The older he gets the more he will remember about us and the harder it will be for him to adjust to his new parents. While he is still a toddler, he will easily make the transition from us to Mitsuko and Harry. He'll be calling them Mama and Papa in no time at all. And think how lucky he'll be to be an American boy. The possibilities for his future are endless there. In Japan life is stratified and a child's success depends too much on the status of his parents, but in America anyone can be president if they put their mind to it."

I thought, *Has Ichiro lost his mind?* I flailed around for one final argument. "Hisashi was conceived in love on our wedding night. Doesn't that tell you he is a very special child? Any child we might have in the future will never be born of the passion of our first union."

"This is true." He twisted my words. "And for this reason, that he is a special child, he deserves a happy life—or what you call a joyous life. I cannot promise him that. I feel as if I do not exist, that I have crossed over into an invisible world where only ghosts live. I am like the 'human vapor' in the horror movie I once saw."

"Wasn't it you who was making love to me, or was that my imagination?"

Ichiro forced a smile. "Lately, I haven't felt capable of making love to you. It must have been the miracle water you sprinkled over my head in the bath."

I slapped Ichiro's face to stop him from mocking me. "Don't ask me to give up our son!" I felt as if burning nettles were stuck in my throat. I was choking on my words. Walking out onto the balcony, I caught the first star peeking through the evening's canopy and the moon hanging low in the sky between the rise and fall of the nearby hills. It felt as if the stars and the moon were mocking me.

Ichiro followed me and whispered, "If you love me as much as I love you, you'll do as I ask. Put aside your feelings and try to understand mine." He then slipped his hand inside my blouse. I pushed his icy cold hand from my breast and turned my back on the moon as it started its climb into the darkening sky.

"You think that you are being magnanimous, Ichiro, but I can't help but accuse you of being selfish. You're trying to take away my right to claim Hisashi as my son, our son. It is inconceivable."

Ichiro dressed in silence. I watched him put on his father's navy-blue tie and straighten it in the mirror over the sink. His face was expressionless, and I clenched my teeth to keep from saying anything more that could irreparably wound Ichiro. But for the first time since we married, I thought of Ichiro as a coward and a quitter.

Chapter 30

I SAT NEXT TO the window on the train ride back from Arashiyama without saying a word to Ichiro. Along the tracks, three-story apartments with bamboo-fenced balconies burdened with wet laundry and glowing hibachis leaned against one another for support. A single ember from a hibachi could pass from one apartment to another, I thought, setting an entire neighborhood on fire like a contagious germ that spreads from one person to another through a single cough. I shuddered to think of the unhealthy conditions these families were forced to live in without the benefit of clean air and ocean breezes.

Ichiro buried his head in the evening's paper. I was too distraught to read it. He reported the news of the day: "Construction plans in Japan's major cities are already underway in preparation for the 1964 Olympics. The journalist predicts that revenue from the Olympics will be the capstone of the country's economic boom." As if speaking to himself, he said, "I wonder how I can take advantage of all these developments. Remaining in Setsuko's employ is not going to get me anywhere." Ichiro was like a teeter totter—up one minute and down the next. He had earlier predicted his death and now he was thinking about what he could do to improve our financial condition. My head throbbed, and I couldn't carry on a conversation with him. All I could think of was the outrageous proposal he had presented to me. Did he think that giving Hisashi away would lead to a better life for us? Or had he totally given up on us—on me?

The train came to a halt at the Namba Station after passing through Kyoto. Neon lights blinked on and off, enticing customers with the promise of fresh sushi, premium sake, and American phonograph records. Climbing the stairs to the Fujiwara's apartment above the Aki-Torii, I heard Hisashi and Kazuko screaming at one another. Hisashi's face was red from crying. When we entered the apartment, he could not get any words out to explain his frustration.

Kazuko sobbed, "I was holding Hisashi and he bit my ear." I asked why. Hisashi was normally such a loving child and adored his cousin, Kazuko.

"I told him he couldn't take the airplane kite home with him. I said he could play with it here with me. It's mine. And that's when he bit me, and so I slapped him."

Setsuko intervened. "Kazuko, you shouldn't hit your cousin. He's just a toddler. He doesn't know how to tell you he's upset, and so he bites. Little ones do this. You must be more understanding, but I'm sorry it happened. Does your ear hurt?"

Kazuko choked back tears and nodded.

"Let me put some ice on it. It will stop hurting in no time." Setsuko scooped up her daughter in her arms and said, "It's been a long day. I think Hisashi needs to go to bed. Don't punish him, Noriko. He just misses the two of you when you're away. Tomorrow all will be forgotten. Children, thankfully, have short memories and are easily bribed. You might just give him some candy." Turning to Ichiro, she said, "I hope your day in Arashiyama was everything you hoped it would be."

Lying, he said, "Yes, it was a breath of fresh air. Noriko and I needed time alone." He put his arm around my shoulder. He sounded like such a hypocrite. He was becoming quite the actor.

I crouched down to Hisashi's eye level and asked him, "Would you like a kite of your own?" He smiled. "Well, how about we go to the store tomorrow and I'll find you another kite? And when summer comes, we can take it to the beach and sail it high above the waves. What do you think of that?" He had never been to the beach or played in the sand. I promised myself that Ichiro and I would find the time to go. When I was a little girl, I had spent some of my happiest times swimming with my father, and I didn't want to deny my son this pleasure.

"Yes, Mama, please."

I said, "We've taken up too much of your time. Hisashi looks like he's going to fall asleep any minute. I better take him home. Ichiro, are you coming?"

"I need to put together the end of the month report for Setsuko. Are you all right going home by yourself?"

"Of course. Why should tonight be different from any other night?" For once, I was glad that Ichiro was staying at work. I needed to sort out my feelings and consider my options. It was easier for me to think through everything without being distracted by Ichiro's glum face and intermittent sighs.

I put Hisashi in his stroller and joined the throng of evening commuters. There were no empty seats on the subway train. I reached for a strap to steady myself, and removing one of my gloves, I touched my forehead. As I suspected, I was running a fever. I could count on the fingers of one hand the days and nights when I felt well recently, but I refused to see the doctor, afraid of what he might tell me. I expected that it was just a bad cold coming on since I had been vaccinated to prevent me from contracting what Ichiro had. I thought, *I can't even name the condition it is so terrifying, this awful disease that has driven Ichiro to such a tortured state.* All I knew was that I couldn't afford to get sick.

I noticed a well-dressed man watching me; without saying a word, he stood up and motioned for me take his seat. As we exchanged places, he looked down at Hisashi and said, "Forgive me for being impertinent, but your little boy is so beautiful, just like his mother."

Embarrassed by his compliment, I looked away. When the subway reached our stop, the man got off. I was afraid he might follow me home, but instead he wished me well and walked in the opposite direction. I was flattered by his compliment, and it reminded me of the times at the tearoom when men looked at me admiringly. I used to pretend that the tearoom was my stage and I was an actress playing the role of a waitress waiting to be discovered by a wealthy businessman who would whisk me away to his estate somewhere in the woods, where we'd stroll among the bamboo and float in a rowboat downstream. My imagination was a gift and a trap! Or that I'd be standing in front of a camera speaking my lines as the crew adjusted the lights to best complement my features and make sure my scar was invisible.

The moment we entered our empty apartment, Hisashi woke up and started crying all over again. I took camphor out of the medicine cabinet and rubbed it on his gums to relieve his teething pain. He usually drank from a cup now, but tonight I gave him a bottle of warm milk to comfort him and carried him in my arms, quietly singing "You Are My Sunshine." It was one of the American cowboy songs on a record Mitsuko had sent us. Before I could sing a second chorus, Hisashi was fast asleep.

I settled him underneath his comforter, locked the door to our apartment, and ran downstairs to the telephone booth on the corner. Pushing the door open, I was assaulted by the terrible smell of stale cigarettes and rotting food. When I caught my breath, I dropped several coins in the slot and instructed the operator to connect me to 07-12-035 in Hiroshima. On the third ring I heard my mother's voice. She sounded half-asleep.

"Mother, I'm sorry to call you so late, but I must speak with you."

"What is it, Noriko? You sound frantic."

"Ichiro told me today that Dr. Shizumi wants to admit him to a sanatorium. He's not responding well to the drugs. He could be away for as much as six months." I felt as if I was suffocating. I opened the door a crack to let in some fresh air. I needed my mother's advice and some words of comfort. She did not disappoint me.

"I'll try to send you some money, and I'll ask your father to help out. His mistress will just have to make some sacrifices for the good of the family."

I gripped the receiver. "I've already suggested that. Ichiro says he won't accept any money from our family. He says it would be too humiliating. We are already getting money from his sister. He's admitted that he feels like a charity case."

"I'll have to figure out a way to send you some money without his knowing about it, then."

I wiped the perspiration from my forehead. The stuffiness of the booth was not helping me. I thought I might faint, but I needed to tell my mother more. "I'm afraid his pride gets in the way of thinking rationally. His father left him a legacy that doesn't serve him well now. 'Always be proud of yourself,' he was told. We are way past worrying about pride. And he has proposed a shocking solution, as he calls it, to our temporary dilemma. He wants to give Hisashi to his sister and her husband, whom I don't even know. He says they can give him a better life than we can. He went on and on about how great life will be for Hisashi in America—all kinds of possibilities for his future that we can't provide. He romanticizes life there when he really knows nothing about it other than what he reads in books and newspapers. And when his sister shares with him her own difficulties he ignores them."

There was silence at the other end of the phone. "Mother, are you still there?"

"Has he lost his mind? And have you lost yours to even entertain such an idea? It's absurd."

"I don't know, Mother. Ichiro swears that knowing Hisashi is well cared for will help him in his recovery. He confessed that he's afraid he's going to die if things continue the way they are. He admits that he is unable to make any provisions for us. Whatever he makes is going right out the door. He says every day is a struggle, and he confessed to me he's been having nightmares and hallucinations. He calls himself Vapor Man."

Kimie snapped, "I'm sure once Ichiro is back from the sanatorium and feels better, he will realize how ridiculous this notion is. You must not agree to this. Hisashi is my grandson and he's your firstborn, which earns him a special place in our family. If you let him go, you'll regret your decision forever."

"That's what I argued, but Ichiro thinks his plan is best for me and for Hisashi. And he says that giving Hisashi to his sister is a way of paying her back for all that she did for him during the war. She can't have children of her own. Something bad happened to her, and she lives with this disappointment every day."

"And you're supposed to sacrifice for his sister? What hogwash." My mother cleared her throat. "Noriko, you must be courageous. We live in the twentieth century. Women have rights, and if it means you must defy your husband to keep your son, so be it. I did not raise you to be a timid woman. You used to be such a daring girl who never shied away from a challenge! What happened to the girl who cut her hair like a boy's so she could be a star? Have you turned into 'a monk for three days,' giving up just because things are difficult? You did not travel this far in life to give up now. You'll always be Hisashi's mother, no matter what happens to Ichiro, and I shall always be his grandmother."

"I need to go. I left Hisashi alone upstairs so I could speak with you. He'll be frightened if he wakes up and I'm not there."

"Think about how he feels when he wakes up in a strange bed in America, and you are not there…then what? Will Ichiro's sister know what to tell him to make him feel better? I doubt it."

"Please listen to me…" I hung up before she could say anything more. Mrs. Masamoto, our landlady, was standing behind the curtain at her window, spying on me. As I passed her door on the first floor, she opened it.

"Mrs. Uchida, how is that sweet little boy of yours? I sometimes hear him on his rocking horse above my head."

"I hope he's not disturbing you. He does so love to ride his rocking horse."

"Not at all." She put her hand on my shoulder to stop me. "Please thank your husband for fixing my clock. I thought I'd have to throw it away, but it's working perfectly now. I offered to pay him, but he wouldn't hear of it. He's quite the handyman."

"He's like that. Always so helpful. I'm very lucky. Whatever it is—the gas stove, a dripping faucet, a running toilet—he knows how to take care of it." Wiping the perspiration from my forehead, I told Mrs. Masamoto, "I've left Hisashi alone. I need to get back upstairs. Please excuse me."

After unlocking the apartment door, I checked on Hisashi; he was fast asleep with Chaya purring contentedly next to him. Relieved, I opened the medicine cabinet, drank some of Ichiro's cough medicine, and got undressed.

I pulled my comforter away from Hisashi so he would not be exposed to whatever was brewing inside me. The cough medicine worked, and I fell into a deep sleep. Immediately, I was aware of being carried into an eerie dream world so real I thought I was awake. I stood in front of a large clock, its hands frozen to 8:15 a.m. when the bomb, Little Boy, was dropped on Hiroshima by the enemy Americans. All around me were buckled cement slabs and people struggling past ruined buildings, the skin peeling off their faces and backs. To my left was the Okawa River; fish were floating upside down on top of the steaming water. Suddenly Ichiro appeared on a bicycle, and in a basket on the handles was Hisashi dressed in his cowboy outfit, a scarf tied around his nose. Ichiro stopped and yelled to me above the din of cries and screams, "I'm taking Hisashi to the mountains where he'll be safe. Then I'll come back for you, and we'll wait together for the storm to be over." A violent wind rose up and the air was filled with ashes from the fires that burned unabated. A river of mud swirled around my feet.

I screamed out, "Don't leave me, Ichiro."

He didn't hear me. Tying a scarf around his mouth, he headed into the manmade storm. I watched as Ichiro and Hisashi crossed a bridge. As soon as they reached the other side, it crumbled behind them. I tried to run after them, but my shoe caught in the mud and I fell down onto a steel spike. I looked in disbelief as the blood drained from my body. I was lying in a pool of my own blood in my nightmare when I jolted awake. Opening my eyes, Ichiro kneeled beside me.

"When I came in you were screaming in your sleep, Noriko."

I felt disoriented. I sat up in bed, trying to gather my thoughts. "I dreamed I was in Hiroshima and it was the day the bomb fell. I haven't dreamed about that in a very long time. You took Hisashi away on a bicycle. I watched you disappear through the smoke and ash. I tried to stop you from leaving me but I was stuck in the heavy mud. I couldn't move, and then I felt myself dying."

Trying to make sense of the dream, Ichiro said, "That's very unusual—to dream your own death. Usually people imagine themselves falling and then they wake up before they hit the pavement. It's part of the survival instinct. Do you know what brought this dream on?"

"I took some of your cough medicine—perhaps it's too strong for me. But I suspect that it's something else." I took a deep breath and went on. "I think I was trying to sort out how I should respond to your proposal. The dream is saying that I cannot live without you and you are right to send Hisashi away, that he will be better off with your sister than with either of us. I can't believe I'm saying this. It is what you want, isn't it?"

"It's not a question of what I want. I didn't choose to get sick. I didn't choose for my mother to die. I didn't choose to be sent away by my father, who left me without a penny to my name." Ichiro was unraveling before my eyes. "I'm sure Hisashi will thank us someday for the sacrifice we made for his benefit. He will be a man who will do great things." His shoulders slumped. "If he stays with us, he could turn out to be like me, a dying man without direction and purpose."

I felt as if Ichiro had stabbed me in the heart. No one was coming to rescue me, and I did not have enough faith in myself to take matters into my own hands—at least not yet. As the time for Hisashi to leave us would grow closer, I would make one last-ditch effort to reverse the course of our lives.

Chapter 31

THE LAW OFFICES OF Charles Dunn were on the second floor of the Dion Building on South Merrill Avenue in Glendive. Harry parked his truck on the street and walked upstairs, anxious to hear Charles's opinion about bringing Harry's nephew from Osaka to the United States in order to adopt him.

A large Christmas tree in the lawyer's waiting room was already shedding its needles although Christmas was still a few days away. It must have been drying out from the radiator. It was only 2:45 p.m. but Harry was early for his appointment—a habit he picked up in the army. He sat down on a wooden bench and flipped through the pages of *Fly, Rod and Reel*.

Fifteen minutes later, Charles Dunn, a tall man with salt and pepper hair and a studious face that elicited confidence from anyone who came to him for advice, strode into the waiting room. He shook Harry's hand. "Hope I haven't kept you waiting too long. I was on the telephone with Governor Babcock. How's Mitzi doing? I haven't been to the Jordan in I don't know how long. Can't seem to get out from behind my desk. End of the year, everyone wants everything tied up in a neat little bow. And I'm not talking about presents." He chuckled at his joke, which sounded to Harry like he had been using it all day.

"Mitzi is fine. She's working too hard, but that's nothing new. She never seems able to sit down, even for a minute. She doesn't know the meaning of the word no. I tell her that 'no' is a complete sentence, but she just looks at me, puzzled. Sometimes I'm not sure her English is as good as I give her credit for. But then other times she catches on real fast. I don't think I would do half as well as she does if we had stayed in Japan and I had tried to learn their language. It's amazing how she's adjusted to life here. Right down to making great apple pie and macaroni and cheese."

Switching from pleasantries to the reason Harry was there, Charles said, "Mitzi must be getting impatient to know what we can do about bringing your nephew to the United States."

Charles opened his tobacco pouch, removed a pinch, then pressed the leaves into the bowl of his pipe. He struck a match and sucked air through the mouthpiece. His office smelled faintly of tobacco, which seemed to fit the season.

"I won't beat around the bush, Harry. It's rather complicated. I received a letter from the Immigration and Naturalization Service. In order that he is deemed eligible for adoption, he must be classified as an orphan according to current law, which means that one or both parents have died, disappeared, or the child has been abandoned, and none of the above fits this situation."

Harry knew from his time in the army there was always "fine print," however, which might point to a loophole. "What if his parents were to waive their parental rights? Is that a possibility?"

"It's a lot to ask of any parent. You're going to have to instruct the Uchidas they will need to check off that box on their application. And there is another problem. Hisashi could be brought to the US by obtaining an immigrant visa, but the quota for Japanese citizens is oversubscribed. Right now, only 180 Japanese are being allowed to emigrate to the US without extenuating circumstances. President Kennedy is trying to increase the quota as part of his plan to improve US-Japan relations, but it could take a long time, so that won't help your nephew. At least not in the time frame you've set for yourself."

"Right you are. According to the letters we have received from Ichiro's wife, he doesn't seem to be responding well to the drugs he's on; and now Noriko writes that she's not feeling well either. We're just praying that she's not heading toward a diagnosis of tuberculosis. It's a bad situation. They're running out of money. Mitzi and I do what we can but unfortunately our means are limited. Mind you, I'm not complaining. Under normal circumstances, I'd say I was making a decent living, but this situation isn't normal."

His voice cracking, Harry added, "It would break Mitzi's heart if we received a denial. All she can think about now is becoming a mother to this little boy, and she's very concerned about her brother's health. You know, her mother died of tuberculosis when Mitzi was just five years old, so all of this dredges up bad memories."

Charles stood up. He turned his worn leather desk chair around a few times as if he was contemplating a problem that needed to be considered from all sides. "There is another option. It's a long shot, but that's what you need. Why don't you contact Congressman Jim Battin, who is on the House Judiciary Committee? You supported him in the election, didn't you?"

"Sure did. He spoke to the VFW. Great guy and a top-notch representative for the state of Montana. Plus, Halliburton has been helpful to him over the years, not that I'm part of the company's top brass. But the fact that I'm a Halliburton man might carry some weight."

"Well, I think you should write a persuasive letter asking for his help. Let's see what he comes up with. If you can, put it on Halliburton letterhead."

"Is there anything that Governor Babcock can do?"

"No. Although the state of Montana will be asked to do their due diligence to assure the Feds that you and Mitzi will be good parents. They'll dig around for ghosts in your closet."

"Ghosts such as?"

"Bankruptcy, drinking problems, anything like that." Charles leaned forward, waiting for Harry's response.

"Innocent on all counts." Then Harry stood up and dug his wallet out of his back pocket. "I thought you might like to see a picture of Hisashi. He's wearing the cowboy outfit Mitzi and I sent him on his first birthday. He's probably outgrown it by now."

"What a cute boy," Charles said after taking the photo. "Looks a lot like you and Mitzi. Good thing, too. The Montana Department of Social Services likes to put like with like, meaning that the child is Japanese and that's your background, too. The boy will fit right in. And of course, he and Mitzi are related by blood, which makes your case even stronger."

Checking his watch, Harry put his parka on and took his Halliburton cap out of his pocket. "I've taken up enough of your time. Thanks for your advice. I'll get right on that letter after Christmas. I don't expect anyone to be doing much business over the holiday—except you, of course." Charles shook Harry's hand. "Charles, please send me a bill. No freebies."

"Let's call this a friendly visit. If you get somewhere with Congressman Battin, I'll start running the meter. He might have something up his sleeve that we haven't thought of that could expedite all of this."

Harry walked to his pickup truck, climbing into the cab as a funeral procession passed, slowly heading toward the cemetery. The *Glendive Ranger Review* had carried the story that morning. A teenager had tried to jump the railroad tracks. His legs had been severed, and he bled to death on the way to the hospital. The article said the boy was sixteen years old and had been living in Glendive with his widowed mother. Harry imagined the cemetery workers lowering the boy's coffin into the ground, and the grieving mother inconsolable at the grave site. It is risky business being a parent, but Harry felt he was prepared for it, the good times and the bad. Wasn't life a gamble anyway? He thought about the day he took Mitzi to the hospital when she lost their baby. She didn't recover from the pain and sorrow for months. He tried to hide his disappointment, but sometimes it came out when she'd look longingly at a mother with a stroller shopping at J. C. Penney's or a dad taking his son fly fishing. Would they really be given a second chance at being parents? For Mitzi's sake—and his too—he hoped so.

∾

AFTER CHRISTMAS, HARRY WROTE to Congressman Battin, and within a few days he received a response:

January 15, 1963

Dear Mr. Mishima:

Thank you for your letter of December 30 outlining your desire to adopt your nephew from Japan and the problems you have encountered with quota restrictions being what they are. I would be happy to introduce a private bill that would circumvent the necessity of applying for a visa and waive some of the ordinary restrictions set in the law. A private bill is normally for individuals seeking asylum in the US, but this case, while most unusual, might qualify for special dispensation. I must have the name of the child. If the House passes this bill, it will go to the Senate and then onto President Kennedy for his signature. The entire process could take up to a year, but I'm encouraged by my initial conversations with the White House and representatives of our Committee and believe we can look forward to a positive outcome. You are doing a very good thing for this little boy.

With best wishes, I am sincerely yours,

James F. Battin, Member of Congress

Harry showed Mitsuko the letter. "You are a miracle worker, Harry."

"Not quite. And I can't believe I omitted Hisashi's name and his address from the letter. I'm usually so careful. Army training. But I guess I was so excited I forgot something that basic. Anyway, no harm. I'll get him the information and then we'll wait for his instructions."

Mitsuko asked, "Do you think there is a chance?"

"Between Charles and me, we'll do our best. He hasn't made any promises, but reading between the lines, I think we might win our case."

Chapter 32

1963

ICHIRO'S ROOM AT THE sanatorium overlooked an allée of cherry trees that had yet to bloom. A wrought-iron gate at the end of the driveway was locked to protect outsiders from exposure to tubercular patients. Ichiro had been admitted in January against his wishes, but Dr. Shizumi told him he had no choice. Sitting at his desk, Ichiro filled out the US immigration forms for his son. He pressed his pen hard to make sure his answers were legible in triplicate.

Are the mother and father of the child deceased? He answered no.

If no, please explain the reason for this application. Ichiro wrote: "Child's father has tuberculosis. His prognosis is uncertain (doctor's report attached). Mother of child in weakened condition. Parents are in dire financial straits. Child's aunt and uncle living in Glendive, Montana, and citizens of the United States, are prepared to take custody of child, nineteen-month-old Hisashi Uchida, born on August tenth, 1961 in Osaka, Japan."

Are parents willing to forego their parental rights so the child can be considered an eligible orphan according to US law? Noriko had already answered yes and signed the forms. Ichiro made sure of that when she visited him at the sanatorium a few weeks earlier. Seeing Noriko weep as she signed the papers, Ichiro almost lost his resolve. Her words still echoed in his ears: "I may be signing this paper that I am giving up my maternal rights, but in my heart I know it's a lie. I will never stop thinking of myself as Hisashi's mother until the day I die, and no government, no person—not even you—can take that away from me."

She went on. "I pray, once Hisashi is gone, the guilt that you feel for not giving him the life you think he deserves will go away and you'll recover. It is only for this reason that what we are about to do makes any sense to me. I am trading my son's life for yours, Ichiro. Don't ever forget that. Your survival will be proof that I have made the right choice. And someday I will see Hisashi again, and I'll have the chance to beg for his forgiveness."

"Forgiveness. You are doing him an enormous favor, Noriko."

If Ichiro could have put his hands over his ears and blocked out Noriko's indictment, he would have. Instead he told her to trust him.

Referring to a calendar hanging on the wall over his desk, Ichiro dated his signature: March 30, 1963. He then put an X through the space on the calendar, marking off one more day of his confinement. Soon it would be spring, and the delicate pink petals of the cherry trees would be blown by the wind like snow falling from heaven. He remembered how Hisashi stretched out his hands in the park trying to catch the petals, which were too delicate to hold.

Neatly folding the application, Ichiro put it in an envelope addressed to the US consulate in Kobe, counted out the correct number of stamps, and gave the envelope to the attendant at the front desk to mail. Then he joined a fellow inpatient for their regular board game of Go.

Joji Yasuda was a ranked Go master but he looked forward to playing with Ichiro because he was a clever opponent and quickly learned from his mistakes. Mr. Yasuda had placed the board on the floor and filled the bowls with black and white stones. "Shall I give you an advantage today, Mr. Uchida?"

"Yes. I'll play the black stones."

"Then you have the privilege of going first."

Ichiro tried to concentrate on the game, but he kept thinking about filling out the application for his son to go to America, so he kept making mistakes an amateur would have committed. One after another Mr. Yasuda captured the black stones from the nineteen-line board, expanding his territory. Ichiro knew he was in trouble. He could see in his mind's eye the end of the game.

Mr. Yasuda said, "You have employed a suicide strategy today."

"A suicide strategy?" Ichiro repeated flatly. "I have certainly played myself into a corner. I apologize. I haven't been concentrating. Let's count the stones to determine the winner, although it's quite obvious to me."

"I can see right now that white wins one hundred and forty-six to one hundred and six," said Mr. Yasuda.

"I squandered my advantage, didn't I? But don't give up on me yet. To-morrow I'll try to be a better pupil."

"That's the attitude. There's always tomorrow. Not only in the game of Go but in the game of life. That's what I like so much about playing a daily game—it reminds me there are always second and third chances to redeem myself. No point in regretting past mistakes. What's passed can't be undone. We just have to forge ahead." Ichiro wondered how Mr. Yasuda had such boundless optimism in the face of his illness and age. He was at least sixty, and anyone of his age with TB was usually taking a slow walk to the grave. But in spite of everything, he looked robust and always had a smile on his face.

Ichiro and Mr. Yasuda put the stones in the silk bag. Bowing to one another, they walked in opposite directions down the glistening white corridor to their rooms. Ichiro turned around expectantly. "Until tomorrow, Mr. Yasuda."

The other bed in Ichiro's room was empty. His roommate, Mr. Yamamoto, had been discharged that morning, leaving Ichiro alone until another patient was assigned to his room. Ichiro already missed Mr. Yamamoto's company. He shared Ichiro's passion for baseball, and the two men spent many afternoons arguing over the future of the Hanshin Tigers and the Yomiuri Giants, Mr. Yamamoto's home team. At seventy-five, Mr. Yamamoto was a retired salary man of the team's owner, Yomiuri Conglomerate. As Mr. Yamamoto packed to leave the sanatorium, he promised Ichiro free tickets to a game. Ichiro expressed his gratitude and added, "When my son Hisashi is older, I'll take him to a baseball game. It's good for fathers and sons to have something in common besides a family name." He was surprised at how easy it was to lie about his son. He wondered what Mr. Yamamoto would think of him if he knew the truth—that he intended to give him away. What would he have thought of this plan? Would he have chided him for giving up too easily or praised him for his sacrifice?

Ichiro opened his red leather diary. He turned the pages and entered the score of today's game of Go with Mr. Yasuda. It was their sixtieth game. He had spent four months in confinement, and Dr. Shizumi was hesitant to predict when Ichiro would be well enough to go home again.

He told Ichiro, "You seem unable to gain any weight. I'm going to increase your antibiotic dosage. And if that doesn't work, we always have the option of removing the infected tissue around your lung."

Stunned, Ichiro stammered, "You mean an operation?"

"I'm hoping it won't be necessary. After all, you have youth on your side. Unfortunately, I had to send your roommate home. He's old, and I can't do anything more for him. He wouldn't be strong enough to withstand an operation or a higher dosage of antibiotics. Consider yourself lucky that this remains an option for you. Get rid of the infected tissue and let the rest of the lung take over."

"But Mr. Yamamoto and I made plans to go to a baseball game together when I get out of here." Ichiro knew he sounded like a child whose father had broken a promise, but that was how he felt. He needed something to look forward to, besides seeing his wife and son again.

"I don't think you should count on that. But who knows? Miracles do happen. Mr. Yamamoto's family paid for a Shinto shrine in downtown Osaka and the gods may grant him one more favor because of that generosity." He laughed. "We Japanese are fortunate to have so many gods and goddesses protecting us. A shrine on every corner makes it easy to be devout. That is one of the strengths of our people."

"Do you believe in the power of prayer? My wife regularly goes to the Tenrikyo church in Nara and prays for me, but as far as I can tell she's wasting her breath."

"Did you ever think she's also praying for herself so that she'll have enough strength for the both of you to get through this difficult time? And maybe she's praying that you'll find your way to prayer."

"Doubtful. I'm more interested in what the Greek and Roman philosophers have to teach me. I have been reading Seneca at your suggestion." He picked up a book lying open on his desk. "I particularly relate to this thought: 'Sometimes even to live is an act of courage.'"

"Ichiro, you do not disappoint. You dwell on the negative. Perhaps it would serve you better if you considered another quotation: 'It is not because things are difficult that we do not dare; it is because we do not dare that things are difficult.' We must all fight against inertia and imagine possibilities in order to lead a fulfilling life."

"I'll try and remember that." Ichiro took a sip of water and was struck with a hacking cough. He sat down and closed the book, fear in his eyes.

Dr. Shizumi, preparing to leave, buttoned his white jacket and straightened his tie. "Dinner will be served soon. I hope you can find your appetite and eat everything you're served. I've instructed the kitchen to give you an extra portion to try to fatten you up a little."

"Nothing tastes good to me. It must be the medication. I seem to have lost my taste buds. Not a good thing for someone in the restaurant business." Ichiro sighed as Dr. Shizumi wished him a good evening and left.

Ichiro finished entering the score of today's game and then closed his diary so his tears would not smear the numbers. He needed to preserve the running score, even today's when he played like a clumsy idiot. Numbers grounded him. He thought about *The Little Prince*, which had been his favorite book and still had much to teach him:

Grown-ups love figures. When you tell them you have made a new friend, they never ask you questions about essentials. Instead, they demand: "How old is he? How many brothers has he? How much does he weigh? How much money does his father make?" Only from these figures do they think they have learned anything about him.

Ichiro could say to himself: "I have played fifty games; I weigh fifty-eight kilos; I'm thirty-one years old." He didn't have to assess his character or his accomplishments, which would have earned him a failing grade from anyone he admired, other than his wife. He couldn't understand how she had not entirely given up on him. Her faith in him felt like a burr under his shirt— reminding him he didn't deserve her loyalty. On his worst days, he thought that she'd be better off with another man, someone who could give her what she and Hisashi deserved. Someone who believed in Tenrikyo, someone with money, someone healthy.

Ichiro stood at the window. Across the way he saw Mr. Yasuda on his knees, praying. *Perhaps his spirituality is a secret to his happiness,* thought Ichiro. He suspected that he had more to learn from Mr. Yasuda than mastery of the game of Go. Ichiro tried to take a deep breath of the fragrant night air but could only manage a shallow gasp. With each passing day, he became more convinced that Death was coming after him. He was so tired that he almost welcomed the idea that he would no longer have to struggle against the inevitable. After all, doesn't everyone die?

Chapter 33

ON MY WAY HOME from the tearoom, I stopped at a sweet shop. Hisashi pressed his hands on the display case, trying to reach for a butter cookie, and got his little fingerprints all over the glass. Embarrassed, I leaned over and tried to wipe the marks off with my handkerchief. The shopkeeper looked over the counter. "Don't bother, Madam. As soon as you leave, I'm going to close up. You're my last customer. What can I get for you?"

I picked out a small cake decorated with a yellow lion balancing on a tightrope. When the shopkeeper told me the price, I hesitated. "It's more than I planned to spend, but it's for my son's second birthday. Do you have time to write his name on the cake? It's Hisashi. And I'll take that candleholder in the shape of a two."

"All of that comes to one hundred eight yen." I shouldn't be splurging like this, but I thought this could be the last birthday I would celebrate with Hisashi, and I wanted to make it special—for both of us. I hadn't truly accepted this, and secretly hoped that something would change the course of events that would take Hisashi from me. If the US government said no, then the matter would be taken out of my hands, and I could not be blamed by Ichiro for the failure of his plan. Ichiro's absence had a profound impact on me. I realized that I could survive without my husband, but that I could not survive without my son. I was ashamed for thinking this way, and didn't voice my thoughts to anyone, not even to my mother or my sister. It was as if I had awakened from the terrible nightmare which had influenced my thinking, and was now looking for ways to hold onto my son and my husband. I didn't want to have to make a choice between the two of them.

I carefully counted out the money and asked the proprietress in the bake shop, "How long will this cake stay fresh?" I explained, "My husband is away on business. I'm hoping there will be some left when he gets back. I expect him any day now. We're both disappointed he's not here."

She cautioned me, "It has cream in it, and so it's best to refrigerate the cake. It was just made this morning so it should last at least a week if your ice box is in good working order. In this heat, it will spoil in no time if you leave it out."

Ichiro had been confined to the sanatorium since January, and as the months ticked by, there was no reason for me to believe this week would bring him home. He had already sent Hisashi a birthday gift—a selection of children's illustrated books—with a note telling Hisashi Dada loved him and missed him. I wasn't sure Hisashi remembered who Dada was after an eight-month separation.

Hisashi tried to pull the boxed cake out of my hands. "Stop that. I'll give you some when we get home."

He yelled, "Lion, lion, I want him." I was losing my patience and felt like slapping Hisashi's hand.

Instead I leaned over and whispered in his ear, "I have a surprise for you when we get home. Your Dada has sent you a special present. If you're a good boy, I'll give it to you."

Hisashi looked at me and his eyes softened. "Okay, Mama. I'll be good."

I wanted to cry. Why was my little boy being subjected to my moodiness? The person I was angry with was Ichiro, who didn't deserve my wrath any more than my son did.

I was assaulted by the fumes from the automobiles and motorcycles and started to cough, and I was so tired I hardly had the strength to push Hisashi's stroller to the subway. The train was packed with early evening commuters, but fortunately, when I stepped on board, a young student wearing a heavy backpack stood up and offered me his seat. I seemed to elicit courtesy and sympathy from her. *Do I look so helpless?* Holding Hisashi on my lap, my legs perspired from his body heat. I opened the collar of my uniform and blew on the back of his neck to cool him off.

By the time we reached our stop, the outside temperature had dropped a few degrees and there was a light breeze coming off the bay. I quickened my steps, feeling refreshed to be out of doors after being cooped up at the tearoom all day and then the train. A man, his face shadowed by a white Panama hat, passed us. Hisashi turned around and yelled, "Dada!"

Stopping, I leaned over the stroller and explained, "That's not Dada, my little angel, but I promise he'll be home soon." What else was there to say?

Mrs. Masamoto held the apartment door open for us. I gritted my teeth as I waited for her saccharine greeting. She didn't disappoint me. "And how are you this warm evening, Mrs. Uchida?"

"Fine, thank you."

"And how's that handsome husband of yours doing? If I didn't know better, I'd think he was a figment of my imagination." Then she laughed lightly.

"Thank you for asking. He's doing much better. I expect he'll be home in a few weeks. Hisashi is getting so big. I'm wondering if my son will recognize his father after all this time."

"Nonsense. Children never forget their parents. You have nothing to worry about." Turning the conversation in another direction, Mrs. Masamoto said, "When Mr. Uchida is back, I have a long list of things that need fixing: The faucet in my kitchen sink is dripping again, there's a small crack in the wall, and one of the spindles on the staircase is coming loose. It's an accident waiting to happen. Be careful going up and down the stairs. If Mr. Uchida is not back soon, I'm afraid I'm going to have to call a handyman."

I wanted to ask her if she was planning to pay Ichiro for all these chores, but I needed to stay on her good side in case we ran short of money and needed to ask for another grace period as we had two months earlier when the money from Ichiro's sister was late. Whatever goodwill Ichiro had bought by giving Mrs. Masamoto a large rent deposit when he signed the lease had long since run out.

"I'm sure he'll be only too happy to help you." She knew the position we were in and was using it to her advantage.

"It must be hard for you, Mrs. Uchida. Working all day, taking care of little Hisashi…You aren't looking so well."

"I have a summer cold, that's all. I'm always exposed to germs at the tearoom. We are so busy and you never know what foreigners are carrying, do you?"

"Yes, you're right. That's why I always make sure my renters are native Japanese. It makes life much easier—safer, too."

"So true, Mrs. Masamoto. And now, if you'll excuse me. It's Hisashi's birthday, and I promised him a few surprises."

"I didn't realize it's August tenth. Imagine, Hisashi is two years old today. I remember when you first brought your little bundle of joy home from the hospital. I never saw two happier parents than you and Mr. Uchida. What a shame that he's not here to help you celebrate your son's birthday."

I put on a brave face. I didn't need Mrs. Masamoto pitying me. "We'll carry on, and I'll make a wish with Hisashi on his cake that his father will be home soon."

Mrs. Masamoto patted Hisashi on the head. I wanted to swat her hand away like an annoying mosquito. "Happy Birthday, Hisashi, and have a good evening, dear."

Hisashi gave her a big smile and put up two fingers, pleased by her attention. I felt intense rage boiling inside me and imagined digging a sharp kitchen knife into her back and watching her collapse in a puddle of blood. I shook off this horrific image, thanked her for her good wishes, and climbed the stairs, trying not to look as if I was struggling from the weight of Hisashi's stroller.

I warmed up some leftovers, and after dinner, I presented Hisashi with his birthday cake. Some of the chocolate icing had melted in the heat, but the image of the lion was still intact. Lighting three candles, I told Hisashi that the third was the one to grow on.

I snapped his picture, and without any help, he blew out all three candles. Pointing to the top of the cake, he said, "That's a lion like in the zoo. We went there with Dada."

"You remember? Do you know that one day you'll be as big and strong as a lion, my Hisashi?"

Hisashi climbed into my lap and patted my face as if trying to comfort me. I opened a package from Ichiro that was sitting on the kitchen table. It had arrived yesterday. There was a selection of books. "Which one would you like me to read to you?" Hisashi looked at the covers and picked out *The Tiny Samurai: Issun-Boshi.*

I didn't know how much Hisashi would understand, but I hoped that when we were no longer together, he might hear my voice and remember me whenever Mitsuko read this story of the tiny hero to him, one of many Japanese folk tales:

"Once upon a time there was a married couple who had no children. They went to a shrine and prayed. On their way home, they heard a tiny cry

224 ～ Loren Stephens

coming from the deep grass. It was a one-inch baby boy who was named Issun-Boshi. They brought him home and took very good care of him, but he never grew."

I stopped reading and said, "That's nothing like you, Hisashi. Look how big you already are." Hisashi nodded and tapped the page for me to continue. "One day he told his parents he wanted to go to Kyoto to become a samurai. They did not say no and gave him a suitcase full of things he would need for his trip. Miraculously, he met the Emperor and his beautiful daughter. He joined the samurai warriors and went with them to protect the princess from a demon. He was swallowed by the demon."

I asked, "And then do you know what happened?" Hisashi shook his head and waited. "The little samurai took out a sword and poked the demon right in the stomach and he was spit out. The demon ran away, leaving behind a magic hammer. The princess hit the little samurai many times on the shoulder, and he grew taller and taller until he was a handsome young man. The princess married him. The End."

Hisashi looked puzzled. "Do you understand the meaning of this story?" Hisashi shook his head. "Even though the boy was tiny, he was very smart; he used his mind to escape from the demon and was rewarded. He grew big and tall. I see why your father picked out this book for you. He believes that a clever and smart person can accomplish anything they set their mind to, and he believes they will be rewarded." Or was this a message from Ichiro to me: that parents must be prepared to give up their son? Could he be that cruel? I didn't know.

Closing the book, Hisashi begged, "Again, Mama. Again."

"Time for bed. We have to be at the tearoom early tomorrow. Get your pajamas."

Hisashi climbed down from my lap and went to his basket in the corner. He pulled out a pair of yellow pajamas. With a proud look, he held the top in one hand and the bottom in the other.

"Bring them here and I'll help you. Soon you'll be able to dress yourself, and you won't need my help at all."

Hisashi stepped into the bottoms and I threaded one arm and then the other through the sleeves and buttoned the front. Laughing, he unbuttoned the top and said, "Again, again, Mama."

"How did you learn how to do that?"

"I watch you. I am smart." I realized then just how much Hisashi understood of the story, and how much he understood of so much more.

Picking him up, Hisashi seemed as if he had gained weight. Or was it just that I was feeling so weak from constantly worrying about Ichiro? The day had gone by and my husband hadn't surprised us by showing up at the door. I knew it was wishful thinking, but I hoped he would make it home for Hisashi's birthday as he did last year. Carrying Hisashi to bed, I kissed his forehead. "Good night, my angel. Happy Birthday."

I sat by my son's side and rubbed his back. The cat curled up next to him and purred happily. Within a short time, he was fast asleep.

I opened a window to feel the evening breeze, took off my damp uniform, and washed myself with a wet washcloth. It was too hot to wear a nightgown. Lying down naked on top of my futon, I listened to the sounds of the street. A woman hummed the melody to a song as she walked by, her high heels clicking on the pavement. I recognized "All of Me" and sang the words as the woman's voice disappeared into the night: Ichiro had two versions of the song in his record collection. One by Louis Armstrong, which we danced to, and the other by Billie Holiday. Her voice, the longing and sadness of every note, always made me want to cry.

I imagined the woman on the street rushing to make the second show at the Takarazuka, putting on her makeup and sparkling costume, standing alone in the spotlight as her adoring fans lifted their faces in the dark, transfixed by her beauty. At one time I wanted to be that woman. What I wanted now was to have Ichiro back, strong and healthy, and for us to stay together as a family by undoing everything that had been put in motion before it was too late. Mitsuko had warned, "You must think about this one hundred times…" I only needed to think about it once to know it was wrong.

Chapter 34

Ichiro asked Dr. Shizumi for permission to leave the sanatorium for a day so he could spend it with his son on his second birthday, but his request was denied. "You're doing much better, but I don't want you exposed to other people's germs, which could cause a setback. Be patient." Ichiro felt despondent and isolated with only Joji Yasuda and their game of Go to distract him from the terrors that invaded his thoughts. He kept imagining the tuberculosis eating away at his organs, one by one, until there would be nothing left of him.

He did himself a further disservice by reading about the progression of the disease: "TB is referred to as consumption because it attacks the body's organs: first the lungs, then the bones and the kidneys and the abdominal cavity, even the brain. In rare cases, it can affect the body's main artery, the aorta, with catastrophic results." He hid the medical reference book from the sanatorium library under his mattress so Dr. Shizumi wouldn't discover what he was up to. And of course, he retained a hazy picture of his mother, Toshiko, and his sister throwing herself over their dead mother's corpse, begging her not to leave them. Too much grief and sadness for one little boy to endure.

Mr. Yasuda waited for Ichiro in the loggia. He had already set up the game board, and when Ichiro sat down opposite him, he greeted Ichiro with a big smile. "Mr. Uchida, I will be going home today so this will be our last game of Go for a while."

Ichiro could not hide his disappointment. He tried to come up with a cheerful remark, but his mind went blank and instead he said in a rather pathetic-sounding voice, "I should congratulate you, but all I can think of is that I won't have anyone to play Go with and it has been my happiest distraction here. As has getting to know you, of course."

"I asked my secretary to buy you a gift to remember me by."

"You should have no worries that I would forget you, Mr. Yasuda. You have been an inspiration to me. I only wish I could model my thinking after yours. You are always so positive about everything. And see, it has paid off. You're leaving while I remain imprisoned here."

"Don't despair, Ichiro. You're looking much better than when you walked in here. I'm sure you'll be going home in no time. But it is a shame to have missed your son's birthday."

The two men allowed a moment of silence to pass between them. Then, clapping his hands, Mr. Yasuda said, "I've gotten you a copy of *The Master of Go*. I think you'll enjoy reading it. The author is knowledgeable about the strategy of the game, and there is much that you can learn to prepare yourself for our next game when you are back in Osaka. The book has more to offer you than just that, however."

"What is it really about?" Ichiro asked.

"The Go master is challenged by a young upstart—someone like you. The two men symbolize old and new Japan and the clash between tradition and modernity. I won't reveal who wins the game, but it goes on for six months. Can you guess who wins?"

"I don't know. Perhaps the match is a draw."

"A very diplomatic answer, Mr. Uchida. I hope I have piqued your curiosity and that you enjoy it."

"Thank you for your thoughtfulness, Mr. Yasuda."

As Mr. Yasuda cleaned his glasses with a monogrammed handkerchief, he asked, "Do you know when you'll be leaving here? Has Dr. Shizumi given you some indication?"

"I hope to be out in December, before my thirty-second birthday."

"That will be a wonderful present. I'm sure your wife and son will be so happy to see you after all this time."

"Hisashi just had his second birthday, and, of course, I have missed it. My wife writes that he's getting so big she can hardly lift him. Unfortunately, he misses me, which makes it hard on me and even harder on her. He asks, 'Where's Dada?' And she can only answer, 'He's away, but he'll be home soon.' But really, what does a toddler know about time? What does the word 'soon' mean to a two-year-old?"

"You're right. Time is relative. When you are a child, five months can seem like an eternity, but when you get to be my age, a year goes by in an instant. It's hard to believe I'm sixty-two. It's only when I look in the mirror that I see the passing of time written all over my face. I see rivers of wrinkles lining my face and I wonder, 'Where did they all come from?' But inside I still feel like a young man. Oh, yes, I have an occasional cough, but I'm still strong and I'm convinced I have a lot more life left in me."

"You see, I need to copy your way of thinking, Mr. Yasuda. I often feel as if I'm about to take my last breath."

"You're wrong, both about your last breath being imminent and to think such things. If you have such thoughts, focus on your son and your wife and you will feel rejuvenated. Now, to our endgame. Will it be white or black?"

"I'll take the white stones."

The board was partially covered with stones as their game progressed when Mr. Yasuda took out his gold pocket watch. He stood up, "Oh, I'm sorry, Mr. Uchida, but I must leave. My driver will be here in a few minutes."

"I shall miss your company, Mr. Yasuda. Thank you for this book. It will give me something to fill my time after you've gone. I've enjoyed our afternoon games very much."

"You're a smart young man, and despite your inexperience, you've become a decent opponent." He handed Ichiro an engraved business card. "I might have an opportunity for you should you decide that the restaurant business is no longer to your taste." He chuckled. "Forgive me for the pun, but I like jokes very much. Anyway, telephone me when you return to Osaka."

"I'm deeply flattered. How shall I enter today's game in my diary?"

"Forfeited, which means you can count it as a win for you."

The men bowed. Mr. Yasuda hesitated and then embraced Ichiro in an unusual expression of affection. "Goodbye, my friend, and good luck."

Ichiro took out his red leather-bound diary and wrote: "Game 170 interrupted." His hands were trembling. He poured a glass of water and swallowed several pills to calm his nerves. Looking out the window he saw a black Mercedes pull up to the porte-cochère below. The chauffeur left the car and returned carrying two large leather suitcases, which he placed carefully in the limousine's trunk. He opened the rear door and a white Akita jumped down from the back seat followed by a tall, slim woman in a red silk dress holding the dog's leash. Her platinum blonde hair glistened in the late afternoon sun.

She had full red lips and was smoking a cigarette, which she tossed on the gravel when Mr. Yasuda walked toward her. They embraced and disappeared into the luxury of the Mercedes. A groundskeeper picked up the discarded cigarette and put it into his wicker basket. Ichiro watched the limousine until it passed through the iron gates of the sanatorium. He wanted to run downstairs and outside and yell, "Don't leave," but he controlled himself.

Ichiro had always been curious about Mr. Yasuda. He presented himself as a man of importance and refinement, and so Ichiro wasn't surprised to read his business card: Chairman of the Board, Allied Metals Industries, Osaka, Japan, and Pittsburgh, Pennsylvania, United States of America. He tucked the engraved card inside his diary for safekeeping. He didn't want to get his hopes up, but perhaps Mr. Yasuda was being more than merely solicitous in mentioning that he might have a job for him. What a strange turn of events if he found himself working at Allied Metals. His father, Hide-Ichi Uchida, had been the president of Izumi Steelworks, and given their respective ages, he and Mr. Yasuda might have crossed paths before and during the war. Perhaps there was some unseen plan at work and fate was guiding him in a new direction when he couldn't see a path toward his own salvation. Mr. Yasuda has the same elegance and nobility as his father, as best as he could remember.

⌒

TWO MONTHS LATER, ON October 9, 1963, to his enormous surprise and relief, Ichiro was discharged from the sanatorium. He had escaped an operation and his drug dosage was reduced. He had managed to put on some weight, and when he looked at himself in the mirror, other than the gray along his hairline, he had not aged to any noticeable degree. Delivering the usual admonitions and recommendations—don't overwork, don't forget your medicine, maintain a positive outlook—Dr. Shizumi informed Ichiro he had already called Noriko at the tearoom to let her know her husband would be home that day. Ichiro asked, "How did Noriko sound to you when she heard the news?"

"She was elated, of course. And then she started crying. From happiness, I'm sure."

"She might have done that for your benefit. She's a convincing actress, you know. I sometimes think she'd be better off without me. She could find herself a rich man who wouldn't be such a burden, like Mr. Yasuda, for example."

"Ichiro, you must not think that way. Besides, he's a bit old for her, don't you think?" Dr. Shizumi cleared his throat and then took a card out of his pocket. "I'm giving you the name and telephone number of a psychiatrist in Osaka. He specializes in treating patients with chronic illnesses. I've sent a number of my patients to him. I think you would greatly benefit from his expertise."

"I'm glad you haven't given up on me yet, Dr. Shizumi, but I have more pressing things to spend my money on."

"What if I were to ask him to see you at no cost? He's successful, so what you would pay him won't make the soup fat. He can get along quite well without your money, and he owes me a favor or two."

"I don't take charity from anyone. Whatever benefit I might receive from him would be annulled by the thought of not paying him for his time."

Dr. Shizumi gave up. "Suit yourself, Mr. Uchida. Be sure to call my clinic to set up your follow-up appointments."

Instead of going home, Ichiro went directly to his office at the Aki-Torii. Setsuko's husband Hideo gave him a disapproving look when he sat down at his desk, which was spotless. Scowling at him, he said, "Setsuko had to hire a part-time bookkeeper to take care of all the bills in your absence. If I were her I would have fired you. You're lucky she is so devoted to your wife or you'd be out on your ass. You're lucky you still have a job."

"Believe me, I'm grateful to your wife for everything she has done for Noriko and me. I'll try to make it up to her. I've been given a clean bill of health, and I intend to work hard to earn not only her confidence in me but yours as well."

"Don't bother about me. You may have fooled Setsuko, but I wrote you off a long time ago, Ichiro."

Chapter 35

I WAITED UNTIL MIDNIGHT for Ichiro, but he didn't show up until almost two in the morning. I spent the time reading from the Tenrikyo prayer book, searching for words of comfort and guidance on how to prepare myself for his return. I wanted to sweep away all the negative thoughts and resentment accumulating in my heart and concentrate on supporting Ichiro's fight for recovery. I put a record on, *The Rhapsody in Blue*, which had inspired Ichiro and me to think about making a trip to America. And now it would be our son who was going away alone—not to the hustle and bustle of a big city, but to an isolated town in the dusty plains of eastern Montana to live in a trailer park with relatives I had never met.

When the record ended, I heard the door open and Ichiro stood there holding a small suitcase. He looked as if the months in the sanatorium had done him some good. The color had returned to his cheeks, and he had gained weight so his jacket was not hanging off him like a prisoner-of-war uniform. I rushed into his open arms, hardly believing he was home at last.

"Where have you been? Dr. Shizumi told me you'd be home by early evening. I've been so worried. I imagined the worst."

"What? Worried that I threw myself on the subway tracks or jumped off a bridge into the Okawa River? The police would have been here by now if I had done something so rash. No, I went straight to the office at the Aki-Torii, and it's a good thing I did. Setsuko's husband was in a foul mood."

"He's all bluster. Setsuko is the one who wears the pants in the family, so you have nothing to worry about. She always says that there is no one who could replace you. I just can't believe that you wouldn't come right home after being away so long."

"What difference does a few more hours make?"

"Waiting for you and not hearing a word from you felt like an eternity. I promised Hisashi that you would be home soon, and every few minutes he was asking me when he would see you. I should probably not have said anything. He was so agitated I had a hard time putting him to bed, and he reverted to hitting me with his fists, which he hasn't done in a long time."

Ichiro poured himself a whiskey and sat down. "He should learn to behave himself and be patient."

Apparently realizing that his earlier remarks to me were insensitive and harsh, he apologized. "I'm sorry to have worried you. I tried calling you at the tearoom to tell you I was back, but you'd already left for the afternoon and I had no way to reach you. When our finances are in order, I'm going to install a telephone in the apartment. It's so awkward going through Mrs. Masamoto, and she's such a busybody. We should have a way of getting in touch with my sister and her husband anyway. Have you heard anything from them?"

"Harry is doing what he can to move things along. In fact, all the approvals have been given to a bill that makes Hisashi eligible for adoption. I don't know the details, but Harry says all that is needed is for President Kennedy to sign the bill and that should happen any day now." I tried to gauge Ichiro's reaction, but he looked at me stone-faced.

I took Ichiro's hand. "Come with me. I want to show you something." I led him to Hisashi's bed. His arm cradled Chaya. I picked up the cat and pulled back the covers. "Can you see how big Hisashi is getting? When he wakes up tomorrow, you can decide if he looks more like you or me. It's hard for me to be objective—all I see is a beautiful little boy any mother couldn't help but adore."

The two of us stood looking down at Hisashi for a few minutes, and then Ichiro leaned over and brushed his hair out of his eyes. Our son stirred but didn't wake up. He was sleeping peacefully, unaware of his father's caress. The autumn moon threw a beam on Hisashi as if he was being blessed by the heavens. I looked into Ichiro' eyes, and they were filled with tears, giving away his true feelings, which he kept locked up in the dark coffin of his mind.

⌢

THE NEXT MORNING, ICHIRO struggled to get up. He said the room spun around and he could only lie back and rest. "I think Dr. Shizumi may have discharged me too soon. He probably wanted to get rid of his most irascible patient."

I brought him a cup of tea and wiped his forehead with a cool washcloth. When Hisashi saw that his father was not getting dressed to go to work, he pulled out all his books, handing one after another to him. "Dada, read this; no, I want this." He held up *The Little Peach Boy*, one of his favorite stories.

"Poor child. He's starving for your attention, Ichiro. Can you at least give him a smile and tell him how happy you are to see him?"

Ichiro groaned. "I will read you that book later. Why don't you try to amuse yourself, Hisashi? Go play with your truck like a good boy. I need to rest."

Hearing his father speak so sharply, Hisashi looked as if he wanted to disappear, but there was nowhere in the one-room apartment for him to hide. Instead, he ran out onto the balcony and pulled a nightgown hanging on the clothesline with such force that it fell on top of him, wooden clothespins flying in the air. The wet cloth filled his nose and mouth. He punched at the nightgown, trying to free himself, but he only became more entangled.

I gasped at seeing my son trapped like an unborn baby kicking against the walls of a mother's womb. "Stay still, my Hisashi. I'll get you out." I untangled the wet laundry wrapped around him and rocked him in my arms. When he calmed down, I tickled him under his chin, chirping, "Peek-a-boo, I see you." Hisashi quickly wanted to engage in our game and put his hands over his eyes and laughed.

Ichiro muttered, "Must you make such a racket?" He then barked at me to lock the door to the balcony. "Hisashi can't go out there again by himself. He's big enough to climb over the railing. I hate to think what could happen. Honestly, what were you thinking leaving the door to the balcony open like that?"

"It's so dark in the apartment and the air is so still…I was just trying to make you more comfortable, Ichiro. Why must you blame me for everything? You're being so cruel. I'm trying to do my best, with and without you."

I could see that Ichiro barely heard me, as if my voice was fading into the distance. He lay on his back with his eyes closed and was soon fast asleep again. I suspected that he had taken more of his medicine.

I changed into my uniform in the early afternoon because I was expected to do a short shift at the tearoom. I brushed my hair, dabbed my nose with face powder, and carefully applied a light coat of red lipstick and rouge to distract the regular patrons from noticing the dark circles under my eyes.

"I wish I could stay with you, but we are shorthanded. Will you be all right?" I asked Ichiro. Then I leaned over and pressed my lips against Ichiro's forehead. It was cool, but the bed sheets were wet from his sweat. "Let me change your linens before I leave. You'll be more comfortable."

"Don't bother. I'm getting up now. I feel much better. I want to give Hisashi my undivided attention. I shouldn't have snapped at him before, but I can't control my outbursts. I'm sure it's the medicine. Once I'm off the drugs, I'll be back to my old self again."

I thought, *Who is that old self? It's been so long I can barely bring you into focus. Is it the man I met the first day I worked at the tearoom, the man who proposed to me? The man I married who made so many promises, who painted a picture of shared happiness instead of inestimable sorrow?*

Pointing to the books strewn all over the floor, Ichiro asked, "Which of these books is Hisashi's favorite? I think I'm up to reading one of them to him."

"He keeps changing his mind, just like a typical two-year-old, but I think he'd be happy if you read him *The Peach Boy*. And then if you could, he likes the book you sent him on his birthday, *Little One Inch*."

"Okay, *Peach Boy* it will be." With a faraway look in his eyes, he reminisced: "I remember when Mitsuko used to read me that story. I can still hear her voice, and from the hallway, my father always had some beautiful classical music playing on the phonograph. And then our stepmother came into our life and Mitsuko read to me to calm me down after the woman had done terrible things to me…like burning my back, and forcing Mitsuko to sit on top of me so she wouldn't miss her target. And then Mitsuko revealing what Madam Tamae had done to me…." Then his voice faltered.

I put my hand up to stop him. Taking my pocketbook off the table, I prepared to leave and then remembered there was a letter for Ichiro from Mitsuko. "It arrived in this morning's mail, but I didn't want to wake you."

"It's addressed to you. What does she say?"

I could barely bring myself to read it out loud. Every word was like a pain in my heart.

October 1, 1963

Dearest Noriko: I am so sorry Ichiro is still away at the sanatorium. The two of you have spent so little time together as husband and wife. I am sure he would have wanted to share your son's birthday with you. Life is full of sorrow.

I know this all too well. Losing a baby of my own made me want to end my life, but I went on and now I am presented with this unimaginable turn of events. Harry has received encouraging news from our attorney that President John F. Kennedy will make everything official soon. If you have any reservations about giving Hisashi to us, you must tell me right now. I would never forgive myself if you were doing this against your own free will to satisfy my brother and to be a dutiful wife. I would understand if you changed your mind at the last minute. But please know that we want this more than anything in the world. Your loving sister-in-law, Mitsuko

"Why would my sister plant a seed of doubt in your mind? Have you written to her that you are still unsure?"

"No, Ichiro. It's a woman's intuition. Your sister is standing in my shoes, I'm sure. But I haven't changed my mind. You have nothing to worry about." How easily I lied to Ichiro instead of telling him that, as each day passed, I felt more unsure of our decision, but I hadn't yet figured out a way out. I thought about running away with Hisashi, but how would I live with no money? I needed to come up with a concrete plan that was realistic.

"It's a good thing because long ago I stopped fooling myself that I could learn to be a good father to our son."

I leaned over and kissed Hisashi goodbye without saying another word to Ichiro. Turning around at the door, I saw our son curled up in Ichiro's lap. He put his hand on his father's face as if he wanted to assure himself Ichiro was not a figment of his imagination. And then I heard him say, "I love you, Dada. Do you love me?"

Chapter 36

I COULD BARELY KEEP up with the customers pouring into the tearoom. Osaka was to be one of the major sites for the Olympic Games beginning next October, and sports managers, architects, and builders jockeyed for seats or stood in line to grab something to eat before heading to their offices. Setsuko had to hire additional waitresses to accommodate the steady stream of customers who usurped the seats of our regulars. I had to be careful not to drop anything from my tray because customers rolled out architectural drawings on the tables or displayed models of buildings under construction.

At the end of my shift, Setsuko stopped me at the front door. "Let me walk you to the subway. I need to speak to you in private."

I had been avoiding my sister all afternoon, afraid that she might bring up Ichiro's latest absence. I had nothing to say to defend him and argue that she keep him on the payroll.

Putting a hand on my shoulder, she said, "My husband is not very sympathetic to Ichiro's situation, but honestly, he is right in one regard. We can't function much longer without a full-time manager for the restaurants. You know I can't rely on my husband. If he pressures me into terminating Ichiro, I'll find a way to give you money. I have some investments of my own that he knows nothing about. It's never smart for a woman to rely entirely upon her husband. I learned that a long time ago."

I said, "Ichiro's job is important to him, not just for the money but for his sense of self-worth. Although, he is so clever that, if he puts his mind to it, I'm sure he could eventually find another job, but the only practical experience he has is as a restaurant manager."

As we neared the subway, Setsuko said, "Now that Ichiro is back, are you and he still intent upon giving Hisashi away? He is such a precious boy. All my children are attached to him, especially Kazuko. It will break her heart to see him leave. I can't understand how you agreed to this."

Setsuko echoed my secret thoughts. I hardly recognized the woman I had become. Where was my independent spirit? Had Ichiro's illness broken my spine? I answered her, "Too much has already been done. There is a saying that fits our situation: 'Spilt water will not return to the tray.'"

"Ugh, an old saying. Nothing is irreversible except death. Need I remind you that Hisashi is just as much your responsibility as Ichiro's and you've spent far more time with him than his father? He is so attached to you, which is only natural. There is a bond between mother and child that is unbreakable."

"I'm not sure I would have the wherewithal to raise Hisashi on my own if I were to lose Ichiro. Doesn't every boy need his father?"

Setsuko bit her lip and then blurted out, "Not if he is incapable of truly being a father. You've been taking care of Hisashi on your own for the past nine months. Granted, you've had help from all of us, but that wouldn't change. We will always be here for you, Noriko."

"What is the future of a widow with a young child in Japan? Nothing. Less than nothing. I'm ashamed to admit it but I lack the courage to face such a bleak fate. Mother called me 'a monk for three days' when I first told her what Ichiro was planning, and she is right. Ichiro's illness has taken a tremendous toll on me. My worry over my sick husband has been an unfair punishment on my son. I find myself distracted and scared. Really, I am convinced that Hisashi will have a better life if he is raised by his aunt and uncle in America." I was aware of how conflicted I sounded—one minute advocating the logic of Ichiro's plan and the next (to myself) ruing the day I had agreed to it.

"What if I take Hisashi and raise him? My children are getting older, and we have plenty of room in our apartment above the Aki-Torii for another child. Before I know it, Mitsuo will be getting married and he'll be looking for a place of his own. Children these days don't like living with their parents. And can you blame them? They want their independence. They don't want to be smothered by doting mothers like you and me."

"You think I'm a doting mother? Working as many hours as I do, I think of myself as negligent. But what choice do I have? I can only trust that Hisashi knows how much I love him even when I'm not by his side." I tried to read

Setsuko's face to discern if she was really sincere in her offer. "I don't think Ichiro could bear to watch Hisashi grow up right in front of him without being able to raise him. And I don't know if I could stand it either."

"You could visit as often as you wished, Noriko. It would be as if he has two mothers—you and me. Wouldn't that be better than sending him thousands of miles away to live with people you don't know?"

"I can't think straight. I feel so confused, and I'm afraid to upset Ichiro. His mental state is precarious. When Dr. Shizumi called to tell me Ichiro was coming home, he raised the possibility that Ichiro should see a psychiatrist. Ichiro carries so much regret over his past that it is weighing him down like a bag of bones. He has been unable to free himself from all the tragedies that happened to him as a child. I feel as if I am wasting my words when I ask him to put all that behind him."

Setsuko sighed. "As Mother has told you, I hope you won't come to regret this decision. If it were up to me, I'd take Hisashi in a heartbeat. And then, when Ichiro is well and can find work, I'd return him to you. And if he were not able to overcome this disease, you would at least still have your son by your side to raise and to love. Is that not more sensible than giving your son to his sister? What if she's an unsuitable parent? At least if I took care of him, you could see him whenever you wished and we could easily communicate with one another about important decisions."

"There's more to the story, Setsuko. As I have already told Mother, Ichiro has promised his sister that Hisashi will be adopted by her. He feels he owes her everything for what she did for him during the war. He doesn't want to go back on his word. And on top of it all, his sister lost a baby—two, in fact—and Ichiro is trying to compensate for these losses."

"You're his wife, and his loyalty to you should be first and foremost. I'm sure his sister would understand if you changed your mind, even now. Why don't you think of yourself for once?"

"My husband's happiness and that of my son are more important than my own." I shocked myself by this admission. Was it true that I thought of myself as a second-class citizen to my husband? When had I sold myself to the loudest bidder, my husband? If Hisashi could express himself, what would he tell me? Would he say, "No, Mama, I belong with you no matter what"?

When we reached the subway entrance, Setsuko said, "Think about what I'm offering you and Hisashi—and Ichiro," and then she embraced me.

I pulled away and ran down the flight of stairs, afraid of turning back because I didn't want Setsuko to see the tears streaming down my face.

⁓

WHEN I OPENED THE door to our apartment, the smell of liquor assaulted me. An empty bottle of scotch sat on the table, and Ichiro was snoring loudly. Hisashi lay curled up next to his father on the floor. When I put covers over both of them, they did not stir.

At that moment I despised Ichiro for drinking while looking after Hisashi. Either of them could have had a terrible accident, and then what? Here was the evidence right in front of my face that Ichiro was an unstable father. I felt like a traitor for having these thoughts, but I couldn't help myself.

The apartment was stone cold. I turned the gas burner on the stove and made a cup of tea to warm myself. The tea was soothing and calmed my nerves. After changing into my bathrobe, I lit a candle so as not to disturb Ichiro or Hisashi by turning on an overhead light. Then I composed a letter to Mitsuko, giving her instructions on how to take care of Hisashi. This was the most painful letter I had ever written, but I forced myself to do it because I wanted to make sure that Hisashi's daily routine would be followed and he would feel as little disruption as possible when he went to his new home in Glendive, Montana. I had only read about it in travel books. What kind of life would Hisashi have and how would he fit in even if his new parents were Japanese? I tried to set aside my concerns and focus on my letter, hoping it would help them:

11 October 1963

Dear Mitsuko: Ichiro is finally out of the sanatorium after nine months, but he is not at all well. I think the doctors have washed their hands of him. He is drinking to bury his worries. I apologize for telling you this about your brother, but I think you should know.

Hisashi is two years and two months old. I took a picture of him on his birthday so that you can see how big he is getting. He has outgrown his cowboy outfit that you and Harry sent him las year; only the hat still fits. He likes to sing and dance and is a happy boy. He is already potty trained and is very conscientious about being clean. If he get his clothes dirty, he wants to have them changed right away. He is speaking in full sentences now and calls me "Mama" and Ichiro "Dada."

He loves chocolate, gum, candies, and fruit; but if you give him too much chocolate, he gets a runny nose. He may be allergic. He loves apples and oranges, fish, eggs, and beans. He doesn't like meat. He has a little tummy from all the sweets he gets at the tearoom. I've tried to limit this, but he is such an adorable child that when he reaches for something, everyone wants to oblige. But I'm sure when he runs around in the park, he'll burn off the baby fat and become very fit and trim like his father.

He likes to play with his car and his big truck and puts all his toys away by himself. If he doesn't like something, he will point and make a sad face. When he sticks his finger in your eye, tell him "owee" and he will stop right away. He is a sensitive and sympathetic child and takes great pleasure in pleasing all the grown-ups he meets at the tearoom. He is really a very social boy, and I hope he will make friends in your town of Glendive, Montana. (All I know of the place you live is you have lots of cows and horses, and it snows in the winter and is hot in the summer. Do you have cherry blossoms as we do here in the spring?)

Hisashi wakes up at six in the morning. As soon as he gets up, you have to feed him. Lunch is between noon and one. He rarely takes a nap now. At three I give him a snack, but I don't give him too much or he will not eat his supper. Supper is between six and seven. Sometimes he starts to fall asleep before his actual bedtime, and we just put him to bed. I'm sure when he comes to live with you he will adapt to your schedule, but this is what I do.

I may have forgotten something, but that's all I can think of right now. If you have any questions you can just write me, or if we can figure out a way to afford one, Ichiro is going to put in a telephone in our apartment and we can speak to one another. I would love to hear your voice, Mitsuko. You may be curious about what I sound like, too. Right now, we can only use the phone booth on the corner if we need to make a telephone call, or you can call me at the tearoom if you want to speak directly with me.

It is getting late, and I need to go to sleep. Fortunately, I still have my job at the tearoom. It looks like Ichiro will be dismissed because he has missed so many months of work. My sister is heartbroken she has to do this, but she cannot run her businesses without a full-time manager.

Ichiro assures me that Hisashi will get used to you quickly and forget about us in no time. I am not so sure, but I am confident you will do your best to be a good mother to him. You asked me if I have changed my mind. My answer is no. Your brother has made it clear that we have no other choice.

Please let us know when you receive the document signed by President John F. Kennedy. Imagine, this great man is going to make sure that our Hisashi will rightfully belong to you.

Please thank Harry for all that he is doing for us and for the money you both have been sending. It will make an even bigger difference if Ichiro is terminated. When he is better, I am sure he will find another job.

Have you thought about what you wish Hisashi to call you? I think it might confuse him if you ask him to call you "Mama" and Harry "Dada." What do American children call their parents because that is what he will be?

I wish I knew you, Mitsuko, and your husband Harry, but believe me when I tell you I am sending you all my love. At least I know Harry's mother and she is a very fine lady.

Noriko

I reread the letter, making sure I hadn't forgotten anything of critical importance and that the tone was not that of a complaining wife and mother. I didn't want Mitsuko to feel sorry for us, but I didn't want to paint a rosy picture either. I was tired of lying about our circumstances and suppressing my sadness and disappointment. I felt envious of Mitsuko that she would be the one to raise Hisashi and watch him grow up while I would be denied the honor and privilege of raising my firstborn son. How I would get through the days, months, and years without Hisashi, I could not imagine. As time went by, would it lessen the pain or make it more unendurable?

I took a sip of lukewarm tea as the candle sputtered. When I blew it out, a trail of black smoke floated into the air, a mournful symbol of what was to come.

In his sleep, Hisashi cried out, "Mama! Mama, where are you?"

I whispered, "I'm right here, my little one."

Chapter 37

Ichiro sat in his office at the Grille Room and read his sister's letter, which had arrived in the morning mail. He calculated that she had written it three weeks earlier. The mail was slow between Glendive and Osaka.

November 2, 1963

Dearest Ichiro: I have good news! President John Kennedy has signed the private bill giving us permission to bring Hisashi to America, bypassing all the quota restrictions. This is truly a miracle but we have my Harry and our attorney Charles Dunn to thank for this. Harry and I spent hours rehearsing just what we would say to the lady who visited us from Child Welfare Services. She wanted to make sure we would be suitable parents. We passed with flying colors, as Harry said to me. I think my almond cookies might have helped win her over. She asked me to send her the recipe! Imagine that I have managed to learn lots of American recipes although I still love to make sushi platters for my customers at the Jordan Hotel on Friday nights. I'll be able to prepare familiar food for Hisashi when he gets here so that it won't be such a shock to his tummy.

We are going to be moving to a bigger trailer home so that Hisashi will have his own room. (This is something the lady asked about.) The trailer is much further from the main road so it is safe and right next to the children's playground. Everyone is anxious to meet "the cute Japanese boy." I have shown my friends pictures of Hisashi, and they are waiting to greet him with open arms. Glendive is a nice town so you should have no worries about anyone being unkind to him.

Harry continues to move things along. We will be sending you Hisashi's plane ticket after all the arrangements have been made.

I don't know what more I can tell you right now, Ichiro, except that my heart is overflowing with love for you and Noriko. I pray every day that we are all doing the right thing, and that whatever burden you feel will be lifted, and that your health and happiness will be restored. I still think of you as my little brother whom I tried to protect from all the horrors that rained down upon both of us. You deserve to be happy and so does Noriko.

With all my love forever, your devoted sister, Mitsuko

Ichiro put the letter in his jacket pocket. He'd have to share it with Noriko that evening. There would be more tears, more sighs, more sadness. He wasn't up to his wife's outpouring of emotions. He went to the bar. It was just noon but he ordered a beer. "To quench my thirst." He shouldn't have had to explain his actions to the bartender but he felt as if he was being judged. The television over the bar was tuned to a rebroadcast of the tribute concert for the slain American president, John F. Kennedy—the chyron underneath the picture said, "*Mahler's Resurrection*, performed by Leonard Bernstein conducting the New York Philharmonic." Customers seated at the bar and in the dining room sat in stunned silence watching the solemn proceedings. After the concert ended, the announcer invited viewers to sign a condolence book at the US embassies in Tokyo, Kobe, and Osaka. Ichiro would try and find the time to write a message to President Kennedy acknowledging his appreciation for what he had done for him and his wife before his untimely death. It came as a terrible shock to everyone around the world. He was especially popular among the Japanese and everyone had been anticipating his state visit in 1964. His brother, Robert Kennedy, had been to Tokyo to plan his brother's visit, and he had impressed his audience with his intelligence, diplomacy, and sense of humor.

Finishing his beer, Ichiro put the empty beer bottle on the bar, paid for it, and went back to his office. He really didn't feel up to working, but he was so behind. He berated himself for not being on top of everything, There was a knock on the door. It was Setsuko. He saw the sadness in Setsuko's eyes and assumed it was in reaction to the news about President Kennedy, but instead it was because of something personal that struck Ichiro like a knife to the heart. He had expected what she said and was surprised that it hadn't come sooner. "I have to let you go, Ichiro. I cannot keep picking up the pieces each time you are out sick. It pains me to do this. I promised Noriko we would stand by you, and we will. But I need to find someone to replace you. It won't be easy. Maybe you could help train them to take over for you."

"Don't worry, Setsuko. You have nothing to apologize for. You put up with me for a lot longer than anyone else would have. When I'm feeling better, I'm sure I'll find another job. I just need to be sure you'll give me a good recommendation."

"Of course. Why wouldn't I? After all, I trained you. I'm going to miss you very much. Everyone will miss you."

Ichiro stood up. "Thank you, Setsuko. It has been an honor to be of service to you. You gave me a job when I was destitute. I still remember when I walked in the door of the tearoom, after sleeping on a park bench the evening before and not knowing what would happen to me. You gave me a chance, a place to live, and a family who embraced me, and I will be forever grateful to you. And if it were not for you, I might still be a bachelor. Who would have ever thought that I could meet and marry someone as lovely and kind as Noriko?"

Trying to remain stoic, Setsuko said, "Who knows? This might be a good thing in the end. You have many talents. Do you know the expression the Americans like to say over and over again? 'You never know when your bad luck is your good luck.' I don't think we have an equivalent saying in Japanese. We should."

"I'll keep that in mind when I'm feeling discouraged."

Setsuko reached into her pocket. "I'd like to pay you for this week. And there's something extra—severance pay for all the years you have worked here, and done such an excellent job. Our waitresses have no trouble finding other work because of the way you trained them, and I hope that when you are ready to look for another job, your prospective employer will value all the time you put in here."

"Normally I wouldn't accept the bonus because I don't deserve it, but I'd be lying if I didn't confess that we need it. If you don't mind, I'll gather my personal effects and go out the back door so I don't have to say goodbye to the staff. And I would appreciate it if you would tell everyone that I resigned so I could spend more time with Hisashi. I'm sure they'll understand when they find out he's going to America."

"So everything has been settled?" Setsuko unconsciously puckered her lips.

"Yes, I just received a letter from my sister. All that needs to be done now is to arrange for Hisashi's travels. It turns out that one of President Kennedy's last official duties before he was killed was to sign the private bill for Hisashi."

"Is there nothing Kimie and I can do to change your mind?"

Ichiro took out a handkerchief and wiped the perspiration from his brow. He felt as if he had a fever again. "No. In my condition, there is nothing you can do."

Ichiro put his arms around Setsuko and hugged her. "Please tell the children I'll come and see them regularly. They're important to me." He smiled weakly, "I still owe Mitsuo a baseball game. He's become quite a fan."

Setsuko nodded and then turned around to leave Ichiro to gather up his belongings.

⁓

ICHIRO SPENT ALL HIS time with Hisashi now that he was unemployed. Noriko was promoted to assistant bookkeeper at the Tesagara Tearoom, picking up some of his former duties while waiting for a new general manager to be hired, and Setsuko gave her a raise to help them out without it appearing like a handout. Ichiro was frustrated and ashamed he could contribute nothing to the household. Fortunately, Mitsuko and Harry continued to send money, but he didn't know how much longer that would last. Once Hisashi was living with them, what reason would they have to send money? Unless they looked upon him as a charity case. That thought depressed him enormously.

He didn't feel strong enough to look for a job, and in his dismal frame of mind, he thought no one would want to hire him, not even Mr. Yasuda, whose card he kept in the red leather diary. When he was up to it, he would telephone him. He trusted Mr. Yasuda's parting words to him at the sanatorium were sincere. He wasn't the kind of man to spoon out pablum, or give lip service just to make someone feel less miserable about their situation. He was a businessman with a big company to run, and he wouldn't pad the payroll just to do someone a favor.

To pass the time, Ichiro bought a few woodworking tools and a bench, which he set up on the balcony. He constructed a ring toss game to amuse Hisashi. Fastening two pieces of wood together in the shape of a cross, he glued posts to each end and one in the middle and painted them red, blue, and bright yellow as he had seen in the toy stores for toddlers of Hisashi's age. Hisashi sat on the floor a few feet from the cross and aimed the brightly colored plastic hoops. Each time one slid down a post, Ichiro encouraged him, keeping score in a notebook with Hisashi's name on the cover.

Ichiro showed Hisashi his notebook to teach him basic numbers. "How did you do today?"

Hisashi studied the page carefully, and then, without hesitating, answered confidently, "Three."

"And yesterday?" He pointed to the number.

Ichiro held up two fingers. "So, you did better today?"

"Yes, better today."

"That's my boy. With practice you will improve. Do you understand?" Hisashi shook his head. "I'm going to have to write these ideas down so you'll follow my orders even if I'm not around to check up on you." Ichiro noticed a change in his voice, and then he started coughing. He swallowed a pill and waited for it to take effect.

Hisashi gathered up the pieces of the game and put them back neatly in his toy box, which Ichiro had also made for him. Then he took out a record and tried to put it on the player.

"No, Hisashi. We have time for songs later."

Hisashi made a face. "I want to hear 'Home on the Range.'"

"Not now. What do you say we go to the playground? Mama wants you to get out in the fresh air, and I could use a change of scenery." Then he mumbled to himself, "I feel like the walls are closing in on me." Forcing a smile, he said, "It looks like a very nice day—a bit cold though so get me your jacket."

Hisashi stuck one arm in the sleeve of his jacket, dragging it across the floor so that his father could help him with the other sleeve. Then he pulled the zipper up right to his chin. Taking a cap out of the pocket, he put it on his head. "Ready for the park, Papa." He had a big smile on his face. Ichiro guessed his son was proud of his growing independence.

Ichiro carried Hisashi's tricycle down the stairs, and then the toddler insisted on riding it. He leaned forward over the handlebars, and before Ichiro could stop him, he took off. Ichiro ran to catch up with him and grabbed him just before he headed into oncoming traffic in the street. Yelling at Hisashi, he said, "Don't go so fast. Stay right next to me. You could get hurt. What in God's name were you thinking?"

Ichiro's heart pounded; he held onto the handlebars of the tricycle to restrain his son. When they reached the playground, Ichiro felt as if his lungs were about to explode. He sat down on a bench and let Hisashi explore the playground on his own. There was a big iron gate so he wasn't worried that Hisashi might try and escape.

Ichiro noticed that Hisashi kept looking over his shoulder to make sure his father had not disappeared. A group of women sat on a nearby bench. Occasionally, they glanced in his direction. He imagined they were gossiping about him: *What is that man doing in the park at this time of day? Why isn't he at work? Where is the boy's mother?* He lit a cigarette, opened the newspaper, and scanned the headlines. Suddenly Ichiro heard screaming from the far side of the playground. He looked up and Hisashi was lying on the ground next to his overturned tricycle. He dropped his cigarette and ran to him, but not fast enough. Tears were streaming down his son's cheeks and his bare knee was scraped and bleeding. One of the women had come to his rescue and was trying to comfort him.

"Thank you, Madam."

Raising her eyebrows, she said, "You should have been paying attention to your son instead of sticking your nose in your newspaper. He's too young to be on his own. But it's none of my business. I apologize for speaking out of turn." She walked away briskly.

Ichiro wiped Hisashi's face and knee with his handkerchief and picked him up. "I'd better get you home and clean you up before Mama sees you this way."

Hisashi stopped crying. "No, I want to stay here." He tried to squirm out of his father's arms.

Ichiro yelled, "Don't argue with me. I'm your father and I make the rules, not you. When I say we're going home we're going home. I don't want to hear 'no' out of your mouth again." The women stared at Ichiro, telegraphing their thoughts that this was no way to speak to a little boy.

Ichiro felt humiliated. He put his son down and righted the tricycle. Hisashi hesitated and then climbed back on. Ichiro noticed that the bell had fallen off the handlebar. He picked it up and put it in his pocket. "When we get home, I'll fix it for you and you can help me." Hisashi gave him a feeble smile, which made Ichiro feel even more guilty for having exploded. It was only normal for a little boy to want to play out of doors, he told himself. It was good for him. Being cooped up all day in the apartment was not healthy for either of them. An image of himself at Hisashi's age floated across Ichiro's mental screen: filling a pail with sand with Mitsuko as the waves lapped against the shore, his mother and grandmother playing a board game beneath an umbrella, and his father, jacketless and his sleeves rolled up, reading a newspaper through dark, wire-rimmed glasses. It was the picture of a happy family, but it wasn't true. They were suddenly forced to go back to their room at the ryokan because his mother was too weak even to lift her head to look at the pieces on the board, let alone continue the game. He could hear his father telling him and his sister, "Play quietly. Your mother needs to rest;" and then he saw his grandmother wiping his mother's brow with a wet cloth, trying to make her comfortable. He shivered as he recalled the pained expression on his father's face and his mother's eyes as she peered off into the distance even though her children were right in front of her.

Retracing their steps back to the apartment, Ichiro mentally inventoried the tools he would need to put the bell back on Hisashi's tricycle. Then he made a list of items that needed fixing around the apartment: the lock on the balcony door was broken, the light over the sink kept blinking on and off at odd moments, and the steam refused to come out of the iron. It seemed to Ichiro as if everything around him was breaking down.

He kept a steady grip on the tricycle handlebars. Pointing to his knee, Hisashi said, "Owee, Papa."

"Can you be very brave? I'm going to wash the dirt off your knee and put some medicine on it. I'll give you a candy as a reward even if your mama doesn't like me doing that. She says you eat too many sweets."

Hisashi bit his lower lip to keep from crying as Ichiro painted his son's knee with mercurochrome. "There you go. All done." He opened the cupboard and looked for a piece of candy, but he couldn't find any. Shrugging his shoulders, he said, "Sorry, Hisashi. Dada has broken his promise. No candy. How about you help me fix this bell?"

Instead of answering, Hisashi handed Ichiro the record he wanted to hear earlier. Ichiro turned on the phonograph player and put the record on. Hisashi climbed up into Ichiro's lap, and before the first song ended, he was fast asleep. Ichiro examined Hisashi's adorable face, his long eyelashes, his shiny black hair, and his hands pressed against Ichiro's chest. How much longer he would have his son he didn't know, but the reality of a future without him was sinking in. It was as if he was living in denial until today. No matter how often he saw Noriko's sad expression crossing her beautiful face, he closed his mind to the thought of Hisashi's absence. Was his sadness over Hisashi's departure now matching hers? He looked in the mirror. A man devoid of hope was reflected back to him.

Chapter 38

I BALANCED A HEAVY tray laden with pastries and cappuccino for the businessmen sitting by the window. Setsuko stopped me and took the tray. "There's a call for you in the office, Noriko. The lady did not say who she is, but she said she needs to speak with you right away. She said she's from Matsue. Isn't that where your father, Ryo, lives?"

"Yes. He moved there a few years ago and set up another sushi shop." Sensing that something was terribly wrong since I never heard from my father, I rushed into the office and picked up the receiver. The woman at the other end introduced herself as Setsue Chang, my father's bookkeeper. "Your father was riding his bicycle and fell off, hitting his head. The doctor who examined him said he's had a heart attack. If you want to say goodbye to him, you'd better come right away. I've checked and there's a train from Osaka to Matsue that leaves in the morning and gets here around noon. Do you have our address?"

"Yes. Please tell my father I'm on my way."

The woman hesitated, then said, "He might not last that long," and then the telephone went dead. I spent the rest of the day struggling to stay focused on my duties, but all I could think of was my pending visit with my father and a proposal I had conjured up that might save our family if my father agreed to it. I don't know why I had not thought of this before. I prayed to God the Parent that he would agree to what I had in mind.

Before I left the following morning, Ichiro had some good news, small consolation for what had happened to Hisashi at the park yesterday. Ichiro spared no details in his confession, however, admitting he wasn't keeping an eye on Hisashi as he should have been, so I couldn't reprimand him. I was concerned about my father and welcomed good news.

Ichiro told me, "Mr. Yasuda, whom I met at the sanatorium, got in touch with me. He mentioned he may have a job for me."

"Where does he work?"

"He's the chairman of Allied Metals. I've called him and set up an appointment with him in three days. I'm sorry I can't go with you to Matsue, but someone has to stay with Hisashi. He's getting to be a real handful. After what happened yesterday, I'm reluctant to leave him with Setsuko and Kazuko."

Looking at my watch I realized, if I didn't hurry, I'd miss my train. Ichiro took a book out of his bookcase. "Here's something for you to read. It's a collection of short stories by an American writer, Lafcadio Hearn. He lived in Matsue for two years and died in Japan at the beginning of the twentieth century. His wife was Japanese, and she inspired him to write some of the stories in this collection."

"I've barely had time to read a newspaper in months. I feel as if the world is just passing me by. I can't believe it's the end of November. Soon it will be your thirty-second birthday and then New Year's will be here and then…"

Ichiro, anticipating that I was about to say something about Hisashi's departure, cut me off. He said, "Wish your father a speedy recovery for me, although he'd probably prefer that you not mention my name." I thought, *Why does everything have to be about Ichiro—the good and the bad?*

"From what his bookkeeper told me, he may not even be conscious. I just hope he's still alive when I get to Matsue so I can tell him know how much he means to me and how heartbroken I have been by our estrangement." I put on my warm coat and tucked the book in my pocket. Hisashi held up his arms for me to pick him up. I held him tightly. He patted my cheek and smiled. "Don't worry, Mama."

"Yes, my sweet boy, everything is going to be all right. I'll be back tonight, I promise." I kissed him again. "You know, you are my sunshine."

He smiled and said, "You make me happy when I am blue."

Closing the door quickly before I burst into tears, I hurried through the early morning crowd. Bicyclists wove in and out of the stream of pedestrians and automobiles. Policemen in stiffly pressed blue and black uniforms directed traffic with their white-gloved hand signals. The days were getting shorter and the air was cold and smelled of winter.

I presented my transportation card at the Japanese Railroad ticket booth. Survivors of Hiroshima and Nagasaki were given free passage. When my card came in the mail, Ichiro commented, "Small compensation for what so many went through during the war. Our government should be doing a lot more." I didn't disagree.

I settled into my seat, and the train took off right on schedule. I didn't have time to spare. I was glad to have a book to read to keep the man sitting next to me from starting a conversation, but I needn't have worried because, as soon as the train pulled out of the station, his chin fell forward and he was fast asleep. His wire-rimmed glasses slipped down his nose and into his lap. I carefully tucked them in his breast pocket. I noticed that his jacket was made of the finest cashmere and his leather shoes were highly polished. From his attire and his barely lined face, I assumed that he must be a very wealthy man.

I glanced at the stories in Lafcadio Hearn's *Kwaidan* and selected a story long enough to last the three-hour journey to Matsue. It was called "A Dead Secret." The title frightened me, but I was drawn into the story about ghosts:

> *A daughter of a rich merchant of Tamba named O-Sono married a wealthy man in Kyoto and they had a son. O-Sono fell ill and died very young, leaving her little boy in the care of her husband and his mother. One evening her son said, "Mama has come back and is in her room upstairs, but she will not speak to me and so I ran away."*

I read quickly so that I would find out what happened to the little boy and his ghost mother before I arrived at my destination. Japanese people believe that children up to the age of five can communicate with angels, but can they also communicate with the dead? It was possible, I decided.

The train slowed down as it approached the Hiroshima station before continuing on to Matsue. The man sitting next to me woke up with a start. He touched his face to adjust his glasses and realized they were missing. Surprised to discover that they were inside his breast pocket, he turned toward me. "I wonder how my glasses traveled from my nose to my pocket. Did you notice that I did this in my sleep, Miss?"

Blushing, I answered, "They slipped off your nose. I took the liberty of placing them in your pocket."

"That was very thoughtful of you. Otherwise, if they had landed on the floor, I surely would have stepped on them, and that would have been a tragedy. I'm blind as a bat without them." He paused and then asked, "May I introduce myself? I'm Toyohito Sugimoto. And you are…?"

"Noriko Uchida."

Mr. Sugimoto glanced at the cover of my book, which I had closed and left in my lap. "I see you're reading Lafcadio Hearn. An interesting writer. We Japanese are always fascinated by what outsiders think of our country. His wife is Japanese born and he speaks our language fluently. In fact, his wife is often considered by many scholars to be his muse. She introduced him to our ancient folk tales and ghost stories. They are very captivating."

I nodded, struck by his sonorous voice and formal manner. "Are you on your way to Matsue by any chance?" I nodded again. "Then you must visit his home."

"I'll only be there for a few hours and then I'll be returning to Osaka. I need to take care of family matters."

"And, if you don't mind my asking, what is it that you do in Osaka?"

"I'm an assistant bookkeeper and waitress at the Tesagara Tearoom in Namba. It is a family business." I didn't mention I was married or had a son because that would have been too personal to share with Mr. Sugimoto.

"I've heard of it. My office is not far from there. Perhaps I shall have the distinct pleasure of seeing you some afternoon. Here is my card."

When the train came to a stop at the station in Hiroshima, Mr. Sugimoto picked up his briefcase and stood up. "This is where I get off. I wish you a good day, Miss Uchida."

"And the same to you, Mr. Sugimoto." I watched him leave the station platform.

I couldn't resist looking at myself in my compact; my dark hair curled softly around my face, and luckily, I had not eaten off my lipstick, which I was in the habit of doing when I was worried. I admitted to myself that I actually looked quite pretty. I had almost forgotten what it felt like to be admired by a man, and he was certainly flirting with me but in a most respectful way. I decided not to tell Ichiro about this brief encounter. I did not want to upset him, but if I was being truthful, I was flattered by this attractive man's attention. If he came into the tearoom looking for me, then I would have reason to tell Ichiro, I decided, but not before then.

I read his business card: Toyohito Sugimoto, Chairman, East-West Trading Company, Osaka, Tokyo, and New York. Maybe when Ichiro is feeling better, I can contact Mr. Sugimoto and ask him if he might have a job for my husband. And if he did, someday Ichiro might be sent to New

York and I could join him and we could see the city that "Rhapsody in Blue" was inspired by and then go to Glendive, Montana, to see our son. I couldn't help myself from dreaming, and grabbing onto every possible opportunity, including the one that was right in front of me now in Matsue.

I was carried away by this fantasy and didn't realize the train had been delayed from leaving the Hiroshima station waiting for a group of uniformed schoolboys who filled up all the remaining seats in the car. They sat quietly, their book bags resting on the floor, and then the conductor announced the train was departing. My heart was pounding at the thought that I might not make it in time to see my father.

An hour later the train arrived at the station in Matsue. I tucked my book into my coat pocket and put Mr. Sugimoto's card in my purse. My father's sushi shop and apartment were just a few minutes' walk from the station, past the Ohashi-gawa River that connected Shinji and Lake Nakanoumi where my father must surely have gotten all the fresh fish he needed to satisfy the appetites of his customers. The narrow street was lined with two-story houses and shops selling various crafts and household goods. Electrical wires strung over the street looked like fish netting. In the distance was the medieval Matsue Castle with its solemn, black-shingled roof. The only time I had been to Matsue was with my mother when I was a child. She told me about the castle, "Some call it the plover castle."

As an inquisitive child I always had questions. "What's a plover, Mama?"

"It's a very clever sea bird with the strange habit of protecting its eggs by sitting on a false nest. In that way predators are confused and don't know where she has hidden her baby chicks."

"And why would anyone take her babies away?"

"Rats and bigger birds find them to be a tasty morsel." And then my mother leaned down and nuzzled me, pretending to bite me. I let out a delighted scream.

"Don't do that, Mama. You're scaring me."

I looked overhead and there was a flock of plovers diving into the river for fish. I pulled out my map to make sure I was headed in the right direction; I didn't want to make a mistake causing a delay in getting to my father's house. Trudging up the hill, I focused on the plan that had been forming in my mind since I received the telephone call yesterday. I would explain to my father how dire our circumstances were, which forced me to give his only grandson up for adoption to people in the United States. I was unsure how my father would react to this news. He might remind me that he was against my marrying Ichiro and thought him unworthy. For all I knew he would laugh in my face and say, "I told you so," but it was a chance I had to take. I couldn't let pride get in the way of begging him for help.

He was my last and final hope. I'd propose, "If you are willing to bequeath your sushi shop to me, I could take it over and earn enough money to support my child and my husband. When he recovers, Ichiro and I will run the shop together. He is a good businessman and an excellent manager. And as a condition for this gift, I will hire your mistress, Setsue Chang, to ensure her future as well."

It all made perfect sense. I hadn't discussed this proposal with Ichiro and I wasn't interested if he objected. It was time I took matters into my own hands. With each step I reminded myself of how much my father had done for me years ago. He would surely want to help me now when I was going to be losing my son forever. I prayed he would find it in his heart to throw me a lifeline instead of pointing out what a mess I had made of my life, through no fault of my own other than loving Ichiro, but a mess, nonetheless.

I spotted my father's shop. There was a line of housewives stretching all the way around the corner as they waited for their turn at the counter inside. It was obvious to anyone passing by that this was a shop to buy quality sushi and that its proprietor must be rich. The prices posted in the window would deter all but the wealthiest of customers from buying there. A separate door from the shop led upstairs to my father's apartment. Chopped wood was neatly stacked in an open shed, and small clay pots filled with carefully tended bonsai trees sat on a wooden bench next to the door. The front stoop was still wet from the morning's mopping. Everything was neat and tidy, as was my father's habit.

A stray mongrel ambled out of the alleyway and licked my hand before I reached for the bronze bell to my father's apartment. I pushed him away and yanked hard on the chain to make sure someone would hear it and come quickly. I looked up to see a young boy peering down at me from the second-floor window. A moment later the door opened and the boy led me up the flight of stairs, without speaking.

The chanting of a sutra and the smell of incense filled the air. The boy took two steps at a time to make sure I hastened my pace, but then he turned around and said, "You're too late. My father is gone." I grabbed the wooden banister to steady myself, not only from the shock of hearing my father was dead but because the boy called him "father." He looked about ten or eleven years old with long, skinny legs and broad shoulders.

"Your father…Do you mean Ryo Ito?"

"Yes, who else do you think I mean? I am very proud to be his son."

He quietly opened the door. I felt like I might faint. Would the boy's existence be an impediment to my plans? And why didn't my father hold on long enough so that I could at least say goodbye to him?

The boy's mother, Setsue Chang, sat in the corner weeping as the priest read from his prayer book. My father's large hands were clasped over the white sheet that covered his body. I was struck by how robust he still looked. Except for the bandage wrapped around his head, a visitor would have thought he was just sleeping.

I walked slowly to my father's corpse and kissed his folded hands, which were cold to the touch. As I examined his weathered face, I sensed he had already attained what my priests called *Denaoshi*: his spirit was leaving his body to be reborn again in another body. I had never seen a dead person before. He looked so peaceful. I whispered in his ear, "Thank you for giving me life, Father, and thank you for saving me from the bomb. I wish you could have saved me now."

Then I thanked the priest for taking care of my father's spirit on its way into the next life. Setsue stood up. When Setsue and I were in the hallway, she introduced herself as Ryo's wife. And then she swept away whatever shred of hope I had, announcing, "The boy is my son, Akinobu. Your father adopted him when we married and has bequeathed the shop to him and me. One day my son will be a sushi maker like Ryo, and he'll provide for me in my old age. He had already started training him. It takes ten years at least to be a master sushi maker. Until my son is old enough, I'll find a way to keep the business going."

We stepped outside. She pointed to the housewives standing in front of the shop, our breath making small puffs of clouds in the cold air. Jangling a few coins in her pocket for emphasis, she said, "As you can see, the shop is doing very well."

I felt like spitting in her face, but I was too proud. "You're indeed fortunate. I wish my father had been mindful of his obligations to me and my family, but he had other ideas." Setsue showed no sign of caring one way or the other. I couldn't help prodding her, "You know he never saw my son, not even once. And he's almost two and a half years old. Couldn't he have found the time to visit us in Osaka?"

"He doted on our son, which is often the case with older fathers, and that's all I really know, to be honest with you, Noriko. Once he severed his ties with your mother and settled financial matters in Hiroshima, he turned his back on his former life and concentrated on making a success of himself here for me and my son. He has been a wonderful father and an excellent provider. I could not have asked for more. He hardly ever mentioned you or your son. I think he just closed that chapter in his life once we were a family."

I tried not to react to this stinging retribution. Trading one family for another. I tried to keep the sarcasm out of my voice. "How lucky for you." I buttoned my coat against a wind that started blowing off the river. "I had better be going. I don't want to miss the train back to Osaka."

Setsue observed, "You haven't been here for very long."

"It's just as well I leave now. I have no reason to stay. My father is gone." I couldn't say "dead." It was too cruel.

"May I offer you some fresh sushi to take with you? You can tell your son...What's his name? Oh, yes, Hisashi. Tell your son that the sushi comes from his grandfather's shop."

"I'm not hungry, and Hisashi hasn't developed a taste for sushi just yet."

"Then if you'll excuse me, I must prepare a package for the priest to take back to the monastery. I want to be sure the priests remain good customers. They shouldn't think that, because Ryo is dead, our business will flounder. Your father taught me how to make money and I intend to do just that."

I bowed and said, "Sorry for your loss." I hurried along the canal toward the railroad station, barely noticing the noisy plovers that swooped down over the dark water. Their cries were so loud no one passing by could hear my sobs.

Chapter 39

THREE DAYS AFTER NORIKO's futile trip to Matsue, Ichiro had his meeting with Mr. Yasuda. He trimmed his hair himself, holding up a mirror to see the back of his head and made sure that no stray strands brushed against his collar. He wore his best suit, and a silk tie that had been rescued from his father's possessions. He was especially careful when he pressed his shirt so that he looked like a successful businessman. He thought, *Dress like one and you'll be one.*

Ichiro had difficulty adjusting his eyes to the dazzling marble floor of the Allied Metals Industries lobby and the glistening Christmas tree decorated with paper origami cranes, fake snow, and tinsel. He gave his name to the uniformed guard at the reception desk and was directed to Mr. Yasuda's office on the twentieth floor. Alone in the elevator, he hummed along with the Christmas carols broadcast over the speakers.

His temperature was normal when he left the apartment, and he felt a surge of energy at the prospect of seeing Mr. Yasuda again. He thought about their last game of Go at the sanatorium, which Mr. Yasuda had forfeited. It was not a true win for Ichiro. Perhaps they would have a rematch and he could win fairly. He reminded himself to thank Mr. Yasuda for *The Master of Go,* which contained much to teach him beyond the strategy of the game.

Ichiro sat down on one of the plush velvet sofas opposite the receptionist. Copies of *The Wall Street Journal* and *U.S. News & World Report* were displayed on a large glass coffee table with the December 10 edition of the *Osaka Shimbun.*

As he picked up the newspaper, Ichiro's hands trembled. The door to a more respectable life was right in front of him. He took three tranquilizers from his jacket pocket and swallowed them—more than he should have, but he needed to stay calm and demonstrate to Mr. Yasuda that he would be a good employee.

A few minutes later he heard his name called by a distinctly American voice. He looked up from the newspaper to find a woman with striking platinum blond hair and bright red lipstick standing next to him. He recognized her as the woman stepping out of Mr. Yasuda's Mercedes limousine parked at the front entrance to the sanatorium.

"Good morning, Mr. Uchida. I'm Miss Smith, Mr. Yasuda's personal assistant. He is ready to see you."

Ichiro followed her down a long, carpeted hallway and through heavy double doors.

Mr. Yasuda greeted Ichiro warmly. "So, my friend, have you been practicing your game of Go?"

Ichiro smiled. "I haven't found an opponent with your skill, Mr. Yasuda."

"Ah, but you must practice. Only after ten thousand games will you begin to operate on instinct. Until then, you're just using your head, which can often get in the way."

"How true. Instinct's often more reliable than intellect."

"Well put."

"I'm pleased to see that you're looking so well, Mr. Yasuda."

"Dr. Shizumi is a miracle worker. Of course, I take good care of myself. I have a lot of people counting on me—my family, my employees, etcetera, etcetera, and so forth. I make regular trips to Arashiyama for the baths, and I always have a scotch and soda at the end of the day. A habit I picked up from my American managers in Pittsburgh. And how are you doing, Ichiro? May I call you Ichiro?"

"Of course, Mr. Yasuda. I'm a lot better than the last time you saw me, and I'm looking forward to a job with better prospects."

Mr. Yasuda leaned over and poured two cups of steaming tea from an elaborate bronze teapot. "When I left the sanatorium, you seemed rather deflated," he said. "Of course, that is understandable." He offered Ichiro a cup.

The two men sipped their tea, and Ichiro took a moment to look around Mr. Yasuda's spacious office. Behind his desk were floor-to-ceiling plate glass windows overlooking Osaka. On a wall to the left was a brightly lit van Gogh painting, *Irises*, one the originals the artist painted of this flower. Staring at it, Mr. Yasuda said, "I see you like my *Irises*."

"It is exceptionally beautiful and strangely cheerful given the artist's state of mind. I believe van Gogh was in a mental asylum when he made this painting," Ichiro said. "I have read about his life. He killed himself about a year after finishing this work. Are you familiar with *Wheatfield with Crows?* I think it was his last painting. The black crows indicate a tortured soul."

"I could have bought that painting as well as this one, but it was too unsettling. I may regret that I didn't purchase it someday. It would have been a good investment, but it displeased me. I only like to own what is beautiful."

Ichiro thought, *Like your personal assistant, Miss Smith.*

Mr. Yasuda continued. "While I was studying in Paris, I used to go to the museums all the time. I learned that many artists, not just our van Gogh, have taken their lives: Gorky, Pascin, and there are others. Artists often lead tortured lives, turning to drugs, alcohol, or death to ease their pain." He sighed. "In fact, it is part of the human condition to struggle. But there is almost always a solution to a problem. Or else why would any of us go on living?"

Ichiro took another sip of tea. "I often wonder about that myself. Even in our darkest moments, others are counting on us to forge ahead, and so we do. All sorrows can be borne if we have someone who will listen to our stories. Somehow, it lightens the burden to tell the truth, to say what really happened, even if it is unpleasant and painful. And the more it is repeated, the less power it has over us until it finally loosens its grip on our mind and we are free."

"To be sure, Ichiro. I was impressed by your intelligence and now I see that you're also very insightful."

"My formal education is rather limited. I only made it through high school, but I have tried to teach myself something about the world by reading and listening to the advice of others. I get carried away and spend more time than I should learning for learning's sake. My wife is patient with me, but she'll gently point out I become easily distracted."

"I get the same reaction from my wife, but it's my prerogative to pursue many interests. And I have the money to do so, which is not your case, not yet, anyway." Mr. Yasuda then changed the subject. "You come from a very honorable family. I've heard of your father's reputation as a brilliant negotiator for Izumi Steelworks before the war. Despite your good bloodlines, I know that life has not treated you very well—and I am not speaking of your illness. You're not utilizing your talents. I'd like to offer you a position here at Allied

Metals as a junior bookkeeper. If you do a good job, there is plenty of room for advancement. The company is in a period of rapid expansion. And, who knows? In time, you can earn a salary that truly reflects your worth. As I see it, your abilities far outstrip what you've achieved thus far. You need someone to champion your cause—someone like me!"

Ichiro, bolstered by Mr. Yasuda's encouraging remarks, sat up straight. "I have read in the newspapers that Allied Metals has the contract to provide steel for the Tokaido Shinkansen Railroad."

"Yes, we are building the rail line for the bullet train. It's scheduled for completion on October tenth, 1964, just in time for the opening of the Olympics next year. It's our biggest contract to date. The chief engineer and I met yesterday to discuss our progress, and fortunately, we are ahead of schedule. But I need more staff to watch our expenditures. That's why I called you to come in for an interview." He cleaned his glasses and then added, "You might say that our reputation is riding on the bullet train." He slapped his knee and laughed at his own joke.

Ichiro smiled. "I'm honored you would even consider me."

"There is a prerequisite, which I am sure will be no problem for you. Our bookkeeping candidates are required to take a test. If you wouldn't mind doing so right now, I'll be able to formalize my offer within a matter of days. Miss Smith will show you to the conference room. No one is using it, and it's a comfortable spot to take the exam."

Mr. Yasuda spoke into the intercom on his desk, and Miss Smith entered his office seconds later, as if she had been hovering outside his door waiting to be summoned.

Ichiro rose and bowed to Mr. Yasuda. "Good luck, Ichiro. I look forward to having you on board." Ichiro felt as if he had been anointed and followed Miss Smith to a wood-paneled conference room. The scent of her perfume made him dizzy. The mahogany table was surrounded by modern, orange swivel chairs and there was an *ikebana* floral arrangement at the center of the table. The room featured museum-quality wood block prints by Utagawa Hiroshige. Miss Smith waited a moment while Ichiro took in these works, which reflected Mr. Yasuda's refined taste. "I forgot to tell Mr. Yasuda how much I enjoyed reading the book he gave me."

"*The Master of Go*. It's one of his favorites. I had quite a time finding it. It's a popular read."

"I learned a lot from the book. It has many themes, but the one that interested me the most was the struggle of tradition versus modernity: *From the way of Go, the beauty of Japan and the Orient had fled. Everything had become science and regulation.* Mr. Yasuda has obviously managed to find a balance between science and beauty."

"I will share your observation with him." Ichiro hoped his remark would impress Mr. Yasuda. He was angry with himself for not having brought it up when he was with him so he could show him how carefully he had read the book, but he was distracted by the van Gogh and the opulent surroundings of a successful man.

"Feel free to use the calculator or the slide rule," Miss Smith said. "We've also given you currency conversion tables, which you may refer to. I'll be in the reception area. Bring the test out when you've finished. Good luck, Mr. Uchida. Mr. Yasuda thinks highly of you and would like to see you at Allied Metals."

After she closed the door, Ichiro wiped the perspiration from his forehead. His teeth began to chatter uncontrollably, whether from nerves or the pills. He scanned the test quickly—only twelve questions. He read the first question:

"Allied Metals needs to buy two hundred tons of nickel from Indonesia. Each ton is 558,250 rupiahs. How much will the purchase cost in yen?"

He turned the button of the calculator on and pressed the keys. The sound of the keys hitting the roll of paper pulsated in his head as if they were jackhammers. He blinked until the disturbance died down.

He skipped the first question. He looked at the next question and decided to answer it without using the calculator. "Allied Metals will charge an interest rate of five percent on all invoices more than ninety days delinquent. How much is owed on an invoice of one million yen?"

Ichiro wrote the answer down in the test book, but his pencil broke and the point flew across the room. He stood up to find the lead point. The room spun around, and he keeled over. When he opened his eyes, he was stunned to realize he was lying face down on the carpet and twenty minutes had gone by. In his present condition, he had no hope of making any headway with the test. He turned off the humming calculator and picked up his test paper.

When he walked into the reception area, Miss Smith looked up from her typewriter. "Mr. Uchida, are you feeling all right? You look pale. Would you like a glass of water?"

"No, thank you. Please tell Mr. Yasuda I greatly appreciate his kind offer, but I have another opportunity for which I'm better suited. I'll look forward to playing a game of Go with him again."

"Don't you want to give me your test?" she asked. "You finished in record time. Mr. Yasuda will be impressed. We can keep it on file should something else open up at a later date."

"No, that won't be necessary." Ichiro stuffed the test paper into his breast pocket and hurried toward the elevator.

Ichiro felt as if a swarm of bees were stinging his eyes. He could barely hear the Christmas music playing in the elevator. When the doors opened to the lobby, he was assaulted by the bright sunlight streaming through the tall glass windows. He hurried outside, sat down on a marble bench in front of the office building, and tried to compose himself.

A man dressed in a gray pin-striped suit wearing an old-fashioned bowler hat sat at the far end of the bench feeding breadcrumbs to a flock of pigeons. He looked like his father, Hide-Ichi, who was always telling his children, "Remember to do your best so that you can be proud of yourself and your accomplishments." Ichiro coughed into his freshly pressed handkerchief and whispered, "I'm sorry, Father. I have disappointed you once again."

A pigeon perched on the back of the bench and pecked at Ichiro's shoulder as if to sharply scold him and then flew off. Ichiro walked toward the subway. He couldn't tell Noriko what had happened. He'd say that the job had just been filled by the applicant ahead of him and he'd look for something else when Hisashi was gone.

⌒

THERE WAS A LARGE envelope in front of his apartment door. When Ichiro leaned over to pick it up he had to grab the doorknob to keep his balance. Opening the door, he was relieved to see Noriko was not home. He sat down at the table, and taking a knife, sliced the package open. Inside was a letter from his sister informing him that everything was in order for Hisashi to come to the United States. There was an airplane ticket with Hisashi's name in the box labeled "Passenger" as well as instructions from the airline. The departure date was February 29, 1964, eleven weeks until he and Noriko would say goodbye forever to their son. He wished it were sooner. Isn't that what a man sentenced to death would feel, he thought? Wasn't it better to just get it over with than to live through one more torturous day in anticipation of the agony that awaited him?

Leaving the apartment, he walked to the nearest newsstand and bought a copy of the *Asahi-Shimbun*. Maybe there was something in the want ads he might be suited for. He could apply now and ask for a reprieve until Hisashi was gone. At least that would give him something to count on later, now that he had failed so miserably at Allied Metals. How could he have made such a terrible mistake as to take three tranquilizers? He should have known better. And to have forgotten to mention the book Mr. Yasuda had given him? Clearly he was not in his right mind.

Returning to the apartment, he poured a whiskey, swallowed another pill, and then sat on a bench on the balcony surrounded by the dying potted plants and a stack of wood and paint cans. He stuck his finger into the dirt. The plants had been neglected and needed water, but he was too tired to get up. Besides, wasn't that Noriko's job? He opened the newspaper; his attention was drawn to the article announcing the death of sixty-year-old film director Yasujirō Ozu. The last time Ichiro saw him at the tearoom, Mr. Ozu was looking forward to completing *An Autumn Afternoon*. The article quoted Mr. Ozu: "I want the Japanese character for Emptiness carved on my tombstone, for Emptiness is 'the dark womb of all creation.' Yes, out of nothing comes something. And if that was true was the opposite also true, 'Out of the fullness of life comes nothingness?'" Ichiro grappled with this puzzle and thought about what characters he wished carved on his own tombstone. Maybe Emptiness might suit him well, because that is how he felt—empty and alone.

～

CARRYING A SLEEPING HISASHI up the stairs, I fumbled for my keys. It was six in the evening and I hoped that Ichiro had made a light meal for us, but when I opened the door it was obvious that he hadn't prepared anything. The table was bare except for a folded newspaper.

"Shall I go downstairs and get us something to eat?" asked Ichiro.

"Don't bother. I'm not really very hungry. I just want to get out of my uniform and put Hisashi to bed. It was a sad day at the tearoom. Everyone was talking about Mr. Ozu's death."

"Yes, I was just catching up on the news myself. Odd that he died on his birthday. I wonder how often that happens. It's as if his life had come full circle. First day, last day. We all know our birthday, but we have no idea of our death day until it arrives, often out of nowhere unless we bring it upon ourselves. Suicide is a form of control over our destiny, isn't it?"

"Or an act of desperation. And selfishness leaving behind the people who love us to mourn their loss."

I noticed Ichiro's half-empty whiskey glass, but he seemed sober, and when he next spoke, his words were clear. Picking up a packet on the table, he said, "This came from Mitsuko today. She says that everything is settled. We have been given permission to send Hisashi to America." I tried to stay calm as I listened to Ichiro read the ticket information: "The Northwest Airlines plane will leave Haneda Airport at ten a.m. on February twenty-ninth, with one stop in Hawaii, and then will continue on to San Francisco." He added, "Everything has been paid for by Mitsuko and Harry and there is extra money in the packet for whatever we want to spend it on."

There it was—February 29, 1964. It seemed like the date of a sentencing. I would become a childless mother, with only my husband to take away the pain of such an unimaginable loss. I felt numb. I couldn't react to this information with anything that might sound cheerful. Instead I turned my attention to Ichiro, wanting to know if he had good news for me about his interview earlier in the day.

"Just my luck. Someone came in right before me and Mr. Yasuda offered him the job. But he said he would contact me if something else should become available. They expect to be hiring right up to the start of the Olympics. At least I did well on the test."

"What did you get?"

"One hundred percent."

"Well, you must be very proud of that."

"I am."

Something about the way Ichiro answered my questions made me think he wasn't telling me the truth, but I felt it best not to question him further. It was of only secondary importance. All I could think about was the devastating reality that soon Hisashi would be gone and I'd have to face life without him. And who could anticipate how that might affect Ichiro? Would his son's departure be another in a succession of body blows that might ultimately crush his spirit?

Taking a beer out of the refrigerator, I sipped directly from the bottle, too tired to wash a glass. Ichiro sat in the dark watching me. I asked, "Why don't you put on the Van Cliburn record? It always reminds me of the second happiest day of my life—when you proposed to me."

"And what is the first?"

"The day Hisashi was born."

PART THREE

Chapter 40

1964

HISASHI LOOKED OVER HIS shoulder to make sure his parents were still standing at the gate. He saw his mother waving to him and mouthing the words "you are my sunshine." His father threw him a kiss, and then they disappeared behind a long line of passengers carrying suitcases and shopping bags. Hisashi kept turning around trying to catch a last glimpse of his parents.

Miss Yume, the stewardess, told him to look straight ahead or he might trip and hurt himself. "And then what will we tell your mama?" Hisashi didn't want to make his mother sad, so he focused his attention on his feet: one step, two steps, three steps, four steps, and then he was on the airplane. The stewardess took Hisashi to the cockpit and Captain Morito saluted the toddler. "Welcome aboard Northwest Flight 237, Master Uchida. And where are you going today?"

"America."

"Very good because that's where we're going too. Miss Yume will take good care of you. She has a special gift for you right now as you're our youngest passenger."

The stewardess leaned over and pinned a set of Northwest Airlines wings onto Hisashi's jacket, then put a lanyard around his neck with his name printed on it. He felt very important because, when he looked down the aisle, none of the passengers wore anything like this.

The airline assigned Hisashi a seat in the first row of economy class right on the aisle so Miss Yume could reach him easily. Putting his suitcase underneath the seat in front of him, she fastened his seat belt and told him not to take it off unless he needed to go to the bathroom; and if he did, he should wave his hand and she would help him. He sat quietly with his maroon wool jacket still buttoned and his red toy truck clenched tightly in his hand.

He swung his legs back and forth and spun the wheels of his truck around. The seat next to him was left empty.

When the airplane took off, Hisashi leaned forward to look out the window. There were fluffy white clouds and then the sun broke through. He squinted against the bright light. When Miss Yume pulled the shade down, Hisashi, tired from all the confusion and excitement of the past few days, fell asleep. As the airplane descended into the Honolulu airport hours later, Hisashi woke up. His ears hurt and he cried out in pain. Miss Yume gave him paper cups to hold against his ears to relieve the pressure.

When the plane reached the gate, Hisashi waved at Miss Yume, "Shee, shee. I need to go to the bathroom." She showed him how to sit on the little toilet, and when he finished she helped him wash his hands and then wiped his tear-stained face with a paper towel.

When Hisashi was buckled into his seat, he pulled out his suitcase and unsnapped the latches. He took out the photograph of his mother and father, which Noriko had placed on top of his clothes. Hisashi held the photograph in his lap. Reaching into his jacket pocket, he pulled out a coin. Pressing it against Ichiro's lips in the photograph, he said, "Play horsey with me, Dada." As the plane gained altitude, he kissed the photograph and then put it back in his suitcase so he wouldn't lose it. Picking up his red truck, he spun the wheels around again, saying, "Faster, faster, Hisashi." Then he took out his favorite book, *Little One Inch*, and turned the pages, telling himself the story. He had heard it so often he knew it by heart. He even announced "the end" when he came to the last page.

Feeling bored, he unfastened his seat belt and slipped out of his seat. Miss Yume was at the back of the plane and didn't notice he had gotten up. He ran down the aisle saying hello to all the passengers. They were enchanted by this charming little boy and engaged him in conversation, but when an older woman asked him, "Where are your mama and papa?" he didn't know how to answer. He started to cry, alerting Miss Yume. She rushed up the aisle and took him back to his seat. "Would you like something to drink, Hisashi? How about a Coca Cola?"

Hisashi shrugged his shoulders. He didn't know what it was. She brought him a plastic cup filled with a bubbly brown liquid. He took a tentative sip, then drank it all and handed the empty cup back to Miss Yume.

Leaning back in his seat, his eyelids felt heavy and he fell back to sleep, dreaming of his parents waving to him and his father promising they would see him soon. When he woke up the plane was on the ground and passengers were standing up to collect their belongings. There was loud talking in a language Hisashi did not understand. Miss Yume told him, "We are here, in America. You can keep your wings, but it's time to get off the plane. You are an excellent passenger."

Miss Yume unfastened his seatbelt and pulled out his suitcase. He buttoned his jacket and put his maroon cap on all by himself.

Hisashi, sure his parents were waiting for him, was eager to get off the plane. Hadn't they said they would be taking another plane? The stewardess took his hand and led him to the head of the line of disembarking passengers. Instead of his parents, two people he had never seen before rushed toward him. The woman picked him up in her arms, saying in Japanese, "My son, my son," between unrestrained sobs.

Miss Yume said, "Forgive me, but I need to check your identification to make sure you are the boy's aunt and uncle. Northwest is fully responsible for his safety from portal to portal."

"Of course." Harry handed her his driver's license.

"Thank you. Your nephew is enchanting."

"I hope he wasn't any bother," said Harry.

"Not at all. It was very brave of him to travel all this way by himself. Too bad his parents could not accompany him."

Harry was not about to explain the circumstances of the situation. "Yes. We want to thank you, Miss Yume, for taking good care of him."

Handing Harry Hisashi's suitcase, she smiled. "We all wish you the best of luck. Goodbye, Master Hisashi. It was a pleasure having you on board."

Hisashi nodded and held onto Mitsuko's hand tightly. At least she spoke Japanese, which was not the case with the other people in the reception area. He kept looking around, hoping to see his parents, but they were not there. He tried to remain brave, but after a few minutes he felt totally lost and started to cry all over again.

Mitsuko tried to comfort him. "Oh, my poor little boy. Don't cry. I promised your daddy Ichiro we will take very good care of you. You will be our precious little boy we will love forever and forever." Hisashi wiped his tears with his hand and looked at Mitsuko, puzzled by what she had just said. He didn't understand her, even if she was speaking Japanese.

Chapter 41

THE DRIVE FROM SAN Francisco to Glendive, Montana, took three days. Harry was relieved when city traffic was in the rearview mirror and they were on the open road. By the time they reached Glendive, Hisashi had learned twenty English words, which Harry practiced with him: car, elephant, snow, and the names of various American cars that were hard to pronounce like Chevrolet, Pontiac, and Ford.

Every time Mitsuko tried to encourage him to call her "Mama," however, he said, "No." Harry wanted to know what they were talking about, but she said, "Oh I just keep asking him if he wants to go potty." Although she was not surprised by his reaction, she didn't want Harry to know that Hisashi was resistant to calling her "Mama." She knew she had to be patient, and she was convinced that he would eventually find a name for her even if it wasn't Mama. Perhaps he'd be happy with "Mommy."

Turning into the driveway of Knauff's Trailer Court Harry woke Mitsuko and carried Hisashi into the trailer. Mitsuko turned the heat up. They had set the thermostat to sixty degrees to save propane while they were away. Their cat, Toby, wound herself around their legs with her tail in the air and howled for attention. "Oh, you spoiled cat. You're going to have to get used to sharing us with someone else," said Mitsuko.

Mitsuko changed Hisashi into a pair of freshly laundered flannel pajamas, tucked him into his cowboy bed, and turned on the nightlight. The light cast a silhouette of the moon and stars on the ceiling. While Hisashi slept, Mitsuko unpacked his suitcase. It gave her a start to see the photograph of Ichiro and Noriko lying on top of his things. She pressed the photograph to her heart, and in a whisper she thanked them for this unimaginable gift of a son. Just saying the words made her choke with a mixture of happiness and sadness.

Underneath freshly ironed shirts and pants was a teardrop box of paulownia wood. Mitsuko had heard of these boxes and so she knew what was inside, but she opened it anyway. There was Hisashi's dried umbilical cord—dark brown and shriveled up. She gasped. The symbolic meaning was clear—the natural bond between mother and child. In giving it away to Mitsuko, Noriko was severing her ties with her son and passing them on to Mitsuko. This gesture must have caused Noriko unimaginable pain, thought Mitsuko, but she did it to fulfill the promise she and Ichiro had made.

Mitsuko made sure Hisashi was fast asleep. Then she fell into bed, exhausted from the trip and all the emotion that welled up inside her. But at three in the morning she woke up to the sound of sobbing. Hisashi stood by her side of the bed. "What's the matter, sweetheart?"

"There is a snake in my bed."

"No, the snakes are fast asleep in the mountains far away."

He cried harder. "I want Mama to take it out of my bed."

"Come. I'll get a flashlight and we'll look under the covers." After taking a flashlight from a drawer in the kitchen, she pulled the quilt off his bed and then shined the light underneath the bed. "See? Nothing there. You were just having a bad dream." And then she touched the sheets. Hisashi had wet his bed and his pajamas were wet too. She took out a clean pair of pajamas, changed him, and changed the bedding while he stood in the corner watching her. He kept rocking back and forth. She thought, "That is just what Ichiro used to do when he was upset." She picked him up and asked, "Would you like me to stay with you for a while?"

"Yes."

Mitsuko sat in the rocking chair and wrapped Hisashi in the quilt. He leaned his cheek against her shoulder and she sang to him a few bars of "Home on the Range." Her voice was not beautiful like his mother's but the words were familiar. He closed his eyes; the rocking and the warmth of Mitsuko's body slowly comforted him and lulled him back to sleep.

Mitsuko hoped Hisashi would get over his frustration. She could not bear to see the child unhappy. But that wasn't the case. He had more accidents in his bed and developed a nervous twitch in his eye. She wondered if there might be something wrong with him. "Noriko told me he was already toilet trained. He seems to be going backward, and I don't like the way he scrunches up his face as if he's tasted a sour lemon."

Harry said, "He's had so many changes in his life. I'm sure all of this is temporary, but if it will put your mind at ease, make an appointment with Dr. Carlson."

⁓

HISASHI SAT ON MITSUKO's lap in the waiting room of the children's clinic at the hospital. She had not been near the hospital since she suffered a miscarriage. Being in the building was a painful reminder of that terrible disappointment. How different things were now.

Dr. Carlson lifted Hisashi onto the examination table. After asking Mitsuko a few questions, he took out his stethoscope and listened to Hisashi's heart and lungs. "All good there." Then he looked in the boy's eyes and tapped each knee to check his reflexes. "I'd say your nephew is perfectly healthy. The eye twitching is probably just a reaction to all the changes. I'd give it a few more weeks. If the tick doesn't go away, we can always do an EEG. But I don't think it'll be necessary."

Mitsuko asked, "Can you check his lungs?"

"I already have. They're clear." Mitsuko breathed a sigh of relief. She had seen the paper from Japan giving him a clean bill of health, but she still worried he might be carrying the tuberculosis virus and that it could erupt someday. She realized she was a bundle of nerves. Maybe that was why Hisashi had this eye twitch and was wetting his bed, she thought.

"Doctor Carlson, do you think you could give me something to calm my nerves?"

"I'll say the same thing to you. You've had a lot of changes. I suspect that, in a few weeks, you'll be a lot calmer. If you aren't better in a few weeks, I'll prescribe something. In the meantime, get some rest. You'll need it to take care of your nephew. He's at an age when he's curious about everything and will want your undivided attention."

"When you speak to me about Dwight, Dr. Carlson, would you call him 'your son,' instead of 'your nephew?' I know it's a little soon for you to think of him that way, but Harry and I plan on adopting him, and as far as we are concerned, he's already our boy and will be from now on. We've also decided to call him Dwight instead of Hisashi, although I have to admit I sometimes forget. Hisashi is an easier name for me. But Harry keeps reminding me, and

I'm sure I'll forget his old name soon enough. Harry picked his name after President Dwight D. Eisenhower."

"That's a very grown-up name for a little boy. But in time—before you even know it—he'll grow into it and it will fit him perfectly. If you have any further concerns, please come back to see me. Otherwise, I'll assume that Dwight is thriving and you're doing fine too."

Mitsuko was proud of herself for speaking up. A few years ago, she wouldn't have dared to say such a thing to an important person like Dr. Carlson. But living in the United States had changed her from an obedient Japanese girl into an independent woman who spoke her mind, whether Harry liked it or not.

Chapter 42

ICHIRO INSISTED WE GO to the family registry in Kobe on our way home from Haneda International Airport after Hisashi left. "I want the family record to be correct." The official pulled out a large parchment paper with the name "Uchida" and the names of his parents, grandparents, and great grandparents entered in the appropriate places on the koseki.

"Why do we need to do this now? Hisashi is still our son until the adoption goes through," I asked.

"Not really. We have given up our parental rights so it's only proper that his name be removed from the koseki." Ichiro put on his reading glasses, and taking a heavy eraser, he removed Hisashi's name. Where his name had been was a black smudge that looked as if someone had wiped an ash-covered finger across the space. He did this in a matter-of-fact way as if he was correcting a column of numbers. "Unless we have another son, this will be the end of the Uchida family line."

"How can you think of having another child? We don't deserve one."

"To the contrary, Noriko. If I get better and our life stabilizes financially, there is nothing more I would wish for than to have another child."

I thought, *So you could give that child away too if something goes wrong in your life?*

As we reboarded the train from Kobe to Osaka, Ichiro asked me to carry our overnight suitcase. He breathed heavily as we walked through the station, and the smoke from the locomotive settled into his lungs, causing him to cough uncontrollably. When we found our seats, I stood on my tiptoes to hoist our bag into the overhead rack. Sitting next to him, I took out the Lafcadio Hearn collection of stories so I could finish the one I started on the ride to Matsue.

The ghost mother returned night after night, and a priest was called to discover why she kept appearing. He discovered a love letter hidden in the *tansu* in her bedroom. He took it, without revealing its contents to the members of the household, and the ghost mother disappeared, her secret kept safe with the priest for all eternity.

As I closed the book, Ichiro said, "Noriko, I think it's best for both of us not to bring up Hisashi's name or to talk about what we've done. It will make it easier on me."

"Have you thought about how it will make me feel, Ichiro? I can't just erase my son from my mind or force myself not think about him: what he is doing, how he is feeling, whether he misses us. I'll try my best, but I cannot promise anything. Who else do I have to turn to for a comforting word but you? I am too ashamed to bring it up with my mother or Setsuko."

"Don't expect it from me. I have nothing to say. You may think I'm not affected by what we've done, but you're wrong. Until I met you, I was told not to show my feelings, and if I did, my father would ignore them. You're lucky in that way, Noriko. You know how to express feelings. Otherwise, how could you have been a good actress?"

"And now you want me to pretend I have no feelings where Hisashi is concerned? That we can just go on with our lives and forget about Hisashi?"

"Yes. It will be your finest role—the mother who forgets." I thought to myself, *No, I would never have auditioned for such a role, no matter how famous it might have made me.*

〜

I WAS RELIEVED TO have an excuse to leave the apartment and go to work. It was difficult to see Ichiro so downtrodden. Even in the morning, when the sun filtered through the shoji screen into the apartment, sadness hung over me like a mourner's shroud. The only chore that gave me some pleasure was to attend to my plants, which came back to life after months of being neglected.

I sorted through all of Hisashi's belonging. Some I sent on to Mitsuko and Harry, and the rest I gave to the Tenrikyo church to dispense to families in need with toddlers. I spent hours in the sanctuary praying for the strength to be a good wife.

On the days when Ichiro felt strong enough, he walked his niece, Kazuko, to school, and he continued on his woodworking projects. As with everything he did, relying on books from the library to teach himself the intricacies of the craft, he was becoming quite a master woodworker. Ichiro spent hours listening to his record collection while he honed his woodworking skills. I saw all of this as a form of therapy, and hoped that, before too long, he'd feel well enough to look for another job. Whatever had happened in his interview with Mr. Yasuda at Allied Metals seemed to have derailed him, and stolen what little motivation he had.

～

WHEN THE CHERRY BLOSSOMS arrived, Ichiro and I joined my family for a flower viewing party in one of Osaka's parks. The riotous beauty of the pink blossoms covering the tree branches and floating to the ground only heightened our sorrow—rain and barren trees would have been more appropriate to our mood. Hisashi had been gone a little over a month, but the days and nights dragged. I found it difficult to see my sister and her family enjoying themselves, and kept imagining Hisashi playing with his cousins. When I saw little boys about his age running through the park chasing a ball or flying a kite I wanted to cry. Kazuko asked me, "Where is Hisashi?" I couldn't answer her honestly and made up a story. "He's visiting his aunt and uncle in America, but he'll be back before too long. Don't worry, sweetheart." Ichiro reprimanded me later, but he had no ground to stand on after the lie he told Hisashi at the airport, "We'll be on the very next plane." It seemed as if the two of us were punishing one another despite our pledge to be understanding.

I was tempted to call Mitsuko from the tearoom so I could hear Hisashi's voice, but I put it off, afraid that I might not be able to hide my emotions. When Mitsuko sent us some pictures, I had a hard time looking at them. Mitsuko wrote that Hisashi was happy, but I was so miserable without him I wondered if she was telling us the truth. He looked well taken care of. But he wasn't smiling.

～

AT THE END OF April, Ichiro went back to the tuberculosis clinic for a consultation with Dr. Shizumi. "The X-ray of your lungs looks rather good. I think you can go back to work."

"I was let go by my employer for too many absences. I probably tried to go back to work too soon. I'm going to apply for a car salesman position once I get my driver's license. I've been keeping track of the newspaper ads and reading up on the Japanese auto industry. It's booming, so I shouldn't have any trouble getting hired. I'm good with people and numbers and my experience at the tearoom and the Aki-Torii proves that. I was going nowhere in the restaurant business anyway. My former employer, Mrs. Fujiwara, has agreed to vouch for my honesty and hard work—that's what prospective employers like to hear."

Dr. Shizumi said, "I'm glad to see you're making plans for yourself. I had begun to think that you'd given up. But you'll have to pace yourself and not allow your prospective boss to put too much pressure on you at the beginning."

Ichiro grimaced. "Being new on the job, I'll have to prove myself, and I can't do that by being lazy. I've been thinking I'd like to buy a car someday— even a used one. I'm tired of always having to take public transportation. And it would be refreshing to take a trip to the mountains or the seashore with Noriko. She needs a vacation even more than I do. A change of scenery is good for the body and soul."

Dr. Shizumi said, "Your boy would like that. I just bought a Toyota, the number-one seller. It handles like a dream. My son loves going for a ride in it with me. I sometimes let him sit on my lap and steer the car when it's parked in front of our house. You should consider applying to Toyota for a job." Glancing at his chart, Dr. Shizumi said, "According to my notes, your boy is two and a half now. How's he doing?"

Ichiro's face clouded over. "I wouldn't know. I haven't seen him for a while." He felt his chest tighten and heard a ringing in his ears, but he continued, "My wife and I sent Hisashi away. He's living in America with my sister and her husband. They plan to adopt him as soon as the paperwork is in order, and then they'll apply for his American citizenship."

Dr. Shizumi sputtered, "You never mentioned this to me."

"And what would you have said?" Putting his jacket on, Ichiro stood in the doorway of the examination room. "Not to be disrespectful, but I didn't need to hear your opinion. I suggest that you stick to my lungs, where you seem to be doing a good job. That's your area of expertise, isn't it?"

"You're right, Ichiro. I was out of line, and that's why I referred you to a psychiatrist. Did you ever follow up? I never heard from him."

"I don't need a psychiatrist. I need a job. And now, if you'll excuse me, I promised my wife I'd pick something up for her at the grocery store. She doesn't have time because she's working long hours. You can imagine how embarrassing it is for me to have her supporting us. I'm shirking my duties as a husband. And I was certainly not living up to my responsibilities as a father."

Dr. Shizumi looked at Ichiro; it was obvious to Ichiro he was stunned by this turn of events and by the disrespectful way Ichiro addressed him. The doctor adjusted his stethoscope as if reminding himself where his attention should lie. He extended his hand, wished Ichiro good luck in finding a job, and instructed him to return to the clinic in three months for a routine checkup.

～

ICHIRO STOPPED AT A newsstand at the entrance to the train station and bought a newspaper. It was noon so the train was nearly empty, and he found a seat next to the window. He opened the paper and glanced at the headlines. Toward the middle of the paper was a full-page advertisement for the Toyota Publica Deluxe; the ad featured a family of four with smiles on their faces seated in the car and waving to the camera. The copy read, "The Deluxe model of the People's car. Go in style for only 389,000 yen." He imagined their fictitious life: the father with a company job and enough money to buy this expensive car, a happy wife staying at home to take care of their children, a boy and a girl. He folded the newspaper neatly and stuck it in his jacket pocket. He would show the advertisement to Noriko.

Several weeks later, Ichiro passed his practical driver's test and was immediately hired as a salesman by the Toyota Motor Company. At thirty-two he was the oldest new recruit, and to Ichiro, some of the salesmen looked like they had just graduated from high school. Was he hallucinating, or did they call him "TB man" behind his back? Had someone uncovered his medical records? Had Dr. Shizumi sent a letter to the dealership warning them of his medical condition? His mind was spinning ridiculous tales. Had Dr. Shizumi broken patient-doctor confidentiality he would not have been offered this job. He told himself, *I'm making no sense.*

He didn't fraternize with the other salesmen. During his breaks, he stayed in the employee lounge and studied the handbook to make sure he knew all the details about the newest car, the UP10 Series. The deluxe model featured a heater, radio, chrome décor, and reclining seats.

In a training session, the general manager yelled out, "Mr. Uchida, tell us again why Toyota offers extended warranties to our customers."

"We offer extended warranties because we are so confident in the quality of our cars. We have the best mechanics and the highest-grade steel to give you the safest, smoothest, and most reliable ride."

"Very good. Now if you would just say it with more enthusiasm, you'll certainly be able to meet your quota. The company has set a goal of four thousand cars a month. And this office is expected to generate five percent of the company's goal."

Ichiro quickly calculated that his division was responsible for selling two hundred cars a month, and with five salesmen, each salesman had to sell forty cars per month. That seemed like an impossible goal. The general manager continued, "I have an exciting announcement. We will be rolling out our convertible model in the next month, in time for summer holidays. Who knows? We might even exceed our goal if we all work hard. I expect you to come in six days a week from now through August, is that clear? Do any of you have a problem with that?" No one said a word, grateful to have a job with a company like Toyota.

The six-day-a-week schedule surprised Ichiro. Such a schedule would be taxing even for a much younger man without an underlying health condition. He started perspiring underneath his company jacket. Turning away, he coughed into his handkerchief and felt lightheaded, but he remained standing until everyone was dismissed. Before leaving the showroom, the manager approached Ichiro.

"Since you are the oldest recruit on the sales force, I expect you to set the pace for the other salesmen. Some of the boys don't know what it means to put in an honest day's work. From what your former employer, Mrs. Fujiwara, told me, you'll do whatever it takes to get the job done. That's why I hired you."

Ichiro said, "You needn't worry, sir. I intend to be the number-one salesman here—all I have to do is show a little more enthusiasm in my presentation as you so aptly suggested."

"Well put. I'm glad you listened to what I was saying and will take my advice to heart. Now, go on home. I'll see you bright and early tomorrow morning!"

Ichiro took off his jacket with the Toyota insignia on the pocket as soon as he stepped outside. He didn't want anyone seeing the insignia broadcasting to all the world he was just a car salesman instead of an important professional man. What if he ran into one of his customers from the tearoom? He'd feel so foolish. He put his hat on to hide his face. He could just imagine the expression on Mrs. Tanaka's face in her cat-eye sunglasses if she passed him on the street. She certainly wouldn't be inviting him on any day trips with her sister to the mountains for her amusement. He thought of his position as a car salesman as a step or two below a restaurant manager. At least there he had a staff to manage and the respect of his customers and coworkers. At Toyota, he was a new recruit who had to prove himself, jumping through hoops to meet a nearly impossible quota.

At the end of June, Ichiro had met half of his assigned goal and there were still two months left before he'd be judged on his results. So, the pressure was on. He told himself, "I'd better put the gas on," and then he laughed at his silly joke. It reminded him of Mr. Yasuda and his ridiculous joke about their future "riding on the bullet train." He wondered if this is what happens to men when they adopt the culture of the company they work for, whether they are a lowly salesman or its president. Does that nonsense start at the top and dribble downhill, he wondered? Maybe someday he'd find out if he went from success to success and ended up in a corner office, with large windows and a view of the Osaka skyline, at Toyota's headquarters. All he needed was luck on his side, which had been to this point surely lacking in his life.

The showroom was buzzing with activity. As the manager predicted, the Toyota convertible was a huge success. A bell rang in the employees' lounge, announcing that a customer had walked through the door. Ichiro rushed out onto the floor. The manager addressed Ichiro, "Mr. Uchida, this is Mr. and Mrs. Suzuki. They are interested in the convertible." Turning to the well-dressed couple, the manager said, "This is one of our best salesmen. He'll take good care of you." Underneath his breath, he whispered in Ichiro's ear, "Enthusiasm, old man! And don't let them get away. They look like they can afford a luxury model."

Ichiro didn't know whether to turn and run from embarrassment or to shake his high school friend's hand. He hadn't seen Norimitsu or his wife Maemi since he and Noriko married. Ichiro remembered Maemi was pregnant with their first child at his wedding.

Norimitsu looked elated to see his former classmate. "Ichiro, we haven't seen you since your wedding. We moved to Tokyo for my job, but we've come back to Osaka. Why didn't you answer any of my letters? We thought you had disappeared."

Ichiro spoke quietly so the manager wouldn't hear his answer. "I had some health problems. It hasn't been an easy time for me or Noriko. But things are turning around. I recently landed a job here. Isn't it just my luck that, of all the Toyota showrooms in Osaka, you'd walk into mine? It's got to be fate."

While talking, Ichiro steered them to the most expensive convertible on the floor. "Would you like to take a spin in the new convertible? She's a real beauty and she handles like a dream. Perfect for family vacations."

Ichiro went through the list of features, being sure to emphasize the warranty as the manager strolled by because this was something he was proud of. The manager nodded as Ichiro gave his pitch. Maemi's eyes seemed to glaze over, but Norimitsu nodded politely as if listening to a waiter telling them the specials of the day. Ichiro then rubbed his hands and pantomimed turning the wheel of a car. "How about I take you out on the open road and let you see how she performs, or if you wish, you can drive the convertible yourself, so long as I'm along for the ride. I never tire of the car's smoothness. You won't even feel a pothole."

Maemi laughed. "Your enthusiasm is infectious, Ichiro, but I'm pregnant and I get carsick easily." She rubbed her belly. "This will be number three. We already have twin boys so we need a bigger car, what with all the paraphernalia an infant needs." Opening the door of the car, she sat in the back seat. "This car is really very roomy, and it has that new leather smell I just love." She breathed in and out.

Ichiro felt encouraged by her comment. Perhaps he'd make a sale right then and there. "So does this car seem like the ticket?"

Norimitsu answered, "Not just yet. We don't want to rush into anything. To be honest, this is the first car we've looked at." Ichiro felt deflated, but he held onto his smile. "Give me your telephone number, Ichiro, and your home address, and we'll call you to come over for dinner with Noriko. We just rented a three-bedroom apartment in Namba, and we'll be there until we find a house to buy."

Handing them his card, Ichiro said, "You can reach me anytime at the showroom. I'm keeping long hours through the summer. It's our busiest season." He didn't want to admit he and Noriko didn't have a private telephone or give them his address, which was in a neighborhood some might consider shabby. Ichiro couldn't let them leave without trying one more time to close the deal. "What do you think of the convertible, Norimitsu?"

"We like it. If we decide to buy one, we'll be sure to give you the order. We're thinking about the model you showed us, but with all the additional accessories available and in white. We're planning on holding onto it for at least five years and so we might as well get the best. Don't you think so, Maemi?"

"Whatever you like. You're paying for it."

Norimitsu gave Ichiro his business card. "If you don't hear from us, you must give us a call. We are right in the middle of unpacking and things are a bit hectic. I'm also just settling into my new job."

Ichiro read his card aloud, "Vice President, Finance, SONY Electronics. Congratulations, my friend. You are doing very well for yourself. I always knew you would be a success."

There was a moment of awkward silence between the two classmates. Norimitsu extended his hand. "Well, it's wonderful to see you again, old man. And you must send our greetings to Noriko. We'll look forward to getting to know her. Weddings are hardly the time to have a friendly chat about what really matters. By the way, do you have children?"

Ichiro wiped his brow. Although the showroom was air-conditioned, he felt his temperature spiking from exerting himself. "No. Not yet. But we're trying. Noriko is getting impatient, but I tell her she just needs to relax and enjoy herself and it will happen."

Maemi smiled. "Take her on a vacation. Nurse's orders. It works for me every time. Maybe in one of these new convertibles."

"Toyota doesn't extend employee discounts, so I don't think that's going to happen any time soon. But if I prove myself, the sky's the limit." He adjusted his tie and then put his hand over his Toyota emblem. Staring into Maemi's sympathetic eyes, he said, "You could really help me out by sending some of your friends and Norimitsu's new colleagues my way. Would you do that?"

Maemi nodded and Norimitsu assured him that he'd do what he could.

A bell rang, alerting the salesmen that another customer had come into the showroom. "Ah, duty calls. Maybe this one is a sure bet." But he stood there for a moment longer. He desperately wanted to turn and leave them with whatever shred of dignity he could muster, but instead he pressed on. "I hope to hear from you about the convertible, and about dinner, of course."

Pushing the heavy door open for his pregnant wife, Norimitsu smiled. "Wonderful running into you like this." Ichiro blinked from the glaring sunlight. The couple seemed engrossed in conversation as they walked down the street. Maemi laughed at something her husband said. Was it at his expense or was she too polite to turn him into a a joke?

The manager swooped down on Ichiro. "Well, how did it go?"

"Mr. Suzuki gave me his business card and asked that I call him in a few days." He waved Norimitsu's card in the air and then carefully tucked it into the breast pocket of his company jacket. "I think they'll buy the convertible with all the accessories—in white." He embellished the story. "He said he'd pay cash. He doesn't need a loan, but he's interested in the warranty, and he promised he'd refer his business associates to me if they're in the market for a Toyota. That would be quite a coup."

"Stay on top of them. We don't want to let a big fish get away, do we?"

"Of course not, sir. You can count on me."

Chapter 43

I SAT IN THE darkness in the rocking chair where I had breast-fed Hisashi, his chubby fingers curled around a strand of my hair, his eyelids becoming heavy once he was sated. I sighed replaying those moments of maternal joy. The cat sat on my lap purring contentedly as I scratched her head. I had cut back on my hours at the tearoom now that Ichiro was working. He seemed well-suited to his job at Toyota, and he was on pace to meet his goals by August. There was talk of his training new recruits, which would mean more money. His health was improving even with the long hours he was putting in. With luck and hard work, he could cut back to five days a week once the summer push was over.

I made a promise to myself to bury all the anger and resentment I felt toward Ichiro. I knew it was not unusual for marriages to break apart with the loss of a child, and I vowed this would not happen to us, that I would do everything in my power to repair the crack that had formed between Ichiro and me. *Love is so fragile and is easily destroyed*, I thought. I wasn't sure what glue and magic dust I would use, but I had faith that like kintsugi—which my father taught me about as we picked through the rubble of the bomb—I would fill the cracks between Ichiro and me and create something stronger than what we had before. The fragments of our love would be rejoined. It gave me hope to think this way. If we couldn't repair our marriage, what was the point of making the ultimate sacrifice?

I dozed off, lulled to sleep by Chaya's purring and the steady sound of traffic on the street below. Ichiro touched my bare shoulder, waking me. "What time is it?"

Throwing his jacket on the back of a chair and loosening his tie, he answered, "It's after ten p.m. The showroom was a madhouse today. I couldn't get away earlier. I'm sorry, Noriko."

"No worries. You must have had a profitable day to have stayed so late."

"I didn't make a single sale today. I've decided that this job doesn't suit me at all."

I felt as if I was riding in an elevator that went into free fall. I tried to remain calm. "I thought you were doing so well, Ichiro."

"I don't like the way the clientele treats me. I feel like I did at the tearoom when I was fourteen years old, opening and closing the door for patrons. All I need is a cap to complete my uniform. I'm going to hand in my resignation."

"Why be so hasty? You're making good money. If you quit, what are you going to do?"

"I don't know. But now that I have some experience in sales, I'm sure I can find a better job—one where I don't have to wear a company jacket that makes me feel like a flunky."

Ichiro leaned over and kissed the nape of my neck. "Don't worry. I'll figure something out." He lit a candle, then closed the shoji screen to block out the streetlight; but he left the door to the balcony open to let in some air. The apartment felt claustrophobic, as if all our unexpressed words were trapped within the four walls. Ichiro poured a gin and tonic and then selected a record.

"What are you going to play?"

"Grieg's *Concerto for Piano*. It is a gorgeous piece of music, so romantic and novel in its orchestration. Do you want to hear a story about the composer?"

I wasn't in the mood for one of Ichiro's lectures, but I indulged him, hoping he would eventually admit what was bothering him. I sat down on Ichiro's lap and he put his arms around me. "You're as light as a feather, Noriko. I hope you haven't been starving yourself."

"That's usually what I accuse you of. I haven't had much of an appetite lately. It seems as though, as each month goes by, instead of missing Hisashi less, I'm missing him more."

Ichiro put his hand over my mouth. "We promised we wouldn't mention his name. Now do you want to hear my story or not?"

I took a sip of his drink and was shocked by how strong it was. The gin burned my throat as I swallowed it. "So…tell me about this genius, Grieg."

"When Grieg played this music for his friend, the composer Franz Liszt, who was a pianist as well, he got so carried away that he played the final movement over and over again. And then he said to himself in a loud voice so that Liszt would hear him, 'Keep on, I tell you. You have what is needed to be a great success; don't let the critics frighten you.' Doesn't that suggest that even someone so talented as Grieg can suffer from self-doubt?"

"That is true of many creative people. When I was acting, I never knew what to think of my performance until I read the reviews. Someday I'll show you what my high school newspaper said about me in *The Thin Man*. Mr. Ozu was right when he said I lacked confidence in myself. Who knows where I might be had I tried harder. I gave up too easily. But all that's in the past, isn't it? What's the point of holding on to regrets?"

"I wish I could have seen you on the stage, but instead I get to listen to your singing—you have a devoted audience of one."

"Where is your story about Grieg going? How old was he when he wrote this concerto, which by the way is exceptionally beautiful, although perhaps a bit haunting for this time of night?"

"He was about your age, in his mid-twenties, and he was not convinced he had a future in music. He was already married and had a daughter who died in infancy. Grieg spent the rest of his life reworking this concerto. He was never satisfied with it, and he never wrote another one. He did write many other pieces of music, but somehow he couldn't bring this concerto to his high standards."

"Perhaps his grief stifled his creativity." I stood up and took off my robe. "I was hoping we could make love, but you'll have to change the music."

"Sorry. I picked it because it reflects my mood. Do you remember my high school friend, Norimitsu Suzuki, and his wife, Maemi? I went skiing with them a few years ago."

I remembered them clearly. "They were at our wedding. I recall she was pregnant at the time. He told a story about you. He said that you wondered if you'd ever find someone to love. You were pessimistic about your chances, and as with so many things about yourself, you were wrong. You underestimate your talent and your charm." I kissed Ichiro on his nose and nuzzled his neck.

"Yes. Well, they came into the showroom today. He's on top of the world with an important job at SONY Electronics. I did just as well as he did in night school, and look where I am—nowhere. Seeing them today, having to grovel for their business…It makes me sick just thinking about it. I can't risk putting myself in that situation again. What if another of my friends or a patron from one of the restaurants comes in? It would be too humiliating."

"Did they have their child with them?"

"You would bring that up. No, but they have twins and another on the way. Maemi said something about wanting a big car for their growing family, and a top-of-the-line Toyota might be suitable. Oh, she sounded so self-important and supercilious. And Norimitsu looked at her so indulgently. It was nauseating, really. They want to invite us for dinner when they get settled. It will be a cold day in hell before I accept an invitation from them. I won't be made a fool of. Not by them. Not by anyone."

"What if they buy a car from you?"

"That's not going to happen. I can usually tell when someone is serious, and they just seemed like casual shoppers. They'll probably take their business elsewhere. They don't owe me any favors."

"Don't give up on them, and don't give up on yourself, Ichiro. Maybe you'll feel differently tomorrow." I rubbed his back, hoping I could change his mood.

Ichiro lifted the needle off the phonograph record. He followed me with his eyes as I slipped under the covers alone, waiting for him. I watched Ichiro fill up his glass with straight gin and a few ice cubes, which rattled around in his glass. He sat in the dark, motionless, and then cradling his head in his hands, he silently cried. His shoulders heaved up and down.

⌒

THE INTERMITTENT SUMMER THUNDERSTORMS washed the streets clean, but the rain also left the city oppressively humid and did little to reduce the sweltering heat. It was early morning, but the sun already broke through the heavy clouds. Ichiro was still asleep. He had not yet left for work at the showroom. I didn't believe he meant to quit without giving sufficient notice. That would have been so irresponsible of him, and he always prided himself on being a reliable employee.

I put on a light dress to make the one-hour trip to the cemetery in Osaka Prefecture where Ichiro's parents, Hide-Ichi and Toshiko, were buried in their family plot. I carried a net bag filled with incense, rice, and fresh fruits as offerings. As I climbed the steep hill from the train station, my damp hair stuck to the back of my neck and my skirt wrapped around my legs. I had to stop to unwind it to avoid tripping. Ichiro should have come with me, but I didn't want to disturb him and today was expected to be a busy day at the showroom. I thought for sure he planned on going, even if he got a late start.

A large stone Buddha sat at the top of the cemetery overlooking the graves crowding one another down the hillside. I walked along the gravel pathway to the Uchida gravesite. Someone had recently placed a big stone to mark the gravesite and a smaller one without a name—just the character for Emptiness. I was puzzled who it was for.

Filling a bucket with water, I scrubbed the stone of dust and pollen, and then I pulled the weeds that had grown since the last time I had tended the plot. It was a few days until Hisashi's third birthday and I wanted to communicate with his grandparents. I would never have imagined this was how I would recognize my son's birthday, but for reasons I could not explain I felt compelled to be surrounded by the spirits of the Uchida family.

Placing the rice and fruit at the base of the stone, I lit several sticks of incense to attract Toshiko and Hide-Ichi's attention. "Ichiro and I have given our son to your daughter, Mitsuko. That is Ichiro's wish. He is convinced that Hisashi will have a better life with her and her husband, Harry, whom you have not met, but you may see them from afar. Please, take care of Ichiro and your grandson, Hisashi. He is almost three years old. Ichiro grows more agitated with each passing day. I think he misses our son as much as I do, but he will not speak to me of it. He hides everything inside, and escapes to stories from books to assuage his anxiety. Composers, animals, philosophers all capture his interest and distract him from focusing on his feelings. I am having a hard time pretending to be interested in his long-winded tales. All I can think of is my lost boy. I am plagued with sadness and sorrow and cannot accept that I have gone along with Ichiro's plan, but what choice did I have? I'll never know if it was for the best, what we have done. Please send me a sign that we have not made a terrible mistake. I pray with all my heart that Ichiro will recover, and that our life together will be filled with joy again, although I cannot fathom what will reverse the river current of our life. I try my best, but it doesn't seem good enough."

I stood over the gravesite for several minutes, praying that my words would carry into the next world and reach Hide-Ichi and Toshiko. I left the incense burning, gathered up my offerings, and carried the bucket back to the entrance to the cemetery for another mourner.

When I walked into the apartment, I was surprised to see Ichiro reading a book. "You didn't go to work today? It's Saturday, the busiest day at the showroom."

"I told you last night I was going to quit. You obviously didn't believe me or you wouldn't look so surprised. I'm going to find something else."

I looked down at my shoes, unable to look Ichiro in the eyes. He stopped for a moment, and then said, "I'm not sure what reason I'll give for quitting. Self-respect isn't a reason, is it? I guess it will depend upon what kind of job I apply for. If I go back into the restaurant business I can always say, enthusiastically, 'I missed the excitement of a restaurant.' How does that sound?"

"It sounds like you're going around in circles, Ichiro."

"Thanks for your vote of confidence." He paused and then asked, "Where have you been? When I woke up at seven you were already gone."

"I visited your parents' grave. Someone placed a new stone at the family plot and engraved your parents' and grandparents' names on it. And there was a smaller stone, too. Where did that one come from?"

Ichiro hesitated and then said, "I have no idea. I ordered the granite stone after Hisashi left for America. When I die, you must be sure to take care of the family plot. Will you do that for me?" Shaking the ice cubes in his glass, he finished his drink in two big gulps. The glass slipped out of his hand, breaking onto pieces on the floor. Ichiro sat frozen in his chair. I got a broom and dustpan and swept up the shards. Where was the gold dust to repair the damage? I didn't have a clue.

Chapter 44

THE WEEKEND AFTER HISASHI'S third birthday, the annual Dawson County Fair opened north of Glendive on Merrill Avenue east of the Yellowstone River. A rising moon hung in the sky as the blazing sun sank slowly toward the horizon. The road out to the fairgrounds on the eastern end of town was packed with cars and pickup trucks. Mitsuko held Hisashi on her lap. Harry drummed his fingers on the steering wheel of their 1962 Chevrolet. "We're not even going five miles an hour. I have a good mind to turn around and go home."

"Harry, I've been looking forward to the fair." She could see the Ferris wheel in the distance. "Don't be so impatient. We're almost there."

The sheriff directed them to the nearest parking space in the dusty lot. Country-western music blared over the loudspeaker, and every few minutes the announcer declared the beginning of another event over the PA. "The ladies' barrel race is about to start. Missy Simpson and Gail Drake, two of the top riders from Billings, Montana, are here competing this afternoon. It's anyone's guess who'll take home the blue ribbon."

Harry got out of the car and lifted Hisashi onto his shoulders.

The announcer continued, "The 4-H Club has just handed out a blue ribbon to Danny Smith for his prized heifer. Gentlemen, drum roll, please."

The microphone let out a high whistle and the announcer tapped on it to make sure it was still working. "Attention, everyone. There's a boy here who's been separated from his parents. In case you can't see him, he's wearing a red plaid shirt and dungarees and has curly black hair. He says his name is Bobby."

The announcer turned to the boy. "What's your last name, son?" In the background, Mitsuko and Harry heard the boy crying, "I want my mommy."

The announcer said, "He doesn't know his last name. Will his parents come up to the podium right away?"

Harry reacted to the announcement, "His parents are probably teenagers drinking too much beer instead of paying attention to their kid. I think this country has got it all wrong. You need a license to go fishing or hunting, but you don't need a license to be a parent."

"You're right, Harry. Maybe it should be inside out."

Harry laughed. "You mean the other way around?"

"Isn't that what I said?"

"Not exactly. But I agree with you."

Mitsuko followed closely behind Harry and Hisashi, afraid she might lose sight of them in the midst of the swelling crowd. The smell of grilling hamburgers and hot dogs, cotton candy, corn dogs, and freshly made popcorn competed with cow and horse manure. Inside the fence of Lou's Petting Zoo, children coaxed the baby goats and pigs with handfuls of carrots. Brightly colored plastic pendants with the names of the fair's sponsors hung listlessly from wires surrounding the fairgrounds: Halliburton, Cross Petroleum, Stockman's Bank, Hell Creek Music, American Ford, and the Jaycees of Dawson County. Mitsuko recognized their names; many of their employees came into the Jordan Hotel bar regularly. She hadn't been there since Hisashi arrived. She missed the people and the extra money her job afforded them. But it was a small price to pay for being a mother, she reminded herself. She and Harry managed to scrape together extra money to send to Noriko and Ichiro. She didn't want her brother to feel she was abandoning him.

Usually Hisashi seemed like such a happy child, but Mitsuko sometimes caught him looking wistfully at the photograph of Noriko and Ichiro that sat on top of his bureau. She never believed in hiding that they were his birth parents, and she didn't want him to forget them. But it nearly broke her heart when he asked, "When are Mama and Dada coming?"

She had told him "not now" without elaborating further. And when a birthday card arrived from Noriko, it nearly broke Mitsuko's heart to read the message: "To my dearest Hisashi. I am sorry that I cannot be with you on your third birthday. I hope it is a good one and that you get lots of nice presents. I lit a candle and sang Happy Birthday to you as if you are right here next to me. With all my love, Mama. P.S. Dada sends his love to you as well. You are his brave hero."

Mitsuko put the card on Hisashi's bureau. He kept reaching up for it and pretending he could read it, ending each time, "With all my love, Mama."

The fair's announcer reeled off the schedule for the rest of the week: "And Friday night the Rednecks and Rough Necks, featuring Corb Lund, and the Hurtin Albertans will be giving us a concert. Don't miss this, folks. It's going to knock your socks off. And on Saturday night the John Drake Big Band will be playing oldies but goodies from the thirties and forties. You can do it up right. Dance, if you get my meaning." He then let out a full-throated laugh.

Mitsuko caught up with Harry and Hisashi. Harry said, "That sounds like a heck of a good time. When was the last time we went out dancing?"

"I remember when you tried to teach me the two-step. I wasn't good, was I?" And then she made her point, "Anyway, now that we're parents, going dancing is not something we can think about. I won't leave Dwight with anyone else. We'll have plenty of time for that when he's a teenager."

"I was just thinking it would be fun. I used to like to do my Fred Astaire routine back in the day."

There was a long line of customers waiting to ride the Ferris wheel and roller coaster. Mitsuko said, "Harry, if you want a ride, go ahead. My ears can't take the pressure." She rarely referred to it, but Mitsuko had gone deaf in one ear from a childhood infection the doctors were unable to cure. It wasn't until she went to the doctor at the US Army base medical clinic after the war that her condition was cleared up, and by then it was too late to save her hearing in that ear.

Harry looked up at the Ferris wheel. "I'm not much for heights either. There's the merry-go-round. We can all ride together."

The carousel held pride of place at the fairgrounds. Mitsuko climbed onto a black stallion side saddle, and Harry and Hisashi sat next to her on a white horse with a gold-painted mane. Hisashi held the reins as the carousel turned and the wooden horses went up and down. The center of the carousel was decorated with mirrors and bright lights, and calliope music played the opening bars of the "Star Spangled Banner" over and over again. When the carousel turned and the horses went up and down, Mitsuko held on tightly. She had never ridden a carousel before.

When the carousel stopped, Hisashi said, "Papa, again, again," and so they stayed on for another round. This time Harry leaned out and caught the brass ring. They dismounted and Harry gave the ring to his son. "Show it to the conductor and he'll give you a prize."

The conductor pushed the lever down to start the carousel up again and then sat down on a bench. Taking off his cap, he wiped the sweat from the bald spot on top of his head with a cotton handkerchief. A horsefly buzzed around his head. He swatted it with one hand and pulled a bottle of Coca Cola from an ice chest with his other, prying the cap off with a church key. Hisashi, holding the brass ring, waited politely.

"What's your name, son?"

"Hisashi."

Harry corrected him. "Tell the man your American name."

"Dwight."

"Well, Dwight, I have a special prize for you—an American flag. Now don't go poking your eye out with it." Hisashi looked at Harry to make sure he could take it.

"Where you folks from?" The conductor seemed to have something on his mind besides brass rings.

Before Harry could answer, Mitsuko said, "Glendive."

"I don't see many Orientals around here. Just Americans."

Mitsuko spoke up. "My husband was a US Army corporal during the Korean War, and I'm a naturalized citizen."

"My mistake. I meant no offense. Here's another flag for you."

Harry intercepted it and handed it back. "One is plenty for us."

The calliope music stopped and the riders got off the carousel. The conductor tipped his hat. "Bye, Dwight. Hope you and your folks come back and see me again next year."

Under his breath, Harry said, "Don't count on it."

Harry jammed his Halliburton baseball cap down over his forehead, jostling his glasses. "One more word out of that guy's mouth and I'd have punched him in the nose."

Mitsuko said, "And he would have deserved it."

Hisashi waved the flag back and forth. Mitsuko took it from him. He didn't say anything, but the sad expression on his face was more than Mitsuko could stand. She gave the flag back to him. "Just be careful, sweetheart."

Harry smiled. "You're a real soft touch, Mitzi. I'm afraid when Dwight gets older, I'm going to have to be the disciplinarian. He'll talk you in and out of anything."

"You're probably right."

As they headed for their car, the announcer called out, "For all of you folks who were here at four o'clock, I'm happy to tell you that our lost boy, Bobby, has been reunited with his parents." The crowd hooted and hollered.

Bobby's mother took the microphone. "I'm so grateful to all of you and to the Lord Jesus Christ for returning our little boy to us safe and sound." A lone fiddle played "What a Friend We Have in Jesus." The audience picked up the tune and sang along:

> *Oh, what peace we often forfeit*
> *Oh, what needless pain we bear*
> *All because we do not carry*
> *Everything to God in prayer.*

Looking down at her three-year-old son, Mitsuko was overcome with joy. The crescent moon floated over their heads as night fell, the stars making their debut one by one. It seemed to Mitsuko as if the voices of the singers could reach all the way to the stars.

Chapter 45

AFTER QUITTING HIS JOB at Toyota, Ichiro was unemployed for a month. He scanned the newspapers every day, and when he needed something to take his mind off his unemployment, he worked on a bookcase for his niece Kazuko. With just a few tools and a woodworking bench he bought second-hand, he followed the plans for American prairie-style furniture designed by Frank Lloyd Wright. It was a complicated project, but Ichiro figured it out without difficulty. He was close to finishing the bookcase when he was contacted by the HELLO Limousine Company where he had applied for a job.

He had little choice but to accept a position as an English-speaking chauffeur, but right from the start he struggled. He had a hard time loading and unloading the passengers' heavy luggage into the trunk, and the gasoline fumes irritated his throat. He resented having to wear a uniform again, which was what he wanted to escape from, but what choice did he have? The work was steady.

He told me, "I'll stick it out through the Olympic Games in October."

On his day off he worked on the bookcase. "It should be ready in a few weeks if I keep at it."

I asked him, "Why don't you take a break? We could take a walk and have dinner somewhere in the neighborhood. The wood stain smells terrible. It can't be good for either of us."

Ichiro rubbed his hands with turpentine to remove the blood-red stain and changed into a fresh shirt and a pair of trousers. I noticed he was losing weight again and had to pull his belt to the last notch to keep his pants from slipping past his waist. Despite his thin physique, he was still handsome and looked distinguished; but I hesitated to give him a compliment. He usually turned it around to point out a fault he thought he had. I put on an old blue silk dress and clasped a string of pearls around my neck. Powdering my nose and applying a new pink lipstick, I asked Ichiro, "How do I look?" I wasn't past wanting an occasional compliment from my husband to pull me out of the doldrums.

He did not disappoint me. "You're just as lovely as the day I married you."

Laughing, I said, "I think you need a pair of stronger glasses. I've already got a few gray hairs." I ran my hands through my hair to rearrange my curls.

"I'm responsible for them. It's from all your worrying about me." He sighed. "I want to give you something to be happy about. Maybe the job at HELLO will lead to a better position, although I can't for the life of me imagine what it could be. You know, when I was a little boy, my father used to call the HELLO Limousine Service to drive us around Osaka, and now here I am working as one of their chauffeurs. What a turn of events."

"You said yourself it was only temporary. I'm sure something else will come along, or perhaps we can think of something to do together. Enough of working for someone else."

"You're right about that, Noriko. Look at all the money your sister has made owning two restaurants." He looked off in the distance as if he was imagining some possibility he hadn't yet shared with me.

As we left the apartment, Ichiro said, "Tomorrow I'm driving an American couple, the Blackstones, to a luncheon with the American ambassador, Edwin Reischauer, and his wife Haru in Kyoto.

"Who's Mr. Blackstone?"

"He runs a US television company. From what I've read in the newspapers, he's here in Osaka for talks with Relay One Satellite Company. They may be cooking up a joint venture of some sort and he probably wants the ambassador's endorsement."

"He sounds like an important person. I'm sure HELLO Limousine Service would only give this assignment to its best English-speaking chauffeur."

Ichiro dropped my hand, which he had been holding tightly in his. "I know what you're trying to do, but stop wasting your breath. Giving me false praise doesn't change the facts. I know my limitations." He stopped walking. "I'm really in no mood to go out. Why don't you go somewhere by yourself? I'd rather be home and work on Kazuko's bookcase."

Gasping at his nasty tone, I said, "You want me to go out by myself? Where will I go without you?"

"Does it matter?" he asked. "Just go." He reached into his pocket and handed me some money. "Buy yourself dinner, and while you're at it, maybe you'll meet a rich guy who'll pay for your dinner. Then you can give me my money back." He left me standing in the middle of the street.

Stunned by his cruelty, I watched my husband disappear into the crowd. Wiping the tears from my eyes, and not wanting to be by myself on the street at this hour, I walked into the nearest restaurant. Romantic music played and couples leaned toward one another, engaged in animated conversation, or they just slurped their food, enjoying one another's company. When the waitress came to my table, I ordered a bowl of noodles and a bottle of Kirin beer. The soup turned cold in front of me and the condensation from the beer bottle made a damp circle on the paper place mat. As the restaurant emptied out, I looked at my watch. I'd been sitting there for two hours. In my misery, time seemed to have stopped. I couldn't even remember what I had been thinking about. I opened my purse to pay the bill. As I took out a few bills, several photographs of Hisashi at his birthday party fell on the floor. I picked them up and slowly studied each one. I knew I was being foolish, but I whispered, "Sorry I missed your birthday, my sweet little boy. I hope it was a happy one," and then I kissed his smiling face.

I appreciated that he appeared to be well taken care of—all those people and presents—but that didn't take away the pain in my heart. For myself, for Hisashi, and for Ichiro. I knew I needed help, but I didn't know where to turn to seek advice on how to give my husband the support he needed. Other than turning to the spirit of his parents, of course, who had not sent me a sign since I visited the cemetery. Expecting a message from them was sheer foolishness.

The priest at the Tenrikyo church had counseled me a few weeks ago, "Avoid being pessimistic about anything. Do not feel depressed by any event in life. Sweep away all negative thoughts."

I had admitted, "Sometimes I think it would have been easier if Hisashi had died than that he's alive and I'm forbidden from raising him."

The priest tsk'd, tsk'd. "You must break yourself of the habit of attachment to all beings and all things, Noriko. If someone is meant to be yours, they will return of their own accord in their own time. Even your son. You may not know when or how, but there is always a possibility. After all, your son will be a man someday, and he may feel the need to meet you, to learn about you and his father. This often happens with adopted children. I wouldn't count on it, but life has many twists and turns. Like a river flowing downstream past boulders."

"Do you believe that?"

"I do. Shall I bless you now?"

I bowed my head and listened to the priest's soothing voice.

When I returned to the apartment from the restaurant, Ichiro, still wearing his shirt and trousers he had changed into, was asleep. He had not bothered to put on a pair of pajamas, and slept curled up in a ball. An empty bottle of gin sat in plain view on the table next to him and an envelope with my name on it leaned against the bottle:

Dearest Noriko, I'm sorry for being rude to you. It was very ungentlemanly of me. I cannot control my temper. I feel frustrated and helpless most days, and I cannot reconcile our present circumstances with the dreams I once had for us. Will you forgive me? Believe me when I say you're all I live for. That must be a big burden on you. Ichiro.

I picked up the empty gin bottle and threw it into the trash underneath the sink. Quietly undressing, I prayed to God the Parent to give Ichiro the strength to fight harder.

The dead air in the apartment was oppressive. I opened the balcony door to let in a fresh breeze. Stripping naked, I curled up against Ichiro, stroking his back. He didn't make a sound but I could feel he was aroused. He slowly turned and carefully lay on top of me. I pressed him against me and opened my legs, inviting him into my body. I had not taken any precautions and risked becoming pregnant. Afterward, I rolled off him and wiped myself between my legs with a damp washcloth. It suddenly struck me that, if we had a second child, it might be the spark Ichiro needed to lift him out of his depression and misery. A year ago, I thought being a widow with a child was a calamity, that I would be regarded as "a cold bowl of day-old rice," but I now believed that, whatever happened, I was strong and could face what fate dealt us. I touched myself. "This is my body, lent to me by God the Parent, and I will do with it what I want, with or without Ichiro's permission."

⌒

THE FOLLOWING DAY ICHIRO picked up his clients, Mr. and Mrs. Blackstone, at the Rihga Royal Hotel in Osaka and drove them to the Hiiragiya ryokan in Kyoto for a private meeting with Ambassador Edwin Reischauer and his wife,

Haru Matsukata. Crowds lined the streets, waving American and Japanese flags to greet the ambassadorial party. Along the route, Mr. Blackstone explained to Ichiro in fluent Japanese, "The ambassador was my Asian studies professor at Harvard. We've kept in touch over the years. Mrs. Blackstone and I are looking forward to seeing him and his wife. Our last reunion was a few years ago in New York."

Ichiro responded, "It's a shame that President Kennedy is not alive to see all the good the ambassador is doing."

Mr. Blackstone said, "It's really a miracle that Japan and the United States have repaired their relationship. In some ways we have the communists to thank for that."

Ichiro answered hoping that Mr. Blackstone would be impressed, "I remember when Kennedy's brother, Robert, paid a visit to Waseda University in Tokyo in 1962. There were demonstrations on campus, but the attorney general faced the rioters head on. Since that time, we have seen a remarkable shift. Too bad the president never got the chance to visit Japan himself. He intended to do so."

Ichiro slowed the limousine down. "As you can see from the limousine in front of us with the American flags, the ambassador and his wife are already here."

Ichiro jumped out and opened the passenger door. "I'll wait here for you. Please enjoy your lunch." A group of photographers and journalists and a television crew stood on the steps of the traditional ryokan hoping for a picture or an interview with the dignitaries and their guests, but the Blackstones were quickly escorted inside.

Two hour later Mr. and Mrs. Blackstone followed Ambassador and Mrs. Reischauer down the steps of the ryokan. A security team surrounded the ambassador; a month ago he had been stabbed by a crazed Japanese protester, and the government was embarrassed by this incident. The ambassador resumed his duties in spite of his wounds, determined to visit every prefecture in Japan before his term of office was over. Ichiro was amazed to see him looking so fit despite what he had been through. The two men embraced and their wives bowed to one another. Ichiro put on his white gloves and opened the limousine door for the Blackstones.

Once they were settled in the back seat, Mr. Blackstone leaned forward and instructed Ichiro to take them back to their hotel. His wife had a fitting with the dress designer Madam Hanae Mori at three. "Do you think you can make it?"

"I'll do my best, Mr. Blackstone." Mrs. Blackstone was an attractive woman for her age who wore her clothes with flair, but Ichiro thought, *Noriko would look wonderful in a Hanae Mori outfit. When I am gone I hope she will find a husband who can buy her fancy clothes from famous designers and take her to the best restaurants and hotels.*

He caught himself thinking similar bleak thoughts daily. He already counted himself a dead man, and his wife's optimism and Dr. Shizumi's encouragement were grating on his nerves. What did they know of how he felt? The pain of his existence was unbearable, and he anticipated the day when he would no longer be forced to struggle against the inevitable. It wasn't that he wanted to die; he just didn't want to live any longer.

Straining to keep his eyes on the road and on the clock, he worried that he wouldn't make it back to the hotel on time because the roads were clogged with cement trucks and flatbed trucks laden with steel pipes and rods destined for Olympic sites nearing completion. He made a mental calculation and turned off the main road, speeding through a warren of narrow back streets. At three he pulled underneath the porte-cochère of the hotel located on an island between the Dojimagawa and Tosaborigawa Rivers, a picturesque location for the exclusive Hotel Rihga.

Mr. Blackstone checked his watch. "Right on time. You don't look like a cowboy, but you drive like one. Give me your card, Ichiro. The next time Mrs. Blackstone and I are in Osaka we'll ask for you by name. I expect to be back again in a few months."

"Thank you, sir. It would be my honor. But I don't have any cards printed up yet. I haven't been on the job for long. You can just call HELLO's main office and ask for me. Hopefully, I'll be available."

Ichiro helped them out of the passenger seats and, bowing, wished them a pleasant afternoon. The hotel doorman held the door open for them and signaled to Ichiro to move along to make way for the line of taxicabs and limousines behind him. He shouted back at the doorman, "I'm moving as fast as I can, you churl." The doorman stared at Ichiro and asked him not to come back unless he was being driven by a hearse. Ichiro shivered at the doorman's haunting remark.

Ichiro took off his white gloves and chauffeur's cap and threw them on the red leather seat. He turned off the air-conditioning to save gasoline, a company directive, and opened the front window. The gas and diesel fumes made his eyes tear and blurred his vision. He narrowly missed a bicyclist who cut in front of him. He honked his horn in protest, but the bicyclist was unaware. Ichiro was so tired he didn't know if he had the stamina to drive to the limousine depot.

When he arrived at the HELLO Limousine office, the dispatcher said, "We received a call from Mr. Blackstone complimenting you, Ichiro. He said not only is your English impeccable, but your driving is excellent and you know your way around the city. He credits making his appointment on time to you. I'm putting his comments in your file so we can flag you when other important American passengers hire us. You should be very pleased."

"I am, but I don't intend to be doing this forever. I've got big plans for myself. Eventually I want to open my own business with my wife." He knew it wasn't smart to confess this, but he didn't care. He was already plotting an exit strategy. "One step. Then another step."

"In what field?"

"Possibly a restaurant, or maybe a woodworking business. Who knows? All I know for certain is that working for someone else doesn't get you anywhere. I'm sure I take home twenty percent of what HELLO made today on the Blackstones. Am I correct?"

The dispatcher blanched and then answered, "I don't see the books and so I can't say, but you are right about working for yourself." He lowered his voice. "Listen, when you decide what direction you are going in, don't forget about me. I might want to join you in something. I like the way you treat people. You're courteous and responsible, and I trust you."

"Thanks. That's the second compliment I've gotten today. When I'm feeling down I'll be sure and repeat it to myself and it will immediately lift my spirits."

The dispatcher looked as if he had received a gold medal. In fact, however, his compliment was meaningless to Ichiro. All that mattered was what he thought of himself, and he gave himself a failing grade.

⁓

THE TOKAIDO SHINKANSEN BULLET train was to begin service between Tokyo and Osaka on October 10, 1964, shaving two hours off the trip. The owner of HELLO made a speech to his drivers, telling them that the new bullet train might negatively affect their long-haul service but that it could also dramatically increase their local business, bringing tourists into Osaka for sporting events at the various stadiums.

Ichiro assured me, "In the end things should balance out and my take-home pay shouldn't really be affected. Once the Games are over, I've decided I'm going to open a custom cabinetry business. My niece, Kazuko, is happy with her new bookcase I made for her, and she tells me that her classmates want one just like hers. Fifty students should be a good place to start. No more working for other people."

"You have given up the idea of opening our own restaurant, Ichiro? The restaurant business is where we've both had the most experience."

"That won't be for a few years, not until I've proven myself in a more modest venture. Right now, cabinet making is the way to go. I don't need much capital to get started. It's all about the marketing, and you can help me with that. You have such a lovely voice that I'm sure you can drum up business for us on the telephone. Which reminds me. I've been meaning to order a private phone for us. I can justify spending the money if it's for business, even if it costs more than I can really afford."

"Where do you think we can find the backing to sign a lease on a workshop and buy the equipment? You can't start a business of any scale in our apartment. It's only been a hobby for you to this point. It wouldn't be healthy for either of us to have all those glues, paints, and whatever else you need lying around here."

"I haven't really thought it through. I can ask Uncle Kiyoshi to lend us the money, strictly business of course. He knows we are both hard workers."

I was afraid Ichiro would be offended, but I wanted him to look at this plan realistically. "It's not the best job in the world being an assistant book-keeper for my sister, but I can count on it."

"Are you saying you're not willing to take a gamble with me?"

"It would be prudent to have my salary coming in until your business is firmly established." What was Ichiro thinking? There was no way I would give up my job to help him in something so risky.

He barked at me. "I'll need you to promote the business, to line up customers. Otherwise what's the point? I might as well keep doing cabinetry as a hobby and think about getting another job and we'll just go around and around like hamsters inside a wheel."

I filled up my watering can and slipped out to the balcony to tend to my plants and flowers, which were in full bloom. When I lifted my head, I felt dizzy and nauseous. It would be too soon for me to feel the first signs of pregnancy. I suspected I was probably coming down with another cold. I came inside and took a few rice grains out of the cabinet and swallowed them.

Ichiro looked up from reading the newspaper. "Your home remedy? Are you sick again?"

"No. I'm just taking precautions. I don't have the luxury of staying in bed all day, although I'd like nothing better."

"Lie down and I'll give you a back rub. For once I should be taking care of you."

I did as he suggested. I closed my eyes and felt Ichiro's hands pressing gently on my back. He rubbed my feet and my neck, and I felt the tightness in my muscles relax. "Why don't you turn over and I'll massage your stomach?" He lightly circled my stomach and inserted his finger into my bellybutton— the place where Hisashi and I were attached symbiotically for nine months. I imagined that the warmth of his hands were penetrating into my womb where another child might have been planted by his seed, but I said nothing, not wishing to break the spell of our intimacy. I craved Ichiro's body. He suddenly stood up and put the kettle on to make tea for me. The burner clicked and released the smell of noxious gas. Turning off the burner, he swore, "This stove is so old that it won't turn on or off properly. I'm going to have to try to fix it. We can't count on Mrs. Masamoto for anything."

I laughed. "She'd just call you. You're the unofficial handyman."

"She's an old spinster who's lucky to own this building. It must be worth a lot of money. I keep expecting her to raise our rent, but I guess she's grateful for my help."

"I need your help, too." I put my arms around Ichiro and kissed him. He barely reacted. He was busy taking out a box of tools from under the sink to fix the pilot light on the stove.

Chapter 46

Ichiro was dispatched by HELLO Limousine on October 7 to the Nippon Paint Company near Osaka Bay, where most of the factories had been located before World War II, including Izumi Steelworks. His customer was Hiroshi Ando, a high-level manager, who had a breakfast meeting at the French consulate in Kobe.

While he waited outside the gates, Ichiro imagined a conversation with his passenger:

Ichiro: Mr. Ando, it may be presumptuous, but I'd like to ask your advice.

Mr. Ando: What is it?

Ichiro: I'm thinking about opening my own custom cabinetry workshop in Osaka. Up to this point it's been a hobby, but I do have some skill and I think I can do well. I have a good network of prospective clients from my time working at the Aki-Torii and its sister establishment, the Tesagara Tearoom, both of which are in Namba. I was the general manager and head bookkeeper for many years. I'm proud to say I have a gift for numbers.

Mr. Ando: I'm familiar with these restaurants.

Ichiro: I'm wondering if Nippon might have an interest in investing in me.

Mr. Ando: How old are you?

Ichiro: Thirty-two, sir. I'll be thirty-three this December. Young enough to have many productive years ahead of me and old enough to have valuable experience. I have done some preliminary cash projections. I've considered equipment costs, as well as rent, supplies, and six months' working capital to get started.

Mr. Ando: I'm glad you asked me about this. Coincidentally, your idea is consistent with the company's strategic plan for a home improvement

division. Call me so we can discuss this. You know where to find me. And
don't mention your ideas to anyone else.

Ichiro: Thank you, Mr. Ando.

Mr. Ando knocked on the window of the limousine, rousing Ichiro from
his daydream. He apologized profusely for dozing off and opened the door.
Mr. Ando lit a cigarette and demanded that Ichiro hand him the limousine
telephone. Ichiro overheard his end of the conversation through the glass
partition because he was yelling. "The meeting with DuPont was a disaster.
I don't know why you sent me on this fool's errand. They have no interest in
doing business with us. They just wanted to cajole me into divulging what
we're up to. But their little game didn't work. Get the team together for a
meeting. I'll be back in twenty minutes." He slammed the phone down.

Mr. Ando tapped on the partition. "How quickly can you get back to my
office?"

Ichiro stared at the red taillights in front of him. "About a half an hour,
sir, given the traffic."

"I've scheduled a meeting in twenty minutes. Can't you get out of this
stream of cars?"

"I'll do my best."

Ichiro's hands were sweating beneath his white cotton gloves. At the next
traffic light, he studied his map to find an alternate route. There was none.

Less than two blocks from Nippon Paint, paramedics were loading
a patient on a gurney into an ambulance; a policeman blew his whistle,
prohibiting Ichiro from passing.

Mr. Ando grabbed his briefcase. "This is intolerable. I can get there faster
by walking."

"But we still have five minutes before your meeting, Mr. Ando."

"Look at this traffic, you idiot! We'll never make it." He jumped out of the
limousine and left the door ajar. Ichiro was forced to get out to close the door.
He noticed that Mr. Ando had left his leather billfold on the seat.

Ichiro drove to the Nippon headquarters and parked in the livery section.
The guard stopped him. "Where do you think you're going?"

"Mr. Ando left something in my limousine. I would like to return it to him."

"Just a moment. I need to locate him and make sure he wants to see you.
Let me see your driver's license." Ichiro did as he was instructed. Taking off
his cap, he wiped his brow.

The guard spoke into the intercom, then addressed Ichiro. "All right. Go to the eighteenth floor. Someone will be waiting for you there."

Mr. Ando stood by the elevator when the doors opened. Ichiro said, "Here is your billfold, Mr. Ando. You left it on the backseat."

Mr. Ando opened his wallet and counted the money. "I see it's all here."

"Of course, sir." Ichiro was insulted Mr. Ando would suspect him of filching money.

Ichiro waited patiently for Mr. Ando to offer him the customary five percent reward, but Mr. Ando put his wallet into his jacket pocket. Ichiro felt cheated, but he would not demean himself by asking for money. Instead he said, "I hope you will permit HELLO to be of service to you in the future," while handing him his newly printed card. The ink was barely dry.

"I'll think about it." Ichiro watched him as he hurried down the corridor. Before entering his office, he tore the card into small pieces and dropped them in a receptacle. Ichiro cringed. "That's what he thought of me for my honesty and effort. I should have kept the wallet, but then he would have reported it missing and I would have gotten into a lot of trouble. At least I won't have a blemish on my record."

When he returned to the HELLO depot, Ichiro cleaned the limousine: he emptied the ashtray, gathered the newspapers, and wiped the mahogany steering wheel and dashboard with a chamois cloth. He took out a feather duster from the trunk to remove the thin layer of dust that had settled on the chassis during the trip from Osaka to Kobe and back. Then he handed the keys to the dispatcher.

"Ichiro, you are scheduled to pick up Mrs. Fukushima and her daughter for the four o'clock show at the Takarazuka Theater. Have you forgotten?"

"I'm sorry. I'm not feeling well. You'll have to find someone else to drive them."

"At the last minute? The Fukushimas are important clients." He scanned the schedule. "Ichiro, all our other drivers are already booked for the day. You'll just have to take them. The curtain goes up in one hour, and with the heavy traffic, you'd better get going right now. Do you hear me?"

Ichiro stared blankly at the dispatcher's face. He saw his lips moving, but it was as if he was submerged underwater and he could not understand what the man was saying. When he surfaced, Ichiro heard the red-faced dispatcher yell, "You're fired!"

Ichiro slipped off his jacket and placed it on the counter with his white gloves and chauffeur's cap. He bowed, and pushing the door open onto the street, felt a wave of panic wash over him. Other than the glass coin jar which Noriko kept hidden under the sink, they had no savings. The only money to keep them afloat was Noriko's salary and whatever Harry and Mitsuko could spare each month. He thought, *What kind of a life is this for Noriko? What kind of man lives off his wife and his sister and her husband? What kind of father sends his only son away?* His unforgiving heart spit back at him, *A half-man, a deadbeat.*

Ichiro could not face going home. The shadow of his son lingered in every corner of the apartment like the shadows burned into the cement buildings of Hiroshima and Nagasaki.

He looked at his watch; if he hurried, he could catch the 4:00 p.m. showing of *Woman in the Dunes* and still be back in plenty of time to prepare something for Noriko to eat when she came home from work. He also had more work to do on a side table. He hesitated to admit that he was improving with each piece he made. Maybe he could get a job as a master's apprentice at one of the boutique workshops in Osaka and after a few years he would be in a better position to open his own shop. Then he laughed to himself. *Here I am fantasizing again, when surely nothing will come of it. Nothing ever does. Look at the way Mr. Ando treated me. I didn't get the opportunity to tell him my idea. Instead he suspected me of stealing his money.*

Ichiro rode the subway to the movie house where *Woman in the Dunes* was showing. The theater was nearly empty. Ichiro settled into the end seat in the second row. He sipped a Coca Cola, enjoying the bubbles sliding down his throat and the sweet, smooth aftertaste. Relaxing into a state of eager anticipation, he waited for the movie to start.

His arm was suddenly jostled and he spilled his drink all over his pants. The ice cubes bounced on the floor as an elderly woman carrying a cane pushed past him. She was blind but detected Ichiro's presence. "Sorry to disturb you, but I always sit in the same seat. Second row, second seat on the right. I count down the rows with my cane. Tap, tap, tap." Her voice sounded rough, as if she had stripped her vocal cords with tobacco smoke. "You have had the misfortune of being in my way. I didn't expect anyone to be sitting here. Only old women and drunks are in the theater at this hour, and they usually sit way in the back so the light from the screen doesn't shine on them, if you get my meaning. They can fiddle with themselves!"

Ichiro froze at the sound of Madam Tamae's voice. It had been two years since he last saw his stepmother at the movie theater. How was it possible he would run into her again? Without saying a word, he stood up to let her pass. She gripped his arm to steady herself; her hand felt cold through his shirtsleeve and his wet trousers stuck to his legs. He took out a handkerchief and tried to dry them off, but to no avail. He felt like a child who'd had an embarrassing accident.

Ichiro smelled liquor on Madam Tamae's breath, and the scent of a perfume strangely familiar. Settling into the seat next to him, she took out a silver flask from her pocketbook and lifted it to her lips. The light from the screen illuminated her heavily made-up face. She took off her dark glasses, and when she turned toward Ichiro, he saw that her eyes were dead. Ichiro tried to concentrate on the movie, but the scenes kept fading in front of his eyes, replaced by flashes of his childhood when Madam Tamae tortured him and his sister or lifted her skirt for his father's pleasure.

Over the dialogue, Madam Tamae whispered, "Ha, ha, not such a bad fate for that silly bug man to be stuck in a sandpit for all eternity with a beautiful woman, *neh*? I was once beautiful, too. Now I don't even know how I look anymore. How do I look?"

Ichiro could not speak. He gripped the arms of his seat. Madam Tamae babbled on without waiting for him to answer. When he was a child, this was her habit—to ask him a question without giving him a chance to respond. She was never interested in him, only in herself and in his father's wallet.

Laughing, she said, "Would you believe I once trapped a rich man into marrying me? He gave up his children to make me happy. Two blind mice— see how they run." She laughed again and then turned her attention back to the screen.

Ichiro deliberated over whether he should say something to her. What would he say that would make a difference to her after all these years, that she had destroyed his family, stolen his father's money, left him and his sister to fend for themselves when they were defenseless children, that she'd ruined any chance he might have had for a happy life? All his misery had its roots in this trauma, and as his life proved, he was unable to bury it once and for all.

Ichiro bolted from his seat and ran into the street. Leaning against a bicycle rack, he tried to catch his breath. His heart was beating uncontrollably and perspiration formed on the back of his neck. He tied his jacket around his waist to hide his wet pants. The pavement on the street undulated like an eel swimming through dark waters, and the puffs of steam rising from the subway grating looked like ghosts in the late gray afternoon.

He was too rattled to take the subway back to his apartment. He opened his wallet and counted the coins. There was just enough money to pay for a taxi, and so he flagged one down. He sank into the leather seat, swallowed a pill, and closed his eyes, waiting for the drug to relieve the burning sensation in his lungs. He coughed into his handkerchief, and when he wiped his mouth, there were spots of blood on the white linen.

Mrs. Masamoto was sweeping the stoop as he paid the driver. "Mr. Uchida, you're early. You must have gotten an important fare to be treating yourself to a taxi."

"Yes, Mrs. Masamoto. HELLO Limousine attracts only the richest clientele, and they treat their English-speaking guides like me well."

"As they should. You're such a polite young man, Mr. Uchida."

"Thank you, Mrs. Masamoto. Now, if you'll excuse me…"

Ichiro quickly realized Mrs. Masamoto was after something. "Mr. Uchida, do you have just a minute to look at my toilet? It keeps running and I don't want to have a big water bill at the end of the month."

"I'm happy to help you, Mrs. Masamoto, but can it wait until tomorrow?"

"All right. But the noise is bothering me. I'm afraid I won't sleep a wink tonight."

Ichiro bristled but retained his composure. Glancing at his watch, he realized Noriko would be home in two hours, hardly enough time to execute his final plan.

"Noriko asked me to fix the temperature gauge on the stove. She accidentally overcooked our dinner last night. If I don't fix it now we won't have dinner, and I was planning something special for her. Did you smell something burning last night?" He embellished his story to make it believable to Mrs. Masamoto.

"No, I was out for the evening, rare as that is. Widows are seldom invited anywhere." She laughed. "Just to baby naming ceremonies, weddings, and funerals. The cycle of life and then it's over." She sighed and picked up her broom.

Chapter 47

I HURRIED UP THE stairs carrying a bag of groceries to make dinner for Ichiro and me. I was excited to tell him that Japan Airlines had called me at work earlier in the day. They wanted me to come in for an interview. The company was looking for a telephone operator and liked the sound of my voice, and they were impressed I had studied acting and singing. I thought, *Perhaps all the money my father spent on me was not entirely wasted, although this is not how I thought I'd put the lessons to use.* The job would pay considerably more than what I was making as an assistant bookkeeper, and there was the possibility of a promotion, company benefits, and flexible work hours. I thought, *We can move out of our apartment and start again somewhere else where we don't have to hide from the bad memories in our apartment.* I imagined a vacation with Ichiro to Wakayama, Arashiyama, or north to Hokkaido to see the snow and soak in an outdoor onsen. And maybe I'd be pregnant; the hot springs were said to be a wonderful balm to a pregnant woman.

I reached into my handbag for my keys and saw an envelope stuck to the door with my name on it. I recognized Ichiro's handwriting and worried that it was another one of his apology notes. I ripped open the envelope and read it before going inside. In big letters was GAS with instructions: Turn off the oven immediately and open the balcony door to let in fresh air.

I dropped my groceries. Melons and lemons rolled down the stairs, glass jars filled with jam and pickled beets shattered, eggs cracked, their yellow yokes seeping into the seams of the black-and-white tile floor. I rushed into the apartment. A hose, attached to the oven, snaked its way through the room. The smell of gas made me gag and my eyes watered so I could hardly see what I was doing. I turned off the oven and ripped the tape off the balcony door and slid it open.

My husband was lying on a blanket on the floor. The end of a rubber hose had been efficiently taped to his mouth, and he wore a surgical mask just to make sure that the gas would do its job. I pulled the hose out of his mouth and screamed out his name, but he didn't wake up. Stepping on the broken glass in the hallway, I ran down the stairs, narrowly avoiding slipping on a ripe melon that had split in two. Rushing to the telephone booth at the street corner, I called for an ambulance to take Ichiro to a hospital.

The paramedics arrived in minutes. After examining Ichiro, they told me there was nothing they could do. "Sorry, Mrs. Uchida. Your husband has been dead for at least an hour. Please accept our sincerest condolences." They handed me a business card for the nearest embalmer and then they were gone.

I found a letter addressed to me lying beside Ichiro's pillow. Cradling his head in my arms, my tears dropped onto his cheeks so he looked as if he was crying with me. My hands shook as I read his last words:

7 October 1964

Dearest Noriko, when I was born I believed the course of my life was already ruined by factors beyond my control. It is for that reason my life has always been twisted and distorted. Unfortunately, my talents are too paltry to triumph over the calamities of my upbringing, but I also lacked the courage to do so. Such being the case, nothing can be done. When I met you, you brought me so much joy and I prayed that your bright spirit and optimism would lift me out of what I can only call a deep and dark hole.

I have failed at everything I have tried, or I quit before I could really make something of myself. I freely admit this. I lacked perseverance and any obstacle became a boulder over which I could not climb. I have only brought hardship on you, Noriko. There is no reason to think that you could ever be happy with me in my mental condition. I feel as if I am destroying your life, but thankfully, you're still young and can undo the traumas I have inflicted on you—but for one. You will be able to start over and find happiness before it is too late. It is in your nature to be joyful, and that is the one tenet that Tenrikyo is right about. I am sorry that you could not share its teachings with me. My mind was closed.

Please forgive me for being a coward. A man must have a strong constitution and talent, and I have neither. I no longer have the will to live. I thought for a while that I should divorce you so that you'd be free, but even in that I did not have the courage to execute my plan.

Do not tell my sister Mitsuko or Harry what has happened to me. Please tell them I died of a weak heart and make sure they take good care of our son. I only want his happiness as I want yours. I didn't consider how my decision to give Hisashi away would affect the two of us. I could not have imagined the great pain I would have to endure in sending him away. My heart has been a lonely and broken place. I couldn't share with you how I was feeling, but you must have sensed it. You are so sensitive. Maybe you should have spoken up, but you would then have broken your promise to me to say nothing of what we had done.

Please ask for forgiveness from the people I have inconvenienced by my actions and relay my most sincere apology from the bottom of my heart to Uncle Kiyoshi and the other members of the Uchida and Fujiwara families. To my beloved Noriko,

Ichiro

I turned the paper over to see if he had written anything more that would make sense of what he had done. He had added these words:

Noriko, please don't panic because it will look bad to the neighbors. Call the doctor, who is a friend of my uncle Kiyushi, and beg him to write a death certificate indicating the cause of my death as a weak heart. That will make sense because of all the medication I have been on. I may not be thinking clearly right now and so I will leave it up to you to handle this in any way you think best, but to say "suicide" would put a black cloud over the family and we have had enough sorrow already. And don't forget to place my name on the stone at the cemetery when the time comes. Perhaps Hisashi will visit me there with you someday.

My body was shaking. I didn't have the strength to stand up and I couldn't think of what more I could do to help Ichiro or myself. I lay down next to my husband's corpse, hoping by some miracle he would come back to life and this would be another one of his bad dreams.

As the early morning light filtered into the apartment, Ichiro was cold to my touch. I kept repeating, "Why, Ichiro? Why?" But the only answer I received was the dripping of the sink faucet and the persistent meowing of our hungry cat, who wound and rewound herself around Ichiro's body.

I sat up and petted Chaya, who had somehow escaped asphyxiation. "All right, little one. Mama will feed you." I opened the cabinet underneath the sink, and next to the cat food was a roll of duct tape, Ichiro's hair scissors, part of the rubber hose, and my glass coin jar, which was empty. I had not spent any money from the jar in several weeks, so Ichiro must have taken what was left of the few coins I had managed to save. Had he used them to buy these supplies? What an irony that he knew about my jar all along and had used it in this way. To me the jar was a sign of security and hope, and to him it was a way out.

I turned on the water and swallowed a few kernels of rice. With what little strength I had, I tried to tighten the faucet so the water wouldn't drip incessantly, but it did no good. I'd have to call a plumber. It was just seven but I knew that Uncle Kiyoshi would already be at his desk at his office at the Osaka Electric and Gas Company.

I called him from the pay phone on the street outside the front door of the apartment building, praying Mrs. Masamoto would not open her door as I passed. I asked Uncle Kiyoshi to bring his friend the doctor to sign Ichiro's death certificate, and in a pleading voice I said, "Uncle Kiyoshi, please ask the doctor to say that it was Ichiro's heart. He doesn't want the shame of having anyone know that he committed suicide. It would be a great indignity to him, although he probably will not know it. But who can say what the dead see and hear?"

"If that is what my nephew wants, I will do my best to convince the doctor." He paused, and then through sobs, he forced these words out: "I'm sorry, Noriko. First you lose Hisashi and now your husband. I wonder if you were born under an unlucky star."

"Please don't think that way. Ichiro always called me 'Star of Mine,' the most beautiful variety of rose. I choose to think of myself that way." And then I hung up.

Opening the telephone booth, I was assaulted by the ordinariness of the day. Pedestrians hurried by with determined looks on their faces as if they had somewhere important to go, mothers not much younger than me passed by holding their children's hand, and young boys dressed in school uniforms chattered to one another as they headed off to school.

I slowly climbed the stairs to my apartment and hesitated before unlocking the door. I wanted to escape, but I willed myself to keep going. I had work to do to plan for Ichiro's funeral and burial. I once heard that suicide was the ultimate act of selfishness because it left those who loved the person to go on living without them. I went over everything leading up to Ichiro's suicide in my mind. Did I miss the signs that he intended to take his life? I knew he had been depressed and had violent mood swings, but I never imagined he had given up on himself, and on us. I'm sure he wrote such a lengthy letter to relieve me of any guilt or blame. Could I have done something differently? What if I had refused to give Hisashi away, might Ichiro still be alive? Would he have found the strength to fight his demons and become the father he wished to be?

∼

FAMILY MEMBERS CROWDED INTO our apartment to witness the solemn task of preparing Ichiro's body for his funeral and cremation. Setsuko helped me wash his face with water to "relieve him of his cares," and then the encoffiner shaved his face and applied rouge to his ashen cheeks. He combed his thick hair peppered with gray. I chose one of his finest ties and shirts for him, knowing that he would want to look elegant in death as he had in life.

Holding up a navy-blue tie, I told my sister, "I think I'm going to choose this one. It belonged to Ichiro's father. Someday I'll give it to Hisashi."

Setsuko looked at me with compassion. "I cannot believe what Ichiro has done to you."

"What do you mean?"

"Don't pretend, Noriko. Uncle Kiyoshi told me how Ichiro died—it wasn't his illness or natural causes that killed him. It was by his own hand. I hope you don't blame yourself for what happened."

"I'm sorry he told you. Please don't tell anyone outside the family. Will you promise?"

"Of course. I know how proud Ichiro was, how concerned about what other people thought of him." She sighed. "I can still see him when he came to the tearoom as a fourteen-year old orphan. He bowed so low when I gave him a job that I thought he was going to fall over. Many other boys had asked me for work, but they did not have Ichiro's earnestness. I made a good choice in hiring him. He melted my heart."

"Mine, too. And now he has broken it—twice."

Ichiro's body was transported by hearse to the Buddhist temple. The ceremonial hall was filled with the comforting scent of sandalwood incense placed in the holders by the mourners who filed into the hall. There was a bronze statue of Buddha and a photograph of Ichiro in his ski clothes, looking cheerful and relaxed, and leaning against the base of the frame, offerings of oranges and bags of rice for him to carry into the spirit world. Ichiro's body rested in a simple open casket in front of the mourners. A bell rang several times to signal the start of the ceremony.

I sat between my sister Setsuko and my niece Kazuko. Behind me were my nephew Mitsuo and his sister Akiko and their father Hideo. In the same row were Uncle Kiyoshi, Ichiro's mother's brother, and his wife, Auntie Chiaru. My Auntie Sanae and my mother sat next to my younger brother Tadashi, a mature twenty-one-year-old who had recently graduated college. Three waitresses from the Tesagara Tearoom showed up, and the cashier Hana and the Aki-Torii's barman were also there to pay their respects. Sitting in the back row was our landlady, Mrs. Masamoto, who wailed loudly as if it was her professional duty.

I listened intently to the priest's words, but they didn't hold an answer to the tragedy that Ichiro brought upon us:

Buddha taught that all life is impermanent and that those who are born must eventually pass from this life. However, everyone has within them the seeds of their past virtues, which have the power to bring a fortunate rebirth in the future. We pray through the power of this virtue, through the blessings of the holy beings, and through the force of our heartfelt prayers, that our dear friend Ichiro will experience great good fortune and everlasting peace and happiness in his next life.

We also pray for the bereaved widow, Noriko, and his relatives and friends that they may be comforted in their loss and find peace of mind and strength of heart.

When I heard myself called a widow, I shuddered at the sound of this word. *Is that the designation I would carry with me for the remainder of my days on earth?* It was what I feared and now here it was, brought on in a way I could not have imagined.

At the end of the service, I looked at my husband lying in his casket, his hands folded over his chest and his face finally at peace. His visage gave no hint of the torment that he had silently endured, and the lines that had marred his otherwise youthful face seemed to have disappeared, making him look even younger than his nearly thirty-three years. I said a few words for the mourners, expressing my gratitude for their attendance, and then I recited two short poems: *Making love with you is like drinking sea water / The more I drink the thirstier I become / Until nothing can slake my thirst but to drink the entire sea.* Ichiro and I had disagreed on its meaning when he read it to me. The other poem was one I don't think he was familiar with: *In love's longing / I listen to the monk's bell / I will never forget you even for an interval short as those between the bell notes.*

The priest gestured for me to take one final look at my husband. Then he closed the lid and six men carried it to the hearse to be transported to the crematorium. Surrounded by my family, I watched the hearse melt into the flow of traffic in front of the temple.

Setsuko asked me, "Do you want to go to the crematorium? When his body has been incinerated, you and I can pick the bones out with chopsticks and put his ashes into an urn for burial."

"Although I know it's supposed to be the duty of the widow to do this, I couldn't bear the sight. I want to remember Ichiro when he was alive, most especially on the day when he asked me to marry him, when everything seemed possible because we were in love. I can still feel his arm around my waist as we walked through the garden across from the concert hall. I felt as if he would never let me go. The moon was particularly brilliant that night." As if repeating a dream, I continued. "The final notes of "Clair de Lune" hung in the air between us. I teased Ichiro, pretending I needed to think about his proposal. Poor boy. Of course, I had every intention of accepting his proposal. I had already made my mind up. Why didn't he believe in our love to carry us through the difficult times? If he had, none of this would have happened. I am sure of it."

Setsuko wiped a tear from my cheek in a sisterly gesture. "If it helps you to believe that then go ahead. But I'm afraid Ichiro wasn't strong enough to fight the demons chasing him."

I said, "I do recall that, as we walked from the garden, I heard the claxon of a pleasure boat floating down the river. It sounded so sad. I wonder if that was a sign I should have heeded."

〜

THE PRIEST RETURNED TO my apartment with Ichiro's navy-blue tie that had once belonged to his father, Hide-Ichi, and the urn wrapped in a white cloth. He placed it on the altar I had decorated with red chrysanthemums, oranges, and sandalwood incense. My mother prepared dishes for the relatives, and after we finished eating, I felt compelled to tell them, "No one is to breathe a word of what happened. Especially not to his sister and her husband. And when Hisashi is old enough to understand, he should never be told. Ichiro does not want his son to be ashamed of him. Maybe someday Ichiro will send me a sign that I no longer need to keep the circumstances of his death a secret, or maybe I will decide of my own accord that it is no longer worth hiding, but until then, please honor his wishes and mine."

∼

A MONTH AFTER ICHIRO's death I still had not gotten my period. I went to the doctor and he confirmed what I already knew—I was pregnant. The baby was due in late July or early August. It was possible that his birthday would coincide with Hisashi's or mine. I kept my pregnancy a secret, praying that I could hold the baby despite all the turmoil in my life. I imagined having a second chance at motherhood. I was certain I could face this alone, that somehow, I would put all the pieces together. This time, if I had to turn to my family for help, I would, and I would raise my child into adulthood instead of having him ripped from me. I would name the baby Ichiro if it was a boy, and Aimi, if she was a girl.

A few weeks after Ichiro's death, I was at the tearoom when I was hit with gut-wrenching pain. I rushed to the bathroom and sat on the toilet. A clot of blood slipped out of my body. I looked at it in horror. For a moment, I wanted to reach in and pull it out and give it a proper burial, and then I flushed it down the toilet. I sat there weeping. When I could get up, I washed my face and tried to look somewhat presentable. I knew I had suffered a miscarriage.

I asked Setsuko if I could leave early. She looked at me strangely. "Is everything all right, Noriko? You look so pale."

"I might be coming down with a cold. I should go home. But I'll be here tomorrow, I promise."

I went back to my empty apartment. Lighting a candle, I prayed to God the Parent and heard a voice telling me, "Each body is lent to us by God for whatever time is preordained. This baby was yours for just a short while. Let it go and be grateful for the joy that you have inside yourself to share with others." I struggled to believe this, but nothing I told myself lessened the loss. I had already begun to imagine becoming the mother of Aimi or Ichiro, a second child, a chance to do over what I had done so poorly.

Chapter 48

Hisashi played on the kitchen floor near the warm stove, building a fort with his Lincoln logs. Picking up a cow, he made a mooing sound and then neighed as he placed the horse inside the corral he constructed by himself. Mitsuko was grateful that he was happy to amuse himself so she could put the finishing touches on the Thanksgiving table. She arranged a centerpiece of cranberry branches and pine boughs like the one she saw in the holiday issue of *Good Housekeeping*. Standing back to admire her work, she asked Harry, "How does it look?"

Harry was watching the ceremony at Arlington National Cemetery for the one-year anniversary of President Kennedy's death on television. He briefly looked up, giving Mitsuko the compliment she was after, and then went back to the ceremony as the bugle sounded the final notes of "Day is Done."

Mitsuko took the turkey out of the oven and then lined up the serving dishes filled with sweet potatoes, homemade cranberry sauce, gravy, green beans, and Harry's favorite, mashed potatoes. "Put Hisashi's Lincoln logs away and then sit him into his high chair. Everything is ready. All you need to do is carve the turkey and we can eat."

"Come on, Dwight. Time for a special dinner."

"No, Daddy. I want to play." Over time, Hisashi chose to call Harry "Daddy" and Mitsuko "Mommy," which distinguished them from his mama, Noriko, and his dada, Ichiro.

"That's enough playing for now. Your mother worked very hard on this dinner. And don't say no to me. I'm your father." Turning to Mitsuko, Harry said, "I don't know when he started saying no, but I don't like it."

"Hisashi's just trying to show his independence."

"Where did you get that idea, Mitzi?"

"That's what Dr. Carlson says. It's normal."

"Mitzi, try and remember not to call Dwight by his Japanese name. It's just going to confuse him if you keep calling him Hisashi. And when he's ready for school in a few years we want all the children to call him Dwight."

"Did I? I didn't mean to, but it comes so naturally to me and I have to think three times when I call him Dwight. I even catch myself calling him Ichiro because he looks so much like my brother at the same age." She let out an involuntary sigh, feeling their separation acutely.

Mitsuko tied a bib around Hisashi's neck to protect his plaid flannel shirt. Hisashi picked up his spoon and tasted the tart cranberry-orange sauce. He made a face. "I don't like it, Mommy."

Mitsuko scooped up a portion of sweet potato pudding covered with marshmallows and put it on his plate. He hesitated and then tried it. "Mmm, good." Mitsuko recalled how Noriko had warned her about Hisashi's sweet tooth in her letter, so it came as no surprise that he preferred the sweet potatoes to the cranberry sauce.

Harry carved the turkey and placed the pieces on a serving platter. Mitsuko poured gravy into a pitcher and carried it to the table, careful to keep it out of Hisashi's reach. She didn't want him to stain the tablecloth. He had already finished the sweet potato and was asking for more. "Sweetheart, leave some room for turkey." She cut a piece of white breast meat into bite-size pieces. Hisashi looked at it cautiously and then put a piece in his mouth. He spit it out.

Harry wiped his son's mouth. "I guess he's not quite ready for turkey, Mitzi, but it sure is good."

Mitsuko scooped up some sweet potato pudding for herself. Holding her fork over her plate, she said, "Something has been bothering me. We haven't had a word from Noriko or Ichiro in more than a month. Do you think there's something wrong? In his last letter to us he sounded very down."

"You worry too much," Harry said.

"I know. I guess if there was something really wrong, Auntie Chiaru or Uncle Kiyoshi would write to me." That was what she kept telling herself.

After dinner, while Harry did the dishes, Mitsuko tucked Hisashi into his cowboy bed, and as she did every night, took out his favorite story, *Goodnight Moon*. When she came to the last sentence, Hisashi chimed in. "Goodnight, moon; goodnight, kitty; goodnight, cow; goodnight, clock; goodnight, Mommy."

"Now, say your prayers."

Hisashi put his hands together. "Now I lay me down to sleep, I pray the Lord my soul to keep, and if I die before I wake, I pray the Lord my soul to take." Mitsuko thought, "What a sad prayer for a child to repeat. Why didn't the church come up with more positive words?"

The Thanksgiving moon cast a beam of light across the floor. Mitsuko pulled the curtains across the window. Hisashi burrowed underneath the covers and the cat curled up at the foot of his bed. Mitsuko listened to her son's even breathing as he drifted off to sleep. She told herself, *Everything is all right with Ichiro*, but she had an uneasy feeling that it wasn't. Brother and sister were so deeply connected that Ichiro visited her in her dreams. His message was always the same: "Take care of my boy, Mitsuko, as you took care of me."

After the Thanksgiving weekend, Mitsuko felt a strange and urgent need to put the teardrop box containing Hisashi's umbilical cord in a safe deposit box at the bank. She had been keeping it in her bureau since she discovered it among the things Noriko packed into Hisashi's suitcase.

Mitsuko bundled her son into his snowsuit and sat him in the passenger seat of the Chevrolet. He looked out the window, calling out the names of the stores along the street as they drove to the First National Bank: hardware store, barber shop, grocery store, flower shop, garage. Then he stopped for a moment. "What's that, Mommy?" It was the funeral home.

Mitsuko hesitated, then answered, "It's where people go on their way to the moon and the stars." Hisashi seemed satisfied with her explanation and didn't ask another question. Instead he played with the zipper of his snowsuit, pulling it up and down. The sound unnerved Mitsuko but she didn't tell him to stop. They would be at the bank soon enough, and if he did it again, she'd point it out to him and give him something else to play with. He was such an active child and had so much pent-up energy. She thought, *Just like me. I can't sit still for a minute. It drives Harry crazy.*

Mitsuko noticed a large poster resting on an easel in the bank lobby announcing a promotion: *Open a Savings Account and You'll Receive a Sunbeam Toaster Free. This Offer Expires on December 24—a Perfect Gift Just in Time for XMAS.*

Mitsuko gave the bank teller the key to their safe deposit box and signed the access card. She lifted the steel lid. A red paper origami crane lovingly made by her mother for her birthday was tucked into a corner of the box. She picked it up and it crumbled in her hand, the paper falling like tears to the floor. She looked through the documents: her Japanese passport, her marriage license from the American consulate in Kobe, her citizenship papers from 1956, the deed to their two-bedroom house at Knauff's Trailer Court, Harry's discharge papers from the US Army.

On top was a thick file marked "Hisashi/Dwight." In the file was the original application to the US Consulate in Kobe, Japan, signed by her brother and Noriko and the published Private Bill with the name "Hisashi Uchida" printed on it and signed by President Kennedy. Mitsuko opened her handbag and gently placed the teardrop box inside the safe deposit box. She closed the lid and slid the box back into the vault.

The bank teller locked the small door with her key and returned it to Mitsuko. They exited the vault and the teller asked, "Is there anything else I can do for you today, Mrs. Mishima?"

"I want to wire some money to my brother in Osaka. It will be his thirty-third birthday on December tenth. When he was a little boy, I thought he used to get cheated since his birthday was so close to Christmas. He'd only get one gift instead of two."

"Just fill out this form with the wiring instructions, and I'll take care of wiring the funds right in time."

Mitsuko clearly and slowly wrote Ichiro's name and the name of his bank in Osaka in English and handed the paper back to the teller with five twenty-dollar bills.

"There is a five-dollar wiring fee, Mrs. Mishima."

"Oh." She opened her wallet. "Lucky I have just enough."

The bank teller hesitated a moment and then put a large cardboard box on the counter. "We're having a special promotion for opening a savings account. Why don't you take this toaster as a special thank you for your business?"

Mitsuko was embarrassed. "I can't do that. I only have a safe deposit box. It wouldn't be fair."

The teller lowered her voice. "We have at least fifty of them back there. I'm sure we won't need all of them. It is my gift for you and your husband being loyal customers."

Mitsuko smiled and thanked her.

Hisashi was curious to know what was in the box. Mitsuko tried her best to describe it. "You put bread inside and wait a minute, and then toast pops up because it's like an oven and it cooks the bread and turns it into toast."

Hisashi said, "Bread in the toaster and out comes toast."

"That's right."

"And how does the toaster work?"

"You plug it into the electricity, that's how."

"Like the lamps, and the TV, and the radio, and…" He'd run out of ideas.

The bank teller chuckled. "Kids can sure wear you out with all their questions."

"I don't mind. Except when I don't have the answers."

Hisashi fell asleep in the car. Crossing the Merrill Street Bridge, Mitsuko glimpsed the dark waters of the Yellowstone River. An eagle soared overhead through the twilight winter sky. Mitsuko felt as if she were suffocating, the musty smell of the safe deposit box lingering in her nostrils and her heart beating hard against her chest, her throat tightening.

Harry's truck was parked outside the trailer. When she stopped the car, Hisashi woke up. He opened the door and ran into the house; Mitsuko followed him, carrying the toaster.

Hisashi yelled out, "Daddy, toaster, toaster."

Mitsuko explained, "The bank teller gave it to us just for wiring money to Ichiro. It's a special Christmas promotion. It was awfully nice of her."

Harry took a knife and sliced the box open and lifted the toaster out of its packaging. "Pretty fancy. It's a Powermatic. You don't have to press a lever. The bread comes up automatically when it's done. No more burned toast." He turned the toaster upside down. "Made in Japan."

Hisashi pulled out his Lincoln logs and sang to himself. Mitsuko recognized the tune as a familiar Japanese lullaby her mother had sung to her when she was a little girl. He must have learned it from Noriko.

Harry said, "I stopped off at the post office and there was a letter waiting for you. After you read it, tell me what Noriko says."

Mitsuko sat down, fearful of what it said.

20 November 1964

Dearest Mitsuko and Harry:

I apologize profusely for my silence, but I have not had the courage to write to you. Even now I find it difficult to put pen to paper. The coroner conducted an autopsy of your brother. He died of a weak heart in early October. Ichiro had not been doing well. I kept hoping he would get better. The doctor says his heart couldn't withstand all the TB medicine he was taking. It came as a terrible shock to everyone. I honestly thought he was getting better!

We had a funeral service for Ichiro. I am keeping his ashes next to an altar in my apartment, and when it's time, I'll put his remains in the Uchida family plot. You have nothing to worry about, my dearest sister-in-law. I will take care of everything appropriately, as Ichiro would have wanted. I will observe all the important holidays and put his ashes in the family gravesite in a year. When I can, I will go to the family registry in Kobe and enter his death date on the koseki.

I sometimes dream he is still alive and then I wake up and my bed is empty. I sing to push him from my thoughts, but then I cry so hard I cannot sing. I sometimes call out my husband's name, and then I am startled remembering he is not here. I would like to move from our apartment to start a new life, but housing is expensive in Osaka, and I don't know if I can find a place to live that I can afford. I am sorry that I write about all this sorrow, but Ichiro never had a very happy life. He never admitted it, but he was despondent when Hisashi went away. It broke his heart, even though he thought he was doing the right thing for everyone.

My aunt and uncle and Setsuko and Kimie are supporting me emotionally and that is of great help. Please take care of yourselves and live a long life for me, so you can write often about Hisashi. Make Ichiro proud of our son. Love, Noriko

Mitsuko cried for three days before she ran out of tears, and then she lay on her bed unable to move. She pulled the shades over the window to block out the light, sleeping fitfully. Ichiro came to her in her dreams: "Do not weep for me. My spirit will always be with you. You have my son, and through him you will be connected to me. Please do not abandon Noriko; she is Hisashi's natural mother, but you are the mother who will raise him. This was our choice."

Hisashi curled up next to Mitsuko. He touched her face. "Mommy, don't cry." She opened her eyes and looked at her son's sad face and in it she saw Ichiro.

Harry put his arms around Mitsuko. "It's time for you to get out of bed. We have a son to raise—you and I together."

PART FOUR

Chapter 49

1980

I was only twenty-six years old when Ichiro took his life. If it had not been for my belief in Tenrikyo and its commandment to live a joyous life, I am not sure I would have survived this blow on top of losing Hisashi.

I never stopped hoping someday I might see Hisashi again. I felt foolish lighting a candle for each birthday that passed and singing aloud as if he were standing right next to me, but I couldn't stop myself because stopping meant I had pushed him out of my mind—and that would never happen. He was part of me, heart and soul.

My last memory of Hisashi was as a toddler dressed in his navy-blue and maroon suit with a matching cap on his head that his father kept taking off so they could play one more game of peek-a-boo before he boarded the airplane and disappeared. I can still feel Ichiro grabbing my arm like a vice to restrain me from running after him.

Over the years, I received photographs of my son from Mitsuko and Harry, which I put in an album, marking each one with the date. The most recent showed a serious-looking eighteen-year-old wearing thick black glasses and hair down to his shoulders. He was dressed in baggy jeans and a University of Montana T-shirt. Mitsuko reported in her letters that he was an excellent student and could have had his choice of colleges, but they didn't have the money so he went to a state school where the tuition was manageable.

Mitsuko admitted that Hisashi had run away from home before his last year of high school. She suspected he wanted to see more of the United States—maybe go all the way to California. She was beside herself with worry, which is why she didn't tell me this story until much later. I can only imagine how she felt wondering where he was. He came home when he ran out of money, never telling her where he had been. When he went to college, he spoke of wanting to help poor people.

Harry still worked at Halliburton, and Mitsuko opened her own bar, which she called Mitzi's, right near the Jordan Hotel. Hisashi worked with her during the summers taking care of inventory. She told me he was a numbers man like his father and grandfather.

Over the years, I worked for my sister as an assistant bookkeeper. I didn't have the heart to change jobs, even though I was offered a good opportunity with Japan Airlines. I couldn't seem to motivate myself to make a change. I felt more comfortable surrounded by my family and familiar coworkers. At one point, however, I took a gamble and opened my own tearoom, but it didn't work out, and I went back into Setsuko's employ and have been there ever since.

I eventually moved out of my old apartment and found a much nicer place to live, high on a hill overlooking Osaka where the air is better and it is less crowded than in the center of the city. My new house was light-filled and airy and lifted my spirits. The only possessions I brought with me from my old apartment were the flower- and plant-filled pots I nurtured on our balcony. Most of them were still thriving, and the ones that died, I quickly replaced.

I was able to move because of Mr. Sugimoto, the man I had met on the train to Matsue. He had seated himself next to me and before he got off the train he gave me his business card and promised to visit me at the tearoom. Some months after Ichiro died, he came looking for me at the tearoom. I was surprised to see him, but he turned out to be a man of his word. He was twenty years older than me, successful, and had impeccable manners. Since I was no longer married, I encouraged his interest in me even though he confessed that he had a wife and three sons. This is not so unusual in Japan. From the beginning of our relationship I made it clear to Mr. Sugimoto I had no desire to remarry, but he convinced himself that in time I would change my mind. He eventually learned after we had been together for several years that I valued my independence. I spared him the pain of telling him I didn't love him. He has been exceedingly generous to me, and has treated me with the utmost courtesy. Only my sister and his closest friends know that we are more than friends, since we have had to hide our relationship. We only go out in public when there are other people with us.

No one could take the place of Ichiro. He was still "My Everything." As the years went by, I dwelled on the good times: singing with him at the piano, our honeymoon, and the day of our son's birth. I felt our marriage was unfinished, however, because it ended so abruptly after fewer than four years. Had we been married for many years I might have felt differently about remarrying, but because our union was cut short, interrupted by an unimaginable disaster, I couldn't bring myself to fall in love again. Besides, I had never fallen out of love with Ichiro. I am sure if he could speak to me, he would have encouraged me to remarry, if not Mr. Sugimoto then someone else. Maybe I was too afraid to give my heart away only to have it broken again.

A few years after Ichiro's suicide, I legally changed my name back to Noriko Ito from Noriko Uchida. Had my son still been with me, I would not have done such a thing. We would have shared the same last name, but as a childless mother and widow I saw no reason to hold onto my husband's name. I would have thought about my losses every time I signed my name.

I continued to worship at the Tenrikyo Church and studied the precepts of their teachings. I reached a level where I was just below that of a priestess, and spent time ministering to the sick and the poor. I worked in their orphanage, taking care of children who were born out of wedlock or abandoned. In most ways I was happy.

On important holidays and festivals, I visited Ichiro's grave, and as I promised to Mitsuko, made sure that it was well cared for. I always cleaned the stones and pulled the weeds that grew in the family plot between the times I visited. There was no one else to perform these duties. Mr. Sugimoto was kind enough to drive me out to the cemetery because even with modern trains it would have taken me half a day to get there and back on my own. He'd wait for me in the car while I presented my offerings and cleaned the stones. I hated knowing Ichiro's ashes were there, buried in the ground with worms and roots winding themselves around the box that contained his urn. Perhaps I should have scattered his ashes into the ocean; they might have reached the shores of America or been carried on a jet stream somewhere close to Hisashi.

Mr. Sugimoto offered to buy me an airplane ticket to America to see Hisashi. Whether out of cowardice or confusion I chose not to accept his offer. I didn't want to insinuate myself into Hisashi's life, or break apart the family bonds between his legal parents and him. How would he feel about seeing me after all this time? I would not have blamed him if he slammed the door in my face.

～

I RECEIVED A LETTER from Mitsuko dated May 15, 1981, saying Hisashi had quit the University of Montana after his freshman year. He hadn't been taking his studies seriously and was confused about the direction of his life. He decided to enlist in the Navy, convinced that a stint in the military would give him the structure and discipline he felt he was lacking. And then Mitsuko told me that Hisashi asked the Navy to deploy him to Japan, hoping he might finally meet me after all these years. I could hardly breathe reading these words. I needed a moment before continuing. I went into the garden and cut some roses, put them into a vase, and filled it with water. The petals were still covered with morning dew. Turning on the radio, I tuned it to what had been Ichiro's favorite classical music station. Leaving the door open, the songbirds seemed to be adding their voices to the orchestra. I picked up Mitsuko's letter again:

At this very moment, our Hisashi is somewhere in the Pacific Ocean on the aircraft carrier the USS Midway, *heading for a naval base on the coast of Japan. I don't know the details, but you can expect a letter from him in the next six months or so. I know that seems like a long time, but in the scheme of things, it's but a minute.*

Switching to his American name, Mitsuko continued:

Dwight has wanted to see you for a long time. I told him everything I know about you, but since we never met, I can't tell him very much—only what Ichiro wrote. Please forgive Dwight if he's misinformed. He has many questions about you and Ichiro only you can answer. I think it's a good idea for you and him to know one another. Please be assured that we never lied to Dwight about his birth. He has known for as long as he could grasp the concept that he's adopted and you are his natural mother. I understand that many adopted children reach a point in their lives when they want to know their natural parents. I hope you will be proud of Dwight. We are. With all my love, Mitsuko

My heart felt as if it might burst open. Was this really true that I would see my son again? I never imagined he would take the first step. I leaned against the table, afraid that my legs were too weak to hold me up. What next? I realized I was still in my nightgown. I got dressed for work, carefully placed Mitsuko's letter in my pocketbook, and checked to make sure I had my transportation card for the subway.

Riding the train into Namba, I thought about all the times Hisashi and I went to the tearoom when I had to work to support our family, and how he tried so hard to please me and comfort me. I could almost hear him say, "Don't worry, Mama. Everything will be all right." I needed those words of assurance now more than ever.

When there was a lull in the stream of customers coming into the Aki-Torii, I showed my sister Mitsuko's letter. Setsuko admonished me, "Don't get your hopes up. I don't want you to be disappointed if you don't hear from Hisashi. Your life is going along splendidly. Mr. Sugimoto takes good care of you, and you have a guaranteed job here so long as you want it. And my children love you like a second mother."

"That's all true. But I can't help wanting to see Hisashi. It's always been in the back of my mind since the day he left. Until now our reunion was just a fantasy. I used to dream about Ichiro and me together with our son. Sometimes we'd be at the beach or playing ball in the park. Ichiro was healthy. I couldn't always hear what he was saying, but he'd be laughing at something Hisashi did or said." Tears ran down my face. "I haven't had a dream like that in a long time."

I went on. "Whenever I saw a boy about Hisashi's age, I'd wonder if he was anything like my son. Not his looks but his expression, his personality, his character. I'd sometimes stand next to a mother and her son at a store or on the subway and listen to their conversation just for a hint of what they shared with one another. It was usually not memorable, but their closeness made me so sad. I knew I was being ridiculous, but I couldn't break myself of the habit. Every now and then I'd be caught eavesdropping and have to apologize."

Setsuko held me in her arms. I hadn't realized how much sadness I still carried inside me. It was like hearing a piece of music that opened a floodgate of feelings I couldn't control. "Oh, my dearest Noriko, I only wish the best for you. If this is what you want, I hope Hisashi writes to you soon. Just don't expect too much from him. After all, you are a stranger to him, no matter how many birthday cards and letters you've exchanged. He might bear resentment toward you and Ichiro. Are you prepared for that?"

"I'm not weak. I can deal with his reaction so long as we can sit down and pour out our hearts to one another. It may take time, but I have faith it will happen so long as I am patient with him—and with myself. I can't expect a miracle overnight. Please be happy for me."

"You're right. I shouldn't be saying these things." She sighed. "You could use some company right now. Why don't you ask Mr. Sugimoto to take you out tonight?"

"I still have invoices to pay. Ichiro always told me I shouldn't wait until the last minute. Vendors appreciate prompt payment." Answering my sister's question about Mr. Sugimoto, I said, "He's with his family this evening. It's his younger son's twentieth birthday. Maybe he'll give me some advice on what boys are like at that age. I have no experience, and I can't call upon my own memories for clues."

"I'm not sure Japanese and American teenagers have much in common other than their clothes and the music they listen to. Their upbringing is so different."

"We'll find out, won't we?"

Climbing up the steep hill to the Kunizuka neighborhood where I lived, I was forced to stop and rest every few minutes. I was exhausted from the highs and lows of the day's emotions.

Every day when I returned from work, I immediately checked my mailbox for a letter from Hisashi. Today it was empty except for the electric bill, which I would turn over to Mr. Sugimoto, an announcement of a sale at Takashimaya, and a government form letter sent to all the survivors of Hiroshima reminding us of routine physical exams. Even after all these years, some victims suddenly developed complications from radiation and, within months, died. I didn't think much about it, but with the prospect of seeing Hisashi, I worried that something could happen to me before I had the chance to see my son again.

Finally, the letter I had been waiting for arrived. Written in Japanese by a translator Hisashi hired at the Navy base, my son told me he was in port in Yokosuka, Japan, a five-hour ride on the bullet train from Osaka. He assured me that he would visit me as soon as he received permission for a leave from his superior, but he didn't know how long that would take and he didn't know the ship's itinerary, which could pull out of port any day. He added, *I almost forgot to date my letter. It's my twentieth birthday, August 10. (But you know the date.) I'm sorry I don't know your birthday. When I see you, you'll have to tell me.*

At the end of the letter was a note from the translator: *Miss Noriko Ito, your son is a most polite young man. You will not be disappointed in him when*

you meet him. He anxiously awaits your response to this letter, which I will gladly translate for him. May your reunion be blessed. Mr. Ichiro Koyama, Experienced Translator.

Hisashi's letter revealed nothing about his state of mind, but I was pleased the translator had made such positive remarks about my son. I entertained the idea of taking a train to Yokosuka the next day or asking Mr. Sugimoto to hire a chauffeur to drive me there, but I realized my son might not be given permission to come ashore and so there was no point. I would have to wait for his instructions. I wrote back immediately and received another letter.

September 12, 1981

Dear Noriko, Thank you for answering my letter so promptly. Mr. Koyama translated your letter for me and is helping me with this one. I'm sorry I don't speak Japanese or write it. It would make our communication much simpler.

I am sorry to tell you that we are going on deployment, so I won't be able to visit you right now. I have requested leave when we return to Japan in January of next year. It seems like a long time but it's only five months away, so we'll have plenty of time to get adjusted to the idea of meeting. I hope you won't be disappointed in me. I haven't made much of my life up to this point, but the Navy will whip me into shape and give me skills to ensure my future success.

My son's humility and ambition reminded me of his father.

I continued reading:

I'll send you a letter when we are in port again. I'll probably have two days off at the most, and so it might be easier for us to meet in Tokyo. That way I won't be wasting time traveling all the way to Osaka. I hope you are up for that. That's all for now.

Your son, Dwight Mishima

P.S. I'm enclosing a recent picture so you'll recognize me when we meet. I have short hair now. I don't like wearing it like this but it's Navy regulations. I've had to give up the hippie look for the time being.

I had to think for a moment. My husband—if he were alive—would be fifty in December. No longer a young man. Looking at Hisashi's picture I could see their resemblance—my son's face was gentle and intelligent, just like his father's.

Chapter 50

Mr. Sugimoto drove me to the cemetery on New Year's Day. His wife and sons had left Osaka for a ski trip to Hokkaido. At sixty-two he had given up skiing so he had a convenient excuse not to join them on holiday—one of the few we could share together without lies. It was a fiercely cold day, and the wind tore down the hillside. I wrapped my mink coat around myself and tied a scarf around my head. Many mourners were lined up, waiting for their turn to use the water pump and bucket to tend to the graves and pay their respects to their deceased loved ones. Children walked in a solemn procession behind their parents, behaving themselves as they had been taught. There was no talking other than the repetition of sutras from one grave to the next, as if a radio were playing the same announcement repeatedly. I stood in front of Ichiro's gravesite and wished him and his parents a Happy New Year.

Suddenly I felt Ichiro's presence behind me. I was afraid to turn around, but I heard his voice whisper in my ear, "My dearest Noriko. Claim our son. Tell him the truth. He's old enough to understand. Be brave and know that I love you both with all my heart and regret everything."

The wind roared past me and then Ichiro's spirit was gone. I wasn't sure if my imagination had been playing tricks on me, or if Ichiro actually sent me a message. It was the first time he had reached out to me.

I found Mr. Sugimoto leaning against his Mercedes smoking a cigarette despite the frigid weather. I said, "I would have thought you'd be sitting inside the car." He answered, "I wanted to keep an eye on you, Noriko. I know how emotional this is for you."

I took his hand and kissed it. I didn't tell him what had just happened, but I felt afraid. I asked him, "Please stay the night. I don't want to be alone."

He hesitated and then confessed, "My wife is returning from Hokkaido tomorrow morning. I promised I would celebrate the rest of the holiday with the family. I wish I could be with you, but it's impossible under our current circumstances."

He dropped his cigarette and stepped on it, and then opened the car door for me. Keeping his eyes on the road, he said, "Why won't you seriously consider what I've asked of you so many times? I will gladly divorce my wife and marry you, and then we'll be free to come and go as we please. My sons are old enough that it won't affect them. I've been a responsible father, and I will continue to be, but shouldn't I have some happiness in my life at my age? I think I've earned it."

I answered as sincerely as I could without being hurtful. "I admire you greatly, but I'm happy with the way things are. I'm not made for marriage, and I would feel horribly guilty to break up your marriage."

"I suspect my wife knows about you no matter how careful we are. Our little ruse of having friends join us whenever we go out can't work forever. In fact, someone has probably figured it out by now and told my wife; although, frankly, so long as I give her everything she wants, I doubt that she would care. There has been no love between us since long before you and I began our affair. I hate to use that word, but that's what we have. I want something more permanent. We deserve it."

I kept my hands folded in my lap. I was walking a tightrope and was unable to respond to him. I cared about him deeply, and I appreciated his generosity. I didn't want to lose what we had together—a deep friendship—but I could never love him and gratitude was not a proper basis for a marriage after I had experienced passionate love with Ichiro.

Mr. Sugimoto continued his argument, which sounded as if he had been preparing it for days. "I don't want to risk losing you, Noriko. Who knows? Someday someone else may come into the Aki-Torii and catch your fancy or your eyes will meet a handsome stranger's eyes on a train, and then where will I be? I'll be sixty-three in a few months. Youth is not on my side."

"You can trust me. There will never be anyone else to replace you. You're such a good man, and you've been so kind to me."

"The happiest moments of my life are when I'm with you, Noriko, and I take the greatest pleasure in giving you whatever you need. You don't permit me to spoil you; otherwise I would do much more for you."

"After you've paid my rent and bought me nice clothes, there is really nothing more that I could ask for. I like working so I have my own money. I just wish I made a better salary so I didn't have to ask you to help me out at all."

"I do it gladly. I wish you would reconsider my proposal. I know you'll never love me the way you loved Ichiro, but we could have a good life together. And I would be able to be with you whenever I wanted."

Being at Mr. Sugimoto's beck and call was stifling. I also felt that I had given everything I had to Ichiro and there was nothing left in my heart for Mr. Sugimoto. "Let me think about it. I don't want to be pressured into doing something I will later regret."

Mr. Sugimoto smiled. "I guess I'll just have to be a little more patient and be satisfied with our time together, as limited as it is." We drove the rest of the way to my home in silence. I felt like a fish let off the hook.

When we arrived at my spacious house on the hill overlooking Osaka, Mr. Sugimoto walked me to the door. Before I went inside, I asked "Will you do me a favor? Will you go with me to Tokyo to see my son? He has written to me that he will be here in two weeks' time. If you don't come, I worry that I won't be able to communicate with him. Your English is good and mine is just tearoom talk. I don't think I'll have much use for 'black tea or green, sir?'" Turning serious I admitted, "There are already many barriers between Hisashi and me. At least language won't be one of them if you're with us."

"Of course. I was hoping you would ask. But how will you explain our relationship? Who am I to you?"

"I'll tell him you're my good friend. He's old enough to come to his own conclusion." Then I repeated my request, "Then, you'll go with me?" Mr. Sugimoto nodded. I gave him a gentle kiss on the cheek, and then he walked back to his car. Before putting my key in the door, I turned around and waved a hopeful goodbye.

～

TWO WEEKS LATER, I SAT on a plush sofa in the lobby of the elegant Tokyo Palace Hotel where Hisashi and I planned to meet at noon. The hotel was directly across from the Emperor's Imperial Gardens, one of the city's major tourist attractions. I tried to pay attention to what Mr. Sugimoto was saying but I was too nervous to focus on anything other than Hisashi's arrival. The clock ticked past noon. "What if he doesn't come?" I asked.

"Why wouldn't he show up? You and he have exchanged letters and he's gone to an awful lot of trouble. Dropping out of college and joining the Navy are not to be taken lightly."

"You're right, but what if he decided at the last minute that meeting me was a bad idea after all? He's probably as scared as I am right now."

"Noriko, he's only five minutes late. Maybe he got lost on the subway. I'm sure he'll be here soon."

"Anyone can tell him where it is—right across from the Imperial Gardens. That's one of the reasons I picked this hotel. It's easy enough to find." I looked at Mr. Sugimoto for reassurance, but he unfolded his newspaper and scanned the January 12, 1982, headlines, engrossed in the celebrations around the city for the Coming of Age Day.

I had a knot in my stomach and my throat was parched. I thought about getting something to drink, but I didn't want to take my eyes off the revolving door leading to the hotel's main entrance from Marunouchi Street. An elderly couple walked into the lobby dragging a long-haired dachshund on his leash. At the sight of the busy lobby, he started jumping up and down frantically and barked until his mistress picked him up in her arms, cooing, "Schatzie, Schatzie, my little angel." A uniformed bellman followed behind them pushing a brass cart laden with suitcases and shopping bags. Still no sign of Hisashi.

A group of Americans, led by their tour guide carrying a flag announcing Tauck Tours, crossed the lobby. There were so many of them, all crowding around to push their way into the dining room, they blocked my view. I stood up on my tiptoes to see over their heads, and then I blinked. There was Hisashi holding his duffle bag. He was dressed in civilian clothes but I recognized him immediately from his picture.

Hisashi scanned the lobby. I waved to catch his attention, and when he waved back, we rushed toward one another, meeting under the crystal chandelier glistening overhead as hotel guests seemed to revolve around us.

I clutched his photograph in front of me like a chauffeur holding up a sign for a traveler he was supposed to pick up at an airport. I looked into his soft brown eyes. Here was my little boy all grown up, the one I had sung "You Are My Sunshine" to, whispered "I love you" to, and broken my promise to care for. I bowed deeply and whispered "Hisashi?" as if I were asking him a question.

He hesitated a moment and then answered in English, "Yes, Noriko, It's me…Dwight."

We both laughed at the awkwardness of this exchange. I tried picking up his duffle bag, but he wouldn't allow me. "Much too heavy."

"So, so." I motioned for Hisashi to follow me across the lobby. I yearned to put my arms around him, to touch him to make sure he was real, but I was afraid he'd be embarrassed. Maybe later, I told myself.

Mr. Sugimoto stood up, his newspaper folded in his hand as we approached him. I made the introductions. "Mr. Sugimoto, my son Hisashi." He bowed and shook Hisashi's hand. "So glad to meet you. I'm honored to serve as your interpreter as I speak passable English. Please accept my card." He handed Hisashi the side printed in English.

Hisashi read it out loud: "Chairman, East-West Trading Company. Impressive, sir."

Mr. Sugimoto smiled and added, "We'll go to Nikko now. The trip will take two hours. Up to the mountains. It will be very pleasant." I thought that a brief visit to the vacation spot would be preferable to staying overnight in Tokyo.

Mr. Sugimoto held out my fur coat. As he did, the diamond in his wedding ring caught the light from the chandelier, and I saw Hisashi staring at it. There was no ring on my hand. I had stopped wearing the one Ichiro gave me years ago. I never felt I needed to justify my relationship with Mr. Sugimoto, but the look on my son's face as he took everything in between us made me uncomfortable and I felt my cheeks turning red. I should have thought more about this, but sometimes in life I took the attitude that "everything will work out."

Mr. Sugimoto picked up Hisashi's duffle bag. "I hope you have a warm jacket in here. It will be cold in the mountains. It might even snow. Altitude. You might have trouble breathing. The air is much thinner, but very refreshing."

"Yes, Noriko wrote to me about the weather in Nikko, but I rarely feel the cold because I grew up in Montana where the temperature drops below zero in the winter. It's pretty rugged country where I'm from, or should I say where I live, because technically I'm from Osaka, I suppose."

Then he added, "As for the altitude, one thing you can say about the Navy is that I'm in good shape. I shouldn't have any problems."

Mr. Sugimoto translated what Hisashi said so I would not feel totally lost. He then uttered, "I've never been to Montana. Only New York City. I wanted to take your mother there to see a show, but she didn't accept my invitation. She enjoys theater, as I'm sure she'll tell you."

Hisashi answered, "I haven't seen much of the world until now because my parents couldn't afford to travel. Otherwise, I'd have come to Japan when I was still a kid. I thought often about Noriko and wondered what she was like."

I was shocked to hear that Hisashi had a desire to meet me long before he went into the Navy. I didn't say anything, hoping that he would say more when we had a chance.

The chauffeur pulled the Mercedes up to the front entrance of the hotel and opened the passenger doors, storing Hisashi's duffle bag alongside our matching luggage. I sat in the back seat between my son and Mr. Sugimoto. It took some time to get through the city traffic and out onto the open road. Hisashi stared out the window with a look of amazement on his face.

"How does anyone live in a city like this with so many people? And such enormous buildings? You can hardly see the sky."

Mr. Sugimoto and I nodded. I pulled down a fold-out mahogany table and poured sake from a decanter into three glasses. I lifted my glass and said, "Welcome home, Hisashi," to which he responded, "*Arigato gozai masu.* Thank you very much."

I smiled at the effort Hisashi made. "Very good. Did your translator, Mr. Koyama, teach you that?"

"In fact, he did, but I hear it all around the Navy base. Most of the clerks who work in the souvenir shops speak pretty good English and are happy to help us learn basic Japanese. That way we feel indebted to them and buy more trinkets."

Hisashi turned to Mr. Sugimoto. "I just used all the Japanese I know, although I've heard some phrases that aren't very polite at the port. It's too bad my mother, Mitzi, didn't insist on my keeping up with Japanese. When I came to the States, I was only two and a half, but I'm told I had a good vocabulary. It must have been because Noriko read to me a lot and so did Ichiro. I don't remember anything, but I still have some Japanese children's books stored away somewhere." Smiling shyly at me, he said, "Do you remember *Little One Inch*? Mitzi said that was my favorite book."

"Yes, and you also liked *Little Peach Boy*."

Hisashi shrugged his shoulders. "That doesn't ring a bell. I love to read."

"Just like your father. He had a bookcase full of books and records. I don't know how he found the time to read so much, except when he was sick, of course."

Mr. Sugimoto interrupted me as if to let me know it was too soon to bring up any details of Ichiro's illness. He said, in a very solicitous tone, "I'll do my best to express your words correctly, Hisashi. Your mother has talked of nothing else but seeing you, hearing your voice, and knowing something about you." He unbuttoned his heavy coat and instructed the driver to adjust the heat. Sliding his hand down his silk tie, he continued, "I trust you won't say anything to upset Noriko."

"Why would I do that, Mr. Sugimoto? I hope we can get past the polite chit-chat."

"As I said, I'll do my best to convey your thoughts to her and hers to you. This is a very delicate situation for both of you." He refilled my cup and offered more to Hisashi.

Hisashi turned it down. "I'm not used to it. It will put me right out. As it is I'm kind of tired. Do you mind if I take a nap? I've been traveling for hours."

I encouraged him to sleep and he leaned his head against the window and closed his eyes. I examined my son's face. He had beautiful long eyelashes like his father's, thick eyebrows, and high cheekbones. He looked as if he was coming out of the awkward stage into manhood. In a few years he'd be a handsome man. He was very thin, perhaps the result of the food they served him in the Navy and the long hours he put in. Mitsuko wrote me that he once stayed up for seventy-five hours to complete an assignment for his squadron.

The limousine slowed down as it climbed up the mountain. Hisashi woke up from his nap.

"Better?"

"Yes, Noriko, better."

I asked Mr. Sugimoto to stop at the Tosho-gu Shrine so I could make an offering before we arrived at the inn in Nikko for our overnight stay. Gesturing for Hisashi to come with me, I explained that it was an important place for the Japanese. Mr. Sugimoto stayed behind to give us some time together.

The Tosho-gu Shrine was set in a lush forest of tall, golden cedar trees that shimmered in the late afternoon sunlight. At the main entrance, Hisashi picked up an English-language brochure with a map of the extensive grounds. The most famous structure was the five-story pagoda.

"The brochure says each story represents a different element: earth, water, fire, air, and ether. Nothingness. How do we know that nothingness exists?"

I was frustrated I couldn't fully understand Hisashi's question. "Ask Mr. Sugimoto. Perhaps he has the answer." From the way Hisashi studied the map and scanned the information, I could tell he was very curious—again a trait he must have inherited from his father. If Ichiro had been with us, he would have given Hisashi a lecture on "nothingness" and I would have become bored. I laughed to myself remembering all the times I put on a listening face to satisfy Ichiro.

I pointed out the path to the Sacred Stable, which Hisashi found on the map. I looked up at the wooden carvings that represented the three wise monkeys: See No Evil, Speak No Evil, and Hear No Evil. Was there a message for me? Clapping my hands, I pantomimed their gestures and encouraged Hisashi to do the same. He imitated me, indulging me in my silly game. His willingness to play along with me made me so happy.

"Now we go to Honjido Hall." I stood outside the praying hall, and taking a handful of coins out of my pocketbook, dropped each one into the offering box. Lighting a stick of incense, I explained, "For happiness." That was a word I knew from all the American songs I used to sing.

Hisashi fished into his jacket pocket and put a coin into the box. "For happiness." And then he added, "For you and I," pressing my hand in his and then placing it over his heart. He smiled shyly and for a split second I caught the same sweet smile he used to give me when he was a little boy, accompanied by "don't worry, Mama," trying his best to comfort me when everything seemed unbearable. I regretted those moments deeply; no child should have to share a parent's pain. I thought, *Ichiro and I weren't able to provide our son with what he needed most—our love.*

Chapter 51

THE SOFTLY LIT RYOKAN sat on a hillside above Nikko's Sea of Happiness, Lake Chuzenji. The lake was covered with a thick crust of ice, and the moon's light reflected on the surface, making a shimmery silver path. As often as I stayed here with Mr. Sugimoto, it had never seemed so enchanting and dreamlike as on this wintery January evening. Skaters glided close to the shore, and others sat near a bonfire, stretching their gloved hands to catch the heat. The snow-capped mountains were silhouetted against the darkening sky, and the first stars were visible to the naked eye.

The chauffeur brought our bags into the guesthouse, bowed, and left with instructions to return the next day by mid-afternoon. I was struck by how little time we would have together before Hisashi had to return to his ship. There was so much to say, so many questions to answer—or to avoid answering. I prayed that our time together would go slowly and that he'd wish to visit me again, but I couldn't be sure after what I had to tell him. Would he understand what his father and I had done? Would he forgive me when he knew the whole truth? Was I hoping he would exonerate me from whatever guilt I held inside my heart? I had to wait and see—and patience was not one of my virtues, as my mother used to remind me.

The general manager greeted us and ushered our little party down the highly polished wooden hallway to our room at the far end of the building, where we would have a splendid view of the lake. When we arrived at our quarters, I told Hisashi this is where we would be staying.

He looked shocked. "All together in one room?"

Speaking in broken English, the manager explained, "This is the way it's done in Japan. Family travelers share. No problem. Three futons and comforters. Private toilet to change clothes. When you are ready, we will bring food. In the meantime, enjoy a good soak."

"I don't have a bathing suit."

Mr. Sugimoto assured him, "No need. Separate baths for men and women."

"No sharing. That's a relief."

"Mr. Sugimoto will show you how to get ready."

"Thanks, but I think I can figure it out on my own." Grabbing a kimono, my son followed Mr. Sugimoto while I unpacked the few things I had brought. I left the gifts for Hisashi hidden so they'd be a surprise. This was the first time I'd be giving my son a gift instead of mailing it three thousand miles away.

I walked out onto our balcony overlooking the lake. A flock of geese shadowed the moon and a shooting star passed across the sky. I interpreted these as hopeful signs. I stood outside trying to clear my head. I felt the beginnings of a headache and the scar on my forehead throbbed, which surprised me since I had not experienced this pain in a long time.

Returning from the onsen to our room, Mr. Sugimoto picked up the telephone and ordered our dinner. He then disappeared into the bathroom. Hisashi, his hair still wet from the onsen, took out his English-Japanese phrasebook from his duffle bag. Thumbing through the pages, he found what he was looking for: "*Watashi wa o ai dekite u r shidesu.*"

I touched his warm cheek and answered, "Happy to meet you, too. So happy." And then we were both at a loss for words. I watched my son unpack. Everything in his duffle bag was neatly folded and pressed. *Nothing out of order. Everything neat and tidy.* Was that a force of habit or something the Navy expected of him?

There was a knock at the door, and the hotel attendant entered and set up our dinner on a lacquered table in the center of the room. I hadn't realized how hungry I was until I smelled the aroma of hot miso soup. The attendant filled our bowls and left a serving dish over the brazier. We all happily slurped our soup, which was filled with cubes of tofu, and then I divided up the noodles from the serving bowl. Hisashi was clumsy using his chopsticks, but he insisted on trying rather than switching to a fork and spoon. I admired his intention. There was a plate of honey cakes, and we all helped ourselves. Before I had even finished mine, Hisashi popped another into his mouth.

I told Mr. Sugimoto, "Hisashi always loved sweets when he was a little boy. In that he hasn't changed. I wrote to Mitsuko warning her to make sure he didn't ruin his appetite with cakes and cookies, but I guess my words didn't make such a difference, did they?"

"Shall I tell him what you said?"

"It's of no real importance. Just ask him if he's had enough to eat. I don't want him to go to bed hungry. He's not used to Japanese food."

Hisashi answered, "Please assure Noriko that everything is delicious. My mother used to make Japanese food for my father and me all the time. And on Friday nights, she made a big sukiyaki platter for her customers at the Jordan Hotel where she worked and she'd dress up in a kimono she brought with her from Osaka. She was a big hit. During the summers I used to help her at the Jordan bar, taking care of inventory. I like numbers and math and so I didn't mind it so much. Other kids worked on their parents' farms."

I hung on to Hisashi's every word. I wasn't sure I should ask, but I couldn't help myself. "Was it hard for you growing up where no one else was Japanese except for Mitsuko and Harry? Did you feel like you stuck out like a nail?" I wasn't sure Hisashi was familiar with our expression: "The nail that sticks out gets hammered down."

"Do you mean I stuck out like a sore thumb? That's what we say in America. I remember when I was six years old right after I became an American citizen, kids in my school called me a dirty Jap. I didn't understand what they meant. I told them, 'No, I'm not a dirty Jap. I'm a clean Jap.' Mom laughed when our neighbor repeated this story. Everyone else thought I was cute to come up with that answer. Mitzi made me promise I would always tell her if someone insulted me, but I didn't. When I was in high school, I got called Chairman Mao, Chou Mein, or Melon Head. I let it roll off my back."

"When you were a little boy, you were very smart. And sensitive."

"I wouldn't know about that. We never talked about feelings in our family. Just keep things simple, stay out of trouble, and get good grades in school so I could go to college."

I told Hisashi, "Ichiro wanted to go to college, too, to become an accountant like his father, your grandfather, Hide-Ichi. But he didn't have the money and had to go to work at the end of the war. He finished high school at night and worked for my sister at one or the other of her restaurants. He had plenty of ambition but there were a lot of obstacles in his way."

The attendant returned and cleared the table. Then she rolled out our futons, placing them at the far corners of the room. Bowing, she wished us *Oyasuminasai*, and then blushing, she addressed Hisashi, "Good night." She must have been told by the manager he was American.

Hisashi stood up. "It's been a long day. I think I'll go to bed if it's all right with you and Mr. Sugimoto."

I stifled a yawn. "Sweet mountain air. It makes us tired. I'm ready for bed too."

While my son was in the bathroom changing into his pajamas, I asked Mr. Sugimoto, "Was Hisashi curious about you and me?"

"Yes. I told him we met many years ago on a train ride and that, after his father died, I visited you at the tearoom and we formed a close friendship."

"Did that satisfy him?"

"I'm not sure, but he's too polite to ask more questions."

"I hope he isn't upset. It is awkward, but I didn't have a choice, did I?"

"Noriko, you have more important matters to sort out than my presence. Isn't that true?"

"Yes. But I worry about everything when it comes to Hisashi."

"Relax. Be yourself."

When we were all settled for the night, Hisashi and Mr. Sugimoto both fell into a deep sleep, their intertwined snoring a chorus. I shut my eyes and heard the distant tinkling of the wind chimes and the scraping of dead leaves on the balcony. I finally went to sleep, but I woke up during the night from a series of bad dreams I could not remember. I felt disoriented and it took me a few seconds to realize where I was and why. I tiptoed over to Hisashi and rubbed his back as I used to do when he was a baby. He stirred at my touch but didn't wake up. I could feel the heat of his body through the comforter, the rise and fall of his back as he breathed in and out, in and out.

Wide awake, I walked out onto the balcony and stretched out in a lounge chair. Wrapping myself in a blanket, I sat in the darkness watching the stars move across the night sky and then fade away as the sun rose over the silver lake. Ichiro used to tell me, "The stars are still there in the heavens; they are just hidden from sight during the day by the sun. Tonight, they will be there again for us once more, my darling Noriko." But there was a night when the stars seemed to fall out of the sky, and there was only darkness and grief.

I heard the balcony door slide open. Mr. Sugimoto was already dressed. He put a hand on my shoulder. "Have you been here all night?"

"Since before dawn. It was pleasant here under the stars, and I watched the sun come up over the mountains. I forget how refreshing it is to be in nature. I couldn't sleep."

"That's understandable. Hisashi is having no problem sleeping—the gift of youth. They can sleep through almost anything. We could have an earthquake and he probably wouldn't wake up. That's how my sons are." He leaned over and kissed me gently on the forehead.

"What would your sons do if you took me on a trip with them? Would they be upset?"

"Is that still on your mind? They'd probably accept it. They know my wife and I are strangers."

"You make it sound so easy." I looked at my watch. "It's already seven a.m. We have only a few hours together before Hisashi will have to return to Tokyo to catch the train. I'd better wake him up."

"You should have breakfast together. I need to take care of some business. I'll just wait for you in the lobby. Take your time."

〜

I TOUCHED HISASHI ON the shoulder and whispered in his ear, "Time to get up. Breakfast. And then we'll take a walk in the sunshine. Nice day." We sat opposite one another at the lacquered table and communicated in broken English and hand gestures. When the telephone rang, I picked it up and told Mr. Sugimoto we would be on our way in a few minutes.

"Mr. Sugimoto says it's cold outside." I mimed to my son he should put on his jacket. He didn't argue. Pulling a maroon woolen scarf out of his duffle bag and tying it around his neck, he said, "Mom knitted this for me. Maroon is my favorite color."

I understood what he told me. "Same color as your goodbye suit, Hisashi."

"Yes, Mom saved it all these years, even the cap. It's still in the closet in a plastic bag in my room. I'm not sure what's she saving it for."

I thought, *What a sentimental thing to do. Just as I have kept a few things that belonged to Ichiro. I didn't have the heart to give them away.*

Hisashi helped me into my mink coat. He ran his hand over the fur. "Nice. Present from Mr. Sugimoto?" I nodded. "He's a very generous man. I can see that. I'm glad you have someone to take good care of you."

I grabbed Hisashi's hand. "Let's go!"

Hisashi and I joined Mr. Sugimoto in the lobby and headed down the hill toward the lake, our boots crunching in the snow. A breeze made the frozen tree branches crackle. My son dug his hands into his jacket pocket. He had forgotten his gloves. A group of school children wearing uniform parkas and pants glided past us on cross-country skis singing the Japanese national anthem. They held up their poles in a friendly salute to us, their cheeks bright red from the cold.

A smile crossed Hisashi's face as he waved back at them. Stopping at the bottom of the hill, he turned toward me. "That could have been me a long time ago if you hadn't given me away." Mr. Sugimoto hesitated as he translated what Hisashi said. It was difficult for him to hear my son pointing this out.

I stiffened and felt as if a heavy stone had been dropped on my heart. Here it was, the moment I had been anticipating. "Do you want to know why we gave you away?"

"Yes, I guess so."

"Your father and I did what we thought was best for you."

"That's what Mom and Dad told me, but it never made sense. I always wondered if there was more to the story. I used to imagine what it would have been like to grow up in Japan with you. When I stepped off the boat at the naval base, everyone looked like me. I felt so comfortable walking around alone on the streets. People spoke to me in Japanese, and I'd have to explain I'm American and I only speak English, and, of course, they'd apologize for their mistake. At least I should learn how to say, 'I don't understand Japanese.'"

"*Sumimasen, Nihongo-ga wakarimasen.*"

"I'll have to practice. It's a lot to remember."

Mr. Sugimoto cleared his throat. After repeating what Hisashi said, he reminded him, "This is very hard for your mother."

I continued, "I was so young when your father and I married. He got sick almost as soon as I was pregnant with you, shortly after our honeymoon. He used to call you our 'love child.' We were married for four years, and during that time we lived together for less than three years on and off because he was in the hospital or a sanatorium. I came to understand that his sickness was not just physical. He was suffering from a cold of the soul. He'd get a job and do well at it—he was good at everything—but he'd quit because he fell ill or something went wrong at work that upset him. Usually, what went wrong was in his head. It has taken me a long time to see clearly. When you are in the middle of something as I was, things are often foggy and confusing."

"Sounds bad."

"It was. But I never stopped loving him. When we first married, he was my whole world, and then you came along and I made room in my heart for you, too. I never imagined I could love someone as much as I loved you. I'd have to take you to work with me at your aunt's tearoom, and you were so well-behaved. You never complained, and all the waitresses and your cousins spoiled you." I hesitated and then added, "If you come again, I would like you to meet your cousins and my sister, Setsuko. You are part of their family, after all."

We had been walking for quite a while. There was a bench with enough room for the three of us. I picked up a broom attached to a chain and swept away the thick layer of snow that had settled overnight. We sat down and Mr. Sugimoto took out his pipe.

He asked Hisashi, "Do you mind if I smoke?"

"Not at all. Thank you for asking." *So polite*, I thought. Turning back to me he asked, "And then what happened?"

"I always held out the hope that Ichiro would get better. He had a good doctor, and as far as I knew he was taking his medicine. But he didn't get better. There were days when he couldn't get out of bed, and he felt embarrassed I was supporting us by working at the tearoom. When he came up with the plan to give you away, I agreed. My mother and sister warned me it would end in disaster, but I didn't believe them. I thought it would save Ichiro."

"So…it was his idea and you went along with it? You chose Ichiro over me."

I paused, taking in what he asked. It was a stinging retribution. "I didn't see it that way at the time. But looking back, that's probably the truth. Maybe I could have defied Ichiro, but I had turned into the obedient Japanese wife because of our troubles. At one time I wasn't like that: passive, obedient. I was a strong-willed young girl who did just as she wished. Believe me, I have regretted my choice every minute since then, and it was the wrong decision, as you will hear."

The school children were coming back. Once again they waved their poles as they glided past us. Their teacher was at the front of the line and yelled out, "One, two, one, two," so they would move in unison.

Hisashi laughed. "Reminds me of the military drills I had to follow in basic training. I don't miss those days."

"And now you're an important man on the ship."

"Not really. I've earned a few commendations and was recently given an assignment helping to coordinate the fire drills. Can you imagine five thousand men caught on a ship in the middle of a fire? Everyone's worst nightmare."

"Your officers must trust you to give you so much responsibility."

"I guess so."

"That makes me proud. It would have made your father proud too."

The icicles hanging off the trees over our heads slowly melted as the sun climbed higher in the sky, reminding me that time was passing. As painful as it was for me, I needed to keep going with my story.

"Hisashi, how do you feel seeing me? Do you remember anything about me up to the time you went away?"

Hisashi spoke slowly, I assumed, in order that Mr. Sugimoto would not misconstrue his meaning. "When I first saw you in the hotel lobby yesterday, I thought, 'I know this person.' Even without the photograph you were holding up I would have known you're my mother. It wasn't a thought, actually, more like a visceral reaction, something inexplicable that hit me like an electrical shock."

Mr. Sugimoto interrupted him. "I don't think there is an equivalent word in Japanese."

"It was a feeling deep within my heart."

Mr. Sugimoto looked relieved. "That's easier."

Hisashi continued, "I was overcome. I could hardly move my feet. I never believed the day would come when I would meet you. When I enlisted in the Navy, I did it with you in mind. Thankfully, they deployed me to Japan as I requested. That was the only way I could have ever gotten here."

I told him, "Yesterday, when you were a few minutes late, I thought you might have changed your mind. Can it really be true that you have wanted this as much as I have?"

"I can't step into your shoes, Noriko. Every time I looked at the picture of you and Ichiro on your wedding day, I wondered, 'Who are these people?' My mother always told me, 'You are a lucky boy. You have two mothers—the one who gave birth to you and the one who raised you.' And then she'd say, 'One is just as important as the other.'"

"That was very kind of Mitsuko. I am not so sure it's true. A child needs the constant attention of his mother—day in and day out, and I couldn't do that for you once you left."

"It was hard to accept you really loved me if you gave me away. And what about Ichiro? There were times growing up when I thought of myself as a throwaway baby. I added that to all the other names kids used to call me when they made fun of me. I'd repeat it over and over again to myself: throwaway baby, throwaway baby…I did not tell Mitzi because she would have been sad or laughed to cover up her sadness. I told you we didn't talk about feelings, but I could tell from the expression on her face how hurt she was, especially when I was being difficult. I went through some tough times growing up and maybe I took it out on her, because she didn't really understand. Neither did Harry."

Turning away, I put on a pair of sunglasses to hide the tears in my eyes. Brushing away an icicle that had fallen from the tree overhead onto my shoulder, I continued, "Before I try to explain more about Ichiro, I want to give you two things." Opening my pocketbook, I removed a pair of scissors. "These were your father's. I have kept them all these years. Ichiro never went to a barber. He always cut his hair himself. He was so fastidious. And he was good with his hands. He could fix anything: a clock, a leaky faucet, your tricycle. He made beautiful furniture without any training. He could look at plans or a photograph and duplicate them exactly. Before he died, he was planning to open a furniture workshop, but as with so many other plans, they amounted to nothing. He had an extraordinary sense of direction and so never bothered to take a map with him. He could look at it once and commit it to memory." I was out of breath. "Did you get all that, Mr. Sugimoto?"

He faithfully repeated what I said. Hisashi looked surprised at something. "Funny, I have a pretty good sense of direction too. At least when it comes to geography. I'm not as sure about the direction of my life. Maybe I'll figure that out sooner or later. That's one of the reasons I wanted to see you, to get clarity about where I'm from so that I can figure out where I need to go."

"Ichiro used to say, 'One step and then another step.' It's from his favorite book, *The Little Prince*. I've brought you his copy. It's in English. You'll see it's very worn. That's because Ichiro used to read it over and over again. I imagine he would have read it to you when you were ready for it. But you'll have to do that yourself now."

"Thank you, Noriko."

"So where was I? Reading...Ichiro always had his nose in a book. He was curious about many things. Anyway, another surprise about Ichiro you may not have heard from Mitsuko is he played the piano. There was an upright at the tearoom and he used to play it for his own amusement and later for mine. He couldn't read a note so he figured everything out by ear, and he had a wonderful collection of American jazz, show music, and classical music too. His records were among the few luxuries he allowed himself. For my birthday, he took me to a concert." I laughed, "I would have preferred to see a movie—I love American films—but I was curious to know what your father found so fascinating about live classical music."

Examining his bare hands, which were getting red from the cold, Hisashi said, "I pretended I could play the piano when I was a teenager. I imagined myself sitting in front of a keyboard, my fingers moving furiously over the keys. I love music. When I was sixteen, I thought about becoming a disc jockey. I went to the local radio station in Glendive because I won a contest, and they let me work there for a day. It was great. The kids at school all heard me on the radio announcing the songs, which I had picked out myself."

Mr. Sugimoto said, "Your mother has a lovely voice. She wanted to be an actress when she was in high school, and when she graduated, she auditioned for a theater company in Osaka, the Takarazuka. Unfortunately, she wasn't accepted, but if she had been, she never would have met your father and you wouldn't be here today. We rarely know the consequences of the decisions we make in life, do we? Life is unpredictable."

Hisashi stood up and kicked an icicle sticking out of the snow with his boot. Then he picked up a shard and threw it toward the lake, following it with his eyes as it flew through the air, landing close to the bank.

I smiled. "Good throw. Do you play ball?"

"I was on my high school football team, but I wasn't good. Too thin and maybe not quick enough. I was better at debate, and when it came time to choose, I chose debate. I got into the state championship. It was kind of a big deal. Mom and Dad never came to see me. I gave her my trophy." He interrupted himself. "Noriko, I asked you earlier if Ichiro loved me and you didn't answer."

"I got carried away telling you a lot of details about Ichiro. Sorry. Yes, Ichiro loved you very much. When I was working and he wasn't, he spent a lot of time with you. He'd take you to the park and read to you and make toys for you. He taught you numbers, and before we knew it you could count to ten. It doesn't sound like much now, but for a toddler it was a big accomplishment. You and he became close. In fact, if you add it all up, he might have actually spent as much time with you as I did, which is why it made our decision so painful for him." I winced at the thought of what came next.

"But Ichiro was worn down by his illness. After you left, Ichiro got worse and worse. He couldn't seem to shake off the black cloud hanging over his head. That's the only way I can describe how distraught he was. His sadness became all-consuming, and sometimes I was grateful to get away from him by going to work. My anger was like a wave that overtook me."

Hisashi asked, "And then Ichiro died of a heart attack about six months after I was given away. Is that right? That's what Mom told me. Every time she says it, she cries all over again as if it were yesterday."

"I'm coming to that part of the story." I took out a handkerchief and wiped the tears streaming down my face. "Sorry, Hisashi. It's just this is very hard for me. I've had to summon all my courage to tell you what happened next."

Even Mr. Sugimoto, although he knew what I was about to confess, seemed uncomfortable. I had taken him into my confidence some time ago, not wishing to hide anything from him about my past.

"Ichiro could not live with the pain and guilt of having given you away. He saw how sad I was, and when I wasn't sad, I was bitter. Even now, after all this time I partially blame myself for what happened next. If I had understood him better or if he had trusted me enough to tell me what he was feeling, perhaps I could have saved him."

Hisashi was confused. "Stopped him from sending me away?"

I rushed on as if I were leaping off the edge of a cliff. "I came home from work. Ichiro was lying on the floor. I tried to revive him, but it was too late. The gas from the stove had already done its job. He left me a note with a confession and his last wish that I never tell Mitsuko or you what he had done to himself. I have hidden his letter. I cannot look at it, although someday I will." I paused to catch my breath and to wipe the tears away once more. Hisashi waited, a look of disbelief on his face. He didn't say anything, waiting for me to continue.

"When I found out you were coming to Japan and we would finally see one another again, I was overjoyed, but I was also afraid. I didn't know if I should tell you what really happened to your father. I was not sure how you would judge us. I prayed that, when you heard the whole story, you might find a way to forgive us."

Hisashi took my hand.

I continued, "Don't pity me. As difficult as it was to accept, I've tried to find joy in life. Some days still haunt me—your birthday or my anniversary, and the day Ichiro died. That is perhaps the most difficult to bear."

Hisashi put his arm around my shoulder and I rested my head on his. I felt him tremble as we touched one another. Mr. Sugimoto stepped away to give us some privacy. Hisashi did not say anything about what I had just revealed, but I chose to interpret his silence as sympathy.

We sat that way for a few minutes as the icicles continued to melt over our heads. While the outside temperature had risen, the sky had started filling with clouds blowing down from the mountains. It might begin to snow soon.

"I know you already have some pictures Mom sent you, but here are a few more I put together for you."

Turning the pages of the small photo album, my son narrated some pictures: "This is me when I became an American citizen. That's the judge with Mom and Dad. I'm wearing a dorky powder-blue jacket and black pants with a bow tie that someone gave my parents before I even got to Glendive. That's a picture of me on the high school debate team." He laughed. "I'm the Japanese kid with the thick black glasses. My parents didn't go to the state championship to see me win. Too busy working I guess."

I interrupted him. "That was a huge accomplishment. Were you disappointed that Mitsuko and Harry weren't there to see you win?"

"I guess so, but we were hardly ever together as a family. My dad worked during the day, and my mom worked at night. And to tell you the truth, I wanted to hang out with my friends." He laughed, "Usually we were pulling typical high school pranks. My parents didn't know much about what I was up to." He then turned another page of the album. "And here's a picture of me at my graduation from Dawson County High School. And here's me with Mom and Dad right before I went into the Navy. Dad was so proud of me for going into the military."

"Did you have a girlfriend, Hisashi?"

"No. Maybe someday."

Looking closely at each picture, I said, "I've missed out on so much."

He shrugged his shoulders, as if words could not convey the pain of the lost years. "I've missed out on a lot too. I think about what it would have been like had I grown up in Osaka. Maybe if I hadn't left, Ichiro wouldn't have done what he did and we'd just be a typical, boring Japanese family."

I had the same thought, but it was too painful to dwell upon.

Mr. Sugimoto interrupted. "It's almost time to leave."

"I have something else I want to give Noriko." He handed me a jewelry box.

"Shall I open it now? It's customary for Japanese not to open a gift in front of the person who gives it to them."

"I think you can break that rule in front of an American."

I didn't want to waste a minute. "I'll open it later."

"You'll tell me if you like it. I went to a bit of trouble picking out something for you since I don't know your taste or what you need."

"Will you come back to see me again, Hisashi? We barely know one another. I want to spend more time with you. Please say yes." My heart pounded and my head throbbed as I waited for his answer.

"When I can. I never know our schedule but I'm sure we'll be back in port again. Maybe you'll come and visit me."

I touched Hisashi's cold cheek. "You aren't sorry you came to see me?"

"No." He paused. "Is it okay if I call you Mom?"

"And I'll try and remember to call you Dwight."

"I like the way Hisashi sounds better. When we're together, call me by my birth name—Hisashi."

"Hisashi Uchida. Hisashi Uchida. Hisashi Uchida. Yes, it suits you." I waved to Mr. Sugimoto. "Please take a picture of Hisashi and me."

Mr. Sugimoto took out his camera and shouted, "Ready." Hisashi and I both smiled into the camera. Then I slipped his father's scissors and *The Little Prince* into the pockets of his jacket. "So you don't forget."

As we climbed up the hill toward the inn, it started to snow. Hisashi turned up the collar of my coat to protect me from the wind, just as Ichiro had done so many times before. Then my son held my hand. I took off my glove so I could feel his fingers wrapped in mine. The lanterns along the pathway up the hill toward the inn turned on and lit our way through the falling snow.

⌒

HISASHI NEARLY MISSED HIS train back to the Navy base. The winding road down the mountain was slick with snow and ice, and the traffic moved at a frustratingly slow pace. Visibility was poor as the winter storm built to a near whiteout. The incessant sound of wipers hitting the windshield unnerved me. We passed several cars that skidded off the road and into an embankment. No one spoke, each of us engrossed in our own private thoughts.

Hisashi looked relieved when we reached the railroad station with a few minutes to spare. He kissed me goodbye and climbed onto the train carrying his duffle bag. I stood on the station platform, the Tokyo-Yokosuka sign brightly lit above the tracks. The public address system announced the departure time, the voice echoing against the tile walls as passengers bundled up against the nighttime cold hurried past me. Settling himself in a seat by the window closest to me, Hisashi waved as the train pulled out of the station. I mouthed the words "you are my sunshine."

I reached into my coat pocket for the box and opened it. A beautiful gold-faced wristwatch was cradled inside. Winding its mechanism, I fastened the clasp, pressing hard so it would be secure on my wrist. I held it close to my ear, hearing its ticking above the din of trains arriving and leaving the station. Time lost, time passing, time ahead—it was all there marked by the hands on the face of my watch.

I didn't know when I would see Hisashi again, but he had made me a promise. In the meantime, I waited.

Acknowledgments

PROFOUND GRATITUDE TO MY husband for giving me permission to tell this story and for sharing many personal details, which I incorporated into the narrative. Thanks also to his birth mother and his adoptive mother and father for opening their hearts to share this journey with me.

Special thanks to Reverend Marlon Okazaki for translating many interviews from Japanese into English and for explaining the tenets of Tenrikyo.

Historical details were derived from numerous films and source material, most especially *Hiroshima* by John Hersey; *Edwin O. Reischauer and the American Discovery of Japan* by George R. Packard; *Embracing Defeat: Japan in the Wake of World War II* by John W. Dower; *At Home in Japan: A Foreign Woman's Journey of Discovery* by Rebecca Otowa; as well as *The Makioka Sisters* by Junichiro Tanizaki; and *Maborosi*, a film directed by Hirokazu Kore-eda.

For editorial advice and a keen eye, many thanks to Jane Rosenman, Michael McIvern, Aviva Layton, and Jennie Nash. For encouragement to keep me going, Barbara Abercrombie, teacher extraordinaire; and Billy Mernit.

Many thanks to my readers who took the time to comment and give advice on one or more drafts on the road to "The End": my sister, Lois Gold; Marcia Helmsley; Bonnie Levin; Wendy Kleinbaum; Judy Chaikin; Lisa Smith; Harry Miyoshi; Celeste Akiki; Marilyn Atlas; and George Kolber.

To my writing group—we've hung together for ten years—and have cheered one another to publishing memoirs, short stories, and personal essays: Cynthia Lim, Deirdre Harris, Yasmin Tong, and Dr. Bob Goldman. You all never failed to encourage me to do my best, and to point out where I needed to dig deeper.

Thanks also to the various literary journals that gave a home to excerpts from this novel in different forms: *The Summerset Review, The Laurel Review, Amuse Bouche, The Write Launch,* and *Colere.*

Much appreciation to Jonathan Kirsch, Esq. for looking out for me.

For taking a chance on *All Sorrows,* my publisher, Tyson Cornell at Rare Bird; Olga Grlic for designing the beautiful book cover; and Rachel Tarlow Gul at Over the River PR for helping to put eyeballs on these pages.

Profound love always to my son, Josh, for the privilege of being your mother.

And finally, a thank you to Yuki, my eighteen-year-old cat, who sat at my feet and kept me company in many a dark night of the soul when I wondered if it was all worth it.